Praise for A

"Gill Paul's fascinating novel sho~~~~~~~~~~~~~~~~
lotions were two compelling, ambitious, and passionate women
who were responsible for the birth of the global beauty industry.
Few women leave such an extraordinary legacy as Helena Rubinstein and Elizabeth Arden, and Paul's impeccable research brings
to life their rivalry and their personal struggles, showing us that,
for two women intent on outdoing one another, they actually had
a lot in common, which makes for a poignant and timeless story."
—Natasha Lester, *New York Times* bestselling author of
The Paris Orphan

"A brilliantly entertaining novel about the ugly side of the beauty
business. With incredible attention to detail, Gill Paul takes the
reader up close and personal with Arden and Rubinstein and
their battle for dominance in the emerging beauty industry of the
1900s. Paul blends fact and fiction as smoothly as Arden's Venetian cream, and with pithy dialogue and a wicked sense of humor,
brings her leading ladies and their outrageous backstabbing and
jealousies roaring to life on the page. An absolute decadent joy
from beginning to end, this is the perfect summer read!"
—Hazel Gaynor, *New York Times* bestselling author of
The Last Lifeboat

"Gill Paul brings Elizabeth Arden and Helena Rubinstein to
life on the pages of her new historical novel, *A Beautiful Rival*.
Exposing the raw, ugly side of the beauty industry, Paul deliv-
ers two headstrong, passionate women willing to do whatever
it takes to build their empires. With meticulous research and
Paul's signature skillful storytelling, readers will be swept up in
this fascinating and intimate portrait of these cosmetic titans."
—Renée Rosen, *USA Today* bestselling author of
Fifth Avenue Glamour Girl

"A delicious look at the high-stakes rivalry that defined a century of beauty. Gill Paul masterfully weaves skillful storytelling with an acute eye for glamour to make *A Beautiful Rival* an utterly compelling read."

—Julia Kelly, internationally bestselling author of
The Lost English Girl

"Glamorous and fascinating. Two businesswomen ahead of their time, a tense rivalry in a beautiful world, an intriguing story expertly told. I was completely riveted."

—Tracy Rees, internationally bestselling author of
The Elopement

"A fascinating insight into two titans of the cosmetics industry, mirror images in business and in love, both insatiable in their ambition yet hobbled by their flaws. Readers will love this juicy and well-told tale."

—Bryn Turnbull, internationally bestselling author of
The Woman Before Wallis

"Scandal, sabotage, and spies. Who knew the beauty industry was so cutthroat! This was a thoroughly compulsive and addictive read. Gill is such a clever writer, deftly peeling back the layers of these two formidable doyennes to reveal their tender, vulnerable cores. It had me up way past my bedtime racing to that enormously satisfying end!"

—Kate Thompson, bestselling author of
The Little Wartime Library

"A fascinating tale of two determined, glamorous businesswomen locked in a battle for supremacy. Gill Paul is a mistress of the fictional historical biography."

—Rachel Hore, bestselling author of
The Love Child and *One Moonlit Night*

"A delicious page-turner of a novel about the rivalry between beauty titans Elizabeth Arden and Helena Rubinstein. Spanning two world wars and full of fascinating period detail, I really enjoyed this story about two formidable women driven by a mutual desire to succeed, no matter what."

—Jacquie Bloese, bestselling author of
The French House

Also by Gill Paul

The Manhattan Girls
The Collector's Daughter
Jackie and Maria
The Lost Daughter
Another Woman's Husband
The Secret Wife
No Place for a Lady
The Affair
Women and Children First

A
BEAUTIFUL
RIVAL

a novel of
HELENA RUBINSTEIN and
ELIZABETH ARDEN

GILL PAUL

WILLIAM MORROW
An Imprint of HarperCollinsPublishers

A BEAUTIFUL RIVAL. Copyright © 2023 by Gill Paul. All rights reserved. Printed in the United States of America. No part of this book may be used or reproduced in any manner whatsoever without written permission except in the case of brief quotations embodied in critical articles and reviews. For information, address HarperCollins Publishers, 195 Broadway, New York, NY 10007.

HarperCollins books may be purchased for educational, business, or sales promotional use. For information, please email the Special Markets Department at SPsales@harpercollins.com.

FIRST EDITION

Designed by Renata DiBiase

Library of Congress Cataloging-in-Publication Data has been applied for.

ISBN 978-0-06-324511-2

23 24 25 26 27 LBC 6 5 4 3 2

For Lucia Macro

CHAPTER 1

Elizabeth

January 1915

E lizabeth Arden held her first meeting of the day in her bedroom while doing her yoga routine, dressed in a loose pink gym top and matching bloomers. Irene Delaney, her personal assistant—known to all as Laney—perched on the window seat, legs crossed and spectacles balanced on her nose. She began reading out messages from a notebook, then scribbling Elizabeth's instructions with a pencil sharpened to a point.

Outside, snow was drifting past the tall picture windows but a brisk fire kept the room cozy. A pot of English tea was brewing on a side table, alongside two rose-patterned gilt-edged cups and saucers and a tiny milk jug.

Elizabeth bent forward into Downward Dog pose, feeling the stretch in her calves. She had broken her hip as a teenager after falling badly while trying to high-kick a chandelier on a dare. She'd spent months bedridden while it healed, and ever since, her joints got painfully stiff without the morning yoga, which had been recommended by a progressive Toronto doctor. It had the added benefit of helping to keep her figure trim. She was in good shape for a woman of thirty-six—an age she would never admit, as she hoped to pass for a decade younger.

"Mr. Pease rang yesterday," Laney said. "From Pease and Elliman. He wanted to tell you they've found a tenant for 673 Fifth Avenue."

Elizabeth hoisted herself into a neat headstand, proud of the strength in her arms. She'd been looking for a new Fifth Avenue salon, one with a street entrance. Her current New York beauty salon was on the third floor at number 509, so it didn't attract passing customers. She had viewed the premises at 673 but felt they weren't spacious enough for her plans.

"Do we know who the new tenant is, dear?" she asked, feeling her skin tingle as blood rushed to her head.

"She's another beauty salon owner," Laney said. "Name of Helena Rubinstein."

Elizabeth wobbled, lost her balance, and let her feet topple to the carpet with a thump. "You're not serious." She sat up, adjusting her top, which had ridden up, exposing her flat stomach.

Laney consulted her notes, and nodded. "That's what he said. Why? Do you know her?"

Elizabeth wrinkled her nose as if at a bad smell. "I visited her Paris salon in 1912 during my trip to Europe, and can't say I was impressed. She calls herself the 'Queen of Beauty Science' and blathers on about 'magical antiaging herbs' she's discovered"— she chortled dismissively—"but the facial I had in her salon was run of the mill. I'm sure her Valaze cream brought me out in a rash. What's she doing coming to New York?"

She was thinking out loud. She knew Madame Rubinstein already had salons in Australia and London as well as Paris. Wasn't that enough for her? She had no place in America; this was *her* territory.

"If she's a charlatan, she won't have a chance of succeeding in Manhattan," Laney said. "New York women are very discerning."

"Last time I saw her she didn't even speak English fluently," Elizabeth scorned, remembering the woman's peculiar vowel sounds and the way she placed emphasis on the wrong syllable of words like "astrin*gent*" and "complex*ion*."

She was worried, though. All things Parisian were in vogue. There was a lot of sympathy for the French because of the war in Europe and, from what she had seen in Paris, Madame Rubinstein didn't hesitate to promote herself. But she, Elizabeth Arden, was founder and sole owner of the most successful beauty brand in America, having outstripped all the other pretenders with her upmarket packaging, her clever advertising, and her stylishly decorated salons. She was well connected in this city. Women knew and trusted her.

Suddenly she remembered that 673 Fifth Avenue was owned by the husband of one of her salon clients. Perhaps she would have a quiet word.

"Is Mrs. Lawrance booked for a treatment this week?" she asked.

Laney dug out the schedule and tapped her pencil as she scanned the names. "Three o'clock on Thursday," she said. "Facial strapping and massage."

That was too long to wait. Contracts could be signed by then. Elizabeth decided to telephone Mrs. Lawrance at home. She glanced at the ormolu clock on the mantel. It was still only eight. She'd wait till eleven. The wealthy women she cultivated as clients took their time over their morning toilette, hairdressing, and outfit choices for the day. It would be seen as uncouth to call too early.

She completed her yoga routine while dictating correspondence to Laney, but all the time there was a sour taste in her mouth. She wouldn't let anyone threaten the success she had achieved; it had been too hard-won. She'd grown up in a drafty, run-down backwoods shack near Woodbridge, Ontario, one of five children of an impoverished tenant farmer and a mother who died so young Elizabeth could only vaguely remember her. Hunger pangs used to keep her awake at night, along with the shifting and sleep-murmuring of the siblings who shared the same worn mattress on the floor.

Step by step she had hauled herself up from poverty to wealth and prestige, taking a lot of knocks along the way. It

wasn't easy for a woman on her own without family money to
fall back on. She certainly hadn't gotten this far without learning
how to see off competitors. In her head, she planned the exact
words she would use when she made the telephone call.

"MRS. LAWRANCE, I couldn't forgive myself if I didn't have
a word about the new tenant your husband is considering for
number 673. You see, I came across Madame Rubinstein in
Europe, and I'm afraid she's not the sort you would want in
your property. . . ." She listened hard, trying to judge how
her words were being received, but could hear only the older
woman's breathing and a slight buzzing on the line. "She's rather
flamboyant . . . bohemian, you might say. I'm not sure it's the
image you want at the street level of such a prestigious building,
where every passing shopper can see." It was on the tip of her
tongue to say, "She's not one of us," but she restrained herself.
Mrs. Lawrance, born into old money and married to old money,
wouldn't consider Elizabeth Arden her equal, not by a long shot.

"My husband has been trying to find a tenant there for
some time. Property lying empty costs him money," Mrs. Lawrance said. "And I believe their lawyers are already discussing
the tenancy agreement. It's rather late in the day to ask him to
withdraw."

Elizabeth bit her lip. It was unthinkable that Madame Rubinstein should open a salon at one of the best retail addresses in
the city with its own street entrance. She wouldn't put up with
it. She played her ace. "What if I were to take on the lease? You
know I would present the right image for the area. My salons are
discreet and tasteful, not loud and anarchistic."

"Anar-*chistic*?" Mrs. Lawrance's voice rose. Elizabeth seemed
to have struck a nerve.

"She's friends with all those avant-garde European artists—
you know, the ones who doodle childishly on a canvas and

charge hundreds of dollars for it, although no one can make out what on earth their doodles are supposed to represent. I believe they want to overthrow the status quo." She sighed. "I'm sure the last thing your husband wants is a troublemaker."

"Certainly, that wouldn't be good." Mrs. Lawrance paused, considering. "I will have a word with Mr. Lawrance. You say that if it's not too late to halt the other contract, you will take on the lease? At the terms offered? You didn't seem keen before."

"I've reconsidered," Elizabeth replied, frowning. She would keep her existing salon at 509 as well; that should give her the space she needed—but it was an expensive decision. She would normally have negotiated reduced rent and more favorable terms, but first it was important to see off the newcomer. "I'm very grateful to you, Mrs. Lawrance. Please allow me to offer you a complimentary gift set when you come to us on Thursday. The new Venetian treatments will be perfect for your skin."

Mrs. Lawrance hung up. An hour later Elizabeth took a call from Mr. Pease, confirming that the lease was hers if she wanted it.

"Have you told Madame Rubinstein yet?" she asked, clenching her fist in triumph.

He cleared his throat. "Ah, no. I was waiting for confirmation."

"Perhaps it's best not to mention my name for now. Perhaps just say that there was a misunderstanding, that the owner's wife had already promised it to a friend." She nodded. That would do. She wouldn't move in for a few months because the property needed complete redecoration from floor to ceiling. "I'm sure you'll find somewhere else for Madame Rubinstein's salon in a district that's more suitable for someone of her . . . *background*."

She knew he would catch her meaning: not on Fifth Avenue. The newcomer didn't belong there. That was Elizabeth's domain. Mr. Pease had arranged the lease of her first Fifth Avenue salon, and had received commission for referring her to the agent who found her premises in Washington, DC. She was expanding and he knew she was good for business.

"Of course, Miss Arden," he said quickly, and she was reassured by his tone that they understood each other perfectly.

CHAPTER 2

Helena

January 1915

"I'm afraid there's been a mistake, Madame Rubinstein." Mr. Pease spread his hands and shrugged in a "what can I do?" gesture. "The landlord tells me his Fifth Avenue property is no longer available."

"How strange." Helena fixed him with her dark eyes. "The lease was sent to my lawyers yesterday and they have spent hours examining it." She paused. "Please tell your client I will pay double the rent."

She heard her sister Manka give a slight gasp, saw the greed flicker across the agent's eyes as he calculated the commission. His suit was good-quality cloth, well cut, but it showed signs of wear: shiny patches at the elbows, sagging at the pockets. She guessed he only had a couple of suits, which he alternated.

He was reassessing her now—her navy-blue Worth gown, her chinchilla stole, her eye-popping diamond ring—and probably assuming she had a rich husband who gave her a generous allowance. Men always underestimated her at first. It could be useful.

"I'll call and make the offer," the agent agreed. "Would you ladies like some coffee?"

Helena made a dismissive gesture and watched him leave the room.

"What are you doing?" Manka hissed in Polish. "The rent was already extortionate."

Helena turned to her. "He won't accept. I bet he decided not to let me have it once he noticed my surname on the legal documents."

Friends had advised her to change her name before launching her beauty business in the States, to avoid anti-Jewish discrimination, but she refused. She wasn't a practicing Jew, didn't keep kosher, and wasn't sentimental about her Polish-Jewish heritage, but she didn't see why she should bow to pressure from bigots. It made her all the more determined to succeed using her own name. She had managed in Europe and Australia, despite discrimination there. After researching the US market, she'd concluded that immigrant women could be a valuable source of customers and the name Rubinstein might attract them. If any potential clients were put off by her Jewish blood, frankly, she didn't want them in her salon.

Mr. Pease came back, full of apologies. "So sorry, he promised it to a friend of his wife's." He wouldn't meet her gaze. "But I have several more properties I can show you."

"On Fifth Avenue, north of Forty-Third Street?" She had heard that area was the most prestigious location for a salon like hers.

He consulted his notes, flustered now. "Perhaps not on Fifth Avenue itself, but just around the corner . . ."

Helena spoke sharply. "How far around the corner? You've wasted my time already. Think very hard before you drag me somewhere else that might also turn out to be *not available*." She had been running a successful business for thirteen years, and she knew how to handle men like this.

"I have the perfect place," he said, his cheeks pink, perspiration beading on his top lip, where there was a nick from shaving. "Please—come with me."

Helena viewed seventeen premises over the following week before choosing one on East Forty-Ninth Street, spacious with high ceilings and a sweeping staircase. She loved a good staircase. Mr. Pease was worn out when they sat down in his office to do the bit she loved best: making the deal. Always she had a price in her mind; always she got it.

She had learned her negotiation skills from her father, who was a kerosene salesman in her native Poland: *Listen hard and never say more than you have to. Control your expression so you give nothing away. Work out your bottom line and stick to it.* His rules worked every time. They hadn't been in touch for over twenty years, since he threw her out of their family home and she left Poland to make her own way in the world, but at least she had picked up his deal-making wisdom before then.

HELENA THREW HER energy into the East Forty-Ninth Street salon, choosing every element of the décor as well as the artworks that would be on display, among them sculptures by the Polish artist Elie Nadelman, and a huge Cubist painting by Georges Braque. A treatment room would have black lacquer furniture and gilt trimmings, while the main salon would have dark blue velvet walls, with contrasting baseboards and moldings in deep rose. She wanted an environment that was plush and visually stunning. When women came for treatments, they should feel like visiting royalty.

Time was short, because she wanted to open for business in three months. There was no point paying rent for a property she wasn't earning money from. She bribed the tradesmen to work longer hours and promised them a bonus for speedy completion. It would be worth it.

Soon after they arrived in the city, she had sent Manka to investigate the other beauty salons, booking appointments under her married name, Czerwinksy. There was Eleanor Adair, Kathleen Mary Quinlan, and the woman Helena was most keen to hear about, the one she considered her main rival, Elizabeth

Arden. Whenever she opened a newspaper or magazine, she saw expensive advertisements for Arden products. *Be Beautiful!* they proclaimed. *Don't Look Old!* Her New York salon was known as the Salon d'Oro—a golden name to match her golden promises of eternal youth. Two could play at that game, Helena thought. Her husband, Edward Titus, wrote her advertising copy and he was a much more skillful writer than anyone on Miss Arden's team.

Helena fingered the pink, white, and gold packaging of a pot of Arden's Venetian Pore Cream. The etched glass was too pretty-pretty for her taste, but it was a decent weight in the palm of the hand. The lettering on the label was old-fashioned, from the last century. She opened the pot and sniffed: lavender and maybe a hint of rose. She dipped the tip of her finger inside, then rubbed the cream onto the back of her hand. It was far too heavy. How could anyone advise Manka to cover her delicate complexion with this *muck*?

"Miss Arden herself gave me a head and shoulder massage," Manka told her. "She has big masculine hands, very strong."

"It's not a good business if she has to treat customers herself," Helena said. "What does she look like?"

Manka tipped her head on one side, remembering. "She's no beauty. Reddish-blonde hair set in waves. Square jaw, big nose, eyes too close together. She has good posture but a limp on the right side. She speaks with a breathy, little girl's voice in an upper-class accent that sounds fake. And she calls everyone 'dear.'"

Helena nodded, pleased at that. "What about the salon?"

"White and gold. Marble, chandeliers, mirrors, nothing re-markable."

Helena examined the other Arden products Manka had brought back. She'd have them analyzed by a chemist, but so far she wasn't impressed. Her own creams were far superior.

She thrived on competition, and planned before long to be the leading beauty brand in the lucrative American market.

As they stood looking around the new salon, watching the men at work, Manka said, "It's only two weeks till Edward and the boys arrive. Will they stay in our hotel?"

Helena shook her head. "I've leased an apartment above the salon. It's not huge but it will do to start with."

Edward had been looking after their two sons, Roy and Horace, in Paris while she prepared for her US launch. Manka had accompanied her, since she was at a loose end after the breakup of her marriage. Thank goodness she'd gotten rid of that waste of space, Helena thought. Manka had appalling taste in men.

"You're lucky you got a good husband," Manka said. "Edward's a gentleman."

Helena smiled but didn't comment. He was charming, intelligent, and universally popular, but he wasn't perfect—not by a long shot. He'd always had an eye for the ladies, and gravitated toward the most attractive one in the room like a compass needle swinging to the north. At parties, she usually found him chatting to some beautiful woman in a corner, standing too close, smiling too intimately.

"I like women's conversation," he'd say if she complained. "What's wrong with that?"

"It's disrespectful," she argued. "It looks as though you are playing around behind my back."

"Who cares how things *look*?" he protested. "You and I know the truth. That's all that matters."

She had never found any evidence of affairs, but still she was suspicious. They had been living apart all winter while she set up the American business, and he was a man who liked women. Although he had written regularly—long, intimate letters—she was skeptical that he had slept alone every night.

"You shouldn't neglect him for so long," Manka commented, as if reading her thoughts. "Aren't you worried his head could be turned by some Parisian floozy?"

"His head turns more often than the revolving door at the Paris Ritz," Helena muttered. "But I hope he remembers which side his bread is buttered on."

CHAPTER 3

Elizabeth

April 1915

Elizabeth hired society designer Elsie de Wolfe to decorate her new salon. She wanted it to be refined and chic, with a style befitting the most high-class of beauty salons, not just in New York City but in the world.

"Have you seen Helen Hay Whitney's Italian Renaissance–style lobby?" she asked, picturing the gilt and marble hallway, with a Michelangelo statue standing atop a tinkling fountain. "Something like that."

Elsie's mouth gave a slight twist of distaste. "Perhaps a tad less ostentatious," she replied. "And more twentieth century."

Subtle beaux arts style was best, Elsie advised, with an American rather than a European feel. Elizabeth's heart was warmed by her assertion that Parisian style was *passé* these days.

"I like the fact that your last salon had a red front door," Elsie continued. She handed her a paint chart, and pointed at a bold shade of scarlet. "But why not choose more of a daring red, like this one? At the women's suffrage march apparently they all wore lipstick this color."

Elizabeth had gone on the march. She was strongly in favor of women's right to vote and it was exactly the image she wanted for her business.

"I love it," she said. "From now on, all my salon doors will be this shade of red."

Next she called her advertising manager and told him to plan a campaign that positioned hers as the *crème de la crème* of beauty salons.

"I want your ideas by the end of the week, dear," she said. "And make them good or I might have to bounce you."

He scurried away. Elizabeth was famous for "bouncing" employees who displeased her, and not giving them a reference either. A little healthy fear kept them sharp.

While she was immersed in plans for the new salon, Mr. Dunlop, the manager of the pharmaceutical company that manufactured her products, rang to say he wouldn't be able to fulfill her orders that month because he hadn't been able to purchase any lanolin.

"Why on earth not?" she demanded.

He was hesitant. "A new beauty business has bought up all the supplies. They seem to be stockpiling."

"What new business?" Elizabeth asked, but she knew the answer before he told her. That woman: Madame Rubinstein. "Why is she stockpiling?"

"The owner said she thinks America will join the war in Europe and she wants to be sure she has enough ingredients to see her through." The manager paused. "Perhaps you could contact her and ask if she will share some with you?"

"Perhaps you could jump off the Brooklyn Bridge, dear," Elizabeth suggested, then slammed the receiver hard into the cradle. Madame Rubinstein hadn't been in New York for five minutes and already she was causing trouble.

"Laney?" she called to the outer office. "Find me some lanolin. I don't care how you do it. Kill some goddamn sheep if you need to."

"Will do," Laney called back.

OVER THE FOLLOWING weeks, Elizabeth found herself thinking obsessively about Madame Rubinstein. She couldn't get her out of her head, like a bluebottle buzzing against a window, or a sharp stone in her shoe. Mr. Pease reported that she had leased premises on East Forty-Ninth Street, only a block from Fifth Avenue, which was not nearly far enough away to Elizabeth's mind. How could she ensure the newcomer's salon failed and she retreated back to the other side of the Atlantic where she belonged? She fantasized about unleashing a plague of rats or termites in her salon but had no idea how one would go about such a thing. Perhaps, as a foreigner, Madame Rubinstein would inadvertently breach some city regulations and could be reported anonymously. She could only hope.

Once a week she wrote to her younger sister, Gladys, in Toronto. Elizabeth had been closest to Gladys of all her siblings, as they were the two youngest and were often left unsupervised while the others worked on the farm. They used to play make-believe games, pretending they were a king and queen hosting balls and decorating their pretend castle—a dusty area of the farm's yard they marked out with rocks.

They hadn't seen each other much since Elizabeth moved to New York eight years earlier, but they still felt close, and she complained to Gladys in a letter about the city's newest salon owner.

"Madame Rubinstein seems aggressive," she wrote. "It's not civilized behavior to barge into someone else's territory." It briefly crossed her mind that she had done the same thing when she started her own business five years ago, but she dismissed the comparison. That had been different.

"You've got nothing to worry about," Gladys soothed in her reply. "Your customers are loyal. They won't want to risk trying unusual new products that could ruin their complexions. It's too much of a gamble."

Gladys went on to write that her husband, Albert, was having a difficult time at the office and it made him bad-tempered when he got home. He was critical of her housekeeping and found fault with meals she served, but she was trying to be patient and understanding.

Elizabeth bristled. She had taken against her sister's husband from the start. In conversation he invariably raised his voice and spoke over everyone else. She'd seen the way Gladys tensed in his presence, as if waiting for him to find fault, and she suspected he was a bully. She wondered if he ever struck Gladys. She feared for her gentle younger sister. The world was full of bullies like Albert—and like Madame Rubinstein.

She confided in Tommy, a beau who took her dancing most weeks at Irene and Vernon Castle's dance school. He agreed with Gladys that she had nothing to worry about. "You're too far ahead in the game for a newcomer to catch up," he said. "Never forget you're Elizabeth Arden, head of the biggest-selling American beauty brand. She's an unknown here."

Elizabeth wasn't mollified. She sent Laney to spy on progress of the building work at East Forty-Ninth Street. When Laney returned, she brought a flyer she'd been handed in the street outside.

A Famous European House of Beauty Announces the Opening of Its Doors in New York, it read, before introducing Madame Rubinstein as *the accepted advisor in beauty matters to Royalty, Aristocracy, and the Great Artistes of Europe*.

"What twaddle!" Elizabeth snapped, fury bubbling up. "You wouldn't catch any self-respecting princess in her salons. They look like bordellos, for god's sake. Did you find out when she is planning to open?"

"The first of May," Laney said. "Two weeks on Saturday."

"Ha!" Elizabeth exclaimed. "That proves she knows nothing about the American market." All her clients left the city for the summer, returning in September, and that's when she would open her own new salon with a fanfare. Meanwhile, Madame Rubinstein would be left with her staff twiddling their thumbs on full salary during the hottest months.

Elizabeth felt reassured. Her rival was an amateur. Surely her position was safe.

A FEW DAYS before Madame Rubinstein's salon was due to open, Elizabeth was alarmed to browse the latest copy of *Vogue* magazine and find a full-page advertisement for the new salon opposite an article about her. Madame Rubinstein was illustrated in a white laboratory coat, peering into a vial of liquid, her black hair pulled into the tight chignon Elizabeth remembered from her visit to the Paris salon.

According to the article, Madame Rubinstein had studied medicine at the university in Kraków and learned about skin from the top experts in Europe, before starting her business in Australia, where the dry heat of the sun meant women's skin was prone to premature aging. She had imported precious Carpathian herbs with antiaging qualities from her native Poland, and these formed the base for her miraculous Valaze creams. She claimed she was the only beauty specialist in the world to understand that there are different types of skin—dry, oily, combination, and sensitive—and that each requires different products.

Elizabeth harrumphed—"Nonsense!"—before continuing to read.

It seemed Madame Rubinstein considered herself a "woman of no country" with houses in Melbourne, Paris, London, and now New York, where she planned to make a home with her "wonderful" husband and two "adorable" sons.

"Blah, blah, blah . . ." Elizabeth said under her breath. She had never married, never had children, and didn't regret it one iota. She hated women who boasted about their offspring, as if they were somehow superior to others who had chosen not to squeeze out a few babies.

She stopped when she came to a paragraph in which Madame Rubinstein was quoted as saying: "Results are what matters. I

don't think American women will be fooled by fancy gold lettering and pink packaging if the cream doesn't improve their skin."
No other US brand had gold and pink packaging: she could only
be talking about Elizabeth Arden products. The cheek of it! If
this was a declaration of war, Madame Rubinstein had picked
the wrong goddamn woman to fight with.

Elizabeth threw down the magazine, feeling a twinge of
betrayal that Edna Woolman Chase, the editor of *Vogue*, had
allowed an article like this to run. She considered her one of her
closest friends. Why hadn't she spiked it, or at the very least
warned her it was coming?

"Laney dear," she shouted through to the outer office. "I want
you to set up a lunch for me with Edna as soon as possible. And
find out all you can about the Rubinstein woman. How did she
start her business? Is she backed by family money? What are her
secrets?" There were bound to be secrets. Launching a business
as a woman was tough. Toes had to be trodden on. Lines had to
be crossed. "Hire whomever you need. I want facts, and I want
them *now*."

"Do you mean a private detective?" Laney asked, scribbling
in her notebook.

"Exactly." Elizabeth furrowed her brow. "And when her salon
opens, I want someone posted outside to tell me who visits."

Laney hurried off and Elizabeth sat back and closed her eyes.
What if some of her society clients were tempted to defect to
the newcomer? Madame Rubinstein's scientific drivel and talk
of royal patronage might sound convincing if you didn't know
better.

She could feel her heart beating beneath her ribs, the in and
out movement of her chest. The fear was still there. No matter
how much money she made, she was still scared that one day
someone would come along and take it all away.

Who are you, Florence Nightingale Graham—a girl who never

finished school, who was shunned by her classmates because she had cooties in her hair—who are you to mingle with high-society ladies? If they knew where Elizabeth Arden had come from and who she had been as a child, they would never so much as give her the time of day.

CHAPTER 4

Helena

April 1915

The week before her salon opened, Helena's eye was caught by a stark advertisement on the front page of the *New York Times*, placed by the Imperial German Embassy: *Travelers intending to embark on an Atlantic voyage are warned that a state of war exists between Germany and Great Britain. . . . Vessels flying the flag of Great Britain or any of her allies are liable to destruction. . . . Travelers sailing in the war zone do so at their own risk.* Her heart skipped a beat. Her husband, Edward, and her two sons had set sail from Le Havre just the day before.

Why the heck hadn't he left Europe sooner? Why did he wait till this war got so serious? His excuse was that the sea could be rough during winter crossings and he was waiting for milder weather. Was that the truth or was there some woman in Paris he'd been reluctant to leave?

She hated telephones. She was never sure which bit to speak into, and she suspected the operators were eavesdropping on her calls. All the same, this was an emergency. She got one of her assistants to dial and ask to be put through to the American Line shipping company. There was a wait of almost half an hour because all their lines were busy. When she finally got a flustered clerk at the New York office, she wasn't convinced by his assurances.

"Your husband is on the *St. Louis*, flying under an American flag. The Germans wouldn't dare attack an American ship."

"Everyone said they wouldn't dare attack Belgium," Helena argued. "Who knows what they're capable of?"

"The *St. Louis* is due to dock at Pier 54 on Thursday evening," he told her, sounding bored, as if he had repeated it many times that day. "We are in regular contact with the captain and he hasn't reported any trouble."

"Can I send a telegram to my husband?" It felt important to warn him about the newspaper advert. He probably didn't know the danger. The lessons learned from the sinking of the *Titanic* three years earlier were that you had to get places on lifeboats to survive. At the first sign of trouble, he must hurry the boys to the lifeboat station and make sure they wore their lifejackets.

"I'm afraid we can't send civilian telegrams," the clerk told her. "Military ones only."

"I can pay you. Ten dollars for just one message," Helena offered. He refused. She increased her offer to fifty, probably more than a month's salary for him, but he was adamantly un-bribable. She slammed down the telephone in frustration.

For three days, she waited for news. She wished she hadn't read those reports about the *Titanic* because now she had visions of her loved ones struggling in freezing water. Twenty minutes was thought to be the longest anyone survived. She wasn't even sure if the boys could swim. Roy was five and Horace was three. Had anyone taught them yet? Edward and the nanny took care of that side of things.

Helena hadn't planned to fall in love, hadn't planned to marry, hadn't planned to have children, but now she couldn't imagine life without them. It was terrifying how vulnerable it made you to love other human beings so much that you knew you would never recover if anything happened to them. She hated situations she couldn't control, but an Atlantic crossing with German U-boats prowling was one—and pretty women with loose morals fluttering around her husband was another.

THE EVENING BEFORE the salon opened, Helena hosted a champagne party there. It had been arranged before she knew about the German threat to shipping, and she decided it would be bad form to cancel. She would have to push her worries to the back of her head, just for one evening.

A selection of women's magazine and newspaper writers were invited, and to each she gifted a pot of Valaze cream suitable for their skin type plus a piece of jewelry. She had researched the women's coloring in advance and chosen appropriately from a selection of jewels she'd bought wholesale in Paris. To a *Vogue* journalist with cornflower-blue eyes she gave a sapphire ring; for a *Harper's Bazaar* one with dramatic dark hair, she chose ruby drop earrings.

"I can't possibly accept such an expensive gift," the *Harper's Bazaar* writer exclaimed, trying to hand back the box.

"Of course you can," Helena said with a grin, thrusting her hands behind her back and refusing to accept it. "I absolutely insist."

The writers wandered around, admiring the opulent décor while listening to Helena tell them about the science behind her treatments, and the press coverage afterward was priceless. Wherever she went in the world, Helena made it her top priority to befriend the press.

Bookings for the early weeks were already better than expected. Edward had written copy for a series of advertisements that played on women's fear of aging. They explained what happened when skin loses elasticity: jowls sag, foreheads furrow, and creases are etched around the eyes. The process starts in the twenties and gets worse over time—but, the advert explained, it's never too late to stop the clock. Her products and treatments, designed with the benefit of her rigorous scientific training, could reverse all the signs of aging, smoothing existing creases and lifting jawlines. She knew that's why women came to her salon—in the hope that it was true.

At each customer's first visit, she stopped by their treatment chair to give a personal appraisal that was always laced with flattery.

"Your skin is dry on the cheeks, oily on the nose and forehead," she told one woman. "I can tell you take good care of your appearance. You have such lustrous hair! I guarantee that with a few weeks' regular use of my products, your skin will look as if you are twenty again."

She made each woman feel special. She also gave away samples of her products, knowing that everyone loves a free gift. Investment of time and money was essential when building a brand in a new market. That's how loyalty was won. These women couldn't tell that beneath the charm she was sick with worry about her husband and children; outward appearances were all that counted.

ON THE EVENING the *St. Louis* was due to dock at Pier 54, Helena got her driver to take her there and she stood behind a rope line with the other waiting families. She gave a little scream of joy and clapped her hand to her mouth as the shadowy bulk of the ship glided into sight. A spontaneous cheer arose from the crowd. They were safe. They'd made it.

Edward walked down the gangplank, holding the boys by their hands, detaching one hand briefly to wave. Before he reached her, he called goodbye to an attractive young lady in Wedgwood blue and Helena frowned. Had there been an onboard dalliance? She kissed the boys on their foreheads, then embraced him, sniffing to see if he smelled of perfume, but all she could make out was his usual cypress cologne.

"I've been tearing my hair out," she said, clutching his arm to lead him to the car. "You heard about the German government's threats?"

"We had a naval escort until we reached American waters," he told her. "I don't think we were in any danger. All the same, I'm glad to be on dry land." He kissed her warmly. "And with you."

The boys gazed in awe as they drove north, the new skyscrapers blinking as sunlight danced off their steel and glass exteriors. Her sons had been raised in the elegant eighteenth- and nineteenth-century terraces of London, then Paris, and had never seen buildings as tall and modern as this.

The driver cut through the West Side, but a collision with a horse and cart had blocked the road and they had to loop farther north toward the park, then turn back down Fifth Avenue. As they passed number 673, the place the owner had refused to lease to her, Helena gasped. A sign had been raised over the front window with the name "Elizabeth Arden" in curly script. She must be the so-called friend of the owner's wife who'd stolen the site from under her nose. It was a much better location than Forty-Ninth Street. Before long, Helena decided, she would do something about that.

THAT NIGHT, AFTER the boys were in bed, Helena poured brandies for Edward and herself and sat beside him, telling him about her New York opening, about the favorable press coverage, about the American women with their gray skin and purple noses, who were far behind their European counterparts in the acceptance of makeup.

"They still associate it with actresses and whores, but are quite happy to leave my salon with some subtle tints and highlights that bring their complexions to life." She shook her head with a smile.

"It's strange they are so shy about improving their appearance. Do you think it's an echo of *Mayflower* Puritanism?" Edward asked.

"Perhaps," she said. "I can't claim to understand them yet. Some clients sneak in a side entrance, as if they are ashamed to be seen at my salon—yet they come in their dozens. Business is better than I dared hope for the opening month."

He told her about life in Paris, the anxiety as German troops marched across the Belgian border, the food shortages, and the difficulty sourcing raw ingredients to manufacture her products in wartime. Her Saint-Cloud factory and her Paris salon were still open but some creams were in short supply.

She had stockpiled all the ingredients she needed in America; she had to make the new salon profitable soon or her cash would dry up. It reminded her of the early hand-to-mouth days after she started her business in Australia—but of course she was wealthy now and could simply transfer funds from another country if need be.

After they finished their brandies, they went to the bedroom and Helena changed into a lace negligee and sprayed on some scent. She climbed into bed and rolled over to kiss Edward and hold him close. He embraced her quickly, then kissed her cheek and yawned, saying, "I'm tired, *kochanie*. Good night."

"I thought we might . . ." she ventured, running her fingers over his chest. "After six months, don't I deserve my conjugal rights?"

"You were the one who left, Helena," he replied. "Besides, I believe it's men who get conjugal rights, not women."

"That's not fair. I demand equality." She poked him playfully in the side.

"And I demand sleep," he replied, rolling over.

She lay awake listening to the sound of his breathing with a mixture of emotions: happiness that he was alive, and here with her at last; but frustration that he hadn't wanted to make love. He loved her, she was sure of that, but he didn't seem to desire her anymore—hadn't for a while, if truth be told—and she had no secret potions in her beauty arsenal to deal with that.

Two days later, the horrifying news broke that the *Lusitania* had been torpedoed by a German U-boat off the south coast of Ireland. The Kaiser would stop at nothing. Over a thousand lives were lost, but not Edward's, thank God, and not her sons'. It was easy to be distracted by business, and especially the competition with Miss Arden, but in that shocking moment she knew her family was infinitely more important.

CHAPTER 5

Elizabeth

May 1915

E lizabeth met Edna Woolman Chase for lunch at the Colony Club on Madison Avenue—a private, invitation-only club for women. Edna was chic as ever, with immaculately set brown hair, a well-pressed gray suit and white blouse, pearl earrings and a matching necklace just visible at her collarbone. Over iced tea, Elizabeth described the plans for her second New York salon, with décor by Elsie de Wolfe and new facial strapping treatments that weren't available anywhere else.

"That's worth an editorial," Edna said. "When can I send a reporter to interview you?"

"You'll be the first," Elizabeth promised. "I hope you'll give it the appropriate amount of space. I noticed you featured another salon this month. . . ." She smiled, graciously. "Of course, I don't mind. . . ."

Edna clasped her hands. "I had no choice. Madame Rubinstein spent a fortune on advertising, so I was under pressure. I haven't met her, of course."

"No, of *course* not." A look flashed between them, an acknowledgment that the Rubinstein woman wasn't the type they should be mixing with; certainly not the type who would ever be admitted to this club. It had a firm policy against Catholics, Jews, and anyone with a skin color other than Anglo-Saxon white.

Elizabeth picked at the fillet of fish a waiter placed in front of her. The dining room had a genteel atmosphere. No pipe or cigar smoke, no loud voices, just well-dressed upper-class ladies of the type she liked to attract to her salon.

"I saw a news story in which Madame Rubinstein claimed that her husband and sons had a 'lucky escape' simply because they crossed the Atlantic a week before the *Lusitania* was sunk." She forced a little laugh. "I crossed the Atlantic three months after the *Titanic* sank so I suppose I had a lucky escape too. I guess we are all lucky if we manage to cross the street without being mown down by a careless driver."

"That's one way of looking at it," Edna replied.

It irked Elizabeth that her rival was grabbing newspaper column inches, especially on such a slim pretext. She read all the stories obsessively.

"I was surprised to hear that her husband owns part of her business," Elizabeth continued. "Perhaps he gave her the money to start it. I founded and built mine all by myself and I intend to keep it that way."

Edna put down her fork. "I've said it before, Elizabeth, and I'll say it again: you would be well advised to find yourself a husband. You must know that people whisper when a woman is unmarried. You will find marriage has *many* benefits for your social status." Edna had a husband, although Elizabeth had never met him, and a daughter, Ilka, who was at boarding school.

Elizabeth shivered. "You must surely have heard the story of Harriet Ayer?" She was a salon owner whose husband had left her to run off with his mistress, then had her committed to an asylum so he could steal her fortune.

Edna nodded. "Of course, but . . ."

"The law is *never* on the side of estranged wives," Elizabeth continued. "It made me resolve then and there that no man would ever get his hands on my money."

"You could make your fiancé sign a legal agreement before

marriage," Edna suggested. "Or perhaps if you found the right man you would *want* to involve him in the business so you wouldn't have to work so hard."

Elizabeth couldn't imagine that. She didn't have a high opinion of men in general. Her father had been weak. He could have raised his family out of poverty if he'd had a spark of ingenuity, but instead he scraped along at subsistence level, growing and harvesting the same old crops, always getting the worst of any deals he negotiated. Why hadn't he taken steps to prevent the countless pregnancies that Elizabeth was sure caused her mother to weaken and succumb to tuberculosis? He certainly hadn't been able to cope with the five children she left behind. The fact they'd received an education at all was down to an aunt in Cornwall who sent money. A man with any pride would have found that humiliating.

Her elder brother, Will, was no better than her father. He had a decent job in finance, but spent his earnings on drink and gambling, and probably loose women if she knew him. She didn't see him often anymore, although he also lived in Manhattan. She didn't want her big brother showing up to embarrass her in polite company.

Elizabeth had received plenty of marriage proposals—especially once she became wealthy—but none that remotely tempted her. Every time she thought about sharing her bed with a man, an image of her dying mother flashed into mind. Her only memory was of her lying in bed, all skin and bone, with red eyes, lank hair, and the awful hacking cough that had squeezed the life out of her. If that's what marriage did to you, she wanted none of it.

But she knew Edna was right, that it didn't seem respectable to be unmarried. Reporters wrote that those who went on the women's suffrage march were "man-hating spinsters," and that certainly wasn't an image she relished. She was also aware some married women saw her as a predator who might seduce their

husbands, and they swooped to intervene if she so much as exchanged two words with the poor helpless dears at a party.

Perhaps if she had a husband she would seem better bred,
but he would have to be the right type. She would only marry
if she could connect with old money . . . but the Social Register
matrons would never in a million years allow their sons to wed
the likes of her.

She had met Tommy, her dancing companion, on the ship
back to America after her 1912 trip to Europe, and had been
stepping out with him for more than three years. He had proposed to her several times, but although he was good company,
and a talented dancer, he didn't have a notable family. He worked
in a bank, at middle management level, with no prospect of advancement as far as she could tell.

"I'll bear it in mind if I meet the right man," she told Edna.
"But for now, I'm firmly wedded to my business." She smiled. "I
don't know how you manage your demanding job plus a husband and daughter. I hear you are also hosting a Fashion Fête
next month. How *do* you find the time?"

It had become impossible to import new French designs because of the war in Europe, so Edna had organized a fête featur-
ing American designers, with the proceeds going to charity.

"I reach out to my closest friends and ask for help when I
need it," Edna replied. "In fact, I was going to ask if you might
lend some of your salon girls to prepare the models for the fête?"

"I'd love to," Elizabeth said. She sipped from her glass of tea.
"I imagine you have a program for the event in which you thank
contributors?" It would be useful to have her salon mentioned
there. She imagined that virtually every distinguished lady in the
city would attend.

"Of course," Edna said. "That goes without saying."

They understood each other: you scratch my back, I'll scratch
yours. Neither of them had been born into wealth or privilege,
but they had made their way through hard work and shrewd

judgment. Elizabeth had taken enunciation classes to shed her backwater Canadian accent. She had studied how the rich dressed, how they talked, and how they behaved in company. She had learned the latest dance styles and the protocols for visiting the theater and opera. She could hold a conversation with the best of them now, and Edna was the same. They were women going places. Their lives were on the same track and Elizabeth hoped they were firm allies. If an interloper—especially an outsider, like Madame Rubinstein—tried to break into their ranks, they would link arms and eject her firmly.

CHAPTER 6

Helena

July 1915

Helena squinted at a story in *Vogue* about the recent Fashion Fête hosted by Edna Woolman Chase. There was an illustration of Miss Arden, posing alongside some of New York's wealthiest women, their names listed in a caption below. Presumably she had no idea that several of them were already regulars at Helena's salon.

She studied the illustration of Miss Arden, which fit Manka's description. Her rival had a good figure—very trim and hourglass. Helena placed a hand over her own belly. She had never lost the weight around her middle after the birth of the boys, and she liked food too much to go on a starvation diet. The very thought made her reach for the container of roasted chicken legs she had brought to the office. Eating always helped her to think more clearly.

She had asked her accountant to find out Elizabeth Arden's turnover and gross profit figures, but he said he couldn't do that, since her company was private.

"Don't you have a friend in the tax office who could tell you?" she asked, and he seemed shocked by the suggestion, saying that wasn't how things worked in America.

"So how will I know when I have overtaken her?" she demanded.

He shrugged. "You can look at the number and size of your

salons, and compare the number of products you market, but as for sales, it's impossible to tell. I believe the bulk of hers are done through mail order."

Helena mused on that. She had six salons worldwide, while Miss Arden just had two in the US, with a third opening soon. She had eighteen products but Miss Arden had twenty-four. Her New York salon was busy and her products were available in stores around the country, but Elizabeth Arden creams were often displayed on the same counters, which irked Helena. She wanted to emphasize the difference between them so shoppers made the right choices. In her salons, she educated clients about their skin types, and explained the need for separate morning and evening routines. In stores they could just pick up any old pot of cream, with no understanding of the science. She frowned, the beginning of a plan taking shape, and started to scribble a letter to her sales manager. It became a very long letter.

Her idea was that she and Manka would tour department stores around the country to train their sales staff. They would explain how to diagnose skin types and how to help women to pick the Helena Rubinstein products right for them. She would outline the curative properties of different creams and the best way to apply them, taking lots of samples so staff could try them out. They would supply uniforms too, with her name printed on the top pocket, and sales staff would be given certificates, turning them into official 'Rubinstein women.' She was in her element when talking about skin care. Her English was more or less fluent now, and beauty was a subject she was passionate about.

Her sales manager agreed it was a good idea and promised to start contacting department store managers. Helena reckoned she could travel down the East Coast and across to Texas, getting back to New York by Christmas, then head out to the West Coast in spring.

"Madame . . ." The manager cleared his throat. "Forgive me, but I'm afraid there are some cities I wouldn't advise. Places where you might have trouble getting a hotel reservation." He was pink with embarrassment.

Helena knew what he was hinting at: places where Jews were not welcome. "Where, for example?"

He cleared his throat again. "Newport, certainly. Miami. Boston maybe. Let me explore the options."

Helena nodded her thanks and dismissed him. She would go to these towns later, once she was such a big name in the States that they couldn't afford to ignore her.

TAKINGS IN HER salons dropped during July and August, but Helena had planned for that. She used the time to develop new products, working in the home laboratory she called her "kitchen," and also preparing her presentation for the tour.

Edward would look after the boys while she was away. He had always done the lion's share of organizing their family life by finding homes and hiring staff. In London and Paris he had hired nannies to steer the boys through baby- and toddler-hood. Helena had never been the devoted kind of mother who couldn't bear the children to be out of her sight. She loved them—of course she did—but her time was better spent earning money to give them comfortable lives.

Since arriving in New York, Edward had found schools for them, he'd rented a more spacious apartment on the Upper West Side, an area Helena hated—"Too Jewish," she said, without irony. He had also found a country home for them in Greenwich, Connecticut: a marvelous Tudor-style house with tree-shaded lawns swooping down to a lake.

Greenwich was an Anglo-Saxon, Protestant area, decidedly not Jewish, and he'd bought the house in his own name, which he had changed from Ameisen to Titus before he met her. He preferred to avoid any discrimination, while Helena had always taken it as a challenge to meet head-on.

Their Jewish roots didn't seem to hold them back socially:

Edward had a gift for making friends wherever they went. He had scarcely been in New York a week before he was part of a literary set based around Washington Square. In the evenings he went to poetry readings, gallery openings, and concerts with his new pals. Writers asked his opinion on their manuscripts and laughed too loudly at his witticisms, while copious amounts of booze were consumed.

Helena was invited to their gatherings, but she was shy in their company. She wasn't an intellectual, didn't have time for reading books, and didn't drink much. She preferred to spend evenings in her "kitchen," mixing new products and experimenting with plant extracts, mineral oils, and foodstuffs such as cucumber, parsley, and grapes. Sometimes the mixtures refused to emulsify, sometimes they smelled rancid, but occasionally she made a breakthrough.

She had learned her laboratory skills from an elderly pharmacist in the Australian town of Coleraine, where she stayed on a sheep farm with some relatives of her mother's. It was a time of her life she didn't care to dwell on, when she was still reeling from the shock of banishment by her father. The scorching heat, the dust, the stench of the sheep, the constant irritation of flies, the isolation, and a cousin who kept trying to get her alone and force himself upon her . . . it felt as if she had made a huge mistake in crossing from Europe to end up there. But that elderly pharmacist took her under his wing, taught her how to mix creams and potions using sheep's lanolin as a base, and gave her the tools to start her empire. She would always think fondly of him.

And now, as she rehearsed the speech she would give on her national tour, she remembered his generosity to a young girl far from home, for which he had asked nothing in return. She hoped she would meet many more like him on her travels.

SHE LEFT NEW York in September, just as Elizabeth Arden was opening her new Fifth Avenue salon. Helena hoped that the headlines she attracted would overshadow any coverage her rival received. She had made sure she was word-perfect. It would be a performance, like a piece of theater.

For her talks, she wore French designer gowns in self colors, such as blue, red, or white, which formed a backdrop for the dramatic, oversize jewelry she favored. On her feet were the highest-heeled shoes she could find; she was only four foot ten in stocking feet, and never let anyone see her without heels. Her black hair was smoothed into a chignon that emphasized her strong features and flawless skin, and she wore bright scarlet lipstick as a finishing touch.

"Every woman has the right to be beautiful," she began her talk, "but some of them don't even try." She surveyed the room, catching eyes with members of the audience of department-store staff. When she knew she had their attention, she continued: "Have you ever noticed that it is easier to persuade a pretty woman to try a skin treatment than a plain one? The plain one says, 'Oh, but my nose is too big so what's the point?' or 'My skin is terrible so why try?' It is our job to show them that *anyone* can be beautiful, and that not trying is pure laziness." There were gasps from the audience. "Yes, that's what I know from my years in the business: any woman can be beautiful. And as Rubinstein women, your job will be to show them how."

She asked Manka to come forward and sit on a chair facing the audience, then she demonstrated techniques on her as she talked. "Beauty begins with the skin. But not all skin is the same, so it stands to reason that not all skin treatments should be the same." She explained her theories about the different types of skin, and the products that should be used for each.

"I'm *horrified*," she said, "just *horrified*, by the other creams on the American market, which are *far* too heavy for American skin. These should be avoided *at all costs* as they block the pores and stretch the skin, making it sag." She always gesticulated when she talked, and there was general laughter as she mimed the way Manka's skin would sag if she used brands other than Madame Rubinstein's.

After skin care, Helena talked about the importance of a healthy diet, fresh air, and exercise, citing her medical training at the university in Kraków and her studies with scientists across Europe. She explained how to choose hairstyles and makeup to flatter different face shapes; then at the end she took questions from the audience.

"Some customers still think it is vulgar to wear makeup, yet they want to look their best. How can we apply it so no one can tell they are made up?" one woman asked.

"Good question," Helena said. "The trick is to apply makeup in a good strong light, then study the effect in a magnifying mirror. Parisian women have been doing this for years. Blend and smooth, blend and smooth. You can't tell they are wearing makeup, even close up," she said. "They just look healthier. Younger." She tilted her face under the light to show off her own youthful appearance.

At the end of each talk, audience members clustered around her asking for personal recommendations. The crowds grew bigger each time, and before long there were local journalists waiting to interview her after events. When newspapers sent photographers, she posed for them: head held high, her face turned to give them a shot of her famous profile. She loved this kind of press coverage.

"Look, Manka!" She pointed to a full-page article in the *Washington Post*. "I didn't even have to pay for it!"

"You're becoming famous," Manka said.

"Do you think so?" Helena was tickled by the idea. *Madame Rubinstein, leading beauty scientist*, the newspapers called her. It set her apart from the competition, she felt. One competitor in particular.

CHAPTER 7

Elizabeth

October 1915

Elizabeth couldn't open a newspaper or magazine without seeing articles about Helena Rubinstein's self-glorifying nationwide tour. Reporters claimed, irritatingly, that she was "the most famous scientist of beauty the world has ever known." They said: "In Paris, London, Sydney, and New York, her Maisons des Beauté Valaze are frequented by those who follow her instructions to the tiniest details." It put Elizabeth in a tetchy mood for the rest of the day, but she couldn't help reading to check what her rival was up to.

Laney had received a report from a private detective in Australia, but he scarcely added any information to what Elizabeth knew already from magazine stories. Madame Rubinstein had been born in Kraków, the eldest of eight daughters of a kerosene salesman. She had studied medicine at the university in Kraków, then traveled to Australia. *Why?* Elizabeth wondered. *Why leave home?* There was no answer to that, but the report said she had started her beauty business in 1902. As far as the detective knew, no one had backed her financially. Women paid in advance and waited up to six weeks to get the precious pots of cream made with Carpathian herbs she imported from Poland, which supposedly worked "miracles."

"'Miracle' is hardly a scientific term," she told Laney, "yet it seems to be her favorite word. And if she studied medicine, why doesn't she call herself Doctor?"

She read on. The report said Madame Rubinstein had married in 1908 and gave her husband half the Australian business as a wedding present. *So he hadn't helped her to start up. In that case, who did?* Her father didn't sound like a wealthy man.

Elizabeth felt as if the report had raised more questions than it answered. She asked Laney to hire a detective in Kraków, but Laney pointed out the war in Europe would make that difficult. It would have to wait. Somewhere, she felt sure, she would find a scandal that could be leaked to the press to compromise her rival. There was something fishy about her. She wasn't all that she seemed.

WHEN A NEW York detective brought Elizabeth a list of clients seen entering Madame Rubinstein's Forty-Ninth Street salon, she was incandescent: Mrs. Loew, Mrs. Harriman, Mrs. Morgan—many of them her own ladies. How *could* they? She had thought she could rely on their loyalty at least, but it seemed their heads had been turned by the latest novelty.

When she wandered into the Bonwit Teller department store, there was the Valaze range on display right alongside hers, even taking up slightly more space on the counter. She charged upstairs to the office of Paul Bonwit to complain but he was less than sympathetic, telling her in a patronizing tone that "business was business."

"Loyalty is good business practice where I come from," she snapped, but he was not to be swayed.

On the way out, Elizabeth rearranged the entire counter so that Madame Rubinstein's creams were hidden behind hers, shooing assistants out of the way when they tried to stop her. *Petty but satisfying*, she thought as she strode out onto Fifth Avenue.

Tommy was the only person with whom she could speak her mind. With his banking experience, he understood business—and he was in love with her so she knew he was on her side.

"Department stores will stock whatever they think their customers want to buy," he advised. "You need to push on that front: get into more stores countrywide, and create stunning displays that attract the attention of passing shoppers."

"How would I go about it?" she asked. "I don't have time for a self-glorifying vanity tour such as Madame Rubinstein is indulging in."

She never used herself as a figurehead for the company. She knew she was no great beauty. Besides, she didn't want anyone from her past popping up to say, "Isn't that Florence Nightingale Graham from Woodbridge, Ontario—the girl with cooties in her hair?" She preferred to use glamorous young models for her advertisements, their hair swept back off their brows to reveal flawless complexions and perfect features.

"Hire a sales director who can talk to the stores' buyers and persuade them to place large orders. I would offer to help you but . . . I have some news for you." He paused, met her eye. "I've signed up."

She couldn't imagine what he meant. A new apartment? Another dance class? "Signed up for what?"

"The American Expeditionary Forces. I'll start training in November, then sail for France early next year."

So far, the war in Europe had scarcely impinged on Elizabeth's consciousness, so she was incredulous that Tommy would volunteer to fight in a conflict that didn't affect him. What was he thinking?

"It's not our war! You mustn't go. You could be killed!" she argued. "Did you consider that?"

"I have considered that," he said. "I've given it a lot of thought. And I know the previous times I've proposed to you, I've been turned down flat, but please forgive me if I have one more try, since I feel we are closer now. May I dare to hope you feel the same way?"

He scraped his chair back from the table and, to her horror, he dropped onto bended knee in front of her. "Elizabeth, would you consider becoming my wife before I go to war? The dream of returning to live by your side would sustain me in the trenches."

It sounded like a speech he had rehearsed. Elizabeth glanced around the restaurant, feeling her cheeks redden. Other diners were whispering to each other. Did any of them recognize her? She hoped not. They wanted her to throw her arms around him and accept, but there was too much to consider. Various answers buzzed around her head. She didn't speak for so long that Tommy took it as a refusal and got back in his chair, looking dejected.

She was fond of him, but she wasn't sure she could love him as a woman loves a man. She'd been on her own for so long, she couldn't imagine anyone moving into her apartment or—ghastly thought—sharing her bed. She dreaded the idea of sexual communion.

What if Tommy died in Europe? At least she'd have the status of a war widow. But if he lived and came back as her lawful wedded husband, he could insist on his conjugal rights. He would have to accept from the start that business came first and she wouldn't compromise on that.

"I don't want children," she said in a husky voice, then cleared her throat. "I saw what it did to my mother. So if you're hoping for a family, please choose another wife."

"I don't care about children. It's you I want," he said, catching hold of her hand, hope in his eyes.

Why did he want her? she asked herself for the hundredth time. *Was he after her money?* She supposed she could take Edna's advice and consult a lawyer to protect her assets. If the marriage failed, she would make sure he'd walk away without a cent.

But maybe the marriage would succeed. In a flash, Elizabeth

allowed herself to imagine what it would be like to come home to someone who understood the pressures she was under, who would pour her a cocktail and listen to stories of her day. The truth was, beneath the tough carapace, she was desperately lonely. She accepted invitations to social events she didn't want to attend because she couldn't bear to be home alone. She often called Laney late at night, inventing some work-related pretext or other, just to have someone to talk to. If she married Tommy, she wouldn't be alone anymore.

Madame Rubinstein and her husband, Edward, had thrown a party that got mentioned in the *New York Times* society column, although they clearly weren't "society" by any stretch of the imagination, yet so far she had never rated a mention when she entertained. She was sure that would change if she had the social respectability of marriage. She tried to imagine cohosting dinner parties with Tommy and realized he would be good at it. He could make conversation with anyone. It was a drawback that he didn't come from a distinguished family and didn't have his own money, but he had pleasant manners and a ready smile.

"You took me by surprise," she said at last, with a forced laugh. "Aren't you the dark horse? Could you give me time to think it over? A week perhaps?"

"Of course," he agreed, but he was subdued during the rest of the meal. She had hurt his feelings, and she felt bad about that. He was a decent man.

The next morning, she called her lawyer and asked whether he could prepare legal documents that would protect her wealth in the event of her marrying. He said he could draft some if her husband-to-be would voluntarily renounce any claim.

"He will," she replied sharply. "If he won't, the deal is off."

TOMMY WAS OVERJOYED a week later when she told him she had decided to marry him, so long as they could agree on a few tiny legal details to protect her company.

"I am the luckiest fellow in the world," he declared, lifting her off her feet and twirling her around. "I'll make sure you never regret it."

He signed the documents without a murmur and they booked City Hall for November 29, 1915. Tommy wore his new military uniform, while Elizabeth wore a dark crêpe suit with a silver fox stole and a cloche. Edna sent a *Vogue* photographer to take pictures.

After the ceremony, Tommy was eager to rush straight to the St. Regis Hotel, where he had booked the honeymoon suite, but she told him she had to return to the office—"Just for an hour or so, dearest." In truth, she was nervous about the physical side of marriage and was trying to put off the dreaded deed. She would have preferred a chaste marriage, but the ardent way Tommy kissed her and held her close made it very clear he couldn't wait for their wedding night.

The act turned out to be every bit as painful, messy, and undignified as she had feared, but she endured it with gritted teeth. She would make sure that wasn't repeated too often. Why did any woman put herself through it unless she was trying for a baby?

The next day she rose at dawn, before Tommy was awake, and took a taxi back to her apartment in time for her yoga routine and her meeting with Laney. Business came first, and if he hadn't realized that yet, he soon would.

CHAPTER 8

Helena

April 1916

Helena and Manka set off on their second tour in the spring of 1916, this time starting on the West Coast. While they were in Los Angeles, the movie actresses Theda Bara and Pola Negri asked for personal consultations, and Helena was delighted to meet them privately and give them samples of her products. Afterward she made sure the news leaked to the press, well aware of the benefit of celebrity endorsements.

She wrote to Edward every few days, and he wrote back with news of their sons, so there were usually letters waiting for her when she arrived at a new city. She had missed Horace's fourth birthday, but Edward wrote that he had taken him for tea at the Plaza Hotel and bought him a train set. Did he like trains? Helena hadn't known that. He had certainly been on plenty of them in his short life.

Their tour took them to San Francisco and Seattle, then back across the Rockies. When Edward wrote suggesting that he might join her in Chicago, Helena was pleased. It had been a long time since they were alone together. The hotel concierge told her Rector's Oyster House was the best restaurant in the city, so she got him to book a table and even bought herself a new gown in emerald green silk, cut low at the bosom.

"Your shy, retiring wife has been treated like a star," she told him. "Some of the women at my talks even ask me to sign autograph books! Can you believe it?"

He smiled and raised his glass to her. "I'm sure they've never met anyone like you. You're hardly the average woman."

"It's been useful visiting all these cities: it's helped me decide where to open my next salons. San Francisco, definitely. I had a great reception there."

They talked about the boys: Roy had started attending a weekly boarding school in upstate New York and Horace couldn't wait to join him.

"They are thriving without their parents. Does that mean our job is done?" she asked.

"Not quite," he replied. "Roy comes home each weekend with mountains of laundry and devours any food in sight as if a plague of locusts has invaded the kitchen. And Horace still likes to be tucked up in bed by his nanny, with his teddy bear under his arm."

She smiled. She would never let on, but Horace was secretly her favorite. Roy was shy and often seemed nervous around her, but her younger son was an entertainer whose clowning could always make her laugh.

That night she and Edward made love for the first time in many weeks and it was passionate and beautiful, just like the old days. He called her his "precious love" and his "princess." He kissed her knees, her breasts, the nape of her neck, and ran his hands over her skin as if she were a sculpture. She loved sex and it disappointed her that she wanted it more often than Edward. It was hurtful being rejected when she made overtures. It made her feel less feminine.

Afterward, she lay awake watching him sleep, grateful that she had married him—eventually. She had run away when he first proposed to her in Melbourne, because she was scared of getting hurt; it was easier not to let herself be vulnerable. Edward had persevered, following her across the world to London, and persuading her they belonged together. In the eight years since they married, they had made homes in London, Paris, and America, and created two darling children. It wasn't a conventional marriage—they didn't live in each other's pockets—but it seemed to work most of the time, thank God.

The next morning, she and Manka were catching a train to Cincinnati, and she asked if Edward wanted to ride with them to the station.

"I'm staying an extra night," he said. "It's a chance to have dinner with an author I respect."

Did he mention the author's name? Looking back, Helena couldn't remember.

She and Manka arrived at their Cincinnati hotel, unpacked, and went to the department store where she was speaking that evening. Helena was inspired; a night of passion had left her in an exuberant mood and she felt she had never performed better.

Afterward they had dinner, then she decided to call Edward in Chicago, to recapture a little of their intimacy of the previous night. It was late; he should be back. Manka dialed the operator for her and read out the number. Helena clutched the receiver, listening to the hisses and clicks down the line. How many people were listening in? She distrusted any technology she couldn't understand.

The Chicago hotel operator answered and tried to put the call through to Edward's room but there was no reply. She heard a muffled conversation in the background before the operator told her: "The receptionist says he's not back. His key's still here."

Suspicion prickled her skin. Helena kept her voice casual as she asked, "I wonder if you could ask the receptionist with whom he was dining?"

The operator was gone for a few minutes before her voice came back on the line. "She's sorry, she can't remember the woman's name."

Helena slammed down the phone, feeling as if her chest

were in a vice. So his author friend was a woman. Was she the real reason for his trip to Chicago? How could he sleep with someone else straight after their romantic evening? Is that why he hardly ever made love to her? Because other women were supplying his needs? She felt winded, as though she had been punched hard in the gut.

LOOKING BACK, THERE had been no sign of Edward's roving eye during their courtship. He was friendly with everyone they met, but she never saw him turn his unctuous charm on anyone but her. And then, during their honeymoon in the South of France, she returned from a stroll to see him standing near the door of their hotel chatting to a slim redhead who looked barely out of her teens. He was leaning toward her, like a tree bending in the wind, and they were both laughing. It was clear they were flirting, their postures mirroring each other's. Her stomach twisted with jealousy.

She didn't charge up to confront them; she wouldn't lower herself. Instead, she turned back into the shopping district and bought herself a double strand of creamy pearls she had noticed in a jeweler's window. She put them on and felt a little better, although she was still furious that Edward could flirt with another woman on his honeymoon. She wouldn't tolerate it; yet she was determined not to debase herself by making a scene.

Helena did what her instinct told her to do: she ran away. Leaving her luggage at the hotel, carrying only a small purse, she walked to the train station, bought a first-class ticket for the next Paris train, and got on board. If Edward wanted to sleep with that redhead, she wouldn't stand in his way.

Two days later he turned up at her Paris salon, laden with luggage, both his and hers.

"What the hell are you doing here?" he shouted. "I've been going mad with worry. I called the police and had them out searching for you."

"I thought you might want to spend some time alone with that girl at the hotel," she said, waving her hand airily, as if it were all the same to her.

"What girl? I have no idea what you're talking about."

He seemed genuinely puzzled, so she explained what she had seen with her own eyes.

He shook his head in disbelief: "We were passing the time of day. Her husband was late for meeting her, and you were late for meeting me. That's all you saw. I don't even know her name."

She shrugged. "That's not how it looked." Had her instinct been wrong? Perhaps, perhaps not.

From then on, whenever she thought Edward was flirting with another woman—and it would happen many times—she charged straight to the nearest jewelry store and bought herself a present. "Quarrel jewels," she called them. He didn't know she did it; that wasn't the point. She was spending her own money, but it never failed to improve her mood.

She hoped Cincinnati had a very expensive jewelry store. There was just enough time to shop before she and Manka caught a train to the next city on their tour.

CHAPTER 9

Elizabeth

April 1916

Elizabeth and Tommy had just two months to settle into married life before he left to start his army training at a camp in Massachusetts. He was allowed home on leave some weekends and Elizabeth made the most of them, arranging dinner parties for guests who were carefully selected from her acquaintances. She didn't dare invite any of her high-society clients; they wouldn't dream of dining with anyone who worked "in trade," and to ask would be seen as presumptuous. Instead, she invited Mr. Dunlop and his wife, and some well-connected neighbors who worked in fashion, automobiles, and insurance. She had an Irish cook, but didn't feel her culinary efforts were grand enough, so she arranged for the food to be sent from Delmonico's, and she purchased expensive French wines and cognac, plus cigars for the men.

"I've been perfecting my cocktail-mixing skills since our marriage," Tommy told the guests as they arrived. "I like to greet my wife with a new concoction when she gets home from the salon. Some of our current favorites are laid out on the buffet and I invite you to try them and see if you can guess the ingredients."

There was a range of different-shaped glasses containing liquids in jewel colors, and the guests picked the ones they fancied. It made for a sparkling start to the evening, with everyone tasting each other's drinks and getting half-sozzled before they sat down to eat. Tommy had a knack for making guests feel at ease. There always seemed to be laughter coming from his end of the table. She smiled as she watched his animation.

Tommy was also proving useful as someone to talk through business decisions with. When Elizabeth heard that Madame Rubinstein was launching a makeup range, with rouge, powder, lipsticks, and eyeshadows in multiple shades, she hesitated to follow in case her upper-class ladies deemed it common, but Tommy urged her to try.

"Don't call it makeup," he said. "Just tell them it will put roses in their cheeks, or bring a sparkle to their eyes. They can't object to that."

"Urging women to wear lipstick seems unpatriotic when you and your fellow soldiers might be about to risk your lives in battle," Elizabeth replied. "Her timing is inappropriate. It leaves a bad taste in the mouth."

"I agree," he said. "Especially since her family is on the wrong side in this war."

Of course! Elizabeth stared at him. She had forgotten that Kraków was part of the Austro-Hungarian Empire, which had allied itself with the Kaiser. Not all Americans were familiar with the geography of Eastern Europe so this fact had not occurred to them. If Helena's father was a kerosene salesman, he might even be supplying the enemy.

Perhaps she would hint to her clients that Madame Rubinstein was on Germany's side in the war. It might be enough to make them reassess their loyalty. As a Canadian, Elizabeth was staunchly, proudly pro-British.

The day was approaching when Tommy was to be shipped overseas and he wanted to make the most of the time remaining. Unfortunately, that meant he tried to make love to her every night he was home on leave. She didn't mind an affectionate cuddle, and at first she was happy to give him a shoulder massage. She prided herself on her ability to ease knotted muscles. Sometimes she would shoo treatment girls away in the salon and take over work on a client herself, feeling in her fingertips where the tightness originated and how to ease it. However, Tommy seemed to view massage as a precursor to sexual congress, which was not her intention at all. Gracious, no! Sex was as repugnant to her as it had been on their wedding night. Elizabeth had to invent headaches, backaches, and the onset of her monthlies as excuses to discourage him.

She knew he was disappointed that she wasn't more enthusiastic about the physical side of marriage. He used prophylactics but still, she told him, she was anxious about a pregnancy, given her mother's early death, and that's what made her tense in bed.

"You could get fitted for a diaphragm," he suggested. "I believe they are a reliable method for married women."

"I'll look into it when I have the time, dearest," she promised, kissing him on the cheek and fluffing his hair. "Soon."

She didn't feel passion for him the way she assumed women were supposed to feel passion for their husbands, and yet she was developing feelings for him that could perhaps be described as a kind of love. There was a lump in her throat on the humid June day when she waved him off on the train with a bunch of other men in uniform. Might she never see him again? When he drew back from their last embrace there was fear in his eyes, and sadness too, and she knew that he was thinking the same thing. They'd only been married for five months. Was that it?

His absence left an emptiness in her life. Coming home felt lonelier than it ever had before marriage. She lay in bed listening to the creaking of the building and wind rattling the panes, and missed their late-night pillow talk. Soon it felt like a dream—as if she had never been married at all.

Where was he now? Was he thinking of her? At least he had the camaraderie of the other soldiers to distract him, while she was alone once more, the way she had felt all her life. She resolved that when—not if, *when*—Tommy got back she would try her utmost to be a better wife for him.

SHORTLY AFTER TOMMY'S departure, Mr. Dunlop telephoned Elizabeth with an apologetic tone. He said he had been ordered by the government to start making medical supplies for the war in Europe and he didn't have enough capacity to continue making her products at the same time.

Elizabeth was furious. Only weeks had elapsed since he'd accepted lavish hospitality in her home. He had drunk her whiskey and smoked her cigars, while sitting in her armchair.

"How long have you known about this government contract?" she asked, with frost in her tone.

His fumbling reply left her in no doubt that he had already known it was in the cards when he came for dinner. The Judas! She couldn't abide disloyalty!

"I had no choice," he protested. "I think you'll find all the biggest laboratories are in the same position as us. But I'm sure some smaller organizations would be able to assist you. I can make recommendations if you like."

"No, thank you," Elizabeth snapped. "I'll manage by myself. I always have."

She hung up without saying goodbye and clutched her head in her hands, feeling alarmed. America wasn't a participant in this war, so why was it affecting an American business? She would lose sales if her stock ran out. She wondered how Madame Rubinstein was faring. She must be facing the same problems. "Laney?" She called through to the outer office to ask.

"Madame Rubinstein is building her own factory in Long Island City," Laney told her, stepping into the room.

Elizabeth picked up the nearest item that came to hand—a weighty McGill paper stapler—and hurled it at the wall, where it chipped a hole in the plaster before ricocheting to the floor.

"Why wasn't I told? That's *exactly* the kind of information I need. What else have you been keeping from me?"

"I'm not sure if it's operational yet," Laney continued, unflappable, bending to pick up the stapler. "But work is under way. Madame Rubinstein always opens her own factories in the countries where she trades so she can preserve the secrets of her Carpathian herbs. At least, that's what she said in an interview I read."

Elizabeth thought quickly. She didn't want to build a factory. She had no idea what equipment was needed, or how to manage a workforce of men in overalls who might threaten to go on strike if they didn't get pay raises every year. She knew nothing about it and there wasn't time to start from scratch.

"I need you to find me a new pharmaceutical company that can take on the manufacture of our products." She considered. "No—wait! Find three. Set each of them the task of copying my Venetian Pore Cream, and I will choose the one that does the best job." She nodded, satisfied with the idea. Three competitors would give her some leverage for negotiating prices. She refused to pay a cent more per unit than she was paying at the moment.

"Oh, and Laney . . ." She remembered what Tommy had told her. "Can you mention to one of your reporter friends that Madame Rubinstein's family is on Germany's side in the war?"

"Certainly, Miss Arden." Laney wrote it in her notebook and retreated.

THE TRIAL POTS of cream arrived a week later, and Elizabeth tested each of them on the back of her hand, sniffing to check that the makers had successfully masked the unpleasant animal scent of the lanolin. The one she liked best was made by a company called Stillwell and Gladding, which was based on Staten Island.

Laney arranged a meeting at the plant, and on arrival Elizabeth was guided into a brightly lit laboratory and introduced to the chief chemist, a bearded, middle-aged Swedish man called Fabian Swanson, who wore gray overalls and thick glasses. He pulled up a chair for her and placed two pots of cream on the bench.

"This is my copy of your existing cream," he said, handing her one.

Elizabeth sniffed, then dipped in a fingertip. It was identical to her product.

He produced another pot. "But try this one," he told her. "A different proportion of oil to water, along with a faster beating technique, could give you a much lighter cream that the skin will absorb more readily."

Elizabeth tested the cream on the back of her hand. It had a luxurious feel, yet it seemed to disappear into the skin soon after application, leaving it soft and plump. She tried more on the other hand.

"So it has the same ingredients but a different way of emulsifying them? Would it cost extra to produce?" She sniffed her hand. It smelled fragrant.

"Not at all," he said. "And I have ideas for ways you could expand your product range if you wish." He produced another pot of cream. "Try this."

Elizabeth dipped a finger in the new one and realized it had a slight powdery texture.

"The powder will have the effect of evening the complexion," he said. "It's not makeup as such, but women will look instantly healthier when they use it." His expression was serious, his spectacles glinting in the light. He was a man who didn't smile, it seemed.

Elizabeth was impressed by the new product. Her brain ticked over the possibilities. She could market it as a "miracle cream," stealing Madame Rubinstein's favorite word.

"Are you sure you can obtain sufficient supplies of the raw ingredients?" she asked. "Aren't there shortages because of the war?"

"We have plenty," he said. "I personally made sure we stocked up."

Elizabeth gave Stillwell and Gladding the contract, on condition that Fabian Swanson be in charge of her product design. His serious, knowledgeable style had won her confidence. Before her driver dropped her back at the office that afternoon, she had decided to call the new product Venetian Amoretta Cream: Venice for beauty and Amoretta for love.

This was how she could fight back against Madame Rubinstein's aggressive tactics: she would improve her creams until there was no question whose products were superior.

Carpathian herbs, my foot! she thought to herself. *I'll show the Queen of Beauty Science who really deserves the crown.*

CHAPTER 10

Helena

May 1916

On the night Helena got back from her department store tour, she and Edward dined together in their Upper West Side apartment. She was wearing an emerald necklace that she had bought in Cincinnati—the latest quarrel jewels—along with a low-cut black velvet gown. She knew she looked striking but he didn't appear to notice, talking instead about a novel he'd read, *A Portrait of the Artist as a Young Man*, by an Irishman called Joyce Something—or was it Something Joyce? Joyce hadn't been able to find a book publisher because the novel was so unusual, but it had been printed in installments in one of the magazines Edward subscribed to. Helena wasn't paying much attention as he raved about it; afterward all she could remember was that Joyce didn't use quotation marks.

She was feeling under par. Jealousy always gave her an attack of stomach acid that left her throat raw and her gut unsettled. Who had the Chicago woman been, and was Edward sleeping with her? That was the question at the forefront of her mind, but she saved it till dessert had been served.

"How was your dinner in Chicago?" she asked, her tone casual, as she lifted a forkful of cherry pie. "The one with that author."

"It was fascinating. Perhaps you've heard of Carl Sandburg? He's just published a collection of poems that—"

"Don't lie to me, Edward," Helena interrupted with her mouth full. She swallowed. "I called you. The hotel receptionist told me you were with a woman."

He threw down his fork with a clatter. "For god's sake, Helena. That was Lilian, Carl's wife. She came into the hotel to collect me while he kept the taxi waiting outside." He took his glasses off and rubbed the bridge of his nose. "Carl and Lilian took me to their home. She made pot roast. We talked poetry. We drank whiskey and I got back late. Did you think I spent the evening with another woman? I'm so tired of your absurd jealousy!"

Helena shrugged and carried on eating, her mind turning over this information. Could it be true? He hadn't hesitated before replying. Every time she questioned him, he made her feel like a madwoman. He had an answer for everything, while all she had was her woman's instinct. Was he being truthful and she was oversuspicious—or was he an accomplished liar? If there was no one else, why did he not make love to her more often?

"Would you like me to call Carl on the telephone so he can confirm it?" He was angry now, his eyes flashing.

"That won't be necessary," she said, and took another bite of pie. She supposed it was plausible enough. Perhaps she had been wrong this time, but one day she would catch him. Her gut told her she would.

Edward put his glasses back on, picked up his fork, and they ate the rest of the meal in silence.

IN THE FALL Elizabeth Arden launched a new face cream—Venetian Amoretta Cream—with a burst of adverts in all the women's magazines. Helena had Manka buy a jar and she examined the pink and gold packaging, then rubbed some on the back of her hand. It was light and had a powder base. This was a much more sophisticated product than any Miss Arden had marketed before.

"Get it analyzed," she told Manka. "Find out how they've done it." Her brain was running through possible recipes: How did they emulsify it without the powder sinking to the bottom?

That afternoon she was interviewing candidates to work in the salon. One of the interviewees, a strapping girl in a mid-calf-length skirt with a long tan scarf tied in a bow, admitted that she had worked at Elizabeth Arden's salon until she was "bounced" three weeks earlier.

"Oh, dear. Why did she fire you?" Helena asked, cocking her head as if in sympathy.

"For coming to work with a cold," the girl admitted. "I couldn't afford to lose a day's pay, so I powdered my nose and tried to hide my symptoms. But then Miss Arden heard me sneeze, and she was furious. She called me every name under the sun, I can tell you, including some cuss words. And she is refusing to give me a reference."

Helena nodded, an idea taking shape. "I guess she must be looking for your replacement now?"

The girl made a face. "Good luck to her. Miss Arden has a terrible temper. She's a very difficult person to work for."

"Difficult? In what way?"

Assuming she had Helena's support, the girl let her words pour out. "She prowls around the building checking up on us, even during our breaks. I've known her to bounce girls simply for smoking on their lunch break." She raised her eyebrows, inviting Helena to agree this was the height of unreasonableness. "We call to warn each other—'Lady Muck is on the way!'—so we can hide the ashtrays and open a few windows. She *hates* her girls smoking."

Helena wasn't surprised. It would be unpleasant for clients to have a treatment girl breathing stale cigarette smoke in their faces. She wouldn't tolerate it either. "Does she fire people often?"

"Oh, all the time," the girl said. "'Bouncing,' she calls it. *'I'm going to bounce you.'*" She imitated a breathy, little-girl voice. "She bounced another treatment girl last month—my friend Dorothy—after she found out that she's living with a married man, Dr. Gray. It's not their fault. They're in love and his wife won't give him a divorce, so what choice did they have?"

Helena nodded as if in sympathy, but she could understand why Miss Arden would have gotten rid of a girl who was committing adultery. Her clients would have been outraged if they found out.

"I think the only one who's been there for years without getting bounced is Laney," the girl said.

"And what exactly does Laney do?"

She wasn't entirely sure of her title. "They discuss everything. Laney's always around and she's more reasonable than Miss Arden. You can talk to her if you have a problem."

Helena made a mental note to remember the name Laney as she worked her way around to the question she most wanted to ask. "Has she changed her chemist recently? The new Amoretta cream seems different from previous products."

The girl leaned forward and lowered her voice as if to impart a secret. "She brought in a new company, and she works with their chief chemist, Mr. Swanson. She says he's a genius."

Helena nodded, thoughtful. "And I suppose there are many more new products planned?"

"I guess so. Miss Arden has long meetings with Mr. Swanson. Sometimes they get us girls to test samples on our own skin. . . ." She faltered and corrected herself. "Used to, I mean."

Helena quizzed her about the new products, then said, "Thank you. You've been very helpful." She stood up. "I have more girls to interview but I'll be in touch soon."

The girl was startled. "Don't you want to test my skills? Clients say I have a wonderful touch. Mrs. Whitney told me my facial massage is heavenly and gave me a dollar tip one time."

Helena smiled. "Not today, but we'll definitely let you know."

She wouldn't dream of hiring someone so indiscreet, but it had given her an idea. She would try to plant a treatment girl in the Salon d'Oro, someone loyal who could spy for her. And she knew exactly who to ask.

One of her girls, Edith Brown, lived with her widowed mother and four younger siblings, and was the sole wage earner for the family. She had asked for a raise recently but Helena had told her she couldn't give one treatment girl a raise without doing the same for all the others. If Edith got a job at the Salon d'Oro and reported back on developments there, she could get an extra stipend every month—say, ten dollars. Maybe more. Edith was smart. She would be good value for the money.

Helena waited until Edith had finished with the client she was working on and called her into the office to explain her plan.

BY CHRISTMAS, HELENA felt satisfied with the foothold she had established in the US market. The New York salon was booked for weeks in advance, she had leased premises for new ones in San Francisco and Philadelphia, and her products were stocked in department stores the length and breadth of the country. Edith had gotten a job at Miss Arden's Salon d'Oro and was already supplying titbits about the operation there. But early in the New Year of 1917, the war in Europe suddenly got a whole lot closer to home.

The Kaiser's decision to resume submarine attacks on shipping in the North Atlantic surprised most Americans, but Helena recognized it as the work of a gambler. It took one to know one. In her view, he was taking the risk that he could force Great Britain, France, and Russia to surrender long before President Woodrow Wilson would declare war, mobilize US troops, and get them across the Atlantic. Both she and Edward hoped Wilson would move fast. Poland had borne the brunt of much of the fighting on the war's Eastern Front, with high casualty figures and towns laid waste. The only hope for their country's future independence lay with a victory for the Allies.

When Wilson got the Senate to agree to his declaration of war on April 6, Helena and Edward celebrated. If only the fighting could be over soon, their families in Kraków would be safe again.

She was shocked and puzzled in equal measure when Edward showed her a diary entry in the *New York World*, headed "Whose Side Is Beauty Queen On?" There were no facts, just an insinuation that Madame Rubinstein's allegiance might be with the enemy since her home town, Kraków, was situated in Austria-Hungary.

"Who would write such a thing?" she thundered. "What does it matter where I was born? The cities where I open my salons show clearly where my loyalties lie."

"Leave it with me," Edward soothed. He wrote a letter to the editor, explaining that Madame Rubinstein considered herself Russian-Polish rather than Austrian, and that she was firmly behind the British, French, Russian, and American alliance. All Poles, he wrote, yearned to be free of the chokehold of Austro-Hungarian occupation and were supporting the Allies to the last man. He was too old or he would be fighting himself. He finished with a masterstroke: *Helena Rubinstein is donating thousands of jars of her miracle healing Crème Valaze to help wounded US soldiers, and they are already being packed for transport across the ocean.*

His letter was published two days later, and the story of her donation of Crème Valaze was picked up by several other newspapers.

"I suppose we had better do it, in that case," she grumbled, calculating the cost in her head. She had perfect recall of figures, and a talent for mental arithmetic.

A reporter from the *New York World* called to ask for more

information about how Crème Valaze helped with wound healing. Helena invited him to the salon for a demonstration, and
plied him with shots of vodka and bite-size blinis topped with
smetana and caviar, underlining her Russian credentials.

"I wonder who could have been behind the story that I was
on the German side in the war?" she mused, once he'd drunk a
few shots. "Such nonsense."

"We had a tip-off," he told her, his tongue made heavy by
vodka.

Helena thought fast. The only person in New York who
could possibly want to harm her was the Arden woman, but she
wouldn't have phoned the press herself. She wasn't the type to
get her hands dirty.

"Let me guess . . ." she said, refilling his glass. "I pride myself
on my guesswork. Was it Laney, by any chance?"

He was startled. "I didn't realize you two knew each other."

"I know *everything*," she told him, with a smile. "Please, take
the rest of this vodka home. And here's a pot of Crème Valaze
for your wife." She brushed away his refusal with an imperious
"No, I absolutely insist."

So Miss Arden was prepared to plant stories to harm her,
was she? She must feel threatened. Helena smiled, a plan taking
shape.

Edith had mentioned that Miss Arden was one of the orga-
nizers of a *Vogue* party to raise funds for the Red Cross. Helena
decided she would attend; it was high time for their paths to
cross.

CHAPTER 11

Elizabeth

June 1917

Elizabeth was thrilled when Edna Woolman Chase asked her to be on the committee for a party in aid of the Red Cross. She devoted many hours to compiling the exclusive guest list, sending out invitations, and liaising with the Ritz-Carlton's manager over catering and drinks, as well as arrangements for the auction. The Grand Ballroom was to be festooned with garlands of fragrant pink roses from which all the thorns had been removed, and she bought herself a drop-waisted silk Paquin evening gown in the exact same shade.

Elizabeth arrived early on the night, feeling a buzz of anticipation. As she stood in the entrance to the ballroom, her diamond necklace and drop earrings caught the light from the overhead chandeliers and created a pleasing kaleidoscope of floating white dots. The scent of the roses wafted toward her. She surveyed the room with satisfaction. It was perfect.

Edna was scolding an assistant over some detail so Elizabeth simply waved hello, then glided around the room, checking that everything was in place: the buffet table heaped with dainty morsels; the waiters with thin black bow ties and sleek black jackets; the hand-painted paddles that would be used to bid in the auction. She felt a sense of proprietorship about this party and as soon as guests began to arrive, she stood by the door to greet them.

Some she knew from her salon; others she recognized from the society pages. She admired the ladies' gowns: lace appeared to be making a comeback, and there was a new style with loose pockets on the hips that gave a baggy appearance. Heirloom jewels were proudly on display and she noticed that many faces bore hints of powder and rouge. Some women were even wearing eyeshadow and lipstick. She was glad she had introduced a pink lip paste and a blue eye shadow in her Venetian range. The time was right.

Once the stream of new arrivals had slowed, she moved from group to group, inviting them to view the auction prizes. She had donated a top-to-toe treatment at her salon, plus a complete set of her Venetian products, and she hoped the lot would fetch a good price. The string quartet playing in the corner could scarcely be heard over the murmur of genteel voices.

Suddenly she sensed a lull in the conversation and noticed heads turning toward the doorway. A striking, dark-haired woman stood poised in a gown made of shimmering gold fabric with a deep V neck and Grecian-style folds. Her hair was pulled back in a chignon. It wasn't . . . it couldn't be Madame Rubinstein, could it? She most definitely hadn't been on the guest list.

Vogue staffers scurried around like squirrels, while the newcomer surveyed the room with a smile playing on her lips. Elizabeth was sure it was Helena Rubinstein: she recognized her from magazine images and from that one time she had glimpsed her in her Paris salon. *Someone should eject her*, Elizabeth thought, but no one was doing anything. She grabbed the arm of a waiter.

"That woman is not on the guest list," she said, her eyes sliding toward the entrance. "Could you please go over and explain to her the ball is invitation-only? If she objects, ask to see her invitation. She doesn't have one, so then you can ask her to leave."

He reddened. "It's not my place . . ."

"Do I need to fetch the manager?" she snapped. "I'm in charge here. Do as I ask."

The waiter sloped toward the newcomer. Elizabeth stepped a little closer to eavesdrop. She could see that Madame Rubinstein was annoyed to be challenged. She was arguing. The waiter was retreating. *Damn!*

Just then, Madame Rubinstein turned and noticed her watching. Elizabeth was startled. Did she recognize her? Yes, she had a feeling she did, because she held her gaze. The expression was inscrutable; not a facial muscle moved. Was she waiting for Elizabeth to intervene and allow her to join the party? Well, she wasn't about to do that, for goodness' sake.

Just at that moment, Edna appeared, hurrying toward the door. *Good! Let her deal with the situation*, Elizabeth thought—and then the unthinkable happened: Edna shook hands with the newcomer. What on earth was happening?

Madame Rubinstein glanced at Elizabeth again, and now her smile was triumphant. What was Edna playing at?

Elizabeth lifted a glass of champagne from the tray of a passing waiter and turned to talk to the woman closest, hardly aware of what she was saying. The drink tasted sour. Was it off? Glancing over her shoulder, she saw Edna leading the newcomer toward the room where the auction goods were on display.

Elizabeth grasped the arm of one of Edna's personal assistants. "Why is that woman here?" she demanded, nodding in Madame Rubinstein's direction.

"Madame Rubinstein?" The assistant was unabashed. "The advertising department added her to the list because she donated a painting to the auction—a Rouault. Would you like me to introduce you?"

"Absolutely not," Elizabeth replied. "I wouldn't dream of it." She shuddered. Why hadn't she been consulted? The guest list had been her responsibility.

Now the evening was ruined for her. She would have to be on guard to make sure she didn't bump into that woman. Out of the corner of her eye, she saw Edna introducing her to Carrie

Astor Wilson and her stomach twisted. The immigrant was trying to steal *her* clients and a woman she considered a friend was
helping.

Later, when she spotted Edna on her own by the buffet, Elizabeth sidled across with a forced smile. "I see Madame Rubinstein wormed her way in," she said, with an arched eyebrow.

"You two should talk," Edna said. "You have a lot in common."

"I doubt it somehow," Elizabeth said. "She doesn't look my
type at all." She felt betrayed by Edna. She thought they'd seen
eye to eye on the subject when they spoke over lunch, but it
seemed not.

"The auction is starting soon," Edna said, after a pause, as
if she'd been thinking of saying something else, then decided
against it. "Come stand with me and we'll try to whip up these
ladies to open their purses."

Bidding started enthusiastically. Among the lots, there was a
silver chain-mail evening purse, a Lalique glass perfume bottle,
a pretty gilt candelabra, and tickets for the opera. Elizabeth was
delighted when her lot raised fifty-five dollars and she clapped
hard for the successful bidder.

The Rouault painting was reserved for the very end. It wasn't
attractive, Elizabeth thought, showing a glum Pierrot figure in
dreary colors. The auctioneer said this was an artist at the beginning of his career whose work would be an investment for the
future.

Elizabeth harrumphed and turned to Edna: "It looks to me
like something you would throw onto a bonfire after clearing
the attic," she said, her voice low.

Edna pursed her lips and didn't reply.

To Elizabeth's amazement, the bidding started at a hundred
dollars. She glanced around to see four different women were
competing. The hammer came down at three hundred and

seventy-five dollars, the highest price reached by any item that evening. Elizabeth clasped her hands together and pinned a fake smile to her face as she scanned the crowd, trying to identify the successful bidder.

And then, as she turned, she realized that Madame Rubinstein was standing just a few feet behind her.

"I'm glad to find New York women have discerning taste in art," the woman said in her funny foreign accent. "Apart from the few who prefer to light bonfires with it."

A handful of women in the vicinity tittered and Elizabeth realized they must all have overheard her comment. She was sure she'd kept her voice low. Edna had wandered off to talk to someone else and was unaware of the confrontation.

Madame Rubinstein caught her eye and several seconds passed while Elizabeth tried to think of a suitable riposte. Certainly she didn't intend to apologize. She wasn't in the wrong.

"I don't know the etiquette where you come from, Madame . . ." She paused, unwilling to utter the woman's name. "But in America, it is considered vulgar to buy your way into elite parties, like a common merchant. Just a little tip for the future."

All those in earshot gasped out loud.

Madame's expression didn't change but anger flashed across her eyes before she glanced down at Elizabeth's chest. "You appear to have spilled your drink," she said.

Elizabeth looked down and was horrified to see a dark patch on the pink silk, right across her breast. How long had that been there? She'd put her glass down on a waiter's tray before the auction so the spill must have happened before that. Why hadn't Edna mentioned it?

"If you'll excuse me." She smiled and nodded at the ladies gathered around them, then turned and walked, head held high, toward the powder room. Once in the coolness of the mirrored marble room, she dabbed at the stain with a towel but the silk had soaked up a splash of champagne and only French cleaning would shift it. She couldn't go back out there in a ruined gown. There was nothing for it but to leave early.

She caught a taxi home in a thunderous mood, asked the maid to bring her some tea, and sat up to write a letter to Tommy describing the evening. *Madame Rubinstein arrived in a gaudy gold gown, which did not suit her figure*, she wrote. *If she wants to represent the beauty industry, she should try forsaking the cookies.*

She laid down her pen. What worried her was that if Madame Rubinstein became accepted in her social circles, she could expect to bump into her at many other such events. Should she have allowed Edna to introduce them and greeted her with good grace, to get it out of the way? But that would make Madame Rubinstein more acceptable in polite society, whereas Elizabeth hoped that most well-bred women would view her as persona non grata. The leaked story about her being on the wrong side in the war hadn't had the impact she'd hoped for, but surely it wouldn't be long before New Yorkers saw the woman's true colors. She was horrified at Edna for inviting her, and felt she had certainly made a miscalculation.

She went to bed but tossed and turned, drifting in and out of disturbed sleep, dreaming of parties at which a malignant presence hovered just out of sight.

When light streamed around the edge of the curtains, she rose straight away, dressed in her pink gym suit, and began her yoga routine, breathing deep into her lungs. By the time Laney arrived for their morning meeting, she had more or less recovered her composure.

Laney read out the schedule for the launch of their new Venetian range, created with the help of Fabian Swanson: Crème Mystique for red and shiny noses; Venetian Lille Lotion to prevent sunburn and heal blemishes; Ultra-Lille Lotion to smooth the appearance of lines and wrinkles; she even had Venetian Eyelash Grower. They were sophisticated high-end products, better than anything she had created before, and she had devised a new advertising campaign to launch them, with the help of one of Manhattan's top agencies. She hoped they would once and for all establish her superiority in the New York beauty world.

"I was here first," Elizabeth told Laney as she arched her upper body backward, pushing her chest out into Cobra pose. "I am the Queen of Beauty in America and I will *not* be usurped. Not by anyone. Certainly not by *that woman*."

CHAPTER 12

Helena

October 1917

Helena had a hunch that Edith Brown would prove a talented spy, but she was amazed to find how well she adapted to the role. When she had information to pass across, she got one of her younger sisters to deliver an envelope to Helena's Upper West Side apartment, rather than risk being spotted at the salon. In the first few weeks on the job, she managed to pass on a price list for Elizabeth Arden's new Venetian range, a schedule of launch dates for the products, and even the advertising copy that Miss Arden was planning to run: *There is just one right way to do a thing and you can always distinguish the Right Way by its success. Many are those who offer panaceas for all complexion defects . . . but no one has achieved a success comparable with Elizabeth Arden.*

"Success" was clearly her watchword, Helena thought. She showed the copy to Edward. "Could you write an advertisement for me about the success of our products? This is running on the twenty-eighth of November and I thought I might steal her thunder by running mine the day before."

Edward put down the sheet of paper and regarded her. "Are you sure you want to declare war? Is it wise?"

Helena laughed. "How long have you known me? I love a good battle."

"I think you should have introduced yourself and shaken hands with Miss Arden at the *Vogue* ball," he said, not for the first time. "That would have been the civilized thing to do."

Helena scoffed at that: "She tried to have me thrown out, Edward. She called me vulgar. No, the gloves are off now."

In that split second when they caught eyes, Helena had seen fear. Miss Arden was the incumbent and she had more to lose than the newcomer. With Edith's help, she hoped she could stay several steps ahead in this battle and eventually win the war. So far, she was enjoying it greatly.

Edward agreed to write some copy about success for her, and she laughed when she read it: *"Nothing succeeds like success" is an old and very true saying. Certainly nothing has ever been greeted with more success than the new and improved Valaze Beauty Preparations, the most successful and efficacious in the history of Beauty Culture.*

"Is this going too far?" he asked. "It almost sounds like a parody of her advert."

"It's perfect," Helena replied. She got her advertising manager to place it across the press on November 27, chortling as she pictured Miss Arden's face when she opened her morning paper.

HELENA WAS PLANNING another of her nationwide tours in the run-up to Christmas. During the war, she had opened salons in five locations: San Francisco, Philadelphia, New Orleans, Chicago, and Atlantic City, while Miss Arden had only opened one, in Boston. She wanted to visit them all, to check the décor and the staff selection, and she was considering six further salons. So far, the business was expanding as rapidly as she had planned, despite the war.

She liked to greet customers personally in each new location. Always she offered a little flattery—"such pretty eyes" or "exquisite bone structure"—to soften them up. She wanted women to feel cherished in her salons, as if their well-being was of the utmost importance.

She had relocated her New York salon to larger premises on West Fifty-Seventh Street and, crucially, she had opened her factory in Long Island City, so her products could be made on US soil. The ingredients she had stockpiled before the war meant she could step up the scale of production. As far as the press were concerned, she still used "miraculous Carpathian herbs" that she grew in a secret location, but in fact she had substituted a mixture of sweet-smelling American plants, whose main role was to disguise the unpleasant scent of the lanolin.

Over breakfast at their Connecticut house one weekend, she told Edward about her latest travel plans.

"I think I'll stay here while you're away," he said. "Get some reading done."

Instantly, Helena was suspicious. What would he do on his own in the country? Both boys were at boarding school. Wouldn't he rather be with his literary friends in New York? She knew several of them had books coming out that fall, so there would be readings and drinks parties to attend. It wasn't like him to miss a party.

Edward folded his napkin and rose from the table, and just at that moment Helena intercepted a look between him and a young housemaid who had started recently. It was only the briefest of glances, less than a second, but she was instantly suspicious. The girl was pretty in a plump-cheeked country type of way, probably not yet twenty. *He wouldn't sleep with a maid, would he?* For the rest of the weekend, she watched the two of them carefully and saw no further interactions. She could have challenged him directly, but he would deny everything and he was always scathing when she voiced her suspicions.

Back in New York, doubt preyed on her mind. Was she being foolish? Why did she not trust her husband after eleven years of marriage? Just because he was charming to every woman he met didn't mean he was sleeping with anyone but her. Still, she kept seeing that look in her mind's eye.

Her attention was caught by a newspaper advertisement for a private detective, who claimed to be "discreet and confidential." He had a Jewish surname, Steinburg. On a whim, she decided to hire him to check on Edward while she was away. If her husband had nothing to hide, the detective's report would set her mind at ease and he need never know.

Mr. Steinburg was a slight, nondescript man of few words, the type of man you would never notice in a crowd. He noted down the details she gave without comment. She lent him a photograph of Edward and paid half his fee in advance, then left his office feeling grubby. Loving wives didn't do this, did they? Sigmund Freud would accuse her of neurosis.

What had made her this way? She was sure her father had never cheated on her mother; he simply wasn't the type, but she knew many men who were. Plenty of married men had tried to seduce her while she was setting up her business, offering help in return for favors. She had grown adept at handling these types. A woman on her own had to. The one thing she couldn't handle was sexual rejection; every time Edward turned down her advances in bed, the nugget of suspicion inside her grew.

DURING THE TOUR, Helena received affectionate letters from Edward at most hotel stops. He wrote that he was enjoying the peace and quiet, except at weekends when the boys joined him and the stillness was disrupted by boisterous games. *Why do they feel the need to shout when I am three feet away? The noise level is horrendous. Yet it's when they go quiet that I worry.* He wrote about plans for the holidays, which they celebrated with gift-giving and festive meals just as Americans did. Helena liked to light Hanukkah candles, because they were so pretty. She had taken some on the tour with her to light in her hotel rooms.

She returned to their Upper West Side apartment a week before Christmas, looking forward to seeing Edward. A letter was waiting for her on the hall table, saying that he and the boys were in Connecticut; it had snowed heavily and they were spending the days tobogganing. He wrote that he had bought the festive gifts and food, so all she need do was join them as soon as she could.

She planned to spend a couple of days at the office first, checking the books and dealing with correspondence. She couldn't relax until she felt she was on top of every detail.

On her first afternoon back at her desk, the telephone rang and she jumped, guiltily, when her secretary told her a Mr. Steinburg was on the line. His investigation had completely slipped her mind.

"Did you find anything?" she asked.

"I don't give out information on the telephone," he told her. "You'll have to stop by the office."

She sighed. It felt like a waste of precious time when she was drowning in work. Why had she ever hired him? It seemed so long ago. She had paid half the fee, though, so she might as well hear what he had to say.

The following evening, she climbed the stairs to his poky office and sat in a chair opposite him, tapping her fingers on the armrest as he pulled an envelope from a desk drawer.

"Your instincts were correct, I'm afraid," he told her. Helena drew in a breath sharply as he continued. "I find women's intuition is almost always accurate in these situations."

What situation did he mean? What could he possibly have found?

"On the fourteenth of December, your husband had dinner with the girl in question at a Greenwich restaurant. I have photographs of them together. I think you'll agree they seem very intimate."

He handed her a print. It was blurred, but clearly them, deep in conversation, leaning across the table. Why had Edward taken the maid for dinner? Helena was baffled. She hadn't expected this.

"They also went for walks in the woods. There's a full report in here and more photographs." He handed her the envelope.

Helena pulled out one photograph, then shoved it back again. Suddenly, she felt as if she couldn't breathe. She rose, stuffing the envelope in her bag.

"Are you all right, Mrs. Rubinstein?" he asked. "Would you like a glass of water?"

"The rest of your fee is here," she said, thrusting a bundle of notes toward him. "That will be all."

She hurried from the office, down the stairs, and into her waiting car. She sat very erect in the back seat, managing to hold in the emotion till she got home and had closed the door behind her.

Was it true? Photographs didn't lie. Did it mean she had been right all those other times she suspected Edward of having affairs? Was her marriage built on deception? Perhaps he was only with her for the money and he looked for passion elsewhere. She bent double with the twisting pain in her gut. *What to do, what to do.*

Perhaps she should burn the photos, forget what she had heard, and carry on as before. It was tempting. Many women ignored their husband's infidelities so as not to upset the status quo. Could she be one of them?

There was a pound of smoked salmon in the icebox. She pulled out the package and started devouring it, the oil coating her fingers and slicking her lips. Next, she grabbed a block of hard salty cheese and broke off one corner, then another, until she had eaten almost the entire piece. Her cook would wonder where it had gone.

She went to bed but couldn't sleep for the acid in her stomach and the bitter thoughts in her head. He might have a plausible explanation; he always did. She could listen to what he had to say, let him tell her once again she was a madwoman—but the evidence was there in black and white. If she turned a blind eye this time, his behavior would continue, and every time she saw him chatting to another woman, she would suspect the worst. She had too much pride to let any man take her for a fool. How could she go to Greenwich for the holidays and look that maid in the eye?

By the next morning—Christmas Eve—she had made her decision: she was going to leave him. What's more, the separation would be on her terms. She called her lawyer at his home and asked him to draw up papers for her to buy back Edward's share of the business. She needed to protect her assets.

Next, she wrapped the detective's report in colored paper, tied it with a bow, and stuck it in an envelope addressed to Edward at the Connecticut house, with a note that read: *A little gift from me. I hope you like it. Helena.* She asked their driver to deliver it to him in Greenwich in time to ruin his Christmas.

After the driver left, she took a taxi to the Cartier building on Fifth Avenue to shop for some suitably extravagant quarrel jewels. A magnificent ruby and diamond necklace caught her eye. Two dozen Burmese rubies, blood-red in color, dangled from a platinum and diamond setting. She fastened it around her neck and admired the effect in the mirror. It was dramatic and regal.

"Would Madame like the matching earrings?" a sales assistant asked.

"I would expect, given the price of the necklace, you will include the earrings without charge," she said.

The manager was called. A discussion took place. She got her way.

Helena went home in a taxi still wearing her new purchases. The twenty-fifth of December was her forty-fifth birthday. She spent it alone in her "kitchen," mixing up creams, trying to incorporate some new plant oils into her base mixture. She ignored the persistent ringing of the telephone and immersed herself in chemistry.

Her throat was tight but she wouldn't cry, not even here where no one could see her. She would concentrate on her business and keep herself busy, and she would make Edward rue the day he calculated that she was a woman who could be deceived.

CHAPTER 13

Elizabeth

December 1917

Since Elizabeth's advertising campaign about "success" had been ruined by a virtually identical one by Madame Rubinstein, she had been frantic to find out where the leak had come from. Its wording mirrored hers so exactly, there could be no doubt Madame Rubinstein had placed a spy in her camp.

It seemed a crucial document had gone missing from her personal office, and her hunch was that it had been taken by one of the marketing team. Junior staff, such as treatment girls, hardly ever visited the office and, if they did, they wouldn't know what to look for.

She and Laney drew up a list of suspects and she summoned them one by one, making them stand in front of her desk as she fired questions at them.

"Do you enjoy working here?" she asked first. "Do you consider yourself a loyal type of person?" As the interrogation progressed, she banged the desk, growing more forceful in her questioning. "Do I pay you enough? Or are you looking for alternative sources of income?"

As they answered, she watched their reactions. Elizabeth considered herself an astute judge of character; she made all her business decisions based on instinct, always had.

The employees were understandably nervous and stumbling over words, but she was looking for the telltale hesitations and inability to meet her gaze that would characterize an out-and-out liar.

A young man in the marketing team, who had been hired only two months earlier, seemed the most likely culprit. He didn't once look at her directly, and he kept fingering his chin, as if trying to hide behind his hand.

"I'm bouncing you," she told him, and ignored his protestations. "Laney will pay you up till today but not a cent more. Think yourself lucky I'm not calling the police."

She hoped that would be the end of the leaks. Madame Rubinstein must have been laughing up her sleeve when that advert fell into her lap. It was alarming that her response had been so openly aggressive. She wanted Elizabeth to know she had inside sources, as if trying to provoke her. Should she place spies in her salon too? Wouldn't that make her just as bad? It might be the way they operated in Poland, but it certainly wasn't acceptable behavior in America.

EARLY IN THE new year, Madame Rubinstein launched a new line called Valaze Novena. Elizabeth got Laney to buy a jar of the so-called miracle skin cream and tested it on the back of her hand. It had the same texture as her Venetian Amoretto and the scent was reminiscent of hers too. She sent it to Fabian Swanson for analysis and he confirmed the products were similar.

Enraged, she telephoned her lawyer and ranted down the line: "Surely this can't be legal? I want you to find grounds for a lawsuit: infringement of my patent, perhaps, or downright theft. I want the products withdrawn. I want damages. I will not put up with this."

"I'm sorry, Miss Arden, but you don't have a patent on your face creams," he replied. "All the products on the market have roughly the same ingredients in different proportions. If you had done something entirely original and that had been copied, it might have given us grounds. . . ."

Elizabeth persisted: "She is making products for sunburn, blemishes, red noses, and freckles—all the same conditions as mine. Isn't that actionable?"

"Are there any differences in the two lines?" her lawyer asked.

"Well, hers has a summer and winter collection, but that's just piffle. . . ."

"It doesn't sound as if you have a case," he concluded.

Elizabeth hurled the telephone across the room with a scream. What was that woman trying to achieve? Did she want to put her out of business? She felt a clutch of fear like a cold hand twisting her heart. She seemed to be constantly on the defensive, despite the wonderful new products she had created with Fabian Swanson's help. What did she have to do to keep her business safe?

When Laney reported that some clients in the salon were asking if she planned to introduce a summer and winter line too, Elizabeth grew hysterical. "Don't they know it's just gimcrack? Whatever next? Spring and fall lines too? Rain and sunshine? I wouldn't put anything past that woman."

Madame Rubinstein was a bully, like the girls at school who used to giggle as they leapt out of her way for fear of catching cooties, and the boys who held their noses and nicknamed her Skunk, because her father only let them bathe once a week even when they'd been laboring in the fields.

If only she had ammunition to counterattack with. That woman was a liar. Elizabeth could feel it in her bones. Everything about her was fake.

ELIZABETH WROTE AND told Tommy of Madame Rubinstein's attempts to sabotage her, but his letters back made no mention of it, making her wonder if hers had gone astray.

Instead, he wrote about other soldiers he had become friendly with in the trenches, about the persistent rain and sticky mud, and about French food—he had developed a taste for snails in garlic, which she thought sounded vile. It made her feel very distant from him. She certainly didn't feel like a married woman. She had to manage everything on her own, just as she always had.

The newspapers kept reporting victories on the Western Front and said the tide of the war had turned but it could still be months or even another year before it was over. She read of soldiers returning home with life-changing injuries. What would she do if Tommy came back minus a leg? They could never go dancing again. Or what if he suffered horrific facial injuries? Or brain damage? She shuddered. They would cross that bridge if they came to it.

She hated to spend evenings alone in her apartment so she accepted every invitation that came her way. Sometimes she bought tickets for Broadway shows, then invited members of her staff to join her. When she got tickets for *Oh, Lady! Lady!!* at the Princess Theater, she asked in the salon if anyone liked musicals, and a new treatment girl, Edith Brown, piped up that she adored them.

Edith was a petite blonde in her early twenties, with a pretty speaking voice and a gentle manner. She arrived for their theater date wearing a purple gown in a style that was several years out of date, seeming nervous and unsure how to act. Elizabeth tried to put her at her ease.

"Where did you get your love of musicals?" she asked.

"My father had a good singing voice," Edith said. "My parents paid for me to have singing lessons when I was younger. They hoped I might sing professionally, but I could never have done it." She squirmed. "I'm far too shy."

"Broadway's loss is my gain, dear," Elizabeth said, with a kindly smile. "Does your father sing on stage?"

Edith shook her head. "He died, almost five years ago. I've got three younger sisters and my mother takes in sewing to earn a little, but they mainly rely on my salary. I'm very grateful to you for hiring me, Miss Arden."

Elizabeth was pleased to be able to help a family in need. "It's my pleasure," she said. "You're a good worker and you're popular with clients."

They both enjoyed the show and thought its star, Vivienne Segal, gave a remarkable performance. As they talked during the interval, Edith hummed a little snatch of the title song and Elizabeth could hear how sweet her voice was.

"We should go to musicals more often, dear," she said. "It's nice to meet another fan."

"I'd love to," Edith exclaimed, her eyes shining. "Thank you, Miss Arden."

Elizabeth felt protective toward her. It was clear her home life was difficult. Perhaps she would give her a bonus. She might even be in line for promotion if she carried on doing so well.

A TELEGRAM ARRIVED from Elizabeth's younger sister, Gladys, who lived in Toronto. "Have left Albert," she wrote. "Can I stay with you?"

"Hallelujah!" Elizabeth cheered, and replied by return, inviting Gladys to stay as long as she wanted. Divorce was a stain on a woman's reputation, but sometimes there was no other option.

Gladys arrived in Manhattan two days later, with just a small suitcase. She had lost weight, her clothes were worn, and her hair needed a good cut. As she hugged her in greeting, Elizabeth decided to offer her a top-to-toe treatment at the salon the very next day.

First of all, she had the maid bring tea and they sat on the couch, feet curled under them.

Gladys was clearly shaken about the end of her marriage. "He didn't hit me," she replied in answer to Elizabeth's question, her voice trembling, "but I was a prisoner. He locked me in the house when he went out, leaving a list of tasks I had to complete by his return. I climbed out a window and ran away while he was at work, but I couldn't bring much with me. I had to leave most of my clothes."

"Don't worry, dear," Elizabeth said. "We'll get you a new wardrobe."

Gladys pursed her lips. "He'll be furious. I'm sure he won't give me any money. I'll have to look for a job."

"Nonsense!" Elizabeth said. "Money's not a problem. You can help in the salon if you like, but first you need to get your strength back."

She felt very protective of her poor fragile sister and furious with Albert. How dare he terrorize such a gentle soul! She wished she could give him a piece of her mind, but the best revenge would be to help her sister start a new life without him.

Gladys insisted she wanted to earn her keep, so Elizabeth said she could shadow her at the salon, seeing how the business operated and deciding which role she fancied. She was there the following morning when Laney arrived for their meeting, and Elizabeth could tell Laney's nose was slightly out of joint. She smiled to herself. She didn't want to upset Laney, but a little competition would remind her that even she wasn't irreplaceable.

Laney reported on a new clarifying lotion Madame Rubinstein had launched, and Elizabeth explained to Gladys that the Polish woman had been copying her products and advertisements ever since she arrived in New York.

"She even planted a spy in my company," she complained. "I bounced him, but the leaks are continuing and I fear there could be another. Meanwhile, my incompetent lawyers can't seem to find any grounds to sue her."

"You don't need to sue," Gladys replied. "You are America's most prestigious beauty business. Don't let her see that you are rattled. Carry on as you are, and sooner or later she'll trip herself up in her desperation to imitate you."

Elizabeth liked that argument, but she didn't believe in turning the other cheek. She would keep her eyes peeled for anything she could use against her rival. Forgive and forget had never been her philosophy.

Last thing at night, no matter how late it was, Elizabeth always put her hair curlers in, then gave herself a mini facial. She invited Gladys to join her in this ritual and they sipped glasses of sherry while they helped each other with their grooming. She grew to love the calm and companionship of sherry time. It was the perfect end to the working day.

A letter arrived from Tommy in August. He said he didn't want to tempt fate by speaking too soon, but they could see the Germans deserting their trenches and taking the road toward the east, so it might not be long before he could come home to his beautiful wife.

Elizabeth frowned. How would he feel about Gladys living with them? She didn't want to forgo sherry time, but Tommy would no doubt be hoping to reclaim his place in the marital bedroom. She tutted. Why had she ever married him? She didn't want to share her life with a man. She would much rather carry on living with Gladys, just as they were.

I've grown to love the French people, Tommy wrote, *and hope we can return together in peacetime. I want to sit outside cafés drinking café au lait with you and play boules with the locals in the village square. We never had a honeymoon. I owe you one.*

A French honeymoon sounds delightful, Elizabeth wrote back, *but can Gladys come with us? She would love to see Europe too.*

CHAPTER 14

Helena

December 1917

Helena heard the front door slam, the sound reverberating around the apartment. She hurried out to the hall to see Edward standing there, suitcase in one hand and the envelope containing the detective's report in the other. She was relieved he didn't appear to have brought the boys; they must have stayed with their nanny. Thank goodness they weren't around to witness this confrontation. She folded her arms, cocked her head, and steeled herself.

"What do you mean by this?" he shouted, waving the report. "Have you lost your mind? How dare you have me followed?" He dropped his suitcase and advanced toward her. "I've always known you had an obsessive jealous streak but this time you've gone too far." He threw the envelope on the floor at her feet.

"Can you wonder that I am jealous when my husband takes our maid for dinner?" Helena retorted. "Don't turn this on me, Edward. You are the adulterer." Always he defended himself by attacking her. This time she wouldn't let him.

His tone was calm and reasonable: "I took the girl to dinner because I fancied some clam chowder and didn't want to sit on my own. She accompanied me for a couple of walks in the woods. That doesn't mean we are sleeping together. You're always nagging, always jealous. It's boring, Helena."

"What am I supposed to feel when you prefer the company of your friends to your wife?" Helena snapped. "When you never surprise me with thoughtful gifts, and only make love to me three times a year at most."

Edward took off his coat and hung it on the rack. His spectacles were sliding down his nose and he pushed them up again. "You look down on me because you make more money than me. You think it gives you the right to control me. Why don't you order me to make love to you? See if that works!"

Helena clutched her head in fury. "If I make demands, don't you think I have a right?" she countered. "I pay for your food, your clothes, the books you read, the roof over your head. What did you do to deserve this?" She gestured around the spacious hallway with a sweep of her arm, taking in the Picasso etching on the wall and the modernist Epstein sculpture on a side table.

"You're proving my point," he said, nodding his head slowly, infuriatingly. "I am not your employee, Helena. I'm your husband. What's yours is supposed to be mine. You've behaved with your usual selfishness, leaving me to ensure that our sons had a decent Christmas although their mother chose not to spend it with them. How do you think that made them feel?"

She couldn't think straight. Accusations and insults were jostling inside her head but there was no arguing with his cold rationality. Instead, she grabbed a silver fox coat from the stand, picked up the oversize leather bag in which she kept day-to-day essentials, and fled the apartment, slamming the door just as loudly as he had on arrival. His parting words rang in her ears: "That's right, run away like you always do."

Helena didn't have a plan but she got the doorman to call her driver and, by the time he arrived, she had made up her mind.

"Take me to Greenwich," she said, sliding into the back seat. *Let's find out if Edward's relationship with the girl is as innocent as he claims.* There was only one way to discover the truth.

WHEN SHE ARRIVED, she found the maid dusting the sitting room, fresh-faced in her lace-edged cap and matching apron. She jumped like a startled chicken when Helena walked in. She wasn't pretty, exactly, but she looked healthy and so young. What was her name? Helena couldn't remember. Had she ever known?

"Will you get some tea for us both, please?" she asked. "Then join me in here."

The girl looked terrified. A few minutes later she placed a tray on the table and sat down opposite Helena. She tried to still the shaking of her hands by clutching them in her lap and she bowed her head as if in prayer.

"Edward has told me everything," Helena began, her tone kind, "and I want you to know that I don't hold you responsible."

The girl's lip quivered. She shook her head quickly. "I don't know what you mean."

"I'm talking about the two of you," Helena continued. "I know you had dinner together. My husband can be very persuasive, but you seem like a well-brought-up girl. I'm sure this is entirely out of character."

The girl looked up as she answered. "He wanted some clam chowder and said he would feel lonely on his own. He promised you wouldn't mind. I'm sorry if I did the wrong thing."

She was reciting what Edward had told her to say, Helena guessed. They'd had time to get their stories straight.

"It's not the dinner I mind about, but what happened after dinner." Helena gave her a penetrating look. "I think you know what I mean."

"I didn't . . . Nothing happened after dinner." She sounded close to tears now. Was it an act? "We came back here and I went to bed alone. I swear that's the truth."

She sounded convincing. Helena wanted to believe her. It was disgusting to think that Edward might have slept with someone almost thirty years younger than he was.

She poured them both cups of tea, then asked about the girl's family and her previous work experience. She tried to make her relax her guard, before she slipped in one final question.

"You won't mind, will you, if I telephone your parents to tell them you had dinner with my husband? I want to ask them if this is the way they brought you up."

Suddenly, without warning, the girl broke down, sobbing so hard she was gasping for breath. Helena watched, horrified.

"P-Please don't tell them," the girl stuttered. She fumbled in her apron pocket, produced a handkerchief, and blew her nose. "I-I don't know what I was thinking. Mr. Titus was kind and . . . I've been a fool. I swear it won't happen again."

Deep down, Helena hadn't expected this. She felt numb. Her face carefully masklike, she asked, "Exactly how many times did you go to bed with my husband?"

"Just three," the girl whispered.

Three times. The number echoed in her head. "Why only three?"

"When the boys arrived for Christmas, he insisted we shouldn't be together anymore because it would be upsetting for them if they walked in on us." She burst into a fresh wave of sobbing.

Helena inhaled deeply and stayed outwardly calm as her world came crashing down. So it was true. Edward was a philanderer, and a very practiced one by the sound of things. She'd been holding on to the hope that he was telling the truth, but all this time, her instincts had been correct. How many girls had there been over the years? It was beyond belief that this one was the first. Were the rest as young? She felt a rush of hatred for him.

"Pack your bags," she said to the girl, with a gesture that dismissed her. "I want you out of here by nightfall."

She stood and walked across to the window. Outside, frost-sparkled lawns led down to the frozen lake. The boys appeared, with their nanny. They were throwing stones at the ice, trying to smash it. Soon she would have to find the energy to answer their questions. If only she could answer her own.

HELENA WAITED TILL she was alone in her bedroom before crying. She loved Edward and didn't want to divorce him, but he had crossed a line from which there was no turning back. She could never trust him again. The girl was just an overgrown child, with her pert breasts and pillowy flesh. If that's what he was attracted to, she couldn't compete. She was more striking, but she would never again have the luster of youth.

She stayed in Connecticut a few more days, watching the boys at play and privately grieving for her marriage. By the time she got back to Manhattan, she was resolved. She checked into a hotel suite while her lawyer drew up a separation agreement.

The deal was that if Edward signed over his share of her business, she would continue to give him an allowance but she would no longer live with him. He could stay in the Connecticut house for now, and return to Paris after the war if he wished; she knew it was his preferred city. The boys could spend school holidays with whichever parent happened to be available. They would scarcely notice the difference since their parents had always spent time apart. Had that contributed to their problems? If they'd spent every night of their married life together, would Edward have stayed faithful? She doubted it. She doubted everything about their relationship. Maybe he'd been after her money all along; maybe he had never really loved her.

She didn't want to see him, in case his dear familiar face made her weaken. She felt as if there was a physical wound in her heart. She had built a life with that man and had expected to grow old with him. She had lost so much, so much.

He responded to the separation agreement with a long, pleading letter, in which he protested his love and devotion: *It's only ever been you in my heart*, kochanie.

Perhaps, but not in your bed, she thought.

He turned up at the salon, gaunt and unshaven, but she locked herself in her office until Manka persuaded him to leave.

What was there to say? What's done was done.

Helena threw herself into work. She had more salons worldwide than Elizabeth Arden but Arden had more products, and she was determined to rectify that. She spent days in Long Island City experimenting alongside her chemists, blending and cooking and sniffing and testing mixtures on the backs of her hands. She designed products that would appeal to women trying to cling to their youth: a bust-firming cream, a lotion for puffy eyes, a skin-plumping cream, and an astringent to shrink varicose veins. Miss Arden didn't have those in her line. They were Helena's gift for all women of a certain age whose husbands were attracted to younger women.

It wasn't the first time Helena's heart had been broken. There had been a boy back in Poland, a student named Stanislaus with hair as black as raven's feathers, but that love was doomed once her father threw her out. She knew from experience that keeping busy and the passage of time were the only cures for heartbreak. She couldn't bear to be idle. All her energies were diverted into the battle to become the top beauty scientist in America. As for love—frankly, she would rather do without.

CHAPTER 15

Elizabeth

August 1918

The *New York Times* reported that a few cases of the deadly Spanish influenza had arrived in the city that summer, brought by sailors on a steamship from Norway. Elizabeth was following the story closely, both because she feared catching the flu herself and because it could be bad for business. She had partitions erected in the salon so that clients could be treated in their own private "rooms," and she asked her treatment girls to wear masks at work. All the same, appointments plummeted as influenza took hold in the city. Most of her clients would rather not risk infection, so Elizabeth had her creams delivered directly to their homes so they could maintain their beauty regimes.

On November 11, Laney brought a copy of the *New York Times* to their morning meeting, with the headline "Armistice Signed, End of the War." Elizabeth read the story, gooseflesh prickling her arms. Unless the dreaded telegram was currently winging its way to her, it meant Tommy had survived and he would be coming home. All that senseless killing would come to an end. The entire country would be jubilant. *She* was jubilant—but at the same time she felt a twinge of apprehension about living with Tommy again.

"Let's hang some stars and stripes bunting outside the salon,

Laney dear," she said. "But don't let the girls join the celebrations in the street. I don't want to risk them being in a crowd."

Tommy wrote that it would be a few months before they would be demobilized. In fact, it wasn't until the end of February 1919 that she received a telegram saying he would be home in two weeks and that he couldn't wait to see her.

Elizabeth tried to picture the moment he walked in the door. Would he look different? She hadn't seen him for more than three years and war was bound to have changed him. He would feel like a stranger. What if he wanted to whisk her straight to bed? She shivered.

After some deliberation, she decided to throw a surprise party for his homecoming. It would show him how much he had been missed by all their friends. She didn't admit it to herself in so many words, but it would also delay the moment when they would be alone together.

Gladys helped her pin up a "Welcome Home" banner and decorate the apartment with streamers. Close friends were invited, including Tommy's sister, and a few trusted staff members, such as Laney and Edith. Everyone arrived early so they could hide, then leap out when he walked into the hallway.

"It's not too late for the two of you to start a family," Tommy's sister hinted to Elizabeth. "But there's not a moment to lose."

Elizabeth smiled politely, although inwardly she was cringing.

When she heard the knocker, Elizabeth walked out to the hall just as her housekeeper opened the front door. Tommy stood there in uniform, carrying his kitbag and looking exhausted. He removed his cap and she saw that his head had been shaved and that lines were etched on his face that hadn't been there before. He held out his arms to embrace her and, just at that moment, the party guests burst into the hall shouting, "Surprise!"

For a moment, Tommy stared, bewildered, as if trying to make sense of it. He looked around the expectant faces, noticed the banner and the streamers, then glanced at Elizabeth again before his lips cracked into a smile.

"No one has thrown a party for me before," he said, and hugged her. "Thank you! Hey, can someone get a thirsty soldier a drink? Doesn't matter what, so long as it's alcoholic."

Party guests surged forward to shake his hand, clap him on the back, and thank him for his patriotism.

"Was it as awful as they say in the papers?" someone asked, and Tommy replied, "Let's not discuss the war. Tell me what I've missed while I've been away. Which are the best shows on Broadway? What dance styles are in vogue? I've got a lot of catching up to do."

Elizabeth introduced Gladys, whom he hadn't met before. Tommy ignored her outstretched hand and gave her a hug instead. "I've heard all about you from Elizabeth's letters," he said. "Thank you for keeping my wife from getting too lonesome."

They chatted for a while, and Elizabeth could tell Gladys liked him. Everyone liked Tommy. No matter what he'd been through in France, he hadn't lost his old bonhomie.

When they went to bed later, Tommy reached across to pull her toward him and she froze.

"I'm afraid I didn't have time to get fitted for a diaphragm," she whispered.

"You had three years!" he exclaimed, but he was smiling affectionately. "Maybe it's just as well. I'm so tired, I don't think I would be up to much." He kissed her. "Soon, my love."

He was asleep within moments, but Elizabeth lay awake, wondering how her life was going to change.

TOMMY WAS DELIGHTED when Elizabeth offered him the post of general manager of international wholesale for her company. Business was thriving in the States, with a turnover of two million dollars, and she had opened more American salons and launched more products during the war, but she felt it was high time she had a presence in Europe. Madame Rubinstein already had salons in Paris and London and her dominance there should be challenged.

"Paris should be first," Tommy said, "and I'm told the most prestigious street is the rue du Faubourg Saint-Honoré. I'll make inquiries."

Elizabeth leased a separate international sales office for him on East Fifty-Second Street, where he could build the team he needed. It would stop them from getting under each other's feet, she told him.

"I'd rather be between your legs," he whispered with a naughty smile.

"Tommy Lewis!" she rebuked. "Don't be vulgar!"

She'd had no choice but to get the diaphragm, a clumsy rubber contraption that sprang out of her grip when she tried to insert it, and had an off-putting medicinal smell. The number of headaches, stomach cramps, and fits of exhaustion she claimed to suffer at bedtime were soon alarming Tommy. He urged her to consult a doctor, but she managed to fob him off.

Sherry time with Gladys had to be dropped, but they still found moments alone during the day when Tommy was at his office.

"He's swell," Gladys told her. "I'm glad you've got better taste in husbands than me."

"Tommy's a hero," Elizabeth replied. "I'm proud that he fought in the war. I hope your next husband will be every bit as brave."

She turned away. Secretly she hoped Gladys would never remarry. She preferred having her at home with them. She felt awkward around Tommy now that they faced spending the rest of their lives together, and Gladys provided a useful counterpoint.

A FRESH WAVE of the Spanish flu pandemic delayed their departure but in March 1920, Elizabeth and Tommy sailed for

France, taking Gladys with them. On arrival, Tommy contacted real estate agents and arranged for them to view several possible locations for a new salon. It seemed that Madame Rubinstein had recently vacated a salon at number 255 rue du Faubourg Saint-Honoré, and Elizabeth decided to take on the lease. She'd have to redecorate to get rid of her rival's garish color scheme and to make it more opulent, but the location was perfect. It would, of course, have the trademark red front door, just like her American salons.

Gladys had never visited Paris and she fell in love with the city straight away. Her ex-husband was French Canadian so she already spoke the language fluently, although Parisians poked fun at her old-fashioned pronunciation. She adored the sense of history in the elegant avenues and ornate buildings of the 8th *arrondissement*. She befriended designers whose ateliers were located near the new salon, and a local café owner kept some *beignets* for her every time he fried a batch of the sweet pastries, since she loved them so.

Elizabeth sent Gladys to check out Madame Rubinstein's two Paris salons, which were just a few blocks away, and she reported that they had the same modern style as her New York premises, with works of avant-garde art on display. She memorized the treatment prices and Elizabeth set hers at the same level, but aimed for an ambience that was far more chic and upscale.

"You'll need a salon manager," Tommy reminded Elizabeth in their hotel suite one evening, "and I can't think of anyone better suited than Gladys. She understands the business, she's charming, and, best of all, she's family."

Elizabeth's first reaction was to argue. She needed Gladys in New York, with her. She couldn't be spared. But when they mentioned the idea to Gladys, she was thrilled.

"I'll miss you terribly, Elizabeth dear, but I need to make my own way. I feel at home in this city, and know I can make your salon a huge success."

The decision was made. An apartment was found for Gladys, a bank account opened, and the keys of the salon handed over. Elizabeth felt melancholy when she and Tommy left to catch the boat train to London. She stared out the window at the flat countryside flitting past, and realized they didn't have anything to talk about except business. She had so much in common with Gladys that the conversation flowed endlessly, but she and Tommy seemed to have lost the easy companionship they'd had before they married.

In the train's restaurant car, she watched a couple at the next table: he reached across to stroke his wife's cheek fondly, and she caught his hand in hers and kissed his fingertips. The whole tableau was natural and unforced, as if they were always touching, always happy. Elizabeth wondered if things would be different with Tommy if the physical side of their marriage was satisfying. Would that make the difference? She couldn't change the way she felt about sexual congress, though. She'd have to find another way.

THEY STAYED AT Claridge's in the heart of Mayfair. Elizabeth was impressed by the aristocratic types wandering the corridors with their expensive furs and plum-in-mouth accents, and decided she wanted her salon to be in this vicinity. An agent found a suitably grand building in nearby Bond Street, which was lined with luxury shops: Asprey, the jewelers; Finnigans, the luggage specialists; and Phillips, the auctioneers, were all there. Browsing the neighboring stores, she gasped at the prices, which were sky-high by American standards, and she yearned for a coveted royal warrant, granted by the monarch to tradesmen who supplied the royal family. It was her dream that one day she might be able to display the royal coat of arms, with the phrase "By appointment to Queen Mary" underneath. For a girl from the backwoods, that would feel as if she had truly "arrived."

Tommy suggested they visit a few London department

stores and speak to their buyers about stocking Elizabeth Arden products. Elizabeth felt it was beneath her, as owner of the business, but agreed to accompany him to Harrods and Harvey Nichols, the two most prestigious London stores.

In Harrods they were greeted by a tall blond man in a sharp gray suit, with a pale pink silk handkerchief arranged just so in his top pocket.

"Teddy Haslam," he said, shaking her hand. "I can't tell you how delighted I am to meet you, Miss Arden. Your fame has long preceded you to these shores."

He sent an assistant to fetch a tray of tea and asked after their journey, their hotel, their comfort. More than his upper-class accent, it was his immaculate manners that showed he was a true member of the aristocracy, Elizabeth thought. There was no question that Harrods would be placing a substantial order for her products, he assured her, before asking if they would like to accompany him to the Chelsea Flower Show that weekend.

"I have tickets for Saturday," he said, "when I believe the royals will be taking tea there. I can't guarantee we'll meet them, but the flowers are rather special."

Elizabeth leapt at the chance. "What a delightful man," she said in the taxi back to their hotel. "Didn't you think he was the perfect gent?"

Tommy agreed that he was polite, but added, "I'm suspicious of any man who admits to liking flowers."

"Nonsense," Elizabeth rebuked. "He's exactly the type I want to manage my business in Great Britain. I may make him an offer."

"You've only met him once," Tommy cautioned. "Let's find out more first."

She glanced at him, wondering if he were jealous, but he was gazing out the taxi window at the stately buildings of Knightsbridge.

Walking around the grounds of the Royal Hospital Chelsea

with Teddy Haslam that Saturday was an education in the ways
of English aristocracy. Elizabeth was introduced to so many
lords, ladies, and honorables, her jaws ached from smiling. All
professed themselves "charmed" to meet her, and the ladies
"couldn't wait" to visit her salon. Teddy was immaculate in a
top hat and Chesterfield overcoat, making Tommy look scruffy
alongside him, although his suit was new.

"I'm afraid Queen Mary is keeping to herself today," Teddy
said, nodding his head in the direction of a tent where the royal
party were taking tea. "Perhaps I will get an opportunity to introduce you at some other event of the Season, if you're staying
in London awhile."

"Do you think the Queen might visit my salon?" Elizabeth
asked.

"I'm sure she will," Teddy said. "She takes good care of her
skin. I'll put in a word when I next see her."

"Would you?" Elizabeth couldn't believe her luck in meeting
this very well-connected man.

Teddy spoke softly, shielding his mouth with his hand: "You
are aware that the royals don't pay for anything, aren't you?"

Elizabeth laughed. "Thank you for the advice. I wouldn't
dream of presenting Her Majesty with a bill."

By the end of the afternoon, she had made up her mind. "I
want you to be my UK manager," she told Teddy. "Please say you
will."

"That's very flattering," he said, carefully, "but we get along so
well. Perhaps it would be a mistake to mix business and friendship."

She could tell he was interested, so she persevered. "You'd
have complete control over British operations, and would report
directly to me."

Tommy cleared his throat and made a face at her, but she
ignored him.

"You'd have far more autonomy than I expect you have at Harrods. As well as running the salon, you'd oversee getting my products stocked in the best department stores, and the building of a factory to manufacture them in this country." Since his return from war, Tommy had persuaded her to imitate Madame Rubinstein in building her own factories, so she could control production costs. He was overseeing it, since she had little interest.

When they got around to talking about money, the salary he asked for was high but she accepted without hesitation. She wanted him to be happy with the deal. They toasted their new arrangement with flutes of Harlaux Vervel champagne.

Once Elizabeth and Tommy were alone that evening, he told her he thought he should oversee Haslam's work, to begin with at least. "Teddy has no experience in running a salon or a factory. He has never done anything but work in department stores."

"Until recently, you had never worked anywhere but a bank. He's a smart fellow. I'm sure he'll work it out," Elizabeth said. "Besides, I'll keep an eye on him."

Tommy pouted at that, but accepted her decision.

As she lay in bed that night, she thought about Teddy's confidence and ease in English society. He came from that background himself—public school, Oxford University—and that's what gave him the edge. If only Tommy had been born into an upper-class family and could provide her with an entrée into American society. He was good-natured but he didn't have an ounce of Teddy's flair.

She let her thoughts take a more dangerous turn: *if only she had married Teddy instead of Tommy* . . .

Nothing could be done about it, of course. Teddy had a wife, he'd mentioned in passing, and she had a husband. They would be close friends and colleagues. She would visit London often and spend time with him.

Perhaps she could extend her stay while Tommy sailed back to New York. It was a tempting idea: just a few weeks longer. Maybe she could wait until the opening of the new salon, to check that everything was shipshape and to help Teddy find his feet. It made sense. Tommy wouldn't like it, but she was the boss.

CHAPTER 16

Helena

April 1921

Helena was poring over the accounts, comparing the revenue from her American salons with that from her European ones. Paris takings weren't as high as she'd expected. She'd thought she'd get double the income now that she had two salons in the city, but it wasn't panning out that way. She'd been cross to hear that the Arden woman had taken over her old premises and no doubt stolen some of her customers.

She slammed the account book shut and Manka popped her head around the door. "Are you all right?"

"What is that woman doing in Paris anyway?" Helena ranted. "Edith told me she doesn't speak a word of French."

"I expect she's hired a local manager," Manka replied.

"She's been opening more US salons too. We have eight each now. She's copying me at every turn."

"They're in different cities from yours," Manka said. "Business is good. It seems there is enough for all."

Helena wasn't appeased. The Arden woman had more products as well: Fabian Swanson was churning them out rapidly. "Did you hear she has a new talcum powder called Venetian Snowdrift? What a ridiculous name!"

Manka rolled her eyes in agreement, then said, "Someone from *Vogue* is downstairs in the salon. She wants to write an article about your art collection. Shall I show her up?"

Helena shoved the account book in a drawer and tidied the papers on her desk before saying, "Yes, of course." She had a quick look in her compact mirror, checking there was no lipstick on her teeth.

The young woman who glided in was extraordinary-looking: tall and slim as a broom handle, with short, waved hair that was snow-white in color, although she couldn't have been more than twenty-five years old. She wore a fawn jersey dress that clung to her lean frame in all the right places.

"My, you have wonderful bone structure—like a sculpture," Helena said as she stood to shake hands.

"That's a subject you know all about," the woman replied. "I've just been admiring your Nadelman pieces. My name's Carmel White," she continued. "I'm an assistant editor at *Vogue*. I started a few weeks ago. Before that I was based in Paris, where I often visited your salon for facials and admired your Epstein sculptures. I'd love to write about your collection—with your permission, of course."

Helena's memory often let her down when it came to names so she tried to memorize this one: White she would remember because of the woman's white hair. What was the first name again? Caramel? "What were you doing in Paris, Caramel?" she asked, gesturing for her to sit down.

"I worked for the Red Cross during the war, serving food for the troops. I had a little canteen in Gare Saint-Lazare." She grinned, showing pretty teeth. "As you can imagine, I had *loads* of fun! Then after the war, I started covering fashion shows for the *New York Times*, and when I got back here Condé Nast hired me. He's a friend of a friend, such a dear man." She spoke rapidly, with an accent Helena couldn't pinpoint. "Anyway, I was keen to meet you because you're a fellow art lover and I just had a feeling we would get along."

Helena was slightly bemused by her high-speed delivery. "I

am sure we will, Caramel. Tell me, where do you come from? You have an unusual accent."

"Donegal, Ireland, originally, but I came to the US when I was six, then we lived all over the place, from Iowa to the Lower East Side, so I have no idea what accent I have. My mother works in the rag trade. She copies Parisian designs for American stores, so I grew up steeped in fashion. How about you?" She paused for breath. "Does your family have a background in beauty? Or art?"

Helena shook her head with a laugh. "Not at all. My father buys and sells kerosene, so his trade couldn't be less artistic or beautiful." She felt uncomfortable talking about her father. She usually tried to avoid mentioning him to journalists. "How are you enjoying *Vogue*? It must be a dream job for someone who loves fashion."

Carmel screwed up her tip-tilted nose. "I was hoping it would be. I love the creative side, but . . . Can I trust you, Helena?"

"Of course you can!" *What an odd question*, she thought. Only a fool would trust someone she had met two minutes earlier.

"Our esteemed editor, Edna Woolman Chase, is a talented woman in many respects, but she's firmly stuck in the past when it comes to the magazine. She comes out in a rash if change is suggested." She widened her eyes mischievously. "Just this week I wanted to run a photograph of a couple standing beside their own private plane, but Edna said no, she has a rule against outdoor photographs appearing in the magazine. I asked why and she said, 'That's just the rule.'" She mock-shivered in disbelief, a naughty expression on her face. "Another picture I wanted to use showed a woman wearing bright red nail polish and Edna said"—she adopted a haughty accent—"'Oh no, dear. It looks as if her fingers are dripping in blood.'"

Helena laughed, but decided it wasn't wise to take the bait and join in criticism of the "esteemed editor" of America's premier fashion magazine. "I found some resistance to makeup among American women when I first arrived, but I showed them how to apply it subtly, and now they are all for it." Carmel was wearing a deep crimson lipstick that contrasted with her pale Irish skin and brought out her green eyes. She clearly didn't give a fig for subtlety.

"I'm sure Edna has never worn makeup," Carmel said. "There's probably an unwritten rule against it somewhere: thou shalt not paint thy face."

"She's friends with Elizabeth Arden, I hear," Helena said. "I suppose they are similar types." Miss Arden had introduced a few makeup items to her line, but tentatively, as if she didn't feel easy with the concept.

Carmel nodded vigorously. "Elizabeth's old-fashioned too. You must have noticed. Her fashion sense stopped evolving around the turn of the century, and she speaks in that ridiculous phony accent as if trying to win a place on the Social Register of 1887."

Helena laughed out loud. She kept up to date with the latest designers: Vionnet, Poiret, and Molyneux. The only time she had seen Miss Arden, at the *Vogue* party, she'd been wearing an old-fashioned drop-waisted gown in a sickly shade of pink, like a little girl's dress.

"You seem avant-garde compared to Miss Arden," Carmel said, cementing her place in Helena's affections. "She's old school and you are like a younger generation."

"Now you are flattering me," Helena said, "and I haven't even offered you a drink. What would you like?"

Carmel tilted her head on one side, as if testing her. "I could murder a martini, and I know a stylish little speakeasy just around the corner. Might I tempt you?"

"I will accept to be tempted by you," Helena said, rising to her feet. "Let's go."

PROHIBITION HAD COME into force the previous year, banning the sale of alcohol, but almost every block had its own speakeasy where you could buy a range of cocktails if you knew the password to get past the doorman. Helena hadn't been to one before, so she was curious to see inside.

They walked through a basement door and down a long corridor to a large, dimly lit room with a bar on one side and wooden booths lining the other. A white-aproned waiter led them to a booth and Helena looked around, curious. It seemed much the same as old-style bars; the novelty lay in the knowledge that this bar was breaking the law by existing.

Carmel ordered two martinis, charming the waiter into giving her a dish of extra olives, which she popped into her mouth, one after the other.

"Are you married?" Helena asked, curious about this quicksilver personality.

"I'm still auditioning candidates for the role of Mr. White," Carmel said with a grin. "I was engaged before, to a darling boy called Arthur—Arthur Fitzgerald. We were crazily, all-consumingly in love. The sun rose and set on him, as far as I was concerned. I genuinely thought the world had ended when he broke off our engagement because his mother didn't approve. What a nincompoop!"

Helena hadn't come across that word but the meaning was clear. "Why didn't his mother approve?"

Carmel sucked in her breath before replying. "Because my mother is in trade. Aren't you shocked by that? Mrs. Fitzgerald certainly was! 'No son of mine' . . ." She imitated a very upper-class accent.

"I am in trade too," Helena said, "and from the sound of it, I disapprove of Mrs. Fitzgerald. It seems unforgivable in the twentieth century for parents to interfere in their children's marital choices." A stab of sadness made her close her eyes for a second but Carmel didn't notice.

"Here, here! I agree," Carmel said, raising her glass and clinking it against Helena's. "Tell me about you. You're married, aren't you? Did your parents approve of your choice of spouse?"

Farther along the bar a drunk man crumpled elegantly to the floor. Helena watched as the waiter rushed to try and help him to his feet. On instinct, she decided to confide in this woman. She might be a journalist, but she had confided in Helena first and it felt as if honesty were required: "My parents banned me from marrying my first love because he wasn't Jewish."

She paused, remembering the agony of that period. She'd been eighteen years old and giddy with love. To have it snatched away had been unbearable. She'd mourned for a long time.

Carmel gasped. "Oh my gosh. I hope you married him anyway. Please tell me you did."

Helena shook her head, with a wistful smile. "We couldn't. We had no money. My father disowned me when I refused to marry the Jewish suitor he chose, a widower who was twenty years my senior. I fled Poland and traveled to Australia, which is where I met Edward, the man who is now my husband." She was surprised at herself; she usually tried not to think about that time but Carmel's open friendliness had breached her defenses.

In fact, there had been months when she stayed with her mother's sister in Vienna and wrote long, pleading letters trying to change her father's mind, but received no reply. He'd shut her out completely. Her sisters wrote that he would not allow her name to be mentioned in the house.

"What does Edward do?" Carmel asked. "Does he work for your company?"

"He lives in Paris. It's rather a distant relationship for now, but we write often." That much was true. He wrote long, chatty letters that made her ache with missing him and burn with anger toward him, both at the same time. She wrote back, telling him about business problems and family news. Their correspondence was much the same as it had always been, but without any endearments on her side.

"Do your parents approve of Edward? Does the story have a happy ending?"

Helena felt a wave of sadness wash over her. "They have never met him, or my two sons. I have been back to Poland since then, to try and make peace, but my father wouldn't let me cross the threshold. It's a shame, but life goes on. I'm close to my sisters at least."

Carmel touched her shoulder. "I'm so sorry."

"The only people who know about this are my family." Helena took her hand and squeezed it. "I don't want it to be widely known, certainly not in the press. You understand? It is better not to look backward."

"Of course." Carmel gave her a penetrating look, but changed the subject. "Do you visit Paris often?" she asked. "I was there for the shows last month and managed to see the Salon d'Automne. I fell in love with the work of Georges Braque—and I notice you have a Braque downstairs in your salon."

Helena smiled. "Georges is a great friend of Edward's and mine. He and the Spaniard, Pablo Picasso, are changing modern art, and I'm honored to own some of their pictures. Art is my passion. You probably guessed."

"This is what I need to ask you about for the article," Carmel said, as if suddenly remembering the purpose of their meeting. She scrabbled in her bag for a notebook and pen, then wrote down Helena's words.

"How do you choose the works you buy?" she asked. "Do you see them as an investment?"

"Not at all." Helena shook her head. "I choose from the heart, not the wallet. There's a particular thrill I get when I see a work I love. If I don't feel it, I don't buy."

They talked about exhibitions they had seen recently, and why France was the epicenter of the revolution in the art world. Helena promised that if they were ever in Paris at the same time, she would introduce Carmel to some of the artists of her acquaintance.

She was wearing a pair of emerald and diamond drop earrings and slipped them off as they spoke. "I want to give you these," she said. "They match your eyes and will look much better on you than me." It was her old tactic: butter up the press so they write flattering stories about you.

"I couldn't possibly take your earrings," Carmel said, waving them away. "But I hope we are going to be friends, and next time I am wearing a gown that would be enhanced by emeralds, I will call you up and say, 'Helena, is there any chance I can rush by and borrow those earrings?'"

Helena didn't have women friends. She was too busy for friendships. She had her sisters, and she had cordial relations with the wives of her male employees, but she didn't have social lunches or teas with other women.

"We should be photographed together," Carmel continued. "We look like day and night, you with your black hair and me with my white—it turned white naturally, you know, when I was nineteen."

Helena laughed. "It's a nice idea but I am far too vain to be photographed with someone as young and slim as you." She patted her belly.

"I'll talk you into it," Carmel said, glancing at her watch. "But now I must fly back to the office before Mrs. Chase comes after me on her broomstick. Let's meet again soon."

She rose, tossing money on the table to pay for their drinks. Helena got the impression that she was always in a rush, that she filled her life to the brim with martinis and friends and adventures. She watched as Carmel sashayed through a crowd of young men to reach the door. Their heads turned in unison to follow her, and one whistled in appreciation.

Helena sat alone in the booth, finishing her drink and musing on the encounter. Carmel asking about her parents had put her in a pensive mood. What if she had stood up to them and married Stanislaus, her first love? Would their marriage have survived? She couldn't imagine he would ever have been unfaithful. He'd seemed a gentle and trustworthy young man, but perhaps she was idealizing him in hindsight.

She could picture him clearly: lounging on the grassy banks of the Vistula, with his unruly blue-black hair and his mischievous blue eyes—that expression he had when he was teasing her. He'd been a medical student, and when Helena said she wished she could study medicine, he agreed to tutor her for the entrance exam. There was already one woman in his course at the university in Kraków, and he didn't see why Helena would not be accepted.

For eight months they met and studied his anatomy and physiology textbooks, kissing and laughing, and falling deeply in love. She took her studies seriously, borrowing extra books to read at home in the evenings, and she hoped to sit the entrance exam the following year. They talked about a future when both of them were qualified doctors: the house they would buy, the dark-haired, intelligent children they would have.

But the door to that future had been slammed shut by her father. When he found out about her romance with a *goy*, he presented her with a stark choice: either marry the middle-aged suitor he had found or leave home never to return. Helena left. Always in the back of her mind she hoped that Stanislaus would wait for her but by the time she came back from Australia, eight years later, as a wealthy, self-made businesswoman, he had married someone else. Of course he had. It had been too much to expect.

She returned to Australia and her sister Regina played matchmaker from the other side of the world. Edward walked into her Melbourne salon one day sporting a cream linen jacket and a complicit smile, as if they shared an amusing secret. He told her he was a writer and that Regina had suggested he call on her while he was in Australia. They had dinner, two Poles far from home, and soon they were seeing each other regularly. He began writing her advertisements and did a great job. She liked him, but he wasn't Stanislaus. She didn't think she would ever love another man like that again; she couldn't risk the pain.

When Edward asked her to marry him, she turned him down flat and set sail for Britain to open her first salon there. He persevered, turning up in London at a point when she was feeling especially lonely, and after two years of wooing he finally got her down the aisle. Two children and fifteen years later, now look where they were. . . .

Helena shook herself. No good was done dwelling on what might have been. She would never know if Stanislaus would have proved a better husband than Edward. She never did get to study medicine properly, although she could remember so much from her lessons with Stanislaus that she felt as if she had. She should live in the present and be grateful for all her blessings. The business was her life now, and that was more than enough.

CHAPTER 17

Elizabeth

October 1921

Laney brought the Kraków detective's report on Helena Rubinstein to the morning meeting, along with the rest of the mail, and perched on her usual window seat.

"What does it say, dear?" Elizabeth asked, her shoulders resting on the floor and her hips tilted upward into Bridge pose.

Laney skimmed it. "A neighbor of the Rubinstein family told him there was a huge argument when Helena refused to marry the man her father had chosen for her. They sent her to stay with her mother's sister in Vienna, then she traveled from there to Australia."

"Why go all the way to Australia?" Elizabeth asked, her brain ticking over. "Maybe she got pregnant," she answered herself. "That's often the reason girls are sent overseas—so they can have the baby adopted quietly. Do you think that was the case?"

"The report doesn't mention anything like that."

Damn! Elizabeth thought. *Still, it could be true.*

"He speculates that the Rubinstein girls' marital options were limited because their father couldn't afford a dowry for all eight of his daughters."

"I'm not paying him for guesswork!" Elizabeth snorted. "Did he discover whether or not Helena studied medicine? And if so, why she doesn't practice as a doctor?"

"Nothing on that," Laney said. "The only extra information

he's found comes from this neighbor. She says that Helena used to help her father in his kerosene business, but she believes they don't speak anymore. She said all the sisters were very close as children and many of them work for Helena at her salons around the world. She is proud that the little girl she used to watch skipping in the street has become famous."

Elizabeth rolled her spine down to the floor. "How much is he charging for this tittle-tattle? I've a good mind not to pay his bill." The Melbourne detective had been a washout too; all the information he'd sent had been gleaned from press archives, so it was merely a summary of the interviews Madame Rubinstein had given, all of them self-congratulatory.

"I'll leave the full report on your desk," Laney said, opening the next letter with a pearl-handled paper knife. She pulled out a card and read: "You are invited to Edna Woolman Chase's wedding next month."

"Her what?" Elizabeth sat up. "That can't be right. There must be some mistake." Edna was already married, although Elizabeth had gotten the impression she and her husband didn't spend much time together. Had they divorced on the quiet and Edna hadn't mentioned it?

She reached for the card: *Richard Newton and Edna Woolman Chase invite Mr. and Mrs. Tommy Lewis to celebrate their wedding on November 12, 1921.* The event was in Philadelphia. Elizabeth felt stung that Edna hadn't told her about it when they'd had lunch just three weeks earlier. She had certainly played her cards close to her chest.

"Shall I accept?" Laney asked, pencil poised.

"Of course," Elizabeth said. It would be a good opportunity to mix with Edna's friends. Surely there would be some society figures there? Of course, several would turn up their noses because it was a second marriage, but others would want to show off their wardrobes at what was bound to be a very stylish affair. It wasn't every day the editor of *Vogue* got married!

She rolled over and thrust her hips up into Downward Dog pose, so the blood rushed to her head. The secrecy was perhaps understandable in the circumstances. At least she had been invited. That's what counted.

ON THE TRAIN to Philadelphia, Tommy read the *New York Times* while Elizabeth gazed out the window. She liked traveling by train; it gave her time to think. She was pleased with her gown for the wedding: salmon-pink satin with a circular-cut skirt, worn with a silky sable stole. It looked suitably expensive. Her best diamond jewelry was packed in a Moroccan leather traveling case in the luggage rack. She was keeping a close eye on it, even though they were in a private compartment.

Elizabeth had commissioned research into her customers, which showed that they were the wealthiest three percent in society, the *crème de la crème*. These were the women she wanted to impress, and perhaps some of them would be at Edna's wedding. It irked her that she still hadn't been invited for tea or dinner in an Astor, Morgan, or Vanderbilt mansion, although the women were charming enough when they visited her salon. They invited her to their charity fundraisers, but she suspected that was because they knew she could be relied on to write a handsome check. The strict Gilded Age etiquette of the Four Hundred, with their visiting cards and Monday evening boxes at the opera, might no longer apply, but she was excluded from their company just as effectively now as she would have been in the last century.

Instead, she and Tommy socialized with theatrical types. They both enjoyed outings to the theater and sometimes dined with the cast. They counted Helen Hayes and Ethel Barrymore among their closest acquaintances. Just a few nights earlier Elizabeth had sat next to Irving Berlin at dinner after the show *Music Box Revue* and found him quite the charmer. She smiled to remember his gentle flirting. Edith Brown had been her companion, and she'd been so awestruck she could barely speak. Elizabeth enjoyed buying tickets to the new musicals for the gentle, unassuming salon girl; she loved music and could never have afforded them herself. It felt good to be charitable.

She and Tommy never went dancing anymore. The clubs were full of young people and all the dance styles had changed. Now and again they threw parties in their apartment, where Tommy still mixed his multihued cocktails to break the ice. Elizabeth was nervous about transgressing the Prohibition laws, but he insisted "everyone" did it, and no one would come to their parties if they didn't have booze.

Their marriage had changed in the two years since his return from war. He was still the easygoing and genial sort of man she had married. She counted her blessings that he hadn't turned to drink or gambling or, worst of all, drugs, as she knew some men had after the war. They rubbed along together well enough now that he had given up his attempts to make love to her and accepted that they slept in separate bedrooms. But it was a bugbear of hers that he didn't share her social ambitions, and was even prone to mocking them.

Just yesterday, he had laughed at the cut-out sheets of newspaper with which she lined her shoes in winter—a very practical technique for keeping your feet warm that she had learned in her Canadian childhood.

"What if one of your society ladies were to see?" he asked.

"I'm sure I'm not the only lady to do this," Elizabeth replied, peeved.

"I'll take a poll of Edna's wedding guests, shall I?" Tommy grinned.

"You'll do no such thing," she rebuked. She was determined to make a good impression at the wedding and in no mood for his teasing. It occurred to her that Tommy didn't know her at all, and never had. They were strangers who coexisted side by side rather than as a loving couple.

They checked into their hotel suite and changed into their finery, then made their way to the banquet room Edna and Richard had hired for the reception. They were greeted at the door by a willowy young woman with short snow-white hair, wearing a long-sleeved beige silk-jersey dress that only reached her calves, accessorized with multiple strands of pearls.

"How are you, Miss Arden?" she asked. "I'm Carmel White. We met at *Vogue*, remember? Edna asked me to show everyone to their places. Please come this way."

Elizabeth and Tommy followed. Her dress was scooped so low at the back you could almost see her bottom, and it was on the tip of Elizabeth's tongue to say that she hoped she'd got it cheap since there was so little fabric. She glanced at Tommy, but his eyes were glued to Carmel's shapely shoulder blades.

"Girls with short hair don't make advantageous marriages," she whispered to him.

He snorted with laughter and said, "Elizabeth, you're an antique."

She glared to silence him.

Six tables were arranged around the room, with posies of lilac and baby's breath in the center of each and pretty painted place cards by the settings. They had arrived a little early and only a few guests were already seated. Their table was toward the back of the room, farthest from the high table where the bride and groom would sit, and Elizabeth frowned at that. She assumed there would be a chance to circulate after the meal.

Other guests filed in, and some joined their table: an art director from *Vogue* and his plump wife, plus a distant cousin of Edna's, an elderly man who used an ear trumpet to make out Elizabeth's questions, then bellowed his replies. She could hear the tinkle of laughter emanating from other tables and felt as though she'd got the short straw. She peered around, trying to recognize other guests, and wishing she had a copy of the seating plan.

Suddenly, Elizabeth realized with a jolt of panic that she was the only woman in evening dress. Everyone else was in smart day wear. Why hadn't she thought of that? It was still afternoon, but she had assumed the wedding would continue into the evening and had dressed accordingly.

Edna and Richard skipped in last, arm in arm. She was wearing a chic rose-pink suit with a black velvet and lace hat—definitely day wear, Elizabeth noted, with mounting embarrassment. Richard was tall with curly graying hair and a luxuriant mustache. They waved and called hello to the guests before sitting down, and the first course of coquilles Saint-Jacques was served by waiters.

Elizabeth did her best to make conversation with the plump wife and the deaf cousin who sat on either side of her, while Tommy and the art director seemed to hit it off. She picked at the fish course of poached salmon in mousseline sauce and sipped a glass of ginger ale, since the hotel did not serve alcohol. She didn't generally drink much, but a cocktail would have lightened the atmosphere.

Between courses, Edna flitted round, stopping at each table to murmur a few words. When she approached theirs, Elizabeth smiled and said, "Aren't you the secretive one? I'm overjoyed for you and Richard."

"Thank you for coming," Edna replied. "It's just a low-key affair today, for my most special friends. Don't you look charming! Diamonds, no less! I see you decided to disregard the rule about not wearing them before dusk. Quite right too." Before Elizabeth could reply, Edna was leaning in to talk to the deaf cousin, then she floated on to the next table.

Elizabeth was horrified. Not only was she in the wrong dress, but she had forgotten the rule about diamonds. It was a huge faux pas! She'd wanted to wear them as a symbol of wealth, but instead she must appear vulgar and showy. She considered slipping them into her evening bag, but that would only draw more attention. She glanced around, wondering if people were whispering about her.

When the *crème au chocolat* bowls had been cleared away, Richard stood to thank everyone for coming and announced they were rushing to catch a train.

"I'm surprising my new wife with a honeymoon in Bermuda," he said, and everyone clapped. Elizabeth was watching Edna's face and could tell she already knew where they were honeymooning. She must have packed for it.

As they left, Edna threw her bouquet over her shoulder and Carmel White leapt to catch it with great athleticism, her pearls swinging. The whole event had taken just shy of two hours.

Was that it? Elizabeth wondered. Had they traveled all the way from New York for a luncheon and a ginger ale? What a disaster! She wished she hadn't bothered. Guests began to trickle out of the banquet room, as though they had other parties to attend, but Elizabeth and Tommy had nowhere to go as they were staying overnight in the hotel.

She caught eyes with a grossly overweight woman in black, who was leaning heavily on walking sticks and turning pink with the effort of walking. The woman gave a slight nod in her direction before Carmel took her arm and helped her to the door. Why did anyone let herself get quite so fat? Elizabeth wondered. Had she no pride? It was only after the woman had left that curiosity led her to wander past the place where she had been sitting, and she saw the name card: Bessie Marbury. Of course! She was a theatrical and literary agent from an old-money family, so well connected that she knew everyone who was anyone in polite Manhattan. If only Elizabeth had found a way to be introduced, diamonds or no diamonds.

As it was, the whole trip felt like a wasted opportunity. She had considered Edna one of her closest friends, but she'd been treated as a second-class guest. She'd felt like an outsider in that room, with the wrong gown and the wrong jewels, like the little girl with cooties in her hair. Were they all laughing at her? She curled her toes, feeling the scrunch of newspaper inside her shoes. No matter how much money she made, no matter how successful her company, she couldn't shed this feeling that she was not good enough.

Elizabeth longed for spring when she would sail to Paris to visit Gladys. How she missed Gladys! Then she would travel to London to see Teddy. Maybe she would even meet Queen Mary this time. Teddy wrote that the Queen had visited the London salon three times. Three! She wondered if she would ever get a royal warrant. Or would her humble background count against her?

As they sat on the train back to New York the following morning, Tommy once again buried his nose in a newspaper. Elizabeth felt a sense of despair. She was one of the richest women in America, with a business she had built all by herself; she had a perfectly acceptable husband, even if theirs wasn't a passionate marriage; she had a beautiful apartment and as many gowns and jewels as she wanted—but still she wasn't happy.

One of the thorns in her flesh was that Rubinstein woman breathing down her neck. Elizabeth thought of the newspaper photographs of her on her insufferable countrywide tours, and realized that she had often been photographed wearing diamond jewelry in broad daylight. She wasn't bothered by etiquette but made her own rules, or so it seemed. It was yet another example of her complete lack of class.

Had she given birth to a baby out of wedlock? Was she lying about her medical qualifications? Why was Elizabeth surrounded by a bunch of imbeciles who were incapable of finding anything she could use to discredit a woman who was clearly telling them a pack of lies?

CHAPTER 18

Helena

April 1922

As far as Helena could tell, Edward was enjoying his bachelor life in Paris. He had leased a building on Boulevard Raspail, with a duplex penthouse apartment and a theater on the ground floor where he held poetry readings and staged plays. Helena could imagine him, surrounded by expat intellectuals, with his glasses perched on his nose, drinking cloudy glasses of pastis. He was bound to have a woman by his side, a sheep in strumpet's clothing, but she tried not to think about that.

Their last meeting had been in a lawyer's office three years earlier, when he had signed the agreement letting her buy back the Australian business. She had refused his invitation for dinner afterward, still livid about his affair with the maid. That whole episode had left her feeling broken.

It was easier to be friendly and civilized when there was an ocean between them. She paid him to scout properties for her in Paris, and when he wrote that he had found suitable premises for her third salon in the city, not far from the Arden salon in her old Faubourg Saint-Honoré premises, she gave him the go-ahead to lease it. It amused her to take the battle to her rival's doorstep.

Why don't you come and inspect the new place? Edward wrote back. *The boys are sailing over for summer when school breaks up and you could accompany them. Please come, Helena. I miss you.*

She snorted at that. It was all very well missing her; if he had behaved honorably in the first place they would still have a marriage. Part of her yearned to see him, but she couldn't let herself be vulnerable again.

Helena weighed the risks and benefits for a few days before deciding to visit Paris to oversee the decoration of the new salon. She didn't trust Edward to manage it, and her sister Stella, who looked after the business in France, was fully stretched. She booked a first-class stateroom on the *Aquitania*, and arranged for the boys and their nanny to have rooms nearby.

Helena had always liked the *Aquitania* for its elegant interiors: the double-height Louis XVI dining room, the garden lounge lined with potted palms, the spaciousness of the suites, with their trademark blue and yellow carpets and silk-lined walls. The food was top-notch as well, with a chef who had been poached from the Ritz Hotel in London. Roy was twelve years old and Horace had just turned ten, so both were old enough to join her for dinner in the evening. She trusted they had learned table manners at their expensive boarding school.

The first evening on board, their nanny brought the boys to her room, suitably attired in striped blazers, flannels, and neatly combed hair. They looked much the same as when she had last seen them—*when was it?*—but taller and thinner, as if they had been stretched on the rack. Roy was almost taller than she was.

"Hello, Mother," they chanted, letting her plant kisses on their foreheads. They flanked her on the walk to the dining room, and she was proud to introduce them to the maître d', whom she knew from previous voyages.

"So," she began once they were seated, "how is school? What are you studying?"

Roy listed the subjects in a bored monotone, and Horace piped up that he was on the baseball team.

"Baseball?" Helena asked, feigning ignorance to amuse them. "Is that the game where you throw a ball and try to hit a base?"

They caught eyes. "It's more complicated than that, Mama," Horace replied with exaggerated patience.

"Which teams do you support?"

"I'm a Yankees fan and Roy likes the Giants," Horace told her, and began to describe the fierce competition for the pennant in that year's Major League. Her attention wandered. Sport was tedious; she would never understand why Americans got so excited about grown men chasing a ball around a field.

Oysters were served and Helena squeezed lemon juice on hers, then picked a large one and tipped it down her throat. She closed her eyes, savoring the taste of the ocean and the creaminess of the flesh.

The boys hadn't touched theirs. "You don't like oysters?" she asked, and they shook their heads vehemently, noses wrinkled in disgust as if she had asked them to eat slugs. She debated whether to insist they try one for the sake of it, but what did it matter? "Excellent," she said instead, reaching for their plates. "I'll have yours."

By the end of the fish course, she had run out of questions. She had asked them about books they were reading—boys' adventure stories by authors she had never heard of—and whether they had given any thought to their futures—neither had any idea what they wanted to do. She wondered what they could possibly talk about for the remainder of the meal, never mind the next four nights of the crossing. She planned they would spend their days with the nanny but dine with her each evening. Then she had the brainwave of asking them to explain the baseball league, and she was able to drift off in her own thoughts as they chattered excitedly.

Helena felt strangely nervous about seeing Edward again. What did he expect? Had she been unreasonable to throw him out for his infidelity? She glanced around the dining room. How many of these respectable, well-dressed men were unfaithful to their wives? How many of these wives turned a blind eye?

But it wasn't in her nature to share. Never had been. She wanted him to herself, as *her* lover, not anyone else's. All or nothing. And he would never change, so she shouldn't let herself fall under his spell again. A fool goes twice where a sensible person doesn't venture once.

Next day a cable was brought to her by a first-class steward: Edward wrote that he would meet them off the ship in Cherbourg. Her heart leapt like a teenager's. What should she read into that? Was it a conciliatory gesture? Could it be he still missed her? Her emotions were a mishmash, and that was alarming. She liked to be composed and prepared for all eventualities.

They docked off the French coast, and tenders took passengers ashore to the main terminal building, where they queued to clear customs. First-class passengers were given priority, so it didn't take long before they were walking out to the waiting area. Roy spotted his father first and set off at a gallop, with Horace close behind. Helena occupied herself with directing the porters and counting once more to make sure they had the correct amount of luggage.

Edward had adopted a monocle instead of spectacles, and was dressed in raffish fashion with a paisley-patterned cravat, a Panama hat, and a cane. He looked good, she had to admit; much younger than his years. He leaned forward and kissed her cheeks, first one, then the other, in the French style. Their eyes met as he drew back and she saw he was searching her expression, trying to judge her feelings toward him.

"Are we catching the train to Paris?" she asked, giving nothing away.

"No, I bought a car," he announced. "Follow me."

The boys were full of questions. What kind of car? How fast could it go? Would they all fit inside? Helena was asking a different question in her head: Who had paid for it? She knew the answer, of course—it must have come from the money she paid him for his share in the company.

Helena sat in the front seat, watching the plane-tree-lined road ahead, and noticing out of the corner of her eye that Edward had lost weight: his cheeks were sucked in and his belly concave.

"There are more Americans in Paris these days than there are Parisians," he told her. "Especially in the literary set. I've become friends with a remarkable woman called Sylvia Beach, who has a bookshop called Shakespeare and Company." He turned to the boys. "How many Shakespeare plays have you both read?"

Roy said three, Horace just one, and when questioned he wasn't sure exactly which.

Helena, meanwhile, was wondering about the relationship with his "friend" Sylvia. "Does Sylvia's husband work in the book trade too?" she asked, trying to affect an air of insouciance.

"She has what is known as a 'Boston marriage' with another bookshop owner, Adrienne Monnier. They live together." He caught Helena's eye and winked. "You catch my drift?"

She did.

"Sylvia is branching out as a publisher. She has just agreed to publish a new novel by James Joyce, one that established publishers are wary of touching."

"He's the writer who doesn't use quote marks," Helena remembered.

Edward laughed. "From what I've heard, *Ulysses* is going to challenge literary convention more drastically than that. Paris is abuzz with gossip about it. This whole town is obsessed with books. I've been wondering if it might be worth my opening a bookshop and perhaps publishing the odd book. I wanted to talk to you about it."

Helena froze. Is that the reason for the warm welcome? Because he wanted her to invest in a new venture? "Send me some figures," she said sharply. "Set-up costs, predicted turnover, and profit for years one to five. Perhaps your friend Sylvia can help by sharing her accounts."

Edward cleared his throat.

"Can we go up the Eiffel Tower, Papa?" Horace interrupted. "You promised we could."

"Of course," he agreed. "I have lots of plans for your vacation."

"Will you teach me to drive?" Horace asked.

"At the age of ten? Perhaps not, old sport," Edward replied. "Maybe at eighteen."

"Are you following the Major League, Papa?" Roy asked, and Helena sighed as the talk turned once more to baseball.

THEY ARRIVED AT Boulevard Raspail unscathed, although Helena's hair had blown loose of her chignon and hung in rats' tails around her shoulders. She laughed when she caught sight of herself in the hall mirror, looking like Medusa with her serpent head.

"I've put you in the guest room," Edward said. "I'll have your trunk brought up."

He showed her to the room, which was comfortably furnished, with a view across the rooftops to an old church steeple. The double bed was neatly made up with a cream lace cover on top. She felt a twinge of emotion. On paper they were still husband and wife, but it would have been presumptuous of him to assume they would share a bedroom after all this time—yet part of her was hurt that he didn't at least suggest it so she could turn him down.

"We're having dinner with Stella and her husband at the Jockey Club," he said. "It's very lively. I think you'll enjoy it."

The boys ate at home with their nanny. Just as well, Helena thought, as they walked into the club and were hit by a fug of whiskey and cigarette smoke mingled with the tang of cheap perfume. The walls were lined with paintings—some of them rather good—and Helena regretted they would be damaged by the smoke. It was only eight in the evening, but a louche crowd was clustered around the bar, looking as if they'd been there all day: women with skirts split to the thigh, lounging over glossy-haired men with trouble written all over them. This was the kind of place where Edward was hanging out?

They were shown to a round wooden table and orders were taken by a waiter who seemed bored, as if he had better things to do. Stella joined them, making apologies for her husband, who was running late. Helena was glad of a chance to talk to her alone. How was she enjoying life in Paris? How was business at the salons?

No sooner had their drinks been served than friends of Edward's trickled over to accost him. A young man with blond hair and an unfeasibly high forehead, whom he introduced as an up-and-coming writer; a girl with a jet-black bob and Egyptian kohl eyeliner, a serpent necklace twined around her arm; an older woman who was so drunk she fell onto Edward's knee, then roared with laughter as if it were a grand joke. They came in a constant stream and Edward introduced them, but the names flew straight out of Helena's head. All she would remember later was a general blur of decadence and the suggestive stage antics of a performer called Kiki who sang that she wanted a sailor to share her bed.

She watched the women's expressions for any sign they might be sleeping with her husband, but decided he wouldn't be so foolish as to bring his mistress here on her first night in town—not unless he wanted to hurt her, and that didn't appear to be the case.

"So, is this where you spend your time?" she asked Edward once their meals arrived. "It's very noisy."

"It's calmer in daytime," he said. "I hold meetings here. At night it can get a bit hectic—but colorful too."

"These people are all at least twenty years younger than you," Helena pointed out.

"Paris is a young man's town since the war. Everyone is an artist, a writer, or a musician, while the women are artists' models, actresses, and performers. My friend Kiki is all three." He grinned.

Helena wondered if there were women writers and women artists. She hoped so. The women in this bar wore styles of dress and makeup that would be frowned on in New York: lips were deep scarlet, cheeks pink, and eyes rimmed in thick black, while blouses were slipping off plump shoulders and, in one case, exposing a hint of nipple. The *grandes dames* of Manhattan would say they looked like streetwalkers, and perhaps some were, but there was an exuberance about them she liked.

The food was terrible, of course—overcooked, underseasoned, overpriced—but they were paying for the ambience. When they finished, Edward asked the waiter to put the bill on his tab. Helena wondered how much he owed, since he was clearly a regular. He was childishly possessive about the place, and wanted her to like it too. She didn't dislike it—she was curious about it—but she hoped they would eat in restaurants with higher standards of cuisine in the days to come.

Back at the apartment, she changed into her nightgown and cleansed her skin. She was stroking Crème Valaze into her neck, watching herself in the mirror, trying to order her emotions about seeing Edward again, when there was a gentle knock on the door.

"Come," she said, with a fluttering sensation in her gut.

Edward poked his head inside, and stood, tongue-tied for several seconds, just watching her. "I wondered if . . ." he said at last. His voice cracked and he couldn't finish the sentence.

Helena didn't think twice. "Yes," she said, rising to her feet and walking over to embrace him.

HELENA HADN'T MEANT to make love with Edward. Afterward, she couldn't decide what made her agree. He was looking good, but it wasn't that. His popularity among the young set at the club reminded her that one of his positive qualities was his openness to modern ideas. His uncertain manner around her demonstrated contriteness. But truly it was lust that made her succumb. She had always loved sex with him. His presence triggered memories of all the magical love-making during the early years of their marriage, and she couldn't stop herself.

It was as good as ever; better perhaps, because they knew each other so well. Afterward he lay on his side, propped up by an elbow, gazing down at her.

"I wish we could live together again," he said. "My dearest wish is that you will make your home in Paris. I want you to be my wife once more. Nothing is the same without you."

Helena contemplated that, and it made her sad. "How can I trust you, Edward? I can't risk being hurt again."

"I've learned the hard way," he said, taking hold of her hand and squeezing. "I'm older now. I was lonely in America when you kept disappearing on your tours. Here I have my own life, and I'd love to share it with you." He kissed her tenderly, smoothed back her hair, then kissed her again.

"The boys are at school in America," she objected. "One of us needs to be on the same side of the ocean as them."

"You're just looking for excuses. There's no reason why the boys couldn't be moved. It would be good for them to finish their schooling here. They'd become fluent in French."

"I need to be in New York to complete my expansion plans," she said. "The US market is the biggest in the world, but once I have established my domination there, I can live anywhere I choose."

Edward rolled onto his back with a sigh. "It's clear where your priorities lie."

Helena looped her arm over his chest. She did love Paris— and she did love Edward. "I can't move here yet," she said eventually, "but maybe soon."

She looked around the guest bedroom. They'd need a bigger apartment if they were going to live together—somewhere magnificent. Perhaps he could start looking. In the meantime, she had asked Stella to keep an eye on him and warn her if she spotted signs that any of the women who hovered around him might be sharing his bed: the casual touch on the arm; eyes meeting, then darting away quickly, guiltily; an air of possessiveness. Stella would know.

CHAPTER 19

Elizabeth

March 1926

Elizabeth couldn't contain her excitement when she received a handwritten note inviting her to Sunday tea with Bessie Marbury, the woman she had spotted at Edna's wedding. Bessie's teas were legendary, mixing political, theatrical, literary, and musical talents along with the very finest New York ladies.

What to wear was her first concern, after her faux pas at Edna's wedding. No diamonds for sure. She consulted *Vogue* for the latest styles, and bought herself a steel-blue suit with a hemline a good fourteen inches from the ground, much shorter than she had ever worn before. She decorated the jacket with a peacock brooch, and bought a matching cloche too: it didn't sit quite right over her permanent-waved curls but everyone seemed to be wearing them these days, pulled down low over the forehead. Fashions had changed radically since 1920 and Elizabeth knew it was high time she caught up.

Tommy laughed at the amount of time she spent in front of the mirror, pulling the hat down firmly, then trying to arrange it so a few artful curls poked out beneath.

"From what I saw of Miss Marbury, appearance is not as high a priority as what she plans to eat next," he said.

"Don't be cruel," she rebuked. "The woman may have a glandular disorder for all we know."

"A willpower disorder, more like," Tommy replied.

She wished he hadn't been included in the invitation, but the envelope had been addressed, mistakenly, to "Mr. and Mrs. Arden."

When their taxi drew up outside the Sutton Place address, Elizabeth was encouraged to see that the front door was painted the exact same shade of red as the front door of her salons. It seemed a good omen.

A butler took their coats and showed them up a staircase wallpapered in a modern palm-leaf design to a bright airy sitting room. Around twelve guests were already there, sitting or standing in clusters, a murmur of conversation filling the air along with a haze of tobacco smoke. By the black iron fireplace, the majestic figure of Bessie Marbury sat in a black taffeta dress shaped like a bell tent that covered her from neck to toes. Her head, poking through the neck hole, seemed tiny in comparison to her body, like the knob on a domed cheese dish.

"Come!" She gestured, without standing up. "My dear Mrs. Arden, I've been simply dying to meet you." Her voice was deep and husky. Elizabeth was surprised to see she was smoking a cigarette in a long black holder. She'd thought no well-brought-up lady would smoke.

"Charmed." She held out her hand and Bessie enclosed it in her plump grip.

Her skin was clear and free of makeup. Elizabeth guessed she must be around seventy but she was unlined, apart from a row of grooves along her top lip, like the teeth of a comb. Her eyes were bluebell blue, her hair dyed a rich chestnut brown, and her expression was lively.

"Please—sit down." She gestured to a chair by her side, ignoring Tommy completely. "I've been watching you from afar, admiring the way you invented an industry that didn't exist when I was a girl. Even twenty years ago, none of us knew that

we needed pore cream and neck lift gels—but you persuaded us
they were essential, and now we buy them religiously."

Elizabeth squirmed at the avalanche of praise and tried to
interrupt, but Bessie talked over her.

"It's rare to meet a self-made millionairess. Most of us women
with money either inherited or married it, but you are the genuine article. And look how pretty you are!"

"Gracious, I'm blushing," Elizabeth said, clutching her cheek.
"What a wonderful welcome. I'm honored to meet you, Miss
Marbury. May I introduce my husband, Tommy Lewis?"

Tommy shook hands and hovered as Bessie pointed out other
guests, sweeping her arm around the room. "That's Toscanini,
the conductor. He's just arrived at the New York Philharmonic,
after leaving Italy because he can't abide Mussolini." Next she
indicated a man with shaggy eyebrows and a mustache clipped
into a rectangle as if he had a ruler balanced on his top lip. "Perhaps you'll recognize Groucho Marx, the vaudeville comedian.
Quite the rudest man I've ever met but so funny you forgive
him everything." She waved at two ladies at the next table. "And
these are my precious Annes: Anne Morgan, daughter of J. P.,
and Anne Vanderbilt, widow of William, both of them neighbors
of mine in Sutton Place and my very dearest friends."

They smiled and called hello. Elizabeth felt a thrill ripple
through her. She'd read about these women in society columns.
Should she rise and shake their hands? They didn't get up, so
she stayed where she was. Should she remove her cloche? She
noticed no one else was wearing gloves so she slipped hers into
her bag. How ridiculous to worry about such things!

Tommy wandered over to join Groucho Marx's circle, leaving her to talk to Bessie. A maid brought her a cup of tea and
offered a tray of sandwiches. Elizabeth took a dainty fish paste
one and balanced it on the edge of her saucer, refusing a spoon-
ful of sugar for her tea.

"We have alcohol if you prefer," Bessie said. "I hear your husband is quite the cocktail mixer. That's a useful skill in a man."

"How did you hear about that?" Elizabeth was surprised.

"We have friends in common, my dear," Bessie said. "Edna, of course—remember we saw each other at her wedding to Dick? And Elsie de Wolfe. She designed one of your salons, did she not?" Elizabeth nodded. "Elsie lived here with me for many years, and is responsible for the décor."

"We have the same red door," Elizabeth commented. "Now I understand why."

She looked around the room, admiring the tall lamps with milky glass shades the shape of flower heads, the caryatids of scantily clad women supporting the mantelpiece, the symmetry of coving and dado rails. It felt both classical and modern at the same time.

Bessie continued: "Of course, Elsie disappointed us terribly by getting married earlier this year, to Sir Charles Mendl. Perhaps you read about it." She exchanged a glance with the two Annes, who were listening in. "We haven't seen a wink of her since. I believe they're living in *Paris* now." She spoke as if this were a quite extraordinary thing to do.

"Paris is a beautiful city," Elizabeth said, then bit her tongue. What a dull comment! She wished she could be witty, but she felt shy in this company. Bessie didn't seem to require anything of her except a listening ear, but she wanted to make a good impression. There was a sudden burst of laughter from the men Tommy was talking with, but they didn't share the joke.

Bessie ignored them: "At Elsie's age, to move to a new city, away from her friends—it seems foolish to say the least. She must be lonely."

"She'll be back," Anne Morgan said. "Before the end of the year, I'll wager."

Elizabeth could sense some undercurrent to their disapproval but felt it would be impertinent to question them.

"Have you met Cecil Beaton, the new young English photographer?" Bessie asked. "He's working for Edna at *Vogue* and his pictures are divine. We should get him to photograph you. I have no idea why your picture doesn't appear more often in the press, when you are so beautiful. You are a living advertisement for your products."

Elizabeth beamed at the compliment. "I'm a middle-aged woman, hardly a young ingénue. I prefer my advertisements to show twenty-year-olds rather than forty-year-olds, although I still *feel* twenty. I think a lot of women my age do."

"I feel a hundred and three," Bessie said. "My hips and knees have given out and my spine is like a gnarled, twisted piece of driftwood. You have no idea the army of servants it takes to lift me from my bed each morning and massage my decrepit body until I can bear to be clothed. I hear you are quite the expert when it comes to massage. I should come to your salon but I fear the trip would be beyond me."

"I'm happy to visit you here and see if I can help," Elizabeth found herself saying. "I've always had strong hands." She'd had to be strong as a girl to catch the horses and drag them to their stables, carry heavy buckets of animal feed, one in each hand, and cut hay with a scythe at harvest time.

"Let's arrange a date," Bessie said. "I'll book Cecil Beaton to photograph you at the same time. We can borrow a gown from my good friend Hattie Carnegie. Her style will suit you: simple and classic. Something blue, to bring out your eyes." She clutched Elizabeth's hand. "You have such sparkle."

Elizabeth didn't feel sparkly at all. She felt overwhelmed that this woman was taking an interest in her, and had a feeling it could prove very useful.

"Do you buy art?" Bessie asked next. Elizabeth shook her head and opened her mouth to explain she was no expert but Bessie interrupted. "You should definitely buy art. It shows good taste and is a sound investment too. I can guide you on what to choose."

By the time she and Tommy left that first day, Elizabeth had gathered this was Bessie's modus operandi: she liked to throw out instructions, couched in flattery, in an attempt to control the lives of those around her. Perhaps that's why she had been disappointed in Elsie de Wolfe: because Elsie ignored her advice.

"I never thought I'd meet a woman who could outdo you for bossiness," Tommy said on the way home. "But now I think I have."

Elizabeth grinned. "She's a woman after my own heart," she said. She admired Bessie and hoped she would soon become a very dear friend.

BESSIE TELEPHONED THE following day to arrange a date when Elizabeth could come to give her a massage, partake of some luncheon, and have her photograph taken. It didn't seem to occur to her this would require Elizabeth to neglect the business for an entire day. She didn't object, though; she was keen to deepen the acquaintance.

On arrival, a maid showed her to Bessie's bedroom, where she sat in a pale blue peignoir, leaning against a cluster of pillows on top of the tangled bedcovers. Her body looked even larger than it had in her black taffeta gown. Her scalp was almost bald, with just a few wisps of gray hair, and Elizabeth realized she'd been wearing a wig at her Sunday tea.

"You will be shocked by the state of my legs, I fear," Bessie said. "I wear braces to support them and the wretched things dig into my flesh like medieval torture instruments."

"You poor dear!" Elizabeth said, adopting the soothing voice she used with her clients. "Do you want me to treat you lying on the bed, or perhaps in an armchair?" She normally gave head, neck, and shoulder massages in her treatment chair, and had never worked on legs before, but that seemed to be what Bessie required.

"I can't get out of bed until after a morning massage," Bessie said. "My joints stiffen up overnight, like a rusty old machine."

Elizabeth helped her to roll onto her front, and ran her hands over the legs first, feeling the grooves cut by the braces, the knots of veins in the bulky calves, the rolls of flesh around the knees. She folded up the peignoir to lower thigh and worked intuitively, starting with one ankle and kneading her way up the first leg. She tried not to think about the fact that she was touching another woman intimately.

Bessie gave a deep sigh. "My sources were right: you have a heavenly touch."

"I've had plenty of practice," Elizabeth said. A smell of sweet talcum powder overlay the fusty scent of an unwashed body. It must be difficult for Bessie to climb in and out of a bath, she imagined.

She worked on the other leg, then slid her hands up to Bessie's back. It was difficult to feel the spine under the quilt of flesh, but she pressed down on one side, then the other, trying to mobilize the vertebrae. Some of them clicked, and Bessie moaned. She worked up to the shoulders, the neck, and finally the head, digging her fingers into the scalp, pressing her thumbs into the points where spine met skull, where eyebrows met nose, and into the indentations in the temples just beyond the outer eye.

"Would you like me to help you get dressed?" she asked once she had finished. Bessie said no, that her maid would help her and she would join Elizabeth shortly.

Elizabeth waited in the sitting room where the Sunday tea had been held. She examined the paintings first, all of them showing women: a lady at her toilette, a laundry maid scrubbing a sheet, a ballet dancer. Next she examined the polished wood furniture with its curls and scrolls, before wandering over to look out the window at the view across the East River, where tugs labored up and down pulling improbably large loads.

She had been there an hour and was thinking of ringing the bell to ask what was happening when a maid appeared and invited her to join Miss Marbury in the dining room. Bessie was already sitting at the head of the table, wearing her bell-tent black dress, the brown wig in place. Elizabeth swallowed her annoyance at the waste of her time. She wouldn't put up with it from anyone else, but Bessie could be her entrée into polite society.

"I have a question for you," Bessie said. "I want to hear all about how you started your business. It's hard for women to find lucrative work in this world and I believe you didn't have family money behind you. You must have been very determined."

Elizabeth tried to brush off the question: "I worked hard, and I was in the right place just as the beauty industry was beginning to gain popularity." She smiled. "I was lucky."

"Not just luck, my dear. You must have a core of ruthlessness."

Elizabeth frowned. Where was this leading? "I'm not sure I would use that word exactly," she said.

"I only use it because others do," Bessie said. "Ruthless, selfish, hard-hearted . . . These are all words I've heard said about you."

"Goodness, I can't think who would have said that." Elizabeth flushed. She had been wrong-footed. She'd given a massage she would much rather not have given, and now she was under attack.

Bessie regarded her, unblinking. "I've heard Elizabeth Hubbard's side of the story," she said. "Now, why don't you tell me yours?"

Mrs. Hubbard! Elizabeth hadn't given her a second thought in almost two decades.

Elizabeth had first met her less than a year after she arrived in New York from Canada, when she was still using her birth name of Florence Nightingale Graham. She was working in a beauty salon owned by a woman called Eleanor Adair, where she had been promoted rapidly from bookkeeper to treatment girl and given the chance to learn about the business from the ground up. She was impatient to make a name for herself, though, and couldn't see any chance of further advancement at Eleanor Adair's.

Mrs. Hubbard had created her own face cream line and was looking for someone to help market the products. Elizabeth grabbed the chance, persuading her that she had the knowledge and experience to run a salon by herself. She'd taken a risk, walking away from a regular salary and earning Eleanor Adair's enmity at the same time because she adopted her techniques at the new salon and undercut her prices.

For Elizabeth, the deal with Mrs. Hubbard had been a partnership of convenience. She had never intended it to be more than a stepping stone to owning her own salon, but she couldn't tell Bessie that.

"Mrs. Hubbard was a dear friend," she lied. "But after six months or so—I can't remember how long exactly—it became clear that we had different visions for the business."

Bessie's expression gave nothing away as she watched with her clear blue eyes. "She says it was *her* business and you stole it."

"That's not true!" Elizabeth's cheeks were burning. "I was under the impression Mrs. Hubbard was inviting me to be her partner in the business, or I would never have left Eleanor Adair's." That was a white lie; she had judged from the start that Mrs. Hubbard was not an astute businesswoman and that she would be able to exert her influence and take over, bit by bit.

"Yet it read 'Elizabeth Hubbard' on the signage. Why was your name not there if you were a partner?"

"A superficial detail," Elizabeth said. "I was the one in charge from the start. My plan was to grow it into a national, then an international business, but Mrs. Hubbard seemed happy to run a single salon and make a small profit." She shrugged. "That's why there was a parting of the ways."

It had been acrimonious: Mrs. Hubbard took every piece of equipment, every jar of face cream with her, leaving Elizabeth with an empty salon—and a bruised cheek from a hard slap across the face. Elizabeth had to rent one of the rooms to a hairdresser to cover the rent, and buy new equipment as cheaply as possible. When redesigning the storefront, she kept the name Elizabeth to save money and merely changed Hubbard to Arden, a name that she felt was reminiscent of ardor and gardens.

"Elizabeth Hubbard told me you had an affair with the salon's landlord, and that's why he let you take over the lease," Bessie challenged.

She gasped out loud. "An affair? What nonsense! Mrs. Hubbard insisted I take care of paying the bills, so I was the one the landlord knew. There was nothing remotely untoward. I'm not that kind of woman." She was rattled by the accusation.

I was hungry, she wanted to plead. *I needed to improve my circumstances or I would have sunk to the depths. This city is not kind to the destitute.*

There had been men who offered to pay her to sleep with them, and times when she was so desperate she nearly considered it, but young Florence was made of stronger stuff. That fear of poverty pushed her to take risks—and yes, perhaps you could say she had been ruthless in casting Mrs. Hubbard aside and stealing Eleanor Adair's techniques, but it was the only route to prosperity that she could see.

Suddenly she felt cross at being interrogated. She was Elizabeth Arden; she needn't put up with this.

"It has not been easy being a woman in business," she continued. "I've been preyed upon by lecherous men, gossiped about by jealous women, let down by lazy employees, and sabotaged by competitors at every turn. I arrived here from Canada a young and vulnerable girl, but I have grown into a woman who can look after herself and I'm proud of that."

"Bravo!" Bessie applauded, nodding approval.

A maid came into the dining room with two bowls of potage, which she placed in front of them. Elizabeth picked up her spoon and took a sip: potato and leek, rather bland. "Don't eat something you're not enjoying" was one of her food rules. She was very careful to stay a healthy weight.

"What do you think made you so ambitious?" Bessie asked. "A woman like you could have married a wealthy husband and led a life of leisure."

"I've always been a hard worker," Elizabeth said. "Maybe it was losing my mother when I was young. My father was overwhelmed by the responsibility of raising five children, and it was clear to me I'd have to fend for myself. I tried training as a nurse, then as a bookkeeper"—she pulled a face—"but when I came to New York and got work in a beauty salon, I knew I had found my calling."

Bessie had finished her potage and rang a little bell, whereupon the maid appeared and collected their plates.

"How did you raise enough money to keep going after Elizabeth Hubbard left?" Bessie asked.

"A very dear cousin helped me out," Elizabeth replied, not mentioning that the cousin, a distant one, had charged her exorbitant interest. "But it was tough. I did most of the treatments myself so I didn't have to pay salaries, and when I closed the salon door each evening, I cleaned the place from top to bottom before updating the accounts. I watched every last cent, and still do. There's no big secret, no affairs with landlords, just sheer hard labor." That much was true.

The maid brought in heaped plates of chicken pot pie and vegetables.

"You must have nerves of steel," Bessie said, tucking in, then speaking with her mouth full. "Many would have given up, but not you."

Elizabeth shrugged, relieved to have won her good opinion. "It is remarkable what a woman can achieve with just a little ambition."

She watched Bessie demolish her plate of food while picking at her own, and thought that if their friendship were to continue, she'd have to have a word with her about her diet. Gluttony rather than hormones was clearly responsible for that figure.

That could wait. For now, she was thrilled to have such a well-connected new friend. It felt as though she had taken a huge leap up the social ladder.

CHAPTER 20

Helena

April 1926

Through most of the decade, Helena visited Edward in Paris two or three times a year, staying for a few weeks on each occasion. It was a marriage and not a marriage, both at the same time. She looked forward to her trips, and missed him when she had to sail home, but the demands of the American business drew her back like a siren's call. How were the salons faring? Had Edith sent any new reports on Elizabeth Arden? Her rival was expanding in Europe, with new salons in Cannes and Biarritz, but Helena had four more than her in the US. Miss Arden had eight more products, though, so Helena couldn't afford to relax.

She had given Edward money to set up his own bookshop, At the Sign of the Black Manikin, and agreed that he might publish a few books under the Black Manikin imprint if the right manuscript came into his hands. Literature was his passion and he was well connected; she had a feeling he'd be a talented publisher. Besides, the outlay wasn't vast and it kept him happy.

She loved shopping in Paris and always returned with several more trunksful than she'd arrived with. She bought gowns, coats, and hats in luxurious fabrics with vibrant colors, and shoes in soft calf's leather. She bought grown-up suits for her sons, and a velvet smoking jacket for Edward. She also went art shopping;

after one trip in the spring of 1926 she returned with a Chagall painting of a couple floating over a rooftop, and a stunning African sculpture called *Bangwa Queen*.

Her most extravagant purchase was a historic, five-story town house on the Île Saint-Louis, overlooking the Seine. Of all locations in Paris, this was the most iconic. The rooms were spacious and the whole building was full of light, with reflections from the water below rippling on the walls. She could tell the sunsets would be stupendous. The only drawback was some elderly sitting tenants who were refusing to move, but her French lawyers assured her they could deal with them.

Would it one day be her home with Edward, the place where they grew old together? As far as she was concerned, he was still on trial. Each time she sailed across, he met her at Cherbourg and they sped back to his apartment and fell into bed with all the passion of young lovers. After the romance of the reunions faded, they bickered, but it was a companionable kind of bickering. When she left again, she missed that intimate involvement in another person's life; those moments when she looked at him and knew exactly what he was thinking, and felt he understood her in return.

And yet, she was wary. It was complicated. There was so much history between them and so much at stake.

HELENA INVITED CARMEL White around for cocktails to show her the Chagall and the *Bangwa Queen* sculpture. The sculpture stood on a plinth in the hallway and was the first thing Carmel saw when she stepped out of the elevator.

"Golly! Look at the power and fierceness of her!" Carmel exclaimed. "She's so scary, she reminds me of you."

Helena laughed. "She's feminine too." The womanliness combined with the raw energy had drawn her to the figure. "But I suppose anyone would think twice about crossing her." She stroked the grooves that represented hair on her elongated head.

"I imagine her having lots of children and lots of lovers: no man would be enough for her."

"Is that the case with you?" Carmel had a cheeky expression. "Are there lots of lovers hidden in your closet?"

"I'm sorry to disappoint you, but there's only one man for me." She led Carmel through to the sitting room, and asked her maid to mix martinis.

"Did you bring him with you this time?" Carmel asked. "I can't believe I still haven't met him."

"Edward becomes more Parisian with each passing year. I can scarcely tempt him out of Montparnasse, never mind across the ocean." She spoke lightly, but the ache of missing him was still there, just behind her rib cage. She pointed to the wall at the end of the room. "What do you think of my floating lovers?"

Carmel walked over to examine the painting close up. "It's stunning," she said. "I know Chagall and his lover, Bella, spent years apart, like you and Edward. Yet here they are together. Perhaps that's what drew you to the picture."

"Are you trying to psychoanalyze me?" Helena asked, with a smile. "My marriage is not traditional, but it suits us for now." Had that been why she chose the painting? Perhaps it had, subconsciously.

Carmel came to sit by Helena on the couch facing the Chagall. "I don't understand how you and Edward can bear to be apart. When I'm in love I think about the man the whole time, and want to see him every day." She spoke in a breathy fashion and hugged herself as she spoke, as if imagining the arms of some absent lover. Helena got a sense there was something she wasn't divulging.

"Caramel White, have you met someone while I've been away?"

Carmel bit her lip before replying, as if to quell her excitement. "I have! He's a lawyer, named George Palen Snow."

"Tell me everything. How did you meet? What he's like? And

144

Gill Paul

does he deserve you?" Helena loved hearing the stories of other people's romances.

Carmel's grin was infectious. "I met him at a house party in Long Island. He turned up late because he'd been playing golf and lost track of time. The rest of us were halfway through dinner and we'd left his place empty, then he walked in, all tall and sporty-looking, with an apologetic smile, and I fell for him at that precise moment." She snapped her fingers. "Before we'd even been introduced, I knew I was in love."

"But you're not sporty," Helena said. "Do you have anything in common?"

"Nothing at all really!" Carmel replied cheerfully. "He likes horses, I don't; he likes tennis and golf and sailing, I don't; I like dancing and he has no sense of rhythm; I like art and he gets bored in galleries. But we have the same sense of humor and we simply adore each other. Look!" She held out her left hand, splaying the fingers, unable to keep the secret to herself any longer.

Helena took her hand and examined the ring on her fourth finger. It featured a radiant diamond, about two carats, in an elaborate platinum setting. It was modern rather than an heirloom, and must have been expensive. She whistled appreciatively. "Did he choose this?" she asked. "It's beautiful."

"He chose a ring, but I changed it." Carmel laughed. "He might as well get an early taste of my fussiness so he knows what he's in for."

Helena hugged her. "I'm very happy for you both. When is the wedding to be?"

"November," Carmel said. "Peggy Hoyt is making my dress as we speak, and I'm counting on your being there."

"I will certainly be there," Helena replied. The martinis arrived and Helena raised a glass: "To you and your George. I look forward to meeting him."

"Edna's reaction was priceless," Carmel told her. "No congratulations, just a warning that if I get pregnant it will be the end of my career. She has great plans for me, she says, and none of them will be possible if I have children. So I didn't tell her that I fully intend to start trying for a baby as soon as the ink is dry on the marriage register. We both want children and I don't see why I can't combine a career with motherhood. After all, you've managed it."

Helena felt a twinge of guilt. She was by no means a devoted mother, but the boys seemed to have survived. She felt she knew them better now that she spent time with them in Paris during the school holidays.

"Edna and I keep clashing these days," Carmel continued. "I asked the art department to do a minor redesign using a more modern typeface for headings, and you'd think I'd murdered her favorite cat. The fuss she made! There are strict rules at *Vogue* that cannot be altered or the sky will fall, according to her." She scrunched her lips to one side.

"Can't you have a word with Condé Nast?" Helena asked. The publisher had a reputation for being progressive.

"It's tricky," Carmel said. "In the office they say that Edna is Condé's wife while I am his mistress—figuratively speaking, of course. We both have influence over him but he can never choose one over the other."

"Of all the magazines on the market, *Vogue* is one that must look modern and stylish," Helena said. "How can you report this season's trends using type that is twenty years out of date?" She curled her feet underneath her. "I have changed the lettering on our products to a Bauhaus typeface. Buyers might not be conscious of the change but it positions us as a modern brand."

"That's exactly what *Vogue* should be doing," Carmel agreed.

They talked about new fashion trends, about Carmel's plans for her wedding, and about George's Long Island house, which would become her main home once they were married. Helena described her vision for the Île Saint-Louis town house, and suggested that once it was finished, Carmel might like to stay there when she visited the Paris collections.

As they chatted, Helena didn't find herself distracted by thoughts of work, as she did in most other company. She loved her friendship with Carmel. Weeks could go by between their meetings, but always they took up the conversational thread where they had left off. Helena confided in her, knowing her confidences would never be passed on, and she treated Carmel's secrets with the utmost discretion. They both enjoyed gossiping about other people, though. Why not?

Carmel sipped her martini. "You might be interested to hear that Elizabeth Arden has taken up with the lesbian set. Bessie Marbury has adopted her."

Helena had heard of the Sutton Place coterie grouped around Miss Marbury. "But Elizabeth's married, is she not? Her husband was a soldier."

"It could be a sham marriage," Carmel said. "I have no idea. I just heard that Miss Arden has been socializing with them. You know Bessie Marbury was bereft when her previous companion, Elsie de Wolfe, got married earlier this year? Perhaps Elizabeth is her replacement."

Helena was all ears. "There must be quite an age difference between them."

"Bessie is in her seventies, while I imagine Elizabeth is some-where in her forties. But Elizabeth is fiercely socially ambitious," Carmel explained, "and Bessie can open doors for her. I say good luck to them."

Helena squirreled away the information, not sure what to make of it. Her rival remained an enigma in many ways, but she was sure she knew more than Elizabeth Arden could possibly know about her, thanks to the espionage of Edith Brown and the chattiness of her dear friend Carmel.

CARMEL'S WEDDING TO George Palen Snow was an en-tertaining occasion. First of all, the Episcopalian minister got confused about their surnames, calling him White and her Snow during the vows, then making the same mistake again even after he'd been corrected. They had asked their guests to wear bright colors and Helena selected a gown in cobalt blue, which she accessorized with cerise shoes and bag. Other guests were wearing equally bold shades, giving a rainbow effect as they clustered together.

The wedding party was in a friend's apartment on Park Avenue, and the toastmaster was Frank Crowninshield, editor of *Vanity Fair*.

"What Marie Antoinette was to eighteenth-century France," he said, "Carmel White is to twentieth-century America. And, fittingly, George Palen Snow has all the swagger of a French monarch. But may they keep their heads on their shoulders for the wedding night—when the rest of us lose ours due to the ferocity of these cocktails." He raised his glass. "To the smugly happy couple!"

A tall, very handsome, silver-haired man approached Helena and introduced himself as Carmel's brother, Tom White. "I saw the tribal mask you gave Carmel and George as a wedding present," he said. "It's stunning. She tells me you have quite a collection of African pieces."

"I do," she agreed. "I love the exaggerated characteristics. They seem to me remarkably modern, and have influenced many painters I'm keen on, like Picasso and Modigliani."

"I know a curator at the Museum of Modern Art who is arranging an African exhibition, and wondered if you would be willing to lend some of your pieces?" he asked.

"Certainly," Helena replied. "I'd be happy to."

They talked for a while about trends in art, then she asked if he worked in that area since he seemed so knowledgeable.

"*Au contraire*," he said. "I am a general manager for William Randolph Hearst's media empire, so I deal with sheets of figures, accountants, and union bosses." He pulled a wry face.

Helena was fascinated by other successful business owners and asked what the infamous Mr. Hearst was like.

"Imperious," Tom confided. "I'd tell him to go jump in a lake but he'd probably delegate that to me, the way he does with everything else." He winked, as if to suggest he wasn't serious, but Helena suspected he was.

"Does he? I tend to oversee most areas myself," Helena said. "I figure no one else cares about my money as much as I do."

"Your business seems to go from strength to strength," Tom said, "but I suppose that is true of many in this never-ending bull market."

They talked about the lightning economic growth of the decade, fueled by new inventions. Helena observed that the public trusted everything scientists told them and set increasing store by scientific progress in everything from iceboxes and automobiles to face creams. That had benefited her business, which was based on the science of skin care.

Tom flattered her by saying, "You're more astute than any man I have discussed the economy with."

She was instantly wary. Was he flirting? He was looking directly into her eyes and standing so close she could smell his hair oil. But she was in her fifties, with a matronly figure, and she was married. He was probably agreeable to everyone he met. She expected it stood him in good stead.

"Your brother is quite the charmer," she said to Carmel when their paths crossed later, while the bridal couple was saying their goodbyes before heading off on honeymoon.

Carmel gave her a quick searching look before she replied: "Oh yes, everyone falls in love with my brother Tom."

CHAPTER 21

Elizabeth

September 1927

Bessie was a creature of fixed habits. She asked Elizabeth to visit her every Wednesday morning at ten precisely, then stay for luncheon, which would last till she had her nap at two. Elizabeth always gave her a massage first, then they chatted. Bessie's style of conversation was direct, as if she were trying to peer into Elizabeth's soul. *Is your marriage happy? What makes you work so hard? Do you have any regrets? Tell me about your political views.*

Elizabeth found the interest in her flattering, and answered honestly for the most part. It was nice to feel noticed and understood; Tommy never bothered to ask how she was feeling. One day she confessed that she was disappointed it had been so difficult for her to befriend high-society women since she moved to New York.

"Oh, that's easy to fix," Bessie said straight away. "I know you already donate to charities, but volunteer for the committees too. These women will be forced to talk to you when you're helping them to raise thousands of dollars for good causes. I heard they're looking for someone at the Friends of the Philharmonic. I'll ask Anne Vanderbilt to nominate you."

Elizabeth knew nothing about classical music, but within a week she was on the committee. Bessie was a powerful woman to have on your side.

She was curious about the very close relationship between Bessie and the two Annes. They had clearly known each other a long time and had a shared set of references that Elizabeth couldn't always follow, but her questions on the subject seldom got a straight answer. One day she asked why they had such a low opinion of Elsie de Wolfe following her marriage.

Bessie offered an explanation: "Anne Morgan invested in Elsie's renovation of the Villa Trianon, outside Paris, but she's lost her head and is spending a king's ransom on it. When Anne said she wanted to pull out, you should have heard the invective."

Elizabeth could understand that. She concluded that the four friends must have been unusually close and that's why Elsie's marrying and moving to France felt like such a betrayal.

BESSIE WAS AN influential player in the Democratic party. At one of the Sunday teas, Elizabeth was thrilled to be introduced to Eleanor Roosevelt, wife of the politician Franklin D. Roosevelt. She was a tall, toothy woman in dowdy clothes, who had an engaging presence and an elite accent. They talked about her campaign to abolish child labor, and Elizabeth was in full agreement. Although she didn't tell Mrs. Roosevelt so, she had worked long hours on her father's farm from the age of five, and strongly believed that laws should be passed to protect children like her. She was less enamored of Mrs. Roosevelt's plan to introduce a minimum wage; it would cost her a fortune if she had to pay her factory workers at the level suggested, but she kept her mouth shut, in awe of this forthright woman.

Talk turned to a politician called Herbert Lehman, who was thinking of running for the chairmanship of the Democratic State Committee.

"Of course, he's a decent man," Bessie said, "but Jews are no more popular than Catholics. It simply wouldn't wash."

"Don't you think we should be encouraging a change in such attitudes?" Mrs. Roosevelt asked, gently, but Bessie disagreed.

"I think we should get into power first," she said, "and worry about the niceties later."

One woman whose name Elizabeth had missed said she found Jews were unscrupulous in their dealings.

Elizabeth agreed with her. "Helena Rubinstein, the beauty salon owner, has been quite unethical in the way she spies on my company and copies my products. I'm not saying all Jews are like her, of course, but it's not the way we do things in polite society, is it?" She glanced at Bessie for affirmation.

"Good breeding will out," Bessie said, and Elizabeth blinked, hoping Bessie never found out the circumstances in which she had been bred.

"Do you think the problem lies in Madame Rubinstein's Jewish origins?" Mrs. Roosevelt asked. "Or is she simply a competitive businesswoman? Perhaps you should discuss your concerns with her."

"I wouldn't dream of it," Elizabeth said with a shiver, wishing she had never raised the subject.

"Surely you must bump into her around town?" Bessie asked.

"Only once," Elizabeth replied, "at a *Vogue* party, and she was quite aggressive toward me."

"She's probably curious about you," Mrs. Roosevelt soothed. "You two should talk."

"I'd rather not risk it," Elizabeth said. "There's definitely something of the savage about her. My husband and I went to the Colony to dine just last week and saw her seated at the center table, and I couldn't stay, I just couldn't. It's horrid to feel I have to keep looking over my shoulder."

She was aware of a shrill edge to her voice, and of Mrs. Roosevelt regarding her with a quizzical expression, so she shuffled toward the tea table to occupy herself in refilling her cup, her hand shaking as she poured.

Since the recent near miss with her rival, she had felt as if she couldn't risk dining at the Colony anymore. At least the Colony

Club, a completely separate establishment for women, still did not admit Jews, so she didn't have to look over her shoulder when she lunched there.

"YOU LOOK TIRED," Bessie remarked one day. "You've been working too hard. You should come for a vacation at my summer home in Maine."

Tommy's name wasn't mentioned. Bessie never asked after him, or invited him to their meetings, but Elizabeth preferred it that way. This friendship was hers alone.

"It sounds tempting but how would I get there?" she asked.

"It's too far to drive so I always travel in a Pullman sleeping berth," Bessie said. "I fall asleep in Grand Central and waken in Augusta. We can ride together."

The decision was made, and they set off in mid-June. Elizabeth slept fitfully on the train, her mind still whirring over business matters: a rise in the cost of sweet almond oil that could force her to raise her prices, a rent increase at two of her salons, the resignation of her Miami salon manager. She hated to leave unfinished business.

A driver met them off the Pullman and drove them north toward the Belgrade Lakes. Everywhere Elizabeth looked, she saw dense pine forest and deep blue water, with scarcely any signs of human habitation. It was incredibly still and silent.

"Do you fish?" Bessie asked, and when Elizabeth shook her head, she said, "Don't worry, I'll teach you. We all fish here."

As they turned down a track, Elizabeth spotted two horses cantering in a field, with the tall slender look of thoroughbreds. She turned her head as they passed. She hadn't been around horses since she left her father's farm at the age of seventeen.

Bessie's house was a huge white clapboard one, with a vast expanse of lawn in front leading down to the edge of Long Pond. It reminded Elizabeth of the countryside outside Toronto where she had grown up.

She climbed out of the car and took a deep breath of the pine-scented air. A cool breeze ruffled her hair. The sun sparkled off the water. Birdsong was all around. The sheer beauty took her breath away. In that split second, she felt at peace.

LIFE SLOWED TO a gentle rhythm in Bessie's house: long, lazy mornings, when Elizabeth gave Bessie a massage to help her loosen up and they chatted over coffee; a leisurely lunch on the verandah; reading in the shade or sitting beside Bessie as she cast her line into the lake—Elizabeth didn't take to fishing—and then cocktails before dinner. There was staff to take care of all the practicalities.

On the third morning, Elizabeth rose early after a sound night's sleep, and decided to walk up the track and see if the horses were still in the field. She scrounged some carrots from the kitchen, and sang under her breath as she strolled in the cool morning sun.

A mare and a colt were there, both bays, and they trotted over when she called. They were majestic animals, with long slender legs and broad chests, clearly very well kept. She loved the gracefulness of horses despite their size, and the jaunty swish of their tails.

"Aren't you beautiful darlings," she whispered, and fed them a carrot each, stroking their velvety noses and inhaling their unique horsey smell. "Has someone put you out to breed? I hope you like each other. You two could have adorable foals." She rubbed her head against the mare's, and blew into her nostrils. Ned and Ollie, the old draft horses on her father's farm, had always liked that. Feeding them had been her favorite part of the day.

A man walking down the road stopped to chat. "The stable is half a mile that way." He pointed up the road. "I reckon Old John will have a horse you can ride if you want."

Elizabeth didn't want to ride. She had never ridden horses.

She just liked being around them, talking to them and petting them. She walked in the direction he'd indicated and found a yard with chickens pecking at the earth, a strong odor of manure, and a black-and-white collie, which barked on her approach and rushed up, tail wagging and tongue hanging out. She bent to pet its head.

She found John in an outbuilding and asked if she might have a look in his stable. "I love horses. I grew up around them," she explained.

"Can't think why not," he said, glancing at her smart clothes with bemusement. "The stalls are that way. Watch out for the one with the white flash on his nose; he's got a temper on him."

Elizabeth stood in the doorway to the stable, breathing in the musky scent of horse sweat, listening to the horses' snorting and shuffling as they eyed her up. She knew they were wondering who this stranger might be. Brushes, grooming mitts, and curry combs hung on a rack inside the door, and she decided Old John couldn't object if she tidied them up a bit. She lifted down a brush and approached the first one, a chestnut with gentle brown eyes.

"Hello, dear," she whispered, letting him see the brush first before smoothing it over his rump. The sensation brought a rush of memories. She knew what horses liked and what scared them; she could sense what they were thinking and feeling. She talked to them in a soft, low voice, always letting them see what she was about to do, making sure they didn't get spooked. By the time she had worked her way around the stable, even the bad-tempered one with the white flash was happy to let her groom him.

A sense of calm settled over her and she sang under her breath. Everything left her head except the focus on the animal she was grooming. She felt happier with those horses than she had in years—possibly ever.

CHAPTER 22

Helena

September 1928

Helena hovered in the corridor between the Manhattan salon and the stairs to her office, listening as two of her wealthy clients chatted at the manicure table while treatment girls filed and polished their nails.

"I've added General Motors to my investments," one said. "Folks are always going to want motor cars. And electricity is another winner: my General Electric stocks keep on rising."

"My husband has lots of stocks in oil, but I prefer products I actually use. Sears Roebuck and F. W. Woolworth are making me a pretty profit."

"Does your husband give you a kitty to invest? Mine does. He says I have very good judgment." The woman sounded competitive.

"I have my own money," came the haughty reply. "The bank loans it to me on the margin. They know I'm a good risk."

Helena was alarmed by this, and similar conversations she heard in the salon every week. Stock trading was the new national pastime and suddenly everyone was an expert. The market had continued to rise through the 1920s and investing seemed foolproof, but Helena would never put money into any business but her own. She would have no control over decisions the managers took and wouldn't have all the facts and figures at her fingertips. It was gambling, pure and simple; you might as well put money on a horse.

Helena had started talking to a few private investment companies about the next stage of her expansion plans. She had almost as many products as her rival—seventy to Elizabeth Arden's seventy-five—and more salons around the US, including ones in all the cities her old sales director had warned her would not accept Jews. That hurdle had been swept away by women's desire to look young and beautiful.

Her products were sold in major department stores, but now she wanted to volumize sales by getting them into drugstores in small towns across the country, and that would require a cash injection so she could build more factories and support a larger sales team. She had long considered going public and making shares in the US company available. If there was a mania for share-buying, why not let them buy hers?

She was biding her time, finding the right team to work with. Many top financiers refused to take a meeting with her, and she never found out whether it was because she was a woman or because she was Jewish. She kept a list of them; Helena was a person who held grudges.

Lehman Brothers was an early frontrunner. It had successfully brought several other firms to market: F. W. Woolworth, Macy's, Gimble Brothers, the Studebaker Corporation, and many more in the retail, tourism, and entertainment worlds. She liked Bobbie Lehman, a smart, articulate man in his thirties, who was one of the trustees of the Met Museum of Art, as well as a money expert. He didn't talk down to Helena as they discussed how a deal between them could be structured, and she appreciated that.

As he spoke, Helena heard her father's voice in her head. *Listen hard. What does the other side want? What will they compromise on?* He used to treat her almost as a son, letting her come to meetings with him and observe how he ran his kerosene business. She felt a pang of missing him for the first time in many years.

When she was fourteen years old, her father had been ill for several weeks and she stepped in to run the business. She visited the suppliers he bought kerosene from and, after struggling to persuade them to deal with her, she negotiated a better price than her father had ever achieved.

She thought he would be proud, but he seemed disgruntled to be outdone by a young girl. "Beginners' luck," he told her. "I expect you flashed your ankles." She hadn't; she had just done her research and worked out what margins the wholesalers needed to make and what competitors were charging, then she had gone into meetings with all those figures in her head. She enjoyed it. Always had. And now the experience stood her in good stead while she was negotiating the biggest deal of her life.

If only her father hadn't thrown her out, she could have discussed it with him. Maybe one day, when old age had mellowed him, she would go back and tell him about it. But her sister Regina, who still lived in Kraków, told her he remained as stubborn as ever.

"What are your views on timing?" she asked Bobbie Lehman.

"Sooner rather than later," he advised. "The Fed is trying to cool the market by cutting off easy credit and there are a few indicators that the economy is slowing, especially in the fields of housing and manufacturing. This bull market is nearing the end of its run."

That was Helena's feeling too. But she had decisions to make first. How much control would she be willing to forsake? How would she present her decision to the public? She had many stipulations if she were to cede even partial authority: one being that the quality of the products must never be compromised, the other that she must remain the company's president, the Queen of Beauty Science.

HELENA MET CARMEL for cocktails and found her in a sub-dued mood. A year after her wedding, she'd given birth to a daughter, her little namesake Carmel, but since then she'd mis-carried two babies, and at forty-one years old she feared she might have left it too late.

"I always wanted a big family," she told Helena, guzzling her martini. "The Whites produce large broods, and I would hate for Carmel to be an only child."

"You will have more children. I'm sure of it," Helena told her.

"That's what my fortune-teller says," Carmel agreed.

"Your *what*?" Helena peered at her to see if it was a joke, but she seemed sincere.

"Dolly has advised me on all my major life decisions. She's a genius. I trust her completely."

"What kind of decisions does she make for you?" Helena had thought Carmel was smart but perhaps she would have to reas-sess that judgment.

"After the war, when I was living in Paris and trying to decide which career I should pursue, I wrote to Dolly and she consulted the cards and told me I should be a writer. And then the *New York Times* asked me to report on the shows that spring, and it all fell into place."

"Did you ask Dolly whether or not you should marry George?" Helena asked, trying to keep the skepticism from her tone.

"Of course! I wouldn't have married him if she didn't recom-mend it." She gripped Helena's arm. "You must talk to her. I know you want to spend more time in Paris with your Edward, but you're torn because of your business here. Why not ask Dolly's advice?"

Helena snorted, then choked on her drink. She coughed to clear her throat, and her eyes watered. "I believe in freedom of thought," she said. "I don't think less of you for consulting a card reader, but these seem rather large life decisions to trust her with. Would you jump off a skyscraper if she advised you to?"

"She would never ask that." Carmel laughed. "I pay her too much!" She regarded Helena. "So what *do* you believe in? I know that parts of my Catholic upbringing still linger. Although I haven't said confession for decades, I feel guilty whenever I sin—not that it stops me, of course. Do you have any vestiges of Jewishness lurking from childhood?"

"They say if you are born Jewish, you die Jewish," Helena said. "But I never really believed in God and religious worship, even as a child."

"Your father must have been very religious, though. Otherwise, why did he kick up such a fuss when you fell in love with a boy who wasn't Jewish?"

Helena had thought long and hard about this over the years. She'd been her father's favorite daughter, then he changed completely when he found out about her relationship with Stanislaus. He couldn't bear that she was becoming independent, and making her own choices.

"It wasn't about religion for him," she replied. "Everyone had to obey him in that house, and I dared to defy him. That's what he found unforgivable."

"I'm sure he is proud of your success, even if he doesn't admit it."

Was her father secretly proud of her? It was a nice thought, but she doubted it. He would never admit to being in the wrong. At least she had the benefit of all the business acumen he had taught her back in her teens. When Bobbie Lehman sent a letter containing his proposal, Helena heard her father's voice in her head and knew exactly what to do.

ANOTHER BEAUTY SALON owner, a relative newcomer called Dorothy Gray, had sold her business the previous year to the pharmaceutical company Lehn & Fink, and they had already begun an expansion program, but Helena was too far ahead in the game to feel threatened by them. She wondered if Elizabeth Arden was talking to private investors, though. It would be galling if she sold her business for a higher figure than Helena got.

She didn't want to let go of the US business completely, but Bobbie Lehman said she would have to forsake at least seventy-five percent to give a new manager the control he needed to make changes. His initial offer was five million dollars.

Helena tore the letter to pieces, stuffed them in the same envelope, and sent it back to him, with a note scribbled on the outside saying, *I thought you were serious about this deal. Seems I was wrong. HR.*

Bobbie arrived at the salon just over an hour later, tall and distinguished in his pinstripe suit, a bottle of champagne tucked under his arm and two coupe glasses protruding from his jacket pockets.

"Let's close this, Helena," he said. "What do you want from me? A Matisse etching? A Rodin sculpture? What will sweeten it for you?" He placed the bottle and glasses side by side on her desk.

"Ten million dollars," Helena said. She knew she wouldn't get it, but it was one of her rules of business: always ask for double the first offer.

He sat down hard on her office chair and clasped a hand to his chest. "Don't give me a heart attack. Let's be serious."

An hour and a half later they had agreed on a figure of 7.3 million dollars for seventy-five percent of the American company. Helena had a long list of conditions. He listened, making notes in a diary, and at the end he told her that none of them were insurmountable.

"Can we put this in the hands of the lawyers and open the champagne?" he asked.

Still Helena had misgivings. It was a huge step to take. This had always been part of her plan for domination of the US market, but now that the time was nigh, she felt a tug on her heart. Was it the right thing to do? Would she regret it?

Bobbie was holding the champagne bottle, thumbs poised to pop the cork, and looking at her expectantly.

"I don't want it announced until we have signed off on the details," she said. That gave her time to change her mind.

"Of course not," he replied. He opened the bottle expertly, and poured one glass, then handed it to her before pouring his own. "To a long and fruitful partnership," he said, clinking his glass against hers.

There were weeks of toing and froing between the lawyers, and Helena stayed on top of every last comma in the final deal. December 11, 1928, was set as the date when the contracts would be signed, and some financial reporters were invited to Lehman Brothers' office to hear the news.

Helena submitted some final demands on the tenth, knowing it was too late for Bobbie to object without canceling the press announcement.

"That was naughty, Helena," he whispered to her as they signed the legal document in front of photographers' flashbulbs.

She gave him her sweetest smile, making sure the cameras got her best angle, and didn't reply.

After the announcement, reporters called out questions to her.

"Why did you decide to sell, Madame Rubinstein?"

"I want to spend more time in Paris with my husband, who runs a bookstore and publishing house there."

"Will there be any changes to your product line?"

"Helena Rubinstein products will continue to evolve to suit the skin of the modern woman," she said. "I will personally test every single new item and guarantee the quality and efficacy will be maintained."

"Do you realize this deal makes you the richest self-made woman in America?" one reporter asked.

She smiled at him, and said, "Does it really?"

But of course that had been part of her calculations all along.

CHAPTER 23

Elizabeth

December 1928

E lizabeth read about the sale of Madame Rubinstein's business with mixed emotions. She was astounded her rival would cede control. Wasn't she worried what the new management team might do to the company? What was she up to? In interviews she claimed she would be spending more time in Paris with her husband, and that was good news. At least Elizabeth could socialize in Manhattan without looking over her shoulder.

It seemed they planned to open new factories to mass-produce Rubinstein products and sell them in drugstores the length and breadth of the States. She would become the bigger of the two beauty brands in terms of volume, and Elizabeth's competitive hackles rose at that. Was that why Madame Rubinstein had sold out? She had a nagging feeling that Helena was up to some kind of skulduggery. The woman had already shown herself to be devious and capable of anything.

Over the next few days, she got Laney to purchase any newspapers covering the story and scoured them for information. Several magazines ran biographical features on Madame Rubinstein. A *New Yorker* profile gave her age as forty-eight, which made her two years younger than Elizabeth. In photographs, she seemed remarkably wrinkle-free. Elizabeth was acutely aware of her own lines and furrows. The pictures taken by Cecil Beaton had made her look middle-aged and she loathed them.

Bessie's opinion was that the sale of Madame Rubinstein's business would play into Elizabeth's hands. "Bigger is not the same as better. She might become the more widely sold brand, but that will make yours all the more exclusive. When she drops her prices, as she will have to, you should raise yours. The elite don't want to buy the same face cream as the hoi polloi, so they will happily pay more and your profit margins will increase."

That argument appealed to Elizabeth. She wasn't interested in a dogfight to see who could get the cheapest face cream into a drugstore in Idaho. Hers were the *crème de la crème* of beauty products. Her brand was bought by the wealthiest of women, and there was no reason for them to switch loyalty if she maintained the quality of the products and continued to innovate.

Tommy didn't agree. "Don't you follow the markets?" he asked. "There's a reason why Dorothy Gray and Helena Rubinstein sold out when they did: because stock prices are at an all-time high and everyone says they are due a tumble. I think I should talk to some money men and listen to their proposals."

"You'd be wasting your time, dear. I will never—*never!*—give up control of my company," Elizabeth replied.

"There are ways it could be arranged so you don't lose control," Tommy said. "You could sell forty-nine percent and keep fifty-one, or whatever percentage makes you comfortable."

Elizabeth was adamant. "I won't sell. I simply won't." She stamped her foot for emphasis.

"You keep complaining you don't have enough leisure time. Just think: you could relax more if you brought in another management team. Take it easy."

"I'm not an octogenarian," she snapped. "Next you'll be suggesting I retire and take up needlepoint."

They argued about it many times that Christmas, and finally

Elizabeth said, "Never forget one little point, dear. It's my business. You only work there."

He left the room, slamming the door. She hoped that would
be the end of it. What a nerve!

Tommy didn't often argue with her so forcefully. Usually they
worked quite separately, him in his office and her in hers. He sent
her a weekly report of results from his division, and she wrote
him memos when she wanted him to do something. There was
seldom any need for meetings or even to talk on the telephone.

At home, they still entertained guests for dinner or cocktail
parties, but not as often because Elizabeth preferred to spend
her free time at Bessie's. She and Tommy went to the theater together if there was a show she fancied, or if a friend of theirs was
opening in a new production, and that was fine. Tommy was still
the good-natured man she had married, except over this one issue, where he genuinely seemed to believe she was in the wrong.

Bessie was fascinated by their marriage, and often asked
questions about their home life.

"Do you two sit down and discuss your days over dinner
each evening?" she wondered. "Analyze sales figures over the fish
course?"

Elizabeth admitted that they seldom ate dinner together.
They finished work at different times, and the cook produced a
meal for each of them whenever they got home.

"You told me you have separate bedrooms," Bessie asked,
"but I wonder if there are many night-time excursions between
the two?"

"Bessie Marbury!" Elizabeth rebuked. "I know you have a
curious streak but some things should remain private between
man and wife." In truth, she counted in her head, it had been ten
years since they last had marital relations.

"Do you love him?" Bessie persevered.

"Well, I suppose I must do after thirteen years of marriage,"
Elizabeth replied. "It's not the giddy kind of love I hear the salon

girls giggling about, but a steady companionship. I'm sorry you never married, Bessie. There's a lot of comfort to be had in the institution."

"Don't worry about me," Bessie said. "I've had my share of steady companionships—and now I consider you my newest special companion. I enjoy our time together very much, Elizabeth."

"I do too." Impulsively, she leaned forward and kissed Bessie on the cheek. "And as your special companion, I advise you not to eat that huge slice of cake in front of you. A second on the lips means a lifetime on the hips."

"Thank goodness I've reached an age when I don't give a damn," Bessie replied, lifting a forkful of cake to her mouth.

ELIZABETH WAS CONCERNED in March when the newspapers reported a tumble in share prices. All the clients in her salon were talking about it.

"John said we lost two hundred thousand dollars overnight," one woman said as Elizabeth gave her a shoulder massage. "But I'm not worried. Everyone knows the market will rise again. Traders are skittish creatures, John says. They take fright at the least little thing, then forget about it the next day and go back to where they were before."

"I'm sure you're right," Elizabeth agreed, digging her thumbs into a tangled knot of muscle in the right shoulder.

The woman winced. "Do you invest in shares, Miss Arden?"

"It's not something I've looked into," she said. "I generally prefer investing in real estate. At least you can see what you're buying."

"Real estate doesn't increase in value so quickly though. We make about twenty percent a year on our shares." She gasped as Elizabeth's thumbs found an especially painful spot. "There might be a few ups and downs, but the American economy is rock solid."

Another client leaned toward them from her treatment chair.

"My husband says too many investors are ignoring the price-to-earnings ratio, and they're plowing money into companies that don't have enough intrinsic value."

"That's just inexperienced investors," the first woman said. "John knows what he's doing."

"Of course he does," Elizabeth soothed. She knew from experience that such discussions could become heated if she let them develop. Everyone thought she knew best. "I'm sure there's nothing to worry about."

Over the summer, the whole stock market story seemed to simmer down. Headlines were about the marriage of Douglas Fairbanks Jr. to Joan Crawford, an unlucky Belgian newspaper editor who fell into a hot spring at Yellowstone Park, and a Zeppelin airship that made the first round-the-world flight.

Elizabeth spent six luxurious weeks at Bessie's house in Maine, and visited the stables every day to groom the horses. She knew exactly what they liked. When it was hot, she sponged them down with cool water and opened the barn doors to try and catch a hint of a breeze. Out in the field they were plagued by horseflies, but Elizabeth found that citronella oil helped to protect them and she had Fabian Swanson send her a case of it. Old John screwed up his nose at the unfamiliar lemony scent but didn't object when he realized his horses were happier.

She talked to them as she worked, totally absorbed in these graceful, athletic creatures. She was getting to know their personalities now—the short-tempered ones, the anxious ones, the lazy ones, the sweet-natured ones. They were like children.

"You should get a horse of your own," John said. "You can stable it here if you like."

"Do you know, I just might." Elizabeth smiled at the thought. "When the time is right."

SHE RETURNED TO Manhattan on Labor Day, arriving on the overnight Pullman in time for her morning meeting. Laney told her that Tommy had requested an urgent talk with her, and she frowned. What did he want now?

"We've had an offer for the company," he announced as he strode into her office an hour later. "A very good offer."

"What makes them think the company's for sale?" she asked, sharply. "I thought we'd had this conversation already."

Tommy sat down and crossed his legs. "Fifteen million dollars, Elizabeth. Just think." He watched her face. "Helena Rubinstein sold three-quarters of her company for seven point three million. You could get more than double that. I thought you'd be pleased."

Now that he put it that way, Elizabeth was tickled. She would ask Laney to leak to her press contacts that her company was worth more.

"We're both in our fifties," he continued. "How long do you plan to keep working at this rate? Another ten years? Then what? I'm curious."

"I expect to keep working into my eighties and beyond," Elizabeth replied. "What else would I do?" A thought crossed her mind: she could keep horses. Breed them, or race them. Perhaps she would do that too. "Are you feeling your age, Tommy? Do you want to sit at home reading a newspaper all day? Be my guest."

"No." He shook his head, irritably. "But we need to make plans. The company has been thriving during the boom years of the twenties but it's clear to anyone in the know that those years are at an end. Bull markets can't last forever. Madame Rubinstein got out in time. So did Dorothy Gray. Are you going to be the one who gets left behind? Your wealthy clients' husbands will stop them spending money on beauty treatments when their incomes drop. Everyone will be economizing."

That was an alarming thought. Would it really come to that? Should she at least listen to Tommy's proposal? She asked which company had made the offer, and didn't recognize the name but noted the telltale "-stein" ending.

"I'm not letting a *Jew* take over my business," she vowed. It's not that she was prejudiced—she treated plenty of Jewish clients at the salon—but she knew most Anglo-Saxon Americans felt the same way. She wasn't alone in her views.

"We work with Jews all the time," Tommy argued, "and they are no different from you and me."

"They stick together and look after their own, at the expense of non-Jews," Elizabeth said. "I will not give them power over me."

"You're going to regret this," Tommy said, meeting her eye. "Believe me, you will."

"You're wrong," she replied. "The subject is closed."

He scraped back his chair and left the room.

A little worry niggled at Elizabeth. What if he wasn't wrong? But she had always made business decisions instinctively, and her instinct this time told her to stick to her guns.

CHAPTER 24

Helena

January 1929

When Edward heard that Helena had sold her American business without telling him, he sent a furious cable from Paris.

Reporter called for my reaction, he wrote. *I am last person to know. Should your husband not be first?*

I was busy, she cabled back. *Negotiating deal took all my time.* Truth was, it hadn't occurred to her to tell Edward. Why would she?

He had more complaints to get off his chest. *I asked for six hundred dollars a month to start a literary magazine and you said you couldn't afford it. Now I hear you have seven point three million dollars.*

Reason I am rich is because I am careful, she replied by return. *Not convinced there is market for lit mag. Circulation likely to be tiny.*

A cable came back within hours: *This is my world. Wish you would trust my judgment. You never have.*

His attitude incensed her. Edward's life was one of sybaritic indulgence. Stella wrote that he spent his days drinking with author friends in the Jockey Club before dining out in top restaurants. She reported that he was publishing a novel that every publisher with any sense had turned down because of its obscenity.

Talking of judgment, she wrote back, *why are you publishing the Lawrence book on sex? Is that the image you want for Black Manikin?*

Edward switched to a long letter for his next communication. *So now you have decided to tell me what to publish—the woman who never reads anything but charts of sales figures.* Lady Chatterley's Lover *by D. H. Lawrence is an extraordinary modern novel and I know we will sell thousands of copies, especially since it is not available anywhere else. We will have the monopoly on a book everyone is talking about. Surely you can see that's a clever sales tactic?*

She shrugged. Frankly, she didn't much care what he published. She was exhausted, worried about the future of her American business, and fed up working hard day in and day out. Her monthly bleeds had gradually been getting heavier and were accompanied by cramps so severe that she once had to excuse herself from a meeting with Bobbie Lehman to crouch in his restroom, knees hugged to her chest, trying not to cry out in pain. Men had no idea what women suffered from their reproductive systems.

You have rather got the better deal of it in our marriage, don't you think? she replied to Edward. *I work my fingers to the bone, and you get to indulge your little hobbies, subsidized by my hard labor. When I look into the future, all I can see is work and more work. That's all I have done since I was eighteen years old and I'm weary of it.*

She felt as if she were being battered in a storm as she finalized the handover to Lehman's and the fresh appointments to the board. The new general manager, Charles S. Welch, had many years' experience with Coty, but she wasn't sure he had the imagination to run her company. She had hoped she might be able to rest when she returned to Paris to live with Edward, but the signs were not encouraging.

And then, while she waited for Edward's response to her letter, he sent a cable that put everything into perspective: *Horace in car accident. Admitted to Addenbrooke's Hospital, Cambridge. On my way. Edward.*

In a flash, Helena realized the only thing that mattered was that her son survived. What use was all the money in the world if she couldn't protect her children? She wouldn't be around forever, but hoped her sons would produce grandchildren and the Rubinstein name would continue through the centuries. Horace had to survive. He had to.

ON LEAVING BOARDING school, both Horace and Roy had chosen to study in England: Roy, aged nineteen, was in his second year of a BA at Oxford University, and Horace, at just seventeen, was studying music at a preparatory college in Cambridge. They both appeared to be turning into capable young men. She gave them a generous allowance, wrote to them once a month with maternal advice and exhortations, and sent parcels of warm clothes in winter.

They'd seemed fine, so the cable from Edward came as a sledgehammer blow. She got her assistant to book her a passage on a transatlantic crossing leaving the following morning, and started packing her trunks. She cabled Roy but got no reply so assumed he was also on his way to Cambridge, while she was stuck on the other side of the Atlantic, five days' sail away.

As she paced her apartment that evening, Helena castigated herself. She'd been such a distant mother, she didn't even know that Horace had started driving. Looking back, she'd been wrong to let Edward do the lion's share of the parenting: he was hardly a shining example of the type of man she wanted her sons to grow into. Why hadn't she gotten more involved in their lives? Work was just an excuse; she'd found them tedious when they were noisy squabbling youngsters, and now that they were in their late teens, she didn't know what to talk to them about.

Helena sat by the window gazing out into the darkness. The

thought occurred to her that she should pack clothes for a funeral, just in case he didn't make it. *Please God, don't let it come to that.*

Was she a selfish, coldhearted woman? Why hadn't she loved her sons more? She wondered if it was because of the way her own father had treated her. Perhaps she stopped herself from caring too much so they couldn't hurt her if they ever rejected her the way he had. When she saw them again, she vowed she would be honest with them and try to establish their relationship on a new footing. Pray God, it wasn't too late.

Before she left the following morning, a cable arrived from Edward: *Broken leg and bruising. Lucky escape. Will stay rest of week.*

Helena's heart leapt. She put a hand on the wall to steady herself, took a deep breath, and blew it out. No one died of a broken leg, but Horace would need help when he was released from the hospital. He would need his mother.

She had been planning a trip to Australia to check up on her business there, and she decided to take Horace with her. He could recuperate on board as they sailed south into sunnier climes. They always had doctors on these ships; they even had their own operating theater for emergencies.

She cabled Edward from the ship and asked him to request that Roy accompany his brother to Plymouth, where she would book cabins on a P&O Line crossing to Sydney.

Roy can't come with you, Edward replied. *He has to return to university.*

Helena didn't mind. She looked forward to having time alone with Horace, her sweet, funny, younger son.

When they arrived on the dock in Plymouth, Roy was pushing Horace in a wheelchair. His leg was in plaster from ankle to groin, and there was a lurid purple bruise on his forehead.

"My poor boy." She threw her arms around him. "Don't worry, Mama will take good care of you. We will fix you in no time."

He rolled his eyes at that, and said, "Yes, Mother," with a long-suffering tone, gazing up at the vast luxury ship that would be their home for the next month.

"How are you, Roy?" she asked, turning to her eldest, who looked more like his father every time she saw him.

"Fine, thank you, Mother."

"Are your studies going well?" she persevered. What was he studying? She couldn't remember.

"Very well," he said, not meeting her eye. "I'm in line for a first."

"Good, good," she said. Why was he so reserved with her? Was he jealous that she was taking his brother to Australia and not him? "It's a shame you can't come with us," she told him, "but the captain says you can join us on board for dinner tonight. We don't sail till morning."

They boarded the ship, and a first-class steward took them to the cabins she'd reserved. Helena glanced around her wood-paneled room with its spacious balcony, and sat down on the bed: very comfortable. The marble bathroom with hot and cold running water was smart. It would do nicely.

She met the boys in the first-class lounge for a cocktail before dinner. Horace ordered a gimlet, which he gulped down quickly, and signaled to a steward to bring him another.

"They didn't let me drink in the hospital," he said, as if that explained it.

"Are you sure it's wise?" she asked, with a frown. Seventeen didn't seem old enough to drink so much.

"It helps with the pain," he said, and she supposed she couldn't argue with that.

"Tell me about the accident," she asked. "What happened? You must have had a terrible fright."

He shrugged. "The road was slippery. The car skidded and wrapped itself around a tree. Everyone says I was lucky to get off so lightly."

"Any other cars involved?"

"No. It was the middle of the night and I was on my way back from a party."

"Had you been drinking?"

"Only a reasonable amount. I wasn't sozzled." He gulped at the fresh cocktail and Helena frowned. How did he get to be such a drinker, so young? It must be his father's influence.

They followed as a steward pushed Horace's wheelchair into the dining hall, a vast room lit by twinkling chandeliers. They surveyed the lengthy menu. There were eight to ten choices for each course, but Helena quickly picked out her favorites: Beluga caviar, green turtle soup, cod in caper sauce, braised venison, and ice cream. She asked the steward to bring them a bottle of Bordeaux.

"I'm planning to teach you bridge during the voyage," she told Horace. "There's always a community of bridge players on these ships. It's a game that requires a good memory and careful assessment of your opponents. I've always enjoyed it and I think you will too." She intercepted a look between him and Roy. "What is it?"

"I'm seventeen, Mother, not seventy." He gulped half his glass of wine in one swallow.

The comment wounded her. "You'll enjoy it once you understand the skill involved." She turned to her other son. "Do you enjoy bridge, Roy? Do they play it at your university?"

"I don't have time," he said. "The studies are challenging. We have to write an essay a week as well as attend lectures and tutorials."

Helena thought that didn't sound like much. Her eldest son was too serious, while it sounded as though her youngest wasn't serious enough. She was about to tell them so but was interrupted when the waiter brought the caviar. She dispensed with the tiny wafers arranged in a fan on the plate and spooned it directly into her mouth, enjoying the sensation of the black salty bubbles bursting under her tongue.

Horace signaled the steward to refill his wineglass and this time she couldn't refrain from a rebuke. "You're drinking too much," she said. "Try to slow down or you'll fall out of your chair."

"You're eating too much, Mother," he replied. "Try to slow down or you'll *break* your chair."

She was astonished. "How dare you talk to me like that? Apologize straight away."

"You're not really our mother, are you?" Horace's eyes were slightly unfocused. "It's just a role you play when it suits your purpose. I wouldn't be surprised if you got someone else to give birth to us because you were too busy to do it yourself."

She threw down her caviar spoon and covered her mouth with her hand, absorbing the hurt. Both boys had been born in the bedroom of their South London house with a midwife and doctor in attendance, and they hadn't been easy births. Long labors, tears, sweat, and blood. She could describe to them the huge metal tongs the doctor used to yank them from her body, ripping her flesh, but they didn't want to hear that.

"I know I wasn't around as much as I should have been when you were younger," she said, looking from one to the other. "I regret that now."

Horace laughed unkindly. "It's a bit late!" he said. "You couldn't wait to shuffle us off to whichever nanny or school or relative was available so you could get on with your own life. Frankly, I'm surprised you even recognize us."

Helena took a sip of her wine, trying to stay calm. "Is that what you think too?" she asked Roy.

He blushed a beetroot color right up to his hairline. "Well, not exactly," he stuttered. "But you were away a lot."

Helena had assumed the boys didn't need her, but maybe they had. Maybe she'd got it wrong.

"It's true I devoted my life to business rather than mother-hood, but it hasn't worked out too badly, has it? You have wanted for nothing. What kind of car was it you crashed, Horace? And how did you afford a car at your age?"

She glanced from one to the other. She hadn't been much older than they were when she traveled on her own to Australia, hoping to make her fortune in that young country on the other side of the globe. Money had been tight so she went steerage class, bunking in a shared cabin near the engine room where the noise and vibrations kept her awake at night. She'd arrived in a vast land with diamond-sharp sunlight, to stay with distant rela-tives she'd never met before, in a sheep station miles from any-where. And despite all the hardships she had managed to create an international business and become a millionairess. Somehow she didn't think either of her sons could have done the same. They were soft; they didn't have her gumption.

Horace had drained yet another glass of wine and he signaled the steward to refill it but Helena caught the man's eye and said, "No more for him." Roy sighed and rearranged his napkin on his lap, while Horace clenched his fists. Perhaps it was a time for more honesty.

"To tell you the truth, I never wanted children," she said. "Your father was keen so I went along with his wishes."

She realized she had miscalculated when she saw the looks of horror on their faces. Horace's eyes filled with tears, which he swiped with the back of his hand, and Roy scraped back his chair as if to stand up and leave.

"No, wait!" she caught his arm. "I want you both now, more than anything." She tried to choose her words carefully, so they understood. "You mean the world to me. But Edward was a good father and you didn't seem to need me when you were younger. I thought it was better if I focused on what I was good at—making money. Had our situations been reversed and he was the one who worked while I was a traditional mama, perhaps you wouldn't be so critical. But that's not who I am, or who he is." *I'm not lazy like Edward*, she thought. *I never relied on anyone else to keep me.*

"I'm sorry if we were an inconvenience," Horace said, in a sarcastic tone. "That's the impression you always gave."

She sighed, shaking her head. "That's not true. I built my business as a legacy for the two of you. You will never be poor, and neither will your children or grandchildren. That's why I work so hard."

It wasn't just that, of course. She had always been driven, long before she had children. Competitiveness was in her nature. But having sons gave her hope that her brand would continue long after her death. Elizabeth Arden had no direct heirs, so strangers would take over her business when she died and do with it as they wished.

The steward came to clear their plates and another wheeled up a trolley with the silver soup tureen, dishing up a bowlful for each of them.

"It's my dream that you will both work in the business after you finish college," she suggested. "With a view to taking over one day."

"I'd like to," Roy said quietly, not looking at her.

"Good. I'll get you a job in one of my factories next summer so you can learn from the ground up. Horace?"

He shook his head emphatically. "Not for me. I'm going to be either a writer, an artist, or a musician. I don't know which yet, but I'll be sure to tell you." His tone was still hostile but she ignored that.

"Your father might be able to help you in those fields," she said, with an inward sigh, thinking of the old saying: "You carry small children in your arms, but when they grow up, they sit on your head."

She had hoped this voyage would be a vacation, where she could relax and regain her strength after some challenging months. Instead, it looked as though she would have a different kind of challenge to surmount—winning the affections of her younger son, and stopping him getting blotto every night. He had said some very hurtful things to her this evening, and she knew it wasn't just the alcohol talking. She didn't ever want her children to become estranged from her, the way she was from her father. If she could build multimillion-dollar business from scratch, she could certainly come up with a plan to win over her own sons.

CHAPTER 25

Elizabeth

September 1929

Elizabeth was cross when Laney told her that Dorothy Gray—a treatment girl she had sacked over a decade ago for having an affair with a married man—was opening a new salon at 683 Fifth Avenue. *The cheek of it!* Fifth Avenue was her domain! She decided to respond with something far more spectacular, right across the street.

The Aeolian Building at 689–691 Fifth Avenue had been designed just four years earlier by the architects who had built Grand Central Station, and the lease was available. Elizabeth loved the French classical details of the building's limestone exterior, the decorative marble spandrels above the windows, and the generous interior spaces. The entrance was right on the corner of West Fifty-Fourth Street, and she would occupy the spacious ground floor and six further floors above. In size and grandeur, it would completely dwarf Dorothy's salon—and Madame Rubinstein's come to that. It would have a black marble storefront and her signature red door, with a smart gray-liveried doorman posted outside.

Inside, she planned to have exercise studios and a dining room where healthy meals would be served, as well as dozens of private treatment rooms. Women could come for an entire day of beauty, and walk out the door scrubbed, rubbed, shampooed, scented, relaxed, and feeling years younger.

She signed the contract to take over the lease on September 13, 1929, without consulting Tommy. He was being a doomsayer these days, and she knew he wouldn't agree with her making such a large investment. She had two motives: she had fallen in love with the building, and she wanted to make a bold statement by leasing it. She hadn't panicked and sold her company, as her rivals had done, because Elizabeth Arden was still at the very pinnacle of her game.

A WEEK AFTER signing the lease on the Aeolian Building, Elizabeth was busy briefing her team of interior designers when Laney rushed in with news that the London stock market had crashed. She'd heard it on the radio. They hurried back to the office to listen to the latest updates.

The newscaster said the crash was being blamed on fraudulent dealing—Elizabeth didn't follow the details, which were still coming to light—but the commentator was clear that it wouldn't affect the American market. It was a one-off incident. All the same, she felt a twisting in her insides. It seemed a harbinger of bad luck, like breaking a mirror or walking under a ladder.

When she got home that evening, she was glad Tommy wasn't there. She was fed up with him quoting so-called experts who predicted a crash could hit the American market and they would all be ruined. What nonsense! Their company was worth fifteen million dollars, according to Tommy's Jewish banker friends. How on earth could she be ruined?

The thought made her anxious, though: that old gnawing anxiety, like a persistent toothache, that she would one day lose everything and have to scrabble to make ends meet, just as she had as a child. She remembered the hunger pains that felt like a rat gnawing her gut, and the cold so severe she lay in bed convinced she would be dead by morning. She couldn't go back to that ever again.

Elizabeth lay awake that night with a tired body but an

overactive brain, tossing and turning, trying to get comfortable. Sometimes she woke with a start and realized she had dozed off, but when she turned on her lamp to check the clock, only ten minutes had passed. She got up and pulled back the drapes to look out at the fingernail moon against a jet-black starless sky. A headache was pressing behind her eyebrows, and she knew she would be exhausted the next day. She never used sleeping capsules, but wished she had some now.

Instead, she decided to pour herself a nightcap, and crept down the hallway. The door of Tommy's bedroom was open and she glanced in to see he wasn't there. Where could he possibly be at this time of night? Maybe he had decided to sleep in the office. He did that sometimes.

The second whiskey did the trick: she fell asleep on the couch downstairs and was wakened at dawn by her housekeeper. At least she'd had a couple of hours' sleep, although she still felt agitated. Surely she would sleep well that night.

But once again, Elizabeth couldn't drop off. She brought the whiskey decanter up to her bedroom and drank a couple of glasses, which sent her to sleep for an hour or two—she wasn't sure how long—before she wakened at just after three. She got up and paced the room while playing out different scenarios in her mind.

What if the market crashed and she couldn't raise the rent for the Aeolian Building, or pay all the tradesmen she had hired to design the interiors? There would be a financial penalty if she canceled their contracts. Could it even bankrupt her? Could she lose everything she'd worked so hard for, while Madame Rubinstein and that whippersnapper Dorothy Gray counted their millions?

Each morning, she checked the financial reports in the papers. It seemed US traders were scrambling to sell their shares. *Why?* She wanted to yell at them. *America is the world's biggest economy. What are they thinking of?*

The drop in the market seemed to level off by mid-October, but on the eighteenth it began to slide again. Elizabeth spent the week glued to the radio set. Traders were trying desperately to sell their shares and convert them into paper money as prices dropped further. By the twenty-fourth of the month, it was reported that the market had lost eleven percent of its value. Bookings at her salons plummeted, and lots of women didn't turn up for appointments. Elizabeth nearly cried as she surveyed the week's dismal takings.

On Friday the twenty-fifth the *New York Times* ran a cover story advising everyone to remain calm; a conglomerate of top bankers was going to buy up enough blue chip shares to stabilize the market. Elizabeth gave a sob of relief. These men were saviors; they would turn around the panic. That's all it was—silly panic. There was absolutely no need for it.

At her Sunday tea, Bessie confided that she had asked her broker to sell her shares three weeks earlier, and Elizabeth snapped at her: "It's people like you who are causing this drop in the market," she said. "We all need to hold our nerve."

Bessie was unrepentant. "I don't trust the money men," she said. "I'm keeping my savings under the mattress until they settle down."

Elizabeth was so cross she made her excuses and left. The insomnia was making her crabby and she was finding it difficult to judge whether she was overreacting. With any luck, Monday would bring better news.

It seemed everyone in Manhattan was glued to a morning newspaper or to a radio set on Monday the twenty-eighth. She saw men standing on street corners, shoulders hunched as they read the latest. The market opened and straight away the radio reported that the slide in share prices was continuing, despite the bankers' rescue plan.

"Why don't they close the stock exchange?" Elizabeth asked Laney in frustration. "Then they can't sell any more."

But they didn't, and on the twenty-ninth there was the steepest fall yet, with sixteen million shares sold in a single day. The value of the American market had fallen by a quarter.

Only a handful of women came to the salon that week, and the crash was the only subject of conversation.

"I heard folks are queuing outside banks to withdraw their money, and the banks are not letting them in," one said in hushed tones.

Elizabeth thought of Bessie; perhaps she had been right to put her money under her mattress. Elizabeth's was all in the banking system. Should she be withdrawing it before it was too late?

"My husband told me that Wall Street traders are leaping off the tops of skyscrapers. Many of them will be ruined."

Elizabeth couldn't listen to any more. She hurried out of the salon and wandered down Fifth Avenue, with no direction in mind, just letting her feet take her where they would. Everyone was rushing, as if they had important business to attend to, although they were miles from the Financial District. She felt numb, and above all exhausted. Sleep deprivation had left her brain befuddled and all she could do was walk.

When her high-heeled shoes gave her blisters, she turned and limped toward home. Tommy was in the sitting room with a newspaper in one hand, the radio set playing in the corner. He looked up at her, contempt etched all over his face, and threw the paper down.

"That's it," he said. "We're ruined." His eyes were cold. "We had a chance to cash in and you turned up your nose, so now we have to suffer the consequences."

Elizabeth didn't reply. She headed for her bedroom to take off these blasted shoes. Her heels were bleeding and her stomach was spiraling with nerves.

There's nothing to be done, she thought to herself. *I'll wait it out. It can't be too bad.*

The image of Madame Rubinstein flashed into her mind. She had known this would happen. That's why she had sold to Lehman Brothers. She'd probably moved all her money overseas. She felt a surge of fierce fury toward her rival, as if she were somehow single-handedly responsible for the entire crash.

CHAPTER 26

Helena

October 1929

Helena was in Paris when the American stock market crashed. She read the news in the press and wasn't surprised it had happened, but was still taken aback by the scale of the collapse. She kept in touch with Charles Welch, her US company's new manager, via dozens of daily cables crisscrossing the Atlantic. He wrote that it need not be a setback for their plans to get products into drugstores. The company's share price had tumbled, like the rest of the market, but it would bounce back up again. He urged her not to worry, but she replied, *Clearly you don't know who you are dealing with: worry is my second nature.*

Increasingly it became clear to her that the entire US economy was shrinking and the repercussions were going to be felt around the world. Unemployment would rise, businesses would go bust, and banks would fail, each putting pressure on the other, like tumbling dominos. Would women still have spare cash to spend on beautifying themselves? Helena knew her own fortune was safe—she would be a millionairess for the rest of her life—but she couldn't bear it if the company that bore her name collapsed. She had a creeping sense that she had made a mistake in selling out. She wished she were still at the helm to steer her business through this crisis. No one understood her customers as well as she did.

Her agitation intensified because she was feeling lousy. Her monthly bleeds were heavier than ever. She often woke in the night clammy with sweat and had to get up to change her nightgown. Waves of giddiness came upon her suddenly. Her ankles swelled and her knees creaked. She was fifty-six years old—eight years older than she had told the *New Yorker* the previous year—and assumed these were symptoms of the change of life. Did every woman go through this? How on earth did they put up with it?

When she had returned to Paris from Sydney six months earlier, at first she had stayed with Edward, but they argued constantly. He hadn't forgiven her for not telling him she was selling the company and resentment soured the atmosphere. There was no sexual reunion, just continual sniping. She called him a lazy bum, he called her imperious. In a fit of pique, Helena sacked him from his role as supervisor of her Paris properties, and that hadn't gone down well. After a month, she moved into an apartment above one of her salons, just to get some peace. The arguments were too draining, on top of her physical malaise and her anxiety about the company.

Horace stayed with his father but met her for dinner once a week. He and Helena had made peace during their trip to Australia, and she had even taught him to be a fairly passable bridge player. His character was weak, like his father's, but Helena adored him all the same. She got him to carry messages back and forth to Edward so she didn't have to be in direct contact.

From what she could gather, Black Manikin Press was doing well. *Lady Chatterley's Lover* had sold several thousand copies. The memoirs of his Jockey Club friend, Kiki de Montparnasse, gave it another bestseller. Helena told Horace to let Edward know she was reducing his allowance forthwith.

"Ask your father why he thinks I should continue to subsidize him," she demanded. "He is making his own decisions for

Black Manikin so he should behave like a grown man and live off his own earnings."

Horace had an unfortunate habit of defending his father. "He's got a lot of overheads," he protested. "And the price of paper and printing has gone up."

"A successful business adjusts its prices to cope with fluctuations," she said. "Your father has good instincts about books but he never had a head for business, more's the pity."

Horace passed on the message and returned with a note in which Edward berated her for being a "spoiled, petulant school-girl."

"Name calling! How very mature!" she remarked.

She knew Horace spent his evenings with Edward in the Jockey Club and worried about the kind of influences he was being exposed to. She had tried to moderate his drinking during their trip to Australia, but still he quaffed alcohol in gulps, as if he was parched. Would he learn to chase girls the way she suspected his father did? Was he bedding any of the scantily clad women who draped themselves over the barstools there? If so, she would rather not know.

Helena was restless. She couldn't start work on her Île Saint-Louis property because the tenants were stubbornly refusing to leave. The European and Australian businesses didn't particularly need her. Charles Welch always responded promptly to her cables, then ignored her advice. She wrote a book of "beauty secrets," *The Art of Feminine Beauty*, with the help of a journalist, and gave interviews to promote it, but still she felt unfulfilled.

Travel helped. She went to visit friends in the South of France; to London to spend time with Ceska, the third-youngest of her seven sisters; she went to the Paris fashion shows with Carmel, a couple of months after the birth of her friend's long-awaited second child; she opened a new salon in Berlin, and traveled through Germany, then checked into a spa in the Alps.

She liked being on the move: unpacking her suitcases in one hotel, then packing them up again to move to the next. Always she stayed in the top places and ate in the best of restaurants.

She was shocked when they weighed her at the spa: she was heavier than she'd ever been. She lost a few pounds during her two weeks there, with a combination of a meager diet and lots of saunas and massages, but she somehow put it all back on soon after.

One night, while in Vienna, she dined with Marc Chagall and his wife, Bella, after bumping into them at an exhibition. It was a rich meal of veal schnitzel followed by Sacher torte. She left early, uncomfortably full, and returned to her hotel room. She loosened her clothing and lay down on the bed, then began to feel a hot stabbing pain in her abdomen. *It must be gas*, she thought, and tried to massage the area, but it felt tender to the touch, as if bruised. What could it be?

She ran a bath and soaked in it for a while, but the pain kept intensifying and she felt feverish too. This was ridiculous. What was happening? It didn't feel like gas anymore; it was as if someone were stabbing her with a dagger.

After suffering for a couple of hours, Helena rang reception and asked if the hotel doctor could visit her. When he palpated the area, she screamed.

"I'm afraid you need to go to the hospital, Madame," he said. "I can't say for sure but I suspect you have appendicitis."

"What will they do at the hospital?" Her words came out in a squeak; the pain was making it hard to catch her breath.

"I imagine they will operate," he said. "The sooner the better."

She began to be very scared. Was she going to die? There was no one in the city she knew well enough to call, certainly not the Chagalls. She had to let someone know, in case she didn't make it. Before they wheeled her out to a waiting ambulance van, she asked the receptionist to send a cable to Edward in Paris. She might be furious with him, but he was legally still her husband and would always be the father of her sons. He bore some responsibility for her, whether he liked it or not.

THE FOLLOWING MORNING, when Helena came around from the emergency appendectomy, she felt as if she had been run over by a tram. Her throat was raw, her head thumping, and she had cramping in her womb, as well as a dull ache in her abdomen where a dressing covered the wound from the operation. She had never felt more alone in her life.

"How did it go?" she asked a nurse. The girl looked blank, then Helena remembered she was in Austria and the nurse probably spoke German.

"*Die Operation—war Erfolgreich?*"

The girl didn't seem to understand; Helena knew her German was rusty. She left the room, and returned some minutes later with a doctor, who fortunately spoke good French.

"We removed your appendix, Madame Rubinstein," he said, "but I am alarmed by the swelling in your uterus and your heavy menstrual flow."

Helena was embarrassed he had noticed that. What did doctors do while you were unconscious on the operating table? She felt exposed.

"Have you had any other symptoms recently?" he asked. "Pain, dizziness, flushing?"

"Yes, all of those," she said.

"How long has it been going on?"

Helena thought back. She had ignored it for a long time, but it had certainly affected her while she was negotiating the sale of the business in 1928.

"Maybe two years?" she said. "It's gotten worse gradually."

The doctor nodded slowly as if that confirmed his suspicions. "I will do further tests, but I suspect you would be wise to have a hysterectomy."

Helena knew what that was—removal of the womb. She

supposed that would be all right. She didn't need her womb anymore, and it would be good to stop these debilitating symptoms.

She looked at the doctor: he was tall and blond, with thick sandy eyelashes and brows, probably in his thirties. Too young. How many wombs had he removed? Could she trust him? She'd have more faith in a Jewish doctor, and she wished there was one in the hospital. But this man must have passed his medical degree, he must be competent.

He left her to think it over, and she closed her eyes. *What to do, what to do.* Was it safe here? She felt vulnerable in a place where the nurses didn't understand her, but she knew she was too weak to travel to Paris.

She dozed for a while, and when she opened her eyes, Edward was by her bedside. Tears welled up. She had never been so pleased to see him in her life, not even when he followed her to London before they were married.

He stroked her hair back from her forehead and kissed her cheek. "How are you feeling, *kochanie?*" he asked.

She gave a weak smile. "Not at all like a spoiled, petulant schoolgirl."

He took her hand and squeezed it. "The doctor told me what he has recommended. I have asked for the hospital's head of surgery, Dr. Erdheim, to give us a second opinion. He's coming to see you soon."

Helena closed her eyes, filled to the brim with gratitude. Erdheim was a Jewish name. There were many matters in which she didn't trust Edward one iota, but here and now, she couldn't think of anyone she would rather have by her side. She would be safe with him around. He wouldn't let her die.

CHAPTER 27

Elizabeth

January 1930

E lizabeth's flagship salon in the Aeolian Building opened
in January 1930, three months after the Wall Street crash.
Her stomach was in permanent knots: What if no clients
came? What if she went bankrupt?

She'd put all her energy and imagination into the salon.
There were several exclusive treatments available: her Youth
Mask with diathermy electric currents to rejuvenate skin cells;
the Ardena Bath, in which clients were coated in a thick layer
of paraffin wax to induce perspiration and weight loss; a giant
roller that could pummel away excess pounds; and her specially
designed exercise and weight-loss programs. Edna ran an article
in *Vogue*, entitled "The Elixir of Youth," and bookings began to
trickle in. That was a relief, but still the tangle of anxiety in the
pit of Elizabeth's stomach made it hard to sleep.

She appointed Edith Brown to manage the new salon. It was
a responsible position, but Edith was remarkably efficient and
organized, and she had a polite and winning manner with clients. Together, Edith and Laney made sure everything worked
smoothly in all her New York salons. Deliveries arrived on time,
staff was hired and trained, the floors and fittings were sparkling clean, and flowers were replaced as soon as they started
to droop.

Teddy Haslam sent encouraging news from London: revenues

were holding up there, despite the crash, and he was optimistic about the outlook. Gladys reported that bookings in Paris seemed unaffected. Thank goodness she could rely on them.

Tommy remained a thorn in her flesh. He kept overstepping his authority and trying to dictate what should happen in areas of the business that were none of his concern. He objected to her launching a new face cream, which Fabian Swanson had devised. It was lavender-colored and remarkably good for calming irritated skin. She came up with the name Eight Hour Cream after one of her staff tried it on her son's grazed knee and claimed it was healed eight hours later.

"It's not the right time to introduce a new face cream, when men are losing their jobs all over the city," he argued. "It makes you look out of touch."

"It's *exactly* the right time, dear," she replied. "Women might be cautious about treating themselves to a new gown but *all* my clients can afford a new skin cream."

She noticed that he was paying some of their top salesmen seventy-five dollars a week, and sent a stern memo: "When men are losing their jobs, we can afford to pay less. No one will complain for fear of being bounced. Cut all sales salaries to seventy dollars *at most*." He objected but had no choice but to comply.

Her brother, Will, lost his job in the city and she agreed, very reluctantly, that Tommy could hire him. She had always done her best to keep the two apart because they got on rather too well for her liking. As she had feared, they were soon hanging around speakeasies most evenings after work. Tommy staggered home in the early hours, crashing and banging in the hallway, then had a foul hangover the following day.

"I don't care what you do in your leisure hours," Elizabeth chastised him, "but I will not have you meeting customers with bleary eyes and stale booze breath. It's totally unprofessional."

He curled his lip in a sneer. "It's all about illusion for you, isn't it? You don't mind if I drink to drown my misery so long as I don't *look* as though I've been drinking. You want us to pro-mote the illusion of a happy marriage, with our cocktail eve-nings and theater parties, but you won't have anything to do with me behind closed doors."

Elizabeth tutted impatiently and turned her back.

"Oh, and I know all the lies you've been telling about your childhood," Tommy continued. "Will says your father was a tenant farmer who barely scraped a living. You want Bessie's circle to think you're one of them, with your hoity-toity man-ners and fake accent, but you're not; you're just a scrappy little urchin from the back of beyond."

Elizabeth whirled around and hissed at him in fury. "If you ever repeat a word of that to anyone, I will throw you out and cut you off without a cent. Listen hard, because I've never been more serious."

"You think you're queen of the whole goddamned world, don't you?" he drawled.

Elizabeth raised her hand to slap him, but he caught her wrist, saying, "Oh no you don't!" She wrenched her arm away and swept out of the room, slamming the door behind her so hard that the mirror rattled.

It had been a mistake letting Tommy and Will work together. Damn! She should have known better.

UP IN MAINE the following weekend, she confided in Bessie that Tommy was drinking too much and she feared he was being led astray by her wayward brother.

"I suppose you two don't have much time alone together if he goes out with Will most nights," Bessie replied. "Or does he come home drunk and demand marital relations?"

Elizabeth shuddered. "Certainly not. That part of our mar-riage has always been a flop."

Bessie reacted with a curious twitch of a smile. She had often asked about their marital intimacy, but Elizabeth had refused to answer till now. She was too cross with Tommy to be discreet anymore.

The peacefulness of the Maine countryside soothed her nerves. It was so quiet that when she stood on the banks of the lake, the only sound was the shushing of the wind and the gentle lapping of water against shingle. Spring was on its way, bringing warmth to the sun and lime-green buds to the trees. She breathed the air deep into her lungs as she performed her morning yoga routine on Bessie's verandah.

"The plot of land next to mine is for sale," Bessie told her. "Why don't you buy it and build your own place there? I can't think of anyone I'd rather have as a neighbor."

The idea appealed to Elizabeth. She could come here any time she wanted, whether Bessie was around or not. Maybe she could turn it into an exclusive spa, like the kind they had in Europe, where women spent a week or two, to lose weight and relax. It would mean another investment straight after the fortune she had spent on the Aeolian Building, but better in bricks and mortar than in the bank. She made an offer for the land and was delighted when it was accepted.

TWO OF THE horses from Old John's stables were racing at Saratoga racetrack, and Elizabeth went with him to watch. Straight away she was hooked on the track: the buzz of excitement when the odds were posted, watching the horses pace nervously in the paddock before being led to the starting gates, then the unpredictable thrill of the chase. Anything could happen.

The horses clearly loved racing. They sprang out of the gate in a burst of hooves, pushing the earth away with their muscular legs, jockeys lying flat along their backs, then there was the strategic jostling for position, and the final sprint to the line. The winning horse swaggered, delighted with itself, while the losers looked dejected, and she longed to rush to the paddock and comfort them. It was riveting to watch.

Before the end of the weekend, Elizabeth had decided to buy herself a thoroughbred and race it. She visited several auctions over the following weeks, rejecting horses if she didn't like their coloring or their temperament, and carefully checking the pedigree of each for indicators of good health.

When she was shown a filly called Leading Lady, Elizabeth knew at first glance this was the one. She was the most beautiful horse she'd ever seen: an Arabian yearling with a pale chestnut coat and blue eyes. She seemed shy, looking up from beneath her lashes as Elizabeth approached, but before long she was nuzzling her.

"Who's a pretty girl?" Elizabeth cooed, stroking her warm, smooth coat. "You are just the best girl in the whole wide world."

She paid over the odds in the auction, but didn't care about the money. Her heart was bursting; she couldn't imagine any new mother feeling more overwhelmed with love than she did for her adorable Leading Lady.

She hired a groom and a trainer to look after her baby and instructed them to follow her methods to the letter. Old John told her that New England clover contained nutrients that were especially beneficial for horses so she arranged regular deliveries. She put potted plants around the stall to make it look pretty. When the trainer told her it was a good idea to massage cream into the hooves to prevent splitting, she insisted they use her Eight Hour Cream. Leading Lady was brushed and combed, massaged, oiled, and perfumed every bit as thoroughly as the customers at Salon d'Oro. She loved being groomed. There was a feminine elegance about her. You could tell she knew how pretty she was.

Elizabeth felt irritable when she had to wrench herself away from Maine to return to the city. She didn't want to be in New York—she missed Leading Lady terribly—but there were meetings she had to take. Each salon had its own manager, and each area of the country had its own sales director, but she knew standards would slip if she didn't stamp her authority on the staff. No scruffiness escaped her sharp eye in the salons: a towel that hadn't been folded precisely, a mirror with streaks, a coffee cup with lipstick on the rim—in all these cases the perpetrator would be roundly chastised. She prowled unannounced, checking for girls making personal calls on the company telephone, or—worst of all—the slightest whiff of cigarette smoke.

As she walked into the Aeolian Building the day after leaving Leading Lady for the first time, she noticed a new treatment girl tapping facial oil onto a client's forehead. When she saw Elizabeth, the girl looked away in a manner that seemed furtive. Why would she do that?

Elizabeth took an elevator to the offices upstairs and popped her head around Edith's door. "Who's the new girl with the dark bushy hair?" she asked. "Working on Mrs. Loew."

"That's Mildred Beam," Edith said. "She's been here three weeks and is doing well. Clients like her."

"Send her to me when she has finished with Mrs. Loew," Elizabeth ordered, then slipped away before Edith could ask why.

"Come in, dear," she said when Mildred appeared. "Take a seat." She waved her to a chair. "I thought we should get acquainted."

The girl was fidgeting. She looked shifty. Her nose was too big for her face, Elizabeth thought.

"Tell me a little about yourself," she asked. "What made you want to work in the beauty business?"

"Well . . ." Mildred hesitated. "I think looks are very important to women. Looking good makes them feel happier and they probably get a better class of husband." She glanced at Elizabeth for approval.

"Carry on," she urged. "How did you get started?"

"I trained in a hairdressing salon but I kept coughing from the hair. Little bits get stuck in your throat." She clutched her throat to demonstrate. "And then I got a job at Helena Rubinstein's salon, but after she left and Mr. Welch started running it, he reduced everyone's salary by a dollar a week. So when I saw the position advertised at your salon, I applied straight away."

"I pay more than her, do I?" she asked, thinking she would have to do something about that. "How much more?"

"I make nineteen dollars and twenty cents a week here, but at Madame Rubinstein's it was just seventeen dollars and forty cents." Her hands were trembling.

"It's all about money for you, is it?" Elizabeth asked. "I'm not sure I like your attitude." There was something about the girl she didn't trust, but she couldn't put her finger on it.

"No, I like it here," she insisted. "Honest, I do. I love the building and the other staff have been so kind." She was casting around for the right thing to say, and a coarser accent broke through her vowel sounds. The Bronx perhaps?

Elizabeth made a decision on impulse. "I'm afraid I don't think you're suitable for this salon, so I'm going to bounce you. You'll get paid till the end of the week and I'm sure Edith will give you a reference, but I want you to take off your uniform and leave immediately."

"What? No! You can't!" She was distraught. "I'll never get another job. Everyone is being laid off. Please, Miss Arden, if you tell me what I'm doing wrong, I'll change. I promise I will."

She started crying, with great heaving sobs. Elizabeth wasn't moved. She couldn't have a girl in the building whom she didn't trust. She looked at her watch. "I have another meeting. Please leave, Miss Beam."

The girl got up and ran out, sobbing loudly. Elizabeth sighed. Sometimes this kind of unpleasantness was the price of leadership.

Ten minutes later, she walked up to a storage room on the top floor to find a new yoga mat. The one she kept at home was getting a little tatty. She opened the door and was stunned to find Tommy inside with his arms around Mildred Beam, her head on his shoulder. He jumped back. It took a few moments to process the scene in front of her.

"What on earth are you doing?" she asked him.

"Mildred's upset," he said. "She can't understand why she's being fired. It doesn't seem very reasonable."

She looked around the eight-by-six-foot room with floor-to-ceiling shelving. "But why would you comfort her in here? I don't understand." She pieced it together. "Are you having an *affair*?"

They spoke over each other. "No, I'm a decent girl, Miss Arden," Mildred protested at the same time as Tommy snapped, "You're being ridiculous, Elizabeth."

She genuinely couldn't think how to react so she turned and walked back toward the stairs. Tommy shouldn't even *know* the salon girls; that wasn't his area. Why would Mildred turn to him? And in a storage room? She had been right not to trust that girl. She had known there was something dishonest about her.

"Ridiculous, am I?" she said out loud, to no one in particular. "We'll soon see about that."

CHAPTER 28

Helena

February 1931

After the hysterectomy, Helena felt very low. Every bit of her hurt. The ugly purple scars that snaked across her lower abdomen were tight, as if the slightest exertion would split her open like an overripe fruit. Her joints ached as if she were ninety years old. Her skin was irritated by the seams of her nightgown, the edge of the pillowcase, even a loose strand of hair brushing her cheek. When the nurses gave her a bed bath, she wanted to scream at them to be gentler.

"Come to Paris and I'll take care of you," Edward said. "Horace will help."

But Helena knew that he would be useless, no matter how good his intentions. This was women's business. It had to be one of her sisters.

She could have stayed with Stella in Paris, but she didn't like Stella's husband. It was too far to reach Manka in New York or Pauline in Australia. Regina offered to look after her in Kraków, but she lived close to their parents, and Helena didn't feel strong enough to be in the same city as her father. Finally, she asked her sister Ceska if she could come to London to recuperate in her Mayfair apartment. Ceska was married to an Englishman, whom Helena liked. She was a gentle soul, and Helena knew she would not be put under any pressure there.

The journey was horrendous, because her scars threatened to

tear with each bump and jolt, but when she arrived, Ceska had prepared her guest room beautifully, with fresh flowers and the softest of sheets. A bay window overlooked a square lined with tall trees, and Helena liked the Cubist painting of a crashing ocean wave on the wall opposite the bed. She slid between the sheets and felt gravity press her down into the mattress. Perhaps she would stay there forever. She couldn't face the world.

Ceska brought her light, invalid meals of chicken soup, blanc-mange, and ice cream that would slide down without effort. She changed the sheets and laundered her nightgowns when night sweat soaked them. She brushed Helena's tangled hair as gently as she could and tried to hide the clumps that came out in the hairbrush, but Helena noticed. The operation had aged her. How could she ever be a Queen of Beauty Science again?

After a week of bed rest, Ceska asked if Helena wanted to read the telegrams that had been arriving, and she grudgingly agreed. One was from Carmel, wishing her a speedy recovery, and others were from family members. There were several from Charles Welch, and her heart felt heavy as she opened them.

Charles wrote that Elizabeth Arden's "Days of Beauty" at her new salon appeared to be successful and that they planned to imitate her by introducing an exercise studio and dining room into Helena's Fifth Avenue salon. She thought this was a terrible idea: it was notoriously difficult to make a profit from restaurants since there was so much wastage. Her rival would discover that before long. It was typical of Elizabeth to open a new salon just as the American economy crashed, she thought: that woman loved a grand gesture.

Charles wrote that they were cutting costs wherever they could, and Helena worried that he would make the products look cheap if he reduced the weight of the glass jars, or skimped on ingredients. She began scribbling her reply. She had too much to say, though, and telegrams were expensive, so she put it aside.

In another cable, Charles reported that the share price, which had been eighteen dollars before the crash, had sunk to just two. Two measly dollars! He urged her not to worry, saying that once their master plan was implemented it would pick up again.

How could she not worry? Elizabeth Arden must be laughing up her sweetie-pink taffeta sleeve. Helena should have been at the helm to guide the company through this market nightmare. She suspected that none of Charles's strategies would work, but she was too tired to get involved.

She lay back on the pillows, feeling the business trying to suck her back in, like a whirlpool. But what could she do? She could make recommendations, but Charles and the board had the final say. Increasingly, she felt as if she had made a huge mistake in selling the company: perhaps the biggest mistake of her career. And she was Helena Rubinstein—she didn't make mistakes.

HELENA LINGERED IN Ceska's guest room, trying to regain her strength and raise her spirits, but it was hard. She had never been prone to depression, but now she felt so low she feared she might not recover.

Her marriage was doomed because although she loved Edward, she couldn't trust him. Her business was doomed, because Lehman Brothers and Charles Welch were going to cheapen her brand beyond recognition. Her son Horace was a drinker, while Roy was a weakling; they took after their father, not their mother, and neither of them was capable of protecting her legacy. All the years of hard work she'd put in would go to waste. Ceska said it was the effects of the operation making her gloomy, and that it would pass as her body recovered, but that's not how it felt.

There was worse to come. Ceska burst into her room one morning, clutching a cable. Regina wrote that their father had passed away the previous night.

"Papa died?" Helena repeated. "How?"

"He was eighty years old," Ceska told her. "Maybe it was his heart."

Helena closed her eyes. An image came to mind of the last time she'd seen him, standing on the doorstep of the family home and refusing to let her in. He had blocked the entrance with his body, his face cold, eyes unblinking.

"What do *you* want?" he'd asked with no smile, no warmth.

At first Helena wondered if he recognized her after eight years. "It's me, Papa. I'm back from Australia. I want to see you and Mama, and spend time with you. I brought presents." She gestured to her suitcase.

"You're not welcome here," he said, and moved to close the door.

In a panic, she caught hold of his arm. "I'm your daughter! You can't turn me away. I love you."

"You stopped being a daughter of mine when you refused to marry the man I chose for you. Don't come here again." He stepped backward into the hall.

She didn't recognize him. He'd always been stern but never cruel, not like this. Over his shoulder, she could see her mother's wan face in the dimly lit hallway. "Mama!" she called. Her mother disappeared. "I've come thousands of miles to see you," she pleaded with her father.

"You disobeyed me and now you must suffer the consequences," he said. "Goodbye, Helena."

The door clicked shut.

That had been twenty-six years ago. In the back of her mind, she had always hoped for a reconciliation, but she had left it too late. She should have gone sooner and forced him to listen to her. She could have fixed it if she had tried her hardest.

"We can travel to the funeral together," Ceska said. "I'll help you."

"I can't," Helena replied, turning her head away. She was too weak to face the journey. Besides, it was a matter of pride. She didn't want anyone back home to see her in such a reduced state. She wanted her family and her old friends in Poland to be proud of her achievements, not to pity her.

"Are you sure?" Ceska asked. "You might have regrets in the future."

"I have decided," Helena said. "But while you are there, please ask our mother if I might visit her when I am recovered from my surgery."

Surely she would agree, and they could make their peace. Helena would enjoy returning to her hometown in summer, when the sun sparkled off the Vistula and university students lounged on the riverbank, just as she used to do with Stanislaus.

Ceska and Stella went to Poland for their father's funeral, and on her return Ceska reported that their mother's face had lit up when she passed on Helena's request. She said it was her dearest wish to see her eldest daughter again. Helena was welcome to stay whenever she felt well enough to travel.

That gave her a goal. She would aim to recover by June. She would have her hair styled and colored, she would have treatments in the salon to get her looks back, she would lose some weight and buy new clothes. She and her mother could have a proper talk, and maybe she would explain why her father had rejected her so cruelly.

"I'm sure he was proud of you," Ceska said. "Mama told me he always read newspaper stories about you."

Helena longed to see their mama and hear it from her lips. She closed her eyes and imagined her mother's embrace.

But then came news so shattering that it hurtled her straight back into the furthest depths of her depression: her mother had passed away, just two months after her father. Helena would never have a chance to make peace with her. There would be no last visit, no last hug, no forgiveness. She sobbed for days and nothing could comfort her. It was too cruel.

CARMEL CAME TO visit that spring, straight after the Paris shows. She didn't give any warning, so Helena had no chance to refuse. She burst into the guest bedroom, looking immaculate in a beige Chanel sports suit, and carrying a large black-and-white bag.

Helena covered her face with her hands. "I don't want you to see me like this," she cried. "I'm not ready for visitors."

"Don't worry," Carmel said breezily. "It's only me." She pulled Helena's hands out of the way and kissed her cheeks in greeting. "Although, frankly, you should get your hair done. Look at those roots!"

She sat on the edge of the bed and opened her bag, pulling out a black wool dress with a *trompe l'oeil* white bow knitted into the collar. "Elsa Schiaparelli," she said. "Name mean anything to you?"

Helena shook her head.

"Her designs are so witty! I love them. Anyway, this is for you. You have the style to carry it off."

"I can't accept a dress from you," Helena objected, fingering it. The wool was soft. It looked loose and comfortable to wear, with no tight waistband that might dig into her hysterectomy scar.

"You don't think I actually paid for it, do you? It's one of the perks of the job." Carmel took Helena's hand. "I've got loads to tell you. I should start with the personal: I had another baby, which makes three at the last count. I am officially beating you on the children front."

Helena laughed at that. "I didn't realize it was a competition. I will have to allow you the victory. Boy or girl this time?"

Carmel scratched her head with a frown, as if she couldn't remember, then she laughed. "A little girl, Brigid. That's me done, I swear. At least we have an army of nannies. That's how you coped, isn't it? How does anyone manage without staff?"

Helena laughed again. The sensation felt unfamiliar. It had been a long time since her lips had curled upward. "It's so good to see you," she said. "You bring a breath of spring with you."

"I'm going to do more than that," Carmel said. "I'm going to help you get dressed and tidied up and we are going to walk to a little Italian restaurant on the next street, where I have a booking for a discreet corner table in one hour's time. Ceska says you haven't been outdoors in months, but the day is warm and I want you to feel the breeze on your cheeks. I won't take no for an answer."

Helena felt a twinge of panic. "I can't walk very well," she said. "And I don't want anyone to see me. Can't we lunch here?"

"Absolutely not. My other news is that I'm leaving *Vogue*."

"You're what?" That came as a surprise.

"I won't tell you any more till we're in that restaurant. Now, let's get you out of bed." She pulled the covers back. "Quick march!"

Helena laughed again. She felt as if Carmel had swept into the room on a tidal wave of energy and it might not be so hard to let herself get swept up in it. Slowly she swung her legs to the floor.

"I will wear my new Schiaparelli dress," she said. "And red lipstick."

"Perfect," Carmel said. "And we will drink martinis and gossip, just like old times.

HER LUNCH WITH Carmel wasn't a complete cure but it marked a turning point. In the days afterward, Helena forced herself to get out of bed and start sorting through the mail that had arrived for her. She hadn't read the newspapers for some time but now she began to flick through the international business pages. Most commentators had been predicting that the downward slide of the market would level out by mid-1931, then begin to climb again, but the key indicators didn't look promising. Consumer prices were rising, dozens of businesses were failing daily, unemployment was mounting, and banks were still collapsing, with thousands losing their entire life savings. It didn't look to Helena as if this recession would turn around any day soon.

Charles Welch had sent her the minutes from all the board meetings since she left the US, and she began to comb through them. Her big gamble had been that they could mass-produce her products and get them distributed more widely around the country without any decrease in quality. If it had worked, there should have been a spike in sales, recession or no recession, but that hadn't happened. Why not?

First of all, she noted that there seemed to be an issue with goods that had been damaged in transit. Bottles had leaked, destroying entire consignments. If Welch was skimping on packaging costs, that was the inevitable result.

Crème Valaze sales had held steady, she noted, but the more expensive premium products had slumped. What was Welch's answer? To cut the prices? "No, no, no!" Helena cried out loud. Did they know nothing? The minute she lost cachet, she would be competing with cheap products like Pond's vanishing cream, rather than rivaling Elizabeth Arden at the top of the market. She was willing to bet Elizabeth wasn't reducing her prices. Her new Eight Hour Cream was expensive but it was selling like hot noodles.

Helena wrote letters to half a dozen American contacts she trusted, asking for their honest opinions: Paul Bonwit, founder of Bonwit Teller department store; her sister Manka, of course; a wholesaler in Miami; a pharmacist at her Long Island factory; a treatment girl called Valerie in her San Francisco salon, whom Helena had struck up a friendship with; and finally a man called Fred Eagleton, an ally of hers on the board at Helena Rubinstein Inc. To all she asked the same question: What was happening with her brand?

When the answers came back, her worst fears were confirmed: Charles Welch had cheapened the packaging and the advertising, making the products look mid-market rather than upscale. *Elizabeth Arden would love that*, Helena thought. It left the top end entirely to her.

She started drafting a long letter to Mr. Welch, complaining about her findings and telling him what he should be doing, but she put down her pen halfway through. It would make no difference because he held the whip hand.

She wanted to go into battle, to rescue her American business, reverse the drop in profits, and once more challenge Elizabeth Arden for the top spot. But could she do that with Welch in charge?

And then, an audacious plan came to her. It would have to be done very quietly, so as not to arouse suspicion—but if she pulled it off, it would be the crowning achievement of her career.

CHAPTER 29

Elizabeth

April 1932

Once she got over the shock of finding Tommy in a storage room with Mildred Beam, Elizabeth decided she didn't mind him having an affair so long as no one found out. Men had certain needs, she supposed, and Tommy's weren't being met by her. She would hate to think that any of the other treatment girls knew and were laughing at her behind her back. Worst of all would be if clients discovered it. But if Tommy and Mildred kept quiet, she would turn a blind eye. All the same, she sent him a stern memo, requesting that in future he refrain from paying "inappropriate attentions" to the salon staff. He didn't reply.

Tommy started sleeping in an apartment above his office and seldom came home. It suited them both, since they only argued when they met. She didn't want a divorce—gracious, no! Divorce would be reported in the papers, and she didn't want any negative stories while she was struggling to weather the recession. Living separate lives while staying married suited her right down to the ground.

Elizabeth was busy preparing for a visit to Paris, where Gladys was getting married to a French count, Henri Maublanc de Boisboucher. She was ecstatic that Gladys had made such a prestigious match and was looking forward to the whole trip, which would culminate with her annual visit to London to see dear Teddy. She planned to invest in a new wardrobe with different outfits for each of the society events she would attend, and when Edna called to ask her for lunch at the Colony Club, she decided it would be a good opportunity to ask for advice. She had heard the dos and don'ts of formal wear in Paris and London were different from those in New York, and she didn't want to fall foul of any etiquette regarding gloves or hats or hemlines, never mind diamonds.

Edna hurried in late for their lunch and threw her handbag down on the table. "Carmel Snow just handed in her notice," she said, slumping into her seat. "The devious shrew got us to keep employing her through all her multiple pregnancies and as soon as her last child is born, she announces she is deserting us for *Harper's Bazaar*."

Elizabeth was shocked. "Why would she go to *Bazaar*? It doesn't have one tenth of the cachet of *Vogue*—or the readership."

"I've been half-expecting this ever since her brother Tom took over as William Randolph Hearst's right-hand man. She was never the loyal type." Edna signaled for the waiter. "I don't suppose you could do me a gin rickey, could you?" she asked him. The answer was no. Other establishments might serve alcohol in coffee cups to dodge Prohibition laws, but the Colony was a bastion of teetotalers. Elizabeth watched in surprise. She had never known Edna to drink at lunchtime. One sherry in the evening was usually her limit.

"Carmel never understood the *Vogue* ethos," Edna continued. "Frankly, she never had the class to work there, but she batted those green Irish eyes at Condé Nast and he persuaded me to hire and then promote her. What a mistake!"

"He must be furious that she's jumping ship."

Edna took a long swallow of the lemonade their waiter had brought in place of gin. "He screamed down the phone. Have you ever heard a man scream? It's a most unpleasant, ear-shattering sound. Then he said he will never speak to her again. He said he wouldn't help her if she lay dying in the gutter. And neither would I, it goes without saying. I'm getting all the staff to sign loyalty pledges because God knows which of them Carmel will try to poach."

"I completely understand," Elizabeth said. "I had the same situation a few years ago with Dorothy Gray. I taught her everything she knows and yet there was no gratitude: she waltzed off and set up her own salon, using all my techniques." She didn't mention that she had bounced Dorothy. Edna didn't seem to be listening anyway.

"I would never have promoted her if it weren't for Condé," Edna muttered. "She wasn't serious about anything. Life is one long cocktail party for Carmel Snow."

Elizabeth tried to distract Edna by mentioning her plans to build a health spa in Maine. Building work was already underway. "You must be the first to visit," she offered. "You'll love the peace and calm."

"I don't know when I will ever get time off again," Edna replied. "I'll have to do Carmel's job as well as my own until we find her replacement."

She didn't offer to run a feature on the spa, but Elizabeth decided not to push for it today. There would be plenty of time closer to the opening, when she hoped Edna would be in a better frame of mind.

GLADYS'S WEDDING WAS a three-day affair in an idyllic little town in the Loire Valley. There was a formal dinner the night before, then the ceremony took place in a five-hundred-year-old church. Straight afterward, a hundred white doves were released, and they flew off into the azure-blue sky in a rush of wingbeats. An open-air picnic luncheon was followed by music and dancing that went on till the early hours of the morning, interrupted by dinner and speeches and umpteen toasts. On the final day, the guests attended a champagne breakfast before Gladys and Henri set off for a honeymoon on the Riviera.

Elizabeth met *ducs* and *vicomtes*, *marquesses* and *comtesses*, and she learned by observing when to extend her fingers for the slightest of handshakes and when to lean in and kiss on both cheeks. She spoke passable French now, enough to get by with guests who didn't speak English. Many of the women promised to visit her Paris salon, although a few said they were already clients of Madame Rubinstein. Elizabeth perfected a very subtle eye roll for such moments.

After the wedding, she did a little shopping in the Paris *ateliers*, delighted to find that prices were marked down. This recession definitely had its benefits. She got herself a silky black Russian sable coat for a thousand dollars, which the previous year had cost three thousand.

Elizabeth arrived in London just in time for Royal Ascot, and Teddy met her at Claridge's, her regular hotel, and announced he had procured tickets for both of them. He even had passes to enter the royal enclosure.

"They're very hard to secure," he told her, "but I dropped a word in an equerry's ear when the Queen visited the salon. She's very keen on your Eight Hour Cream, I hear."

"Is that so?" Elizabeth squeaked, with a little skip in her step.

"I'll have to check you know how to curtsy for when I present you." He gave her a sideways smile.

"I'm actually going to meet her!" Elizabeth squeaked again. She cupped her face in her hands, momentarily overcome. "That's too, too wonderful! Can we arrange for a photographer to capture the moment?"

"Not in the royal enclosure, I'm afraid. It's a private, not a formal presentation. But maybe another time."

Elizabeth was nervous about the introduction, but she found

Queen Mary warm and lacking airs and graces. She was an attractive woman in her sixties, with good skin, and she was wearing the subtlest of tints on her cheeks and lips.

"Are you interested in horses?" the Queen asked, and Elizabeth told her about Leading Lady, her beautiful Arabian thoroughbred, whom she missed terribly. They had a cozy chat about training methods, one horse owner to another, until the first race was announced and the Queen slipped off to watch.

Elizabeth felt a little giddy afterward. Imagine if she could go back and tell young Florence Nightingale Graham that she would one day meet the Queen of England!

"How can I thank you?" she asked Teddy, clutching his arm. "You've been a godsend to the business, and to me personally."

While profits had fallen in the States, they were still rising in England, despite the recession. Teddy managed every detail there and, as far as she could tell, he hadn't put a foot wrong.

"We aim to please," he said. "I have such a delightful boss that nothing is too much trouble."

"Doesn't your wife mind all the time you spend at work?" She gave him a coy look. "And entertaining your boss when she visits? Perhaps I should meet her sometime, to thank her for her sacrifice."

"Oh, my wife doesn't mind at all," he said. "She prefers to stay in the country with the children."

He hadn't mentioned children before and it came as a surprise. He didn't seem like the type of man who would have children.

In her suite at Claridge's that night, Elizabeth couldn't get to sleep, but this time it was excitement rather than anxiety causing her insomnia. She relived the events of the day, determined to set every detail in memory: the Queen's floral tea dress and wide straw hat, the bowls of sweet strawberries, Teddy's immaculate champagne-colored summer suit. If only she had married him instead of Tommy, this lifestyle could have been hers all year round.

She allowed herself to fantasize about being Teddy's wife, about going home with him at the end of the evening and chatting over a nightcap. Her fantasy stopped there, though; she couldn't imagine going to bed with him. That wasn't his appeal. He was good-looking but his compliments never felt flirtatious; there wasn't any sense that he would ever try to seduce her. No, she loved his gentle manners, his impeccable grooming, and his empathy. She could talk to him almost as frankly as she spoke to Bessie, and she was sure he was every bit as loyal.

Trust was very much on her mind the following day when a cable arrived from a senior Arden salesman who was touring department stores in the Midwest. *Mr. Lewis has asked us to send correspondence to his address instead of the head office. Thought I should check with you.*

Why would Tommy do that? Elizabeth sent him a cable, querying the order.

Trying to relieve you of pressures of work, came the reply.

She responded sharply that all letters should go through the head office, as usual, then she cabled Laney, asking that her orders be relayed to the regional sales teams.

What was Tommy up to? Was he trying to take over in her absence? It was time she got home and found out exactly what was going on—both within and outside office hours. She cabled Laney again, asking her to hire a private detective to investigate Tommy and have a full report on her desk by her return.

Ask him to find out about Mildred Beam too, she added, a memory of that too-intimate-to-be-innocent embrace still vivid in her mind's eye.

CHAPTER 30

Helena

October 1931

Helena sailed back to New York in the fall of 1931, her head abuzz with plans. She sat on the balcony of her suite scribbling ship-to-shore cables, and she drafted long memorandums on the backs of menus in the first-class dining room. Bit by bit her old energy was returning. She had always thrived on activity; it was enforced idleness after the operation that had made her sink into depression.

On arrival in Manhattan, she ordered two typewriters to be delivered to her apartment, and two extra telephone lines to be installed in her dining room. She hired two secretaries, both of whom she asked to sign contracts in which they promised to keep their work confidential. And she persuaded Fred Eagleton, her ally on the board, to give her a list of the names and addresses of all the shareholders in Helena Rubinstein Inc.

She targeted the women first. Their shares were now worth only a fraction of what they had paid for them in 1928, scarcely the cost of the paper the certificates were printed on. Helena couldn't compensate them for their losses but she offered to buy their shares for twice what they were currently worth on the stock market, cash in hand. As the recession deepened countrywide, most families were counting every cent, and she hoped they would be happy to exchange a virtually worthless share certificate for some real dollars and cents.

The first batch of letters went out and she waited anxiously for the replies. If any of them warned Charles Welch what she was doing, he could block her. That would be a disaster. Within a week, though, she had a postbag of letters: some of the women wanted to know more about her plans, but most wanted the money straight away. She paid them in return and discreetly arranged the share transfers.

Another batch of letters went out and another batch of shares was bought. The thrill of the chase was invigorating to Helena. This wasn't about money. It was about something far more valuable: her reputation.

She wrote more letters, bought more shares, keeping her actions stealthy, until she owned fifty-two percent of the common stock. She had sold the company for 7.3 million dollars and bought back control for just 1.5 million. She opened a bottle of champagne and gave her secretaries a glass each.

Soon after that, Charles Welch got wind of it and the call came. "What do you think you're doing, Helena?" he demanded.

"I'm buying shares in my own company," she replied. "Do you have a problem with that?"

"I hope you're not planning to undermine our strategies," he said.

"Your strategies aren't working," she told him. "Profits have been plummeting under your management, and I get letters from store owners saying they no longer want to stock Helena Rubinstein products because of their 'vulgarization.'" That word resonated for her, as she remembered Elizabeth Arden calling her "vulgar" at the *Vogue* ball.

"You haven't given us enough time," he protested. "We took over just before the crash. Sales would have been affected by the recession even if you were still at the helm. We are on track to get back into profit either later this year or early next."

"Yes, by cheapening my company beyond recognition," she hit back. "You chose the wrong strategy. Elizabeth Arden's sales have held up since the crash because she remained at the top of the market, while you abandoned it, leaving the field clear."

"How do you know her sales held up?" Welch demanded. "She's not publicly listed. You can't assume that."

Helena couldn't tell him that she continued to get reports from Edith Brown. The monthly sales figures passed across her desk at the Aeolian Building, and she forwarded them like clockwork.

"I have my sources," Helena said. "New York's upper-class ladies have continued to buy face creams and lipsticks over the last two years—they just haven't been buying mine, and I intend to change that. I'm taking charge again."

WHEN WORD REACHED the financial press that Madame Rubinstein was back at the helm of her own company, it was hailed as a major coup d'état. Reporters compared her to Henry Ford, Charles Schwab, and George Getty, all of them remarkably canny self-made millionaires. It was flattering, of course, but for Helena the battle was only just beginning. Now it was time for the next step.

She'd had her eye for a while on a sales executive called Harry T. Johnson, a man who was highly regarded in the beauty and cosmetics industry, with twenty-five years' retail experience under his belt. She invited him for a meeting at her apartment, where she outlined her plans.

"I want to start by reversing the price-cutting strategy and reestablishing my products at the top of the market," she explained. "I plan to stop supplying low-end retail outlets, and offer local monopolies to the most prestigious retailers so long as they order enough stock. And I would like you to spearhead this campaign."

He immediately had some ideas on how to make it work. "We could hand-select the outlets we want and offer them incentives, then cut off credit for the ones we don't want."

"Precisely," she agreed. He had used the word "we," she noted. He was already thinking of himself as part of the team.

"I think it's important to establish you as the company figurehead once more," he said. "I noticed a rather lovely portrait of you in your hallway. Perhaps we could offer framed prints to the stores we want to work with?"

Helena liked the idea. The painting, by George Kesslere, was a favorite of hers: she looked serious and regal in a gold skirt and scarlet cloak, every inch the Queen of Beauty Science. She already knew she wanted Harry on board. The only question was how much she would have to pay.

He named his price. It was as steep as she had expected; she didn't respond at first, just wrote the figure in her notes and pretended to consider it.

He kept talking, explaining why he was worth that sum and what he would bring to the company. She made more notes, listening hard, not giving away what she was thinking, just as she had done at age fourteen when buying kerosene for her father's business.

He finished by saying that if the salary he suggested was beyond her budget, he supposed he could come down a few thousand.

"No," Helena said. "I will hire you for the initial sum you asked for, and I'm sure you will be worth every cent." She wanted him to start working for her with enthusiasm. She wanted his loyalty. She would make sure he earned his inflated salary many, many times over.

WHILE HARRY BEGAN contacting retail outlets around the country, Helena turned her attention to opening a new Manhattan salon. She got Harry to deal with the real-estate agent and he secured the lease on a building at 715 Fifth Avenue—her first Fifth Avenue address. By the time the owner realized his new tenant was Jewish, it was too late for him to object.

Helena took personal charge of the design. She wanted it to be avant-garde and European in style, showcasing some of the gems of her art collection. In the front window, she planned to hang a giant painting by Surrealist artist Man Ray of bright red disembodied lips against a gray sky. Let Elizabeth Arden keep the matrons and dowagers with her old-fashioned classical style; this was a new and different salon for the modern 1930s woman.

Her advertising campaign would focus on discovery, innovation, and advancement; from now on, she decided, her salon girls would be called "beauticians," as they were "technicians of beauty." Helena Rubinstein products and treatments were scientific and looked to the future, not the dusty old past.

A LONG, AGGRIEVED letter arrived from Edward. Helena had omitted to tell him she was traveling to New York, and hadn't mentioned anything about buying back the business from Lehman Brothers.

Yet again, I learn your news from the press, he wrote. *In 1928 you told reporters that you had sold the American business in order to spend more time with me in Paris. I hoped it meant that we could revive our marriage. But now you are back in New York again, am I to assume that you have no further interest in being married to me? I was by your side in Vienna, and I would be with you now if you asked. I love you, Helena, but I'm sad that you haven't given our marriage a chance.*

Helena frowned. She was far too busy to deal with him, and it irked her that he was portraying himself as the wronged party. *Did you forget why our marriage foundered in the first place?* she replied. *Some little maid in Connecticut whose name I forget, but who was probably one of your many mistresses in the twenty-four years we have nominally been husband and wife. Stella reports that you are publishing the erotic diaries of a young woman called Anaïs Nin, thereby firmly establishing Black Manikin as a publisher of smut. I'm sure this has many fringe benefits for a man who likes bedding girls who are still in their teens.*

Edward replied with a spirited defense of the books he was publishing. He wrote that his life's work, getting great literature into the hands of readers, was of far more value than getting pore-reducing cream onto the faces of spoiled rich women with too much time on their hands.

Helena was enraged by this. *Too much time on their hands? There speaks a lazy bum who spends his days in the Jockey Club with a bunch of useless people, idlers, little zeros. What is the point of your stupid publishing company, except to make you feel as if you are a Big Man? But this Big Man is subsidized by his wife's hard labor and don't you forget it.*

You are a monster, he cabled back.

Helena lost her temper completely. If he had any idea how hard she was working to claw her way back, inch by inch, to the top of the American market . . . Every waking hour was spent on it. She was designing new products, personally supervising every word of each advertising campaign, walking through the salon spending a few moments with her clients, giving them personal advice and compliments, sending thoughtful gifts to journalists. . . . This was the company that bore her name. This was her life and Edward had no part in it. She was done with him.

She sent a cable to Stella: *Buy the Jockey Club,* she wrote. *Then bulldoze it.*

Are you sure? Stella cabled back.

Yes, do it, Helena replied.

CHAPTER 31

Elizabeth

June 1932

Laney met Elizabeth when she disembarked at the East
River docks, and briefed her while a chauffeur drove
them to the Aeolian Building.

"The detective's report is on your desk," she said, "along with
the latest sales figures. The salon is fully booked this week. Our
clients want to get spruced up before traveling to their summer
homes."

Recession or no recession, Elizabeth's wealthiest customers
still spent July and August in Newport. Bookings increased for
her Rhode Island salon during the hottest months, while they
dropped in Manhattan. She sent some of her "beauticians," as
she now called them, to cope with demand—a posting that was
very popular among the girls because they could go to the beach
on their days off.

"Oh, and Helena Rubinstein is back in town. You probably
heard." Laney gave Elizabeth a worried glance.

Elizabeth dug her fingernails into the palms of her hands and
didn't comment. Like everyone else, she had read about Madame Rubinstein buying back control of her American company
and still retaining a personal profit of almost six million dollars. And she knew about the Fifth Avenue salon her rival was
opening. She'd invested heavily in her own Fifth Avenue salon,
and she was pouring even more money into the building of her

health spa in Maine, yet still the Rubinstein woman was snapping at her heels. It was insufferable to think she would have to watch out for her again whenever she set foot in a restaurant.

"Where's Tommy?" Elizabeth asked, and noted that Laney didn't meet her eye as she answered.

"He's been around," she said, hesitating as if choosing her words carefully. "He often dropped by the salons while you were away, saying he was keeping an eye on things. I imagine now you're back he won't need to."

"I don't want him to keep an eye on anything but his own responsibilities," Elizabeth said sharply. "I'll be sure to tell him so."

She painted on a gracious smile as she waltzed through the salon, greeting clients with a wave and a "How do you do?" but not stopping to chat, because she was anxious to get to her desk and read the detective's report.

It ran to several pages. He wrote that he had interviewed many members of her staff, and discovered that Tommy had been diverting information from different areas of the business that weren't his concern: lists of the prices paid to suppliers for raw ingredients, the packaging costs, the markup from wholesale to retail, staff salaries, and a complete list of all her clients countrywide.

It looked as if he was amassing information either to attempt to take over her business or to set up on his own—or both. Maybe he was spying for Madame Rubinstein; she wouldn't put it past him. Elizabeth turned the page, her fury mounting. If Tommy planned to undermine her, he must know he would never win. She was far richer and far smarter than he was.

"As you requested, I looked into the circumstances of Miss Mildred Beam," the detective continued. "I suspect you are not aware that she was named in a notorious court case eight years ago. One Clarence Baring attempted to poison his wife in order to marry his much younger mistress—your Miss Beam. She was terribly distressed in court and claimed she had believed him to be divorced. No blame was attached to her by the judge, but Mr. Baring was found to be insane and committed to an asylum."

Elizabeth was horrified. She would never have employed the girl if she had known that. Not in a million years!

The report continued: "I investigated whether Mildred Beam has found alternative employment since leaving your company, and discovered that she plans to start her own beauty salon next year, on the ninth floor of 754 Fifth Avenue, under the trading name Jane Cloud."

Another Dorothy Gray, setting up in competition! Elizabeth would destroy her, she vowed. She would swat her like a mosquito.

"I have several photographs of your husband in the company of Miss Beam, but no indisputable evidence of an affair."

Elizabeth felt sure they were sleeping together and her hunch was that Tommy had passed confidential information to Mildred to help her start her own business. She couldn't prove it, she supposed. Nevertheless, she vowed to divorce him and leave him destitute. He could sleep in a cardboard box on the streets as far as she was concerned.

The detective's report continued that Tommy—and her brother Will—appeared to entertain other girls from her salons on a regular basis. There was an envelope with blurred photographs of them emerging from bars, getting into taxis, and entering Will's apartment.

Elizabeth screamed in rage and threw the report across the office. Laney came rushing in, asking if she was all right, but Elizabeth was so furious she couldn't speak. Every morning when she walked into the salon, her girls must have been sniggering behind her back. As far as she was concerned, they were all whores who might as well have been working in a brothel!

"I want you to bounce these girls," she said to Laney, handing her the photos. "Each and every goddamn one. Sack Will too and tell him I don't want to hear from him again. As for Tommy—leave him to me."

She telephoned her lawyer with a set of instructions: "Inform my husband that he is forthwith relieved of his responsibilities at the company and must not return either to his office or to my apartment. I will be changing the locks at both addresses. You can also tell him that I am divorcing him. If he doesn't agree to the terms I offer, I will press criminal charges against him for theft of company property. Is that clear?"

There was a moment's silence at the other end of the line and she heard the scratch of a pen. "All clear, Miss Arden," her lawyer said.

ELIZABETH ACCEPTED AN invitation to dinner at Bessie's that evening. She didn't want to go home in case Tommy turned up and made a scene, and she had missed Bessie during her stay in Europe.

She was hoping for a tête-à-tête but when she arrived the two Annes, Morgan and Vanderbilt, were already there.

Bessie didn't look well. Her eyes were pink and puffy, and her complexion had a grayish tinge.

"You should be up in Maine, getting some fresh air," Elizabeth told her. "You look as though you need it."

"I can't. I'm having surgery next week on some veins in my legs," Bessie said. "It has to be done but I'm rather dreading it. I haven't been sleeping well, I'm so worried about going under the knife."

Elizabeth had seen the way her veins bulged through the skin, like bunches of grapes. She'd taken care to avoid touching them when giving massages. "It will be good to get those veins seen to," she said. "Perhaps you'll walk more easily afterward."

"I don't think I'll ever walk again." Bessie sighed. "I'm not strong enough."

"Nonsense," Elizabeth chided. "I'll help you. Once you've recovered from the operation, we can go to Maine together. I'll put you on a Week of Beauty program and you'll feel better in no time."

She wanted to tell Bessie what she had discovered about Tommy, but not in front of the two Annes. They would find out in due course that she was getting divorced, but she needed to get used to the idea first. She hoped to linger after the Annes left and talk to Bessie on her own, but straight after dinner, Bessie announced she was tired and needed to go to bed. She rang the bell for her footman and Elizabeth had no choice but to leave.

She entered her apartment cautiously. She had told the staff not to let Tommy in, but feared he might have forced his way past them. The maid said he had telephoned several times but hadn't turned up, which was a relief. Elizabeth planned to give him a wide berth while the legal paperwork was tied up. Her original reservations about the scandal of divorce remained, but if she told her own version of the story, she was sure her clients and friends would understand she'd been left with no choice.

The next day, she decided to start by confiding in Edna and gauging her reaction. Edna had divorced her first husband to marry Richard Newton, so she couldn't possibly criticize.

She told her that Tommy had been seducing the beauticians and committing fraud, and she'd been left with no option but to bounce him from the business and file for divorce.

"I'm glad to hear it," Edna said straight away. "Frankly, I never thought he had enough class for you."

Elizabeth was gratified. If everyone reacted like that, she had nothing to worry about.

BESSIE CAME OUT of the hospital a week after her operation, but she was still bedridden when Elizabeth went around to visit, taking an extravagant fruit basket.

"I don't know what that surgeon did to me, but I feel worse

than ever," Bessie groaned. "I can't bear to move my legs. Every-thing is swollen and aching."

"It will take time. Eat sensibly, get some rest, and we'll be in Maine soon." Elizabeth's heart filled with joy at the thought. In her head, she could hear the shushing of wavelets at the lake-shore, and smell Leading Lady's horsey scent, feel the warmth of her coat. If only they could leave straight away.

Bessie seemed unusually gloomy. Elizabeth started to tell her about Tommy, but Bessie closed her eyes mid-sentence and began to snore with a wheezing sound. She waited a few mo-ments, but Bessie had clearly sunk into a deep sleep, so she stood up, kissed her cheek, and tiptoed out.

Later, she wished she had waited for her to waken. If only she hadn't been so impatient. She'd had no idea that she would never get the chance to talk to her again.

ANNE MORGAN CALLED the following Sunday with the news that Bessie had passed away in her sleep. Her heart had been failing and it wasn't unexpected, Anne said. Elizabeth was so shocked, her legs gave way and she crumpled to the floor in her hallway. How could Bessie be dead? She'd been in her seventies, but she was such a forceful, dynamic personality, she simply couldn't be gone. It was unthinkable!

Elizabeth felt the bereavement deeply. She'd lost the person to whom she was closest in the entire world. She'd only known Bessie for seven years, but in that time she'd become her advisor and dearest friend, almost like a mother. Yes, that was it: she felt as if she had lost another mother. The first one died when she was five years old, the second when she was fifty-four, and the grief was overwhelming. She felt lost.

The funeral was held in St. Patrick's Cathedral and everyone who was anyone was there, from Eleanor Roosevelt to Condé Nast and Noël Coward. Elizabeth struggled to retain her com-posure, her face hidden behind a heavy black veil. Sobs kept slipping out, like hiccups, and she dabbed her eyes with a silk handkerchief. She was in the same row as the two Annes, but they were absorbed in their own grief and didn't offer any comfort. Loneliness was a state Elizabeth was familiar with, but she had never in her entire life felt more lonely than she did that day.

Condé Nast was hosting a gathering afterward at his Park Avenue apartment and normally Elizabeth would have been thrilled to be invited, but she couldn't face it. Other guests would be sharing memories of Bessie, and she knew she wouldn't be able to listen without breaking down.

She had lost her closest friend and she'd lost her husband, and she felt washed up and rudderless. All she had left was the business and she couldn't bring herself to care about that anymore, not the way she had in the beginning. Going to Maine used to lift her spirits, but she couldn't face it without Bessie. It would be wonderful to see Leading Lady—she yearned to see her—but that was all she had to look forward to in the decades stretching into the future.

Her driver dropped her outside her apartment building and there, waiting for her on the sidewalk, was the person she least wanted to see—Tommy.

"Please, not now." She raised her hand to fend him off and tried to push past but he caught hold of her arm.

"What makes you think you can discard me like an old coat and I won't make a fuss?" Tommy asked. She could smell drink on his breath. "I'm going to make the divorce very expensive for you, Elizabeth. I might even take the company away from you."

"Talk to my lawyer," she said. "I'm not discussing it here."

"Have you been at the funeral of that fat old lesbian?" he asked, tugging her black veil. "I always thought you were frigid, but once you started hanging out with Bessie's set, I realized you had preferred women all along."

"What the hell do you mean?" she snapped. "Bessie wasn't a lesbian."

He laughed, harshly: "You must be the only person in New York who didn't know. Why do you think she and Elsie de Wolfe lived together for so long? And why was she so upset when Elsie got married? Because they were lovers, stupid."

"That's ridiculous!" Elizabeth tried to yank her arm from his grip but he held tight.

"And then she took up with you," he continued. "All those cozy little tête-à-têtes in Maine. I should have guessed. Perhaps I'll sue *you* for divorce on grounds of infidelity."

Elizabeth signaled for the doorman of the block to come and help. He rushed out.

"Please let go, sir," he said to Tommy, polite but firm. He was a good six inches taller, so Tommy released her arm.

"I'm talking to my wife," he told the doorman. "No need to butt in."

Elizabeth rubbed her arm. "Could you please escort me indoors?" she asked the doorman, and he stepped between her and Tommy so she could walk to the entrance.

"You're a snob, Elizabeth," Tommy called after her. "A snob with poor taste and no morals. And you're shallow. Being married to you well nigh bored me to death."

She whirled around. "And you are a failed, talentless good-for-nothing." She signaled to the doorman to close the door behind her and walked to the elevator without looking back, her entire body trembling.

Could it be true that Bessie and Elsie had been lovers? Did the two Annes know? Would everyone think she had been Bessie's lover? Visions of those intimate massages came to mind and made her cheeks burn. Had they meant more to Bessie than she intended? Had people been gossiping about their relationship behind her back? She gave an involuntary shudder.

As she closed the apartment door behind her, she decided to close her mind to the whole idea. It was disgusting and simply not true. Theirs had been a close and stimulating friendship. Let anyone dare to say otherwise and she would set her lawyers on them before they could draw their next breath.

Meanwhile, she would instruct them to get more aggressive in the negotiations with Tommy. Somehow or other she needed to shut him up for good.

CHAPTER 32

Helena

February 1933

Helena was fascinated to hear from Edith Brown about the vitriolic collapse of Elizabeth Arden's marriage, amid accusations her husband had been sleeping with her beauticians. Edith reported that he burst into the salon one day hurling insults at Elizabeth, and Laney had to intervene to stop them coming to blows.

Helena felt a touch of sympathy. Maybe it was impossible for successful women to have happy marriages. Always the men felt threatened. Always they sought younger women to bolster their fragile masculinity.

According to Edith, Elizabeth had also sacked her brother Will, and Helena thought that a mistake. Family could be a pain in the neck but it was better to keep them close. They knew too much about you to turn them into enemies.

The Arden-Lewis divorce had been settled out of court so no details would be reported in the press apart from the fact they were no longer married. Helena got the inside scoop from Edith though: after almost twenty years of marriage and fifteen years as her sales director, all Tommy would receive was the sum of twenty-five thousand dollars. He had never owned any part of the business and would have no future earnings from it. He didn't even get one of the couple's properties to live in. In return, he'd promised never to talk to the press about Miss Arden, and not to take any other work in the beauty industry for five years.

It was a bad deal for him, Helena thought, and she wondered why he had accepted. How would he earn a living during these five years? Unemployment was endemic. On every street corner there were grown men holding signs begging for jobs. She'd seen one that very morning that read: *Out of work for three months. Have five children. Will do anything.*

It was impossible to live in New York without seeing the effects of the recession. On her drive to the office every day, Helena passed queues of gaunt, stooped men and women standing outside soup kitchens or employment exchanges. She saw men sleeping in alleyways, sheltered from the elements by a few sheets of cardboard. And she saw shanty towns spring up in Central Park and Riverside Park, with dwellings built from discarded odds and ends of wood and metal. Women nursed babies while perched on boxes outside these makeshift homes, and young children played in the mud. What was the country coming to?

Helena kept a supply of dollar bills in her handbag and when she spotted anyone who looked especially desperate, she asked her chauffeur to stop and distribute them. She gave to women in particular, because she guessed they would spend it on food for their children. What more could she do? She couldn't solve the problems of the world. When beggars lingered outside her salons, she had to ask the doormen to move them along, because walking past them made her wealthy clients feel uncomfortable.

HELENA HAD RECENTLY brought her niece Mala over to New York to work with her. Mala was Regina's daughter, a striking beauty with the flawless creamy skin and dark luxuriant hair that were family trademarks. She had been working with Stella in Paris, where Helena had spotted her winning smile and natural friendliness with clients, as well as her fluent English, and decided she could make good use of her talents in America.

Helena had just passed her sixtieth birthday—a fact she wouldn't admit if her life depended on it. She was aware that she no longer photographed as well as she would have liked: the contours of her face were sagging like molten wax, the jawline and neck getting softer, and two grooves were indelibly etched on her brow. She was still happy to sit for artists' portraits, something she had always loved doing, but she no longer wanted to be photographed because she had no control over the outcome. That's where Mala came in: she was young and glamorous, perfect as the face of Helena Rubinstein for a new generation. They looked similar; the girl could almost have been her daughter.

Mala moved into Helena's apartment initially and proved very agreeable company. They gossiped about family members, and Mala told her about her fiancé, Victor, who was still in Paris but planning to join her soon. Helena had an insatiable appetite for the stories of other people's relationships, and quizzed her in such detail she felt she knew Victor inside out long before she met him.

Mala teased her for the little eccentricities she had developed over the years of living alone: spraying her bed with clouds of expensive perfume, leaving gowns by top designers crumpled in heaps on the floor, and eating handfuls of smoked salmon while standing in front of the icebox without bothering to find a plate or a fork.

"You eat salmon like a wild bear," Mala told her, laughing.

"At least I don't have to catch it myself," Helena replied, not even remotely ashamed.

Helena tended to leave her jewelry lying around wherever she took it off, then could never find the piece she was looking for. Mala came up with an ingenious solution. She bought her aunt a filing cabinet and stuck a letter of the alphabet on the front of each section before filing the jewelry. A was for amethysts and aquamarines, C for carnelian, D for diamonds, E for emeralds, and so forth. Helena laughed out loud when she saw it.

"Where does the imperial topaz go?" she asked. "Under I or T? And what about my diamond and ruby necklace?"

"It's not a perfect system," Mala admitted. "But better than rummaging through the entire collection and never finding what you are looking for."

"I guess," Helena agreed, tickled by the effort she'd gone to.

She liked Mala's fashion sense, and her chatter about movie stars and the latest dance styles. It made Helena feel in touch with a younger generation. Life was never dull when Mala was around.

THE NEW FIFTH Avenue salon opened and photographs of the Man Ray lips appeared in newspapers and magazines. After hearing how popular Elizabeth Arden's "Days of Beauty" were, Helena had introduced her own version. She matched the price of twenty-five dollars for a day-long rejuvenation program, but she eschewed the exercise and diet components of the Arden regime: her days were about pampering, not punishing. She added some of her own treatments, using a new range of "Hormone" products she had designed.

The idea had come to her as she recuperated after her hysterectomy. All women went through those difficult years when they got hot flashes and night sweats, their hair got thinner, and their skin aged. Menopause was something shameful you endured on your own, at home, and never discussed, but why should women be ashamed? Helena decided to train her staff to refer to it obliquely.

"For women over the age of forty, we recommend our special Hormone Beauty Masque to rejuvenate the skin," they might say. Or "Anyone can have beautiful hair, no matter what their age, if they use our Hormone Scalp Food." Her favorite mantra was "There is no such thing as an ugly woman, only a lazy one." The message was: put in the effort and you too can still be beautiful.

The new product line included a Hormone Throat Balsam, Youthifying Hand Cream, and a Beautilift Mask. It was more expensive than her standard line, but the packaging was classy, and the text on the boxes and in adverts was convincingly scientific. All women of a certain age would catch the implication; it was designed for them.

Meanwhile, Mala helped her to stay in touch with what young people wanted. Helena had always been careful to keep her face out of the sun, having seen its aging effects on Australian women's skin, but Mala told her suntans were all the rage in the 1930s. After some thought, Helena designed a "sun-proof" cream for young people to help protect their faces from the sun's harming rays while sunbathing. She also introduced a tropical tanning lotion to color the skin without the need for lying on the beach for hours. She created new lipsticks and eye shadows to match the fashion colors each season, and she started a "Beauty Problem" advice service, whereby anyone could write to her for help; her solution, of course, always involved buying a Helena Rubinstein product.

She kept a close eye on the turnover and profit figures, and knew the energy she was pouring into the business was paying off. Harry Johnson had proved a great asset, and they'd achieved their growth targets every quarter since he arrived. He spent much of his time on the road, but the two of them had a monthly meeting to discuss the figures.

"America's a country of two halves," he reported. "The ones on their uppers who are living in cardboard boxes, and the wealthy who are living in mansions."

"Not halves," she said. "There are also those in the middle who are still in work but are merely scraping by without money for extras. Fortunately my top-end customers are still prioritizing skin care."

"And makeup," he said. "Chinese Red lipstick and your cake mascara fly off the shelves."

Her business was growing, so she was astonished when Edith reported that Elizabeth Arden was in debt to the tune of half a million dollars. Helena invited her to her apartment, avid for every detail.

"How did it happen?" she asked.

"She's diverting a lot of money into her new health spa, Maine Chance," Edith explained. "And she also invested in a line of makeup for stage and screen, only to find those areas are already dominated by Max Factor and it was difficult to break through."

Helena nodded. She wouldn't have tried that herself, since Max Factor was so well established with his pancake makeup and dark eye shadows, most of them too heavy for everyday use.

"Business is also suffering without Tommy Lewis," Edith told her. "She hasn't appointed another sales director yet and revenues are dropping off a cliff. Basically she's been spending freely and not earning enough. Laney told me she doesn't know how they're going to pay the tax bill."

Helena rubbed her hands in glee. Nothing cheered her so much as hearing that her rival's business was in trouble. When she arrived in America in 1915, it had been her goal to beat Elizabeth Arden and, for now at least, she was in the lead.

CARMEL AND HER husband invited friends for a housewarming party at their spacious new apartment on Seventy-Second Street, overlooking the East River. Helena went alone because Mala's beau, Victor, had arrived and the lovebirds were spending all their time together.

She was pleased to see that the African mask she'd given Carmel as a wedding present was prominently displayed. The whole apartment was tasteful and elegant, with minimal decoration, so the focus was on the works of art.

"I copied you!" Carmel confessed. "I love your style."

As Helena stood admiring a Grant Wood painting of a farmer's wife, Carmel's brother Tom came up behind her.

"You feel his characters could step out of the paintings, don't you?" he asked.

"I was thinking that she looks Polish," Helena replied. "A practical woman of the soil."

"And you? Are you a woman of the soil?" he asked. A waiter walked past with a tray of champagne, and he took one for each of them, and handed her a glass.

"No, but I am happy to get my hands dirty. I do a lot of mixing and testing of new products in my kitchen. I like to stay involved in the science side of the business." Helena clutched the champagne but didn't drink it. It made her gassy and bloated.

"I don't know how you find the time," Tom said. "I haven't seen you to congratulate you on your masterstroke of buying back control of your company. Tell me, did you foresee the crash and plan this from the start?"

Helena laughed. "No, I don't have a crystal ball. I was disappointed in Charles Welch's running of my company, and so . . ." She spread her hands. "What could I do?"

Tom grinned at her. "My boss, Mr. Hearst, thinks you are a genius. Did you know economics professors are teaching classes about you at Harvard?"

Helena was flattered. "Surely they have better things to do with their time?"

They talked about the effects of the recession on their businesses. Magazine revenues were drastically reduced, he told her, both sales of printed copies and advertising. She said this was exactly the time when advertising was crucial. She had increased her budget. When there was less money being spent, it became even more vital to make sure it was spent on *your* products.

"You're incredible," he said. "If you ever want to leave the beauty industry, we'd have a role for you on the board at the Hearst Corporation. Although I doubt you would have the patience to work with my esteemed boss, who changes his mind every five minutes."

"I can be very patient," Helena said, "if the prize is worth it."

Tom touched her arm and looked directly into her eyes. "Yes, me too," he said, his voice low.

She stepped backward, startled. Could he be flirting with her? Surely not! He was married, and so was she—on paper at least. The compliments were oozing out of him like honey from a jar. Perhaps he was unctuous with everyone? But he seemed to be giving her special attention. He monopolized her for the entire hour and a half she spent at the party.

When she decided to leave, Tom went to fetch her coat as she said goodbye to Carmel.

"Do you find my brother attractive?" Carmel asked, a finely plucked eyebrow raised in question. "I noticed you were inseparable."

"He's a good conversationalist," Helena replied, "But I wouldn't dream of commenting on his attractiveness since we are both married."

Carmel shrugged. "You have a stronger moral code than most New York women, in that case. He's very popular."

Helena was cross to hear it. Unfaithful husbands made her mad. As Tom walked her to her car, he asked if she would dine with him sometime.

"Of course," she said, with a tone like crystal. "Do bring your wife along. I'd love to meet her."

He smiled, tight-lipped, and said he would be in touch, but she knew he wouldn't.

Helena thought about it on the way home. She had no interest whatsoever in bringing another man into her life, but if she did, she would first make sure he was not a philandering type.

What would she want a man for anyway? Since her hysterectomy, she no longer missed sex. She liked her own company, liked living alone. Roy was doing a business degree at Harvard and sometimes came to the city on weekends, but Horace remained in Paris with his father. Mala was getting married and moving out soon, but Helena was so busy, she never got lonely.

She supposed she and Edward would divorce at some stage, but she was in no hurry. After she destroyed the Jockey Club, he cabled that he had "washed his hands of her," and that suited her just fine. They had a separation agreement, and she didn't intend to remarry, so why bother divorcing?

But on a trip to Paris not long after the conversation with Tom, she discovered a very compelling reason to change her mind.

CHAPTER 33

Elizabeth

May 1934

Maine Chance, Elizabeth's health farm, opened in May and was quickly booked up for the summer months. She felt sad going to Maine without Bessie but she had plowed so much money into the venture, she had no choice but to make it a success. She had overseen every detail, from lampshades to towels and bed linen, so that guests could enjoy all the creature comforts they would expect in their own homes.

On arrival, they had a private consultation with Elizabeth herself, at which they were given a diet and exercise plan to suit their particular concerns. She could be blunt in her instructions: "Move around more, dear, and don't let so much food pass your lips," she told her overweight clients. "Every woman has the right to be beautiful," she told the traditional ones who still refused to wear makeup, "and with my help you will achieve your rights."

Guests were wakened each morning with a healthful breakfast on a tray, which was decorated with a posy of flowers from the garden. An exercise class followed. If weather permitted, it was held on the lawn sloping down to the lake, where the water provided a stunning backdrop and they were accompanied by a trill of birdsong. Elizabeth often taught classes herself, wearing a pale pink gym suit. She enjoyed showing off her svelte figure, and knew her fitness and flexibility were unparalleled for a woman of her age. After luncheon on the terrace, the women had an afternoon of top-to-toe beauty treatments: massage, facials, hair styling, makeup classes, manicures, depilation—whatever was required to make them look and feel younger.

At between two hundred fifty and five hundred dollars for a week's stay, it was an expensive luxury in Depression-era America, but very popular with Elizabeth's clientele. She soon realized she wouldn't make much profit, because the running costs of Maine Chance were so high, but she reckoned she earned the lifelong loyalty of every woman who visited, and that made the investment worthwhile.

Every afternoon she left her clients to their treatments and slipped off to see Leading Lady, her precious baby. She should have been racing by the age of two, but Elizabeth struggled to find a trainer and jockey with whom she saw eye to eye. The first trainer had been bounced after Elizabeth caught him using a whip. No one would whip her darling! She didn't like blinkers either, considering them ugly. Several subsequent trainers had been sent packing because they didn't agree with her mollycoddling approach, leading one to complain that her stable had a revolving door.

When, at last, she found a trainer who said he thought Leading Lady was ready for the track, she had her driven to stables near the Saratoga racecourse and entered for a race in her age class. When the starting bell rang, Elizabeth stood in the owners' stand peering through her binoculars and cheering her heart out. There was a lot of scuffling for position on the field, and Leading Lady got trapped behind a bunch of frontrunners with no route through.

"Oh, the rotters!" Elizabeth cried. "That's not fair!"

Leading Lady came in an undistinguished fourth, but that wasn't bad for a first outing, Elizabeth told herself.

"Good girl," she cooed in the stable afterward, as she massaged her legs with Ardena Skin Lotion. "Mama is very proud of you. You'll have better luck next time."

Far from being discouraged, she bought three more racehorses to be stabled with Leading Lady, and asked her new trainer to prepare them for the track, using the unique methods she insisted on: clover from Maine, hanging baskets in their stalls, soothing music in the background, Elizabeth Arden Eight Hour cream for their hooves, perfume for their manes, cashmere blankets, and absolutely no use of the whip or blinkers. The trainer clearly thought she was a crazy lady but agreed to follow her regime in order to keep his job.

She preferred horses to people, Elizabeth decided. You knew where you stood with them. They were sensual creatures who never betrayed you, and they had absolutely no guile.

HER ANNUAL TRIP to Europe had to be delayed until October each year, when Maine Chance closed its doors for winter. It was always a wrench to leave her horses behind and sail across the ocean, but Elizabeth missed Gladys and she couldn't wait to hear the London society gossip from Teddy Haslam.

When they were apart, she and Gladys kept up to date with each other's news in long chatty letters. Elizabeth had written to her about the horrors of her divorce from Tommy, her sacking of their brother Will, the death of Bessie Marbury, and her new racehorse purchases. Still, there was no substitute for sitting side by side, legs curled beneath them, and nattering for hours on end. There was salon business to discuss, family business to chew over, and all their most private feelings to confide as well.

On the first day of Elizabeth's stay in October 1936, they sat in Gladys and Henri's stylish apartment in Saint-Germain-des-Prés, drinking tea from delicate china cups, and talking a mile a minute.

"You two would never run out of conversation if you were marooned on a desert island for the rest of your lives," Henri commented, and they giggled, knowing it was true.

In the evening they dined out with some of Henri's friends. Elizabeth generally didn't pay much attention to European politics, but she listened with interest to talk of the new German chancellor, Adolf Hitler, since her Berlin salon was thriving.

"I'm glad Germany has a strong leader again," Henri said. "It's about time someone dealt with the Jewish problem."

Another man, whose name Elizabeth hadn't picked up, said he believed Jews had been responsible for the Wall Street crash. "They could have prevented it, with their viselike hold over the American financial market, but it suited them to let shares plummet. You can bet they all came out of it with their fortunes boosted," he said.

Elizabeth thought of the way Helena Rubinstein had sold her company in 1928, then bought it back at a profit in 1931; had she known there was going to be a crash? She found it far-fetched to think the entire affair was a Jewish conspiracy, but perhaps it was true that certain Jews had too much control over the markets. Henri and his friends certainly thought so.

One evening they were joined for dinner by Hermann Goering, president of the German Reichstag. He greeted Elizabeth effusively and insisted on sitting next to her.

"Your fame precedes you," he said. "My fiancée gave me an article from *Die Dame* magazine about the weight-loss programs at your health spa. I think she may have been hinting. Tell me, what are your methods?"

"We teach self-discipline," she said, eyeing the bulge at his waistline. "Before putting any food in your mouth, poke yourself in the belly and decide whether you can afford to add more blubber."

"Isn't it dull to deny yourself the good things in life?" he asked, amusement in his eyes.

She leaned over and touched his belly with the tip of a pink-varnished fingernail. "Come for a week's stay at my spa. You would be vastly outnumbered by women so I can guarantee it wouldn't be dull."

He leaned his head back and roared with laughter. "Perhaps I will," he said. "You never know."

He asked which were her bestselling products, and she told him about her new Ardena Velva line, which was popular for younger skin, and the Orange Skin Food that her mature clients preferred, as well as the great success of her Eight Hour Cream for all ages.

"I'm looking for a Christmas gift for my fiancée—the actress Emmy Sonnemann. Perhaps you've heard of her?" he asked.

"Of course," Elizabeth said, although she hadn't. She didn't have time to watch American movies, never mind German ones.

"I haven't a clue what to get her," Goering said. "Women are so fussy. Perhaps you could advise?"

Elizabeth realized he was dropping a broad hint, but she didn't mind. This was how the world worked. "Where are you staying?" she asked, and he told her. "I'll send a gift set of products to your hotel in the morning," she promised. "If Miss Sonnemann likes them, I hope she will tell her friends to come to my Berlin salon."

"I guarantee she will," Goering replied, with a wink. "Leave it to me."

TEDDY HASLAM MET Elizabeth off the train at London's Waterloo station and guided her to his car. She noticed the sleight of hand with which he tipped the porters and remembered that Tommy always used to fumble and drop his loose change. He'd never had an ounce of Teddy's class.

"I hope you're feeling energetic," Teddy said. "I have a full program of socializing lined up with the great and the good."

"It sounds exciting," she said. "I can't wait."

"Tonight," he said, "we are invited to what is known as 'KT hour' with an American woman named Wallis Simpson, who is the new queen of London society. Cocktails only, from six till eight. We'll dine at the Savoy afterward."

"Why is she the queen of London society?" Elizabeth asked, and Teddy shot her a sideways glance.

"I'll let you wait and be surprised," he said. "But be sure to dress *très chic*, my dear."

The woman who greeted them at KT hour was rake-thin, with dark hair scraped severely back from a striking face, and intelligent cornflower-blue eyes. She had good skin, and wore little makeup apart from a bold red lipstick.

"I'm a fan of your Eight Hour Cream," Wallis said, handing her a turquoise cocktail in a pretty coupe glass. "I use it every night."

"I use it on my horses' hooves," Elizabeth told her, "and they get nothing but the best."

Wallis cackled. "It's good to have a fellow American here," she said. "English women are terribly polite to your face and vicious behind your back. At least you and I call a fig a fig."

Elizabeth didn't correct her assumption that she was American. "I hear you are the uncrowned queen of London society, so you must be doing something right," she said.

Wallis looked amused, as if at a private joke. "I do hope so," she said. "Now I want to introduce you to my absolute favorite German man. This is Joachim von Ribbentrop. Joachim—Elizabeth Arden, the beauty expert."

A tall, fair man with a disproportionately high forehead took her hand and bent over it in greeting. "Charmed," he said.

"How do you do," Elizabeth replied. "You Germans are getting around these days. I met Hermann Goering in Paris last weekend and now you."

She noticed his smile didn't reach his close-set eyes and got the impression he didn't like Goering. "We aim to make international friends," he said. "I consider myself very lucky to have been posted to London. Do you know the city well?"

"Not really, but Teddy is a wonderful guide," Elizabeth said, introducing him.

They chatted about their favorite parts of the city, and Elizabeth let her gaze wander around the room, taking in the extremely stylish women in long slender gowns. Wallis herself was wearing a narrow blue tunic printed with pink Chinese roses over a skirt so slim that she had to walk with tiny shuffling steps—a feat she achieved with poise.

A new guest arrived and all heads turned, Elizabeth's included. She realized with a frisson of excitement that it was David, the Prince of Wales, whose face often appeared on magazine covers with the headline "The World's Most Eligible Bachelor." He was shorter and slighter than she'd expected, with baggy eyes and yellow hair in a neat side parting. He kissed Wallis on the cheek and she whispered something in his ear that made him chuckle.

Elizabeth was desperate to be introduced but unsure of the etiquette, so she was delighted when Wallis led him over.

"David, this is Elizabeth Arden, who made her fortune by persuading us girls we need to spend outrageous sums of money on creams and potions in order to stay young-looking. A stroke of genius, don't you think?"

He met her eye. "Do you have anything to help aging men, Mrs. Arden?" he asked.

"You don't look as though you need any help from me, sir," she replied, then worried whether she should have called him "Your Majesty." And should she have curtsied?

"An American!" he exclaimed, hearing her accent. "Americans are by far my favorite type of women," he said, his pale blue eyes fixed on Wallis, who laughed gaily.

Elizabeth was no expert on such matters, but it seemed clear that he was in love with her. That explained why she was queen of London society. Wallis was definitely a connection worth cultivating.

"THEY'RE HAVING AN affair," Teddy told her over dinner in the Savoy. "It's an open secret in London society. He's single, of course, but she is married to Ernest Simpson, a shipping man, who turns a blind eye to their trysts. He was there this evening, but I doubt you were introduced."

"Gracious, what will become of them? Do you think she might divorce Mr. Simpson and be queen one day?" Elizabeth was fascinated.

Teddy began to explain the difficulties they could face under English law. A waiter brought their drinks.

Their table was right in the center of the bustling dining room. As Teddy spoke, Elizabeth was dimly aware of two women rising from a table behind her and walking toward the door. Truth be told, she was shortsighted but too vain to wear spectacles, so it was only as they passed her table that she recognized one of them as Helena Rubinstein.

"Too much hair color," she heard in a distinctive foreign accent as they swept past. The comment could only have been directed at her.

Elizabeth gripped her fork in fury, as if it were a weapon. *How dare she! What a bitch!*

She glanced at Teddy but he carried on talking and didn't appear to have heard.

CHAPTER 34

Helena

October 1936

"That was naughty," Ceska chided Helena, as they stood outside the Savoy waiting for a doorman to hail them a taxi.

It was surprising their paths did not cross more often, Helena thought. It could be because their social sets were quite different: her friends were modern and arty, while Elizabeth Arden's were old-fashioned and snobbish. When they happened to be in the same restaurant for once, she couldn't resist having a little snipe.

She was only on a quick trip to London to oversee the opening of a new factory, then she was traveling to Paris to talk to the architects working on the Île Saint-Louis house, where her lawyers had finally managed to evict the sitting tenants. She would see Stella, of course, but planned to avoid Edward entirely. The way she felt now, she had no desire ever to see him again.

ONCE WORK WAS finished, the Île Saint-Louis house was going to be the most magnificent of all Helena's homes. It had been built in 1641 by Louis Le Vau, chief architect to the Sun King, but had fallen into disrepair after flooding of the river over several decades. She was rebuilding from the ground up, only retaining the glorious front entrance with its original sculptures by Étienne Le Hongre.

It was a narrow house, five floors tall, and Helena planned to occupy the upper three. In the vast stairwell, she would hang a Brancusi bronze sculpture she had bought specially, entitled *Bird in Space*. Its smooth, elegant curves thrusting upward imitated a bird's body in flight. A glass bridge would connect two parts of the building, and the large roof terrace would be planted with a profusion of her favorite flowers. She planned to hold parties there for up to three hundred guests at a time, who could look out over the river as the sun set and the last boats chugged to their moorings for the night. The house was all about light and air and water.

Work on one floor of the building was already completed so Helena moved in. She sent notes to her favorite Parisian friends to say she was in town and began accepting invitations to dine out.

She found the talk on everyone's lips was of the new German leader, Adolf Hitler, who was passing laws curtailing the lives of Jewish citizens. Over the decades, Helena had encountered anti-semitism in many forms, but not with the shocking vitriol that was now being openly voiced. Jews were a convenient scapegoat for the world's economic woes, especially since there were a few wealthy figures, like herself, in the public eye. But the level of hatred was inexplicable when she looked back on the history of Judaism; Jews were one of the most persecuted of races yet they caused the least harm.

A cable arrived from the manager of her Berlin salon, who was handing in her resignation. Graffiti had been daubed on the salon window that read *"Kauft nicht bei Juden"*—"Don't buy from Jews"—and she claimed she was nervous that her family would be targeted if she continued to work there. Helena hired a replacement manager, but the graffiti still appeared and the German police would do nothing about it.

In a cinema one afternoon she watched a newsreel of Hitler speaking at a rally, and felt the hairs stand up all over her body at the harsh, angry tone of his rhetoric and the hysteria of the baying crowds, almost like a lynch mob. Europe was changing, and definitely not for the better.

WHILE IN PARIS, Helena was invited by her friend, the designer Jeanne Lanvin, to a card party at the home of her daughter, Marie-Blanche, Comtesse de Polignac. There were twenty-four guests, who dined around a long table in the Louis Quinze dining room, before Marie-Blanche split them into fours for bridge.

Helena was paired with a dark-haired man with craggy features and smiling eyes, who was introduced as Artchil Gourielli-Tchkonia.

"How on earth do you pronounce that? Tell me again." Helena listened hard, but knew she would never remember the name, so she announced, "I'm going to call you Archie."

"Archie sounds like a dog's name," he said, "but I will gladly answer to it. I'll even bark if you like."

"You should be more respectful," Marie-Blanche told Helena. "He's a Georgian prince in exile."

"A prince indeed?" She reappraised him. Perhaps he had the demeanor of a man born to privilege, but his face was warm and open.

"Where I come from, anyone who owns a few sheep has the right to call himself a prince," he explained, with an amused expression.

Helena suspected he was being modest. "I hope you play bridge well," she told him. "I'm very competitive and hate to lose."

"I hate to disappoint a lady, so I'll do my best," he promised, his eyes meeting hers.

Helena soon found he was a worthy partner. He watched her moves carefully and calculated what cards she held, leaving the game open for her at the right times and stepping in to take tricks when she couldn't. It felt as though they had been partners for some time instead of having just met that evening. They were betting small sums on the games, and soon she and Archie had amassed respectable winnings.

"It's not enough for a Bugatti, a Chanel gown, or a decent diamond, so I suggest we spend it on dinner tomorrow evening," he said. "How about it?"

Helena considered. She liked his warmth and good manners.

"Why not?" she agreed, and gave her address so he could pick her up.

Archie took her to a Left Bank bistro, with wooden floors and lamps that shed a cozy orange glow over the closely packed tables. They ordered snails in garlic, followed by beef tournedos, and he had a long discussion with the sommelier about grapes and vintages.

"Wine was first invented in Georgia," he explained once the bottle he favored had been ordered. "We are all experts there."

"I know very little about your homeland," Helena said, "except that it is presently under the control of the Soviet Union. I suppose that's why you are in exile."

"It is," he said. "I would love to show you my country, but sadly princes are not welcome under communism."

Helena noted the implied invitation. He clearly wanted their friendship to continue. She wasn't sure if his intentions were romantic—at the age of sixty-three, she made no assumptions, especially since he must be at least a decade younger. Was he a married womanizer, like Tom White?

"Georgia has its own unique alphabet," he told her, "so no one else can read our literature—although they certainly should." He talked about the art, the musical traditions, and told her it was a land of great natural beauty divided by the towering Caucasus Mountains. "There are hot springs where Georgians take health cures for everything from rheumatism to broken hearts. Perhaps you could steal the secret minerals for one of your face creams?"

"I like to call it borrowing rather than stealing," she said, noting that he must have done his research on her. "Thank you for the suggestion. A cream to cure broken hearts is an intriguing idea."

He knew Poland well and had many friends there. As they chatted, Helena mused how easy it felt to be with him, as if they had known each other for a long time. When she asked if he was married, he told her his life in exile had been too unsettled for him to wed. Helena didn't trust easily or often, but her instinct told her she could trust this man.

Before saying good night, they agreed to meet the following day at an exhibition of works by Pablo Picasso and Marie Laurencin. Helena had already arranged to sit for a portrait by the latter, and hoped to persuade the former to paint her too.

The short, arrogant Spaniard said he was far too busy to accept a portrait commission, but she was impressed when Archie persuaded him to do a pencil sketch of her on the spot. She didn't even have to pay for it!

Helena had been planning to sail back to New York before Christmas, but Archie convinced her to stay in Paris till the New Year. Lots of friends were throwing parties, and both her sons were going to be in town so she could introduce them. Above all, she was reluctant to leave this man, who was such good company. He asked nothing of her. She could just be herself.

She invited Horace and Roy for dinner with Archie, but they made excuses why they couldn't come, and she realized they were being loyal to their father. They seemed to have swallowed his story that he was the innocent party in the marital breakdown. *Poor Edward, abandoned by their heartless mother!* She hadn't told them about the maid in Greenwich, and all the other women she suspected he'd been unfaithful with, but perhaps she should one day.

"Don't worry about introducing me," Archie said. "You should dine with them on your own."

Helena made a date with them for the fourth of January, the first evening all were free, but two days before that, a telegram arrived from Harry Johnson that changed everything: *Please accept my resignation, effective immediately*. Helena cabled back asking why, and he replied that Elizabeth Arden had persuaded him to work for her.

Helena was incandescent. How dare she? She cabled Harry straight away: *Is this about money? I will pay more*. She changed her mind when he replied that Miss Arden had offered him the unprecedented salary of fifty thousand dollars a year. *Fifty!* No one was worth that! Instead, she got her New York lawyers to draw up a document asking Harry to guarantee not to divulge any professional secrets learned while in her employment. They sent it for him to sign but received no reply.

"I have to go," she told Archie. "My assistant has booked me a sailing for tomorrow morning. I'll have to cancel that dinner with the boys."

He nodded gravely, and didn't try to stop her. "Which is your favorite New York restaurant?" he asked.

She told him it was the Colony.

He took her hand and kissed it, letting his lips linger. "I promise to invite you for dinner at the Colony very soon," he said.

Helena stretched her arms around his neck and stood on tip-toe to kiss him on the lips. "I will hold you to that," she said—but her thoughts were already back in New York, as she worried about the damage that Harry's defection might cause, just when profits were rising. Just when she was winning.

Elizabeth Arden had taken their rivalry to a whole new level. Helena wasn't yet sure how, but she would deal with her in due course.

CHAPTER 35

Elizabeth

January 1937

P oaching Harry T. Johnson cost Elizabeth dearly. It wasn't just the unheard-of salary; he also insisted on a watertight contract for five years.

"Forgive me," he told her, "but a little bird told me you have a reputation for bouncing your staff."

"Only when they deserve it," she replied with a glare. "I want people around me who can achieve the impossible."

She was anxious about making such a long and expensive commitment, but she had arrived back from Europe the previous year to the direst sales figures yet. Since she divorced Tommy, she hadn't found the right sales director to take over and profits were plummeting. She summoned her acting manager for a meeting to explain himself, and ended up bouncing him after losing her temper when he implied that she had made some "unwise investments" without Tommy's "moderating influence."

"How dare you!" she yelled, throwing a teacup at him. "My husband *never* influenced me. Everything you see around you was built by me, and me alone."

She was aware that others in the company thought the same: that the company's success had been down to Tommy, not her, and it drove her around the bend. If only they knew!

The manager she bounced had been popular and several other key members of the sales team walked out in his wake, leaving her in dire need. Laney scoured the industry searching for a suitable candidate to head a new team, and Harry's name came up.

Elizabeth was wary at first. She had been furious about Madame Rubinstein's remark at the Savoy, and her aggressive tactics over the years, but was she ready to declare all-out war by poaching her staff? Where would that end?

Laney arranged a discreet preliminary meeting with Harry at Elizabeth's apartment, asking that he come in via the service elevator to avoid anyone spotting him. At first glance, Elizabeth liked the look of him. She preferred men who were tall and clean-shaven, with well-cut suits and impeccable manners, and on all those counts he fit the bill.

She gestured for him to sit and asked him to tell her why, in his opinion, her sales were floundering.

He didn't hold back: "According to my research, women buy your products as gifts for other women, because they have pretty packaging, but they buy Rubinstein products for themselves, since the perception is that they work just as well and cost slightly less. That means they make repeat purchases of hers through the year, but save yours for special occasions."

Elizabeth narrowed her eyes. He was probably right. Just the previous week, she had wandered into Saks Fifth Avenue to have a look at the beauty displays. Her packaging was by far the best. She insisted on printers matching the exact shade of "paradise pink" she favored, and would send labels back time and again till they achieved it.

Jars of her Eight Hour Cream were piled high and she picked one up. A sales assistant came over and said, "Between ourselves, it's good but it's very expensive. I can offer you another one that does the same for less." Before Elizabeth could reply the girl had picked up a jar of Helena Rubinstein's herbal cream. "Bring me your manager!" Elizabeth demanded, her voice shrill, and she insisted that he fire the assistant on the spot.

"What would you do about that?" she asked Harry. "Are you suggesting I reduce my prices?"

He shook his head. "No, definitely not, but perhaps you could launch some promotions: a free trial of a new product when customers spend more than ten dollars, for example. Women love free gifts. And some of your older packaging could benefit from an update."

"Which products?" she asked.

He listed them, and she nodded, agreeing with his assessments. He'd clearly given it some thought before the meeting.

"If I were to offer you the role of my sales director, what conditions would you require to accept?" she asked.

He sat back, crossing his legs. "Madame Rubinstein has given me a free rein over many areas of her business," he said. "In particular, I deal with the hiring and firing of her sales team. Would you allow me the same latitude?"

Elizabeth hesitated. She tended to be dictatorial over staff recruitment, but if her rival trusted this man, perhaps she could too. "I've lost most of my sales team recently," she said, "so if you accept the job, replacing them would be one of your first tasks."

"That should be easy enough," he said. "I have a very close-knit team at Madame Rubinstein's. If you can guarantee increased salaries for all, I'm sure they will come with me."

"How many are you talking about?" she asked.

He counted on his fingers, then said: "Eleven to start with."

Elizabeth gasped. Madame Rubinstein would go berserk if she stole eleven of her sales team. Her stomach twisted. Dare she do this? Was it worth the risk?

Harry was impressive. He had answers for all her questions, but he would not divulge details of her rival's operations. "You'll have to hire me if you want to know that," he replied in response to her in-depth probing. She liked the fact that he had professional discretion.

Before their second meeting, she had decided she wanted him. Then came the negotiations over his contract: money, terms and conditions, hours of work—his demands seemed never-ending. Elizabeth had never met such a tough dealmaker, but she told herself that was all for the good if he did the same on behalf of her company.

Finally, they reached agreement, Elizabeth wrote down the terms on a sheet of paper, which they both signed, then she offered him a whiskey to toast the deal. Once business was out of the way, the talk became personal. She asked about Harry's home life, and approved that he had a wife and two school-age children. Married men were much more stable employees. She asked about his family background: white, Protestant, middle-class folk from Chicago. That was fine. And then she worked around to asking about his soon-to-be ex-boss.

"I'm curious that Madame Rubinstein's husband lives in Europe while she lives in the States," she said. "One minute she is giving up her business here to spend more time with him, and the next she's bought it back again. What's the inside story?"

"She and Edward live separate lives," Harry told her. "I don't think she speaks to him much, except when it concerns their sons."

Elizabeth asked about the boys, and Harry told her they were now in their twenties. Roy was doing a business degree at Harvard while Horace was a tearaway who drank too much and crashed cars.

"Really?" She was surprised her rival didn't keep a tighter rein on her younger son.

"I think Horace is Madame's favorite," he told her. "He's a risk-taker, like her. A gambler."

Elizabeth stored that away. "Does she have a temper?" she asked. She imagined her rival being fiery and tempestuous.

"On the contrary, I don't think I've ever heard her raise her voice," Harry said. "She keeps up appearances in front of staff and clients and is always civil to me."

"If she's such a saint, I've got no idea why you're leaving," Elizabeth said, a tad sharply. "Is it just the money?"

Harry shrugged. "Children are expensive. Of course it's the money."

At least he was honest. Elizabeth decided to test his commitment to her with one further question. "I've often been curious about how Madame Rubinstein manages to copy my advertisements even before they have appeared, and launch new products that are remarkably similar to mine. Does she have a spy in our camp?" She had thought the leaks would dry up after she fired that marketing man during the war, but they appeared to have continued and it drove her crazy.

Harry made a face. "I'm not sure it's a good idea to tell you."

"Why not?" she asked, instantly wary.

"Because I suspect you will rush to react instead of handling the matter discreetly."

So there *was* someone. She knew it! "Tell me who it is!" she demanded. "I will react appropriately, you can be sure of that."

"Oh-kay," he agreed, looking doubtful. "Edith Brown has been reporting to Madame Rubinstein for as long as she has worked for you."

"Edith?" She was stunned. "You must be mistaken. She's a friend of mine."

He just looked at her, lips pursed.

"But she's been with me since the war," Elizabeth continued. Her brain was whirring as she thought of all the confidential documents that had passed across Edith's desk—sales figures, new product designs, everything. "Are you *sure* it's Edith?"

He gave an almost imperceptible nod. "I'm sorry."

In a fit of temper, Elizabeth hurled her glass across the room. It shattered against the wall, raining splinters. "Goddamn Judas!

I'll kill her with my bare hands," she shrieked, leaping to her feet. "I'll make her wish she'd never been born." She paced up and down, beside herself with fury, and Harry rushed to catch her arm and stop her from cutting herself on the broken glass.

"That's exactly why I didn't want to tell you," he admitted. "Don't do anything rash. It will make you look foolish if word leaks out that one of your most trusted employees has been spying on you. Perhaps we could use the situation to our advantage, by feeding her misinformation." He led her back to her chair. "Please try to calm down."

Elizabeth knew he was right, but she scarcely got any sleep that night as her mind raced over all the occasions she had taken Edith to the theater, bought dinner for her, promoted her, given her bonus payments at Christmas so she could buy something nice for her elderly mother . . . the betrayal made her sick to her stomach.

The next morning, she didn't bother with her yoga routine or the early meeting with Laney. She got dressed and hurried to the Aeolian Building so she was waiting just inside the door when Edith arrived.

"You evil, traitorous bitch," she shrieked, slapping her hard across the face.

Edith leapt back, clutching her cheek in shock.

"You know what this is about, don't you?" Elizabeth continued. "All those years of betrayal! How can you live with yourself?"

Edith gathered her wits and when she spoke, her voice was surprisingly steady. "I assume I'm being fired. Please can I collect my personal possessions from my desk?"

"You certainly cannot," Elizabeth replied. She realized Edith was wearing a coat she had given her, one she had bought for herself, then had second thoughts about. "And I want that coat back." She grabbed the lapel and tugged, hard.

Edith unfastened the coat and let it drop to the sidewalk, then turned and trotted off along Fifth Avenue, heels clicking.

"Don't think about setting foot in any of my salons ever again," Elizabeth screamed after her. "I'm calling my lawyers. I'll sue you. I'll make you wish you'd never been born."

She was trembling with rage when she got back indoors and her legs felt weak. She went to Edith's office and swept everything from her desk onto the floor, then sank down in her chair. How could she have been fooled by that goddamn Judas? Why hadn't she recognized the signs? Who else might be stabbing her in the back? Laney? Fabian Swanson? Could she trust Harry Johnson?

It wasn't just employees—she had been betrayed by her husband too. Edna scarcely ever called. And Bessie may have had an ulterior motive in befriending her. The only people she could trust were Gladys and Teddy Haslam. She had complete faith in both of them—but they were far away on the other side of an ocean.

She laid her head in her arms and wanted to weep, but stopped herself. No tears in the office—staff mustn't see her in a moment of weakness.

Instead she picked up the telephone and summoned her personal driver to collect her from the salon. She would go to her horses. Quiet time with them would calm her soul.

Besides, on reflection, it seemed a good idea to be out of town when Madame Rubinstein heard the news that she had poached eleven of her sales team.

CHAPTER 36

Helena

January 1937

"That woman is stealing all my people!" Helena wailed to Manka. "What to do, what to do."

She paced the floor of her Manhattan office, contemplating the resignation letters on her desk. Eleven of them, all at once! Harry had sabotaged her, and Elizabeth Arden had declared all-out war.

She would think about that later. The first priority was to get in touch with her wholesalers and retailers to assure them a new sales team would soon be in place. Meanwhile, Madame Rubinstein herself would be at the helm.

Edith turned up at the office the day after Helena's return, and she greeted her with a warm hug, then drew away, noticing a bruise on Edith's cheek.

"Did someone hit you?"

"Miss Arden found out I was working for you. I guess Harry told her."

Helena had suspected he would, but she was shocked that Miss Arden would resort to violence. "Did she hurt you?" She gestured at the mark. "Do you want to sue? I'll pay the legal fees." Helena would never hit anyone, no matter what the provocation.

Edith shook her head. "I'm fine. I don't blame her. But I

wondered if you have a job for me? I find myself unexpectedly unemployed. . . ."

"Of course, of course," Helena cried. "Take your pick. What would you like to do?"

"I enjoy management," Edith said. "I'm good at it, and I have an address book full of contacts. I kept a copy at home, in anticipation of the day Miss Arden would fire me." She didn't seem particularly shaken about it. She clearly had strong nerves.

"Welcome to the team," Helena said. "It will be a shame to lose the information you supplied, but I guess Miss Arden would smell a rat if we tried to place another spy there any time soon."

"She has a suspicious mind at the best of times," Edith agreed.

"How about her home?" Helena asked. "Do you know any of the staff there?"

Edith thought for a moment. "There's a maid called Molly who might report to us if we pay her. Shall I ask?"

"She won't have access to business documents," Helena mused, "but she can tell us who Miss Arden entertains, and how her mood is."

That would be interesting. Helena suspected that far from reveling in her triumph at luring Harry to work for her, Miss Arden would be feeling anxious. She had launched an attack and she must know enough about Helena to realize there would be a counterattack. She couldn't know when, or what form it would take, but she must know it was coming.

HELENA SETTLED DOWN to work. She was selling more products and making more money than Elizabeth Arden, and she intended to keep it that way. Harry had known her current sales figures and the customers she had special deals with, but she planned to shake up her operation long before he got comfortable at his new desk.

She knew how his mind worked: he would suggest special promotions, so she would preempt him with deals Miss Arden couldn't afford to match. Her Hormone line and her Herbal line were selling strongly, but new advertising campaigns for each would give them an extra boost, and she could offer trial sizes as a special incentive. She called in a different ad agency, because Harry had been in cahoots with the old one and she wanted a fresh approach.

Helena worked long hours in the office, from seven in the morning through to late evening, bringing in food prepared by her cook so she needn't take time off for meals. She thrived on challenges. This was her forte. She would take on Harry Johnson and Elizabeth Arden, and she would win.

Edith quickly became her closest advisor. Helena often asked her to read advertising copy or memoranda she was sending to retail managers, as her opinions were frank and wise.

"How many years did you work for Miss Arden?" Helena asked, hovering over her desk. "Almost twenty? I don't know how you put up with her."

"She always treated me well." Edith grinned and touched her cheek. "Until now, that is. She is generous to employees she trusts. One ex-beautician is wheelchair-bound after a car accident and can't work, but Elizabeth still pays her salary." She paused. "To be honest, I feel sorry for her. She's the loneliest woman in the world."

Feeling sorry for her hadn't stopped Edith from selling her secrets, Helena mused. Money came first for her. That was worth remembering.

Helena thought that she might have felt a wee bit sorry for Miss Arden until she poached her sales team; that had been a very big mistake. Now, there would be no sympathy and no mercy.

ONE AFTERNOON MALA told her there was a telephone call for her from someone who called himself "Prince Archie." Helena grinned. He must be in New York.

"Hello?" she bellowed down the receiver, never quite sure if she were speaking loudly enough. She hadn't shaken her dislike of telephones. "Is that you, Archie?"

"It is I," he said. "And I have a table for two booked at the Colony restaurant for eight this evening. I had to bribe the maitre d' a scandalous amount to secure it, so I'm begging you to join me."

"There's no need to beg." She laughed. "How can I refuse?"

She sent Mala to her apartment to pick an outfit and some jewels from the filing cabinet. She returned with one of Helena's favorite gowns, in lapis blue, and heaps of diamonds.

"I can't possibly wear all of these," Helena exclaimed. "I'll look like a chandelier."

"Aunt Helena, you know you love being the center of attention," Mala said. "Just wear them."

When she entered the restaurant, Archie rose and hurried over to kiss her on both cheeks, European style. She glanced around, mindful that she had once seen Elizabeth Arden there, but there was no sign. She wouldn't dare, not now.

"I crossed the ocean to have dinner with you," Archie told her as he took her arm and led her to their table. "And seeing you now, so radiant, has already made it worthwhile."

"You don't have other business in New York?" Helena asked, sliding into her seat.

"No, none," he said. "I'm staying with friends near Washington Square. I don't know the city well but they helped me to get here without being attacked."

She laughed. "It's not as dangerous as some folk make out, unless you happen to be a gangster. A few years ago, wars broke out among the types who earned their fortunes from bootlegging during Prohibition and have been forced to find new sources of livelihood now that alcohol is legal. But you're not a gangster, are you, Archie?"

He rolled his eyes. "I'm forty-two, far too old and far too cowardly for a life of crime."

Only forty-two! Helena was surprised. She'd thought he was perhaps a decade younger than her but that made him twenty-three years her junior. His interest in her was flattering but she hoped he never found out her true age. "I'm sure you're not a coward," she said. "Being forced into exile by the Soviets must have been difficult."

"It was," he said, darkness flashing across his eyes. "When Stalin led the Red Army across the Georgian border in 1921, I sent my mother and sisters to safety and stayed to fight, but it was a lost cause. Our cowardly government fled, and there was no overall leader of the resistance. Western powers didn't want to get involved so soon after the end of the Great War, so we were on our own."

"How did you escape?" Helena asked, trying to picture him as a young soldier.

"I was injured during a raid in 1923 and taken to safety. I have an impressive scar I hope I will have the chance to show you sometime." He winked suggestively.

Helena wondered where it might be but didn't presume to ask. "So you have disproved your earlier claim to be cowardly. Did your family manage to take much with them? Money and heirlooms and such like?"

"Most of it was seized," he said. "I'm no longer wealthy . . . but I checked the prices here before you arrived and I'm sure I have enough to pay for dinner, if that's what you're worried about."

Helena laughed. "I'm not worried," she said. "But I must warn you that I am very busy with work and I'm not sure how much time I can spend with you."

"I know you are under pressure," he said, "but if you can slip away from time to time, it will be my mission to make you laugh. Have I ever told you I love the sound of your laugh?"

On impulse, Helena reached across the table and took his hand. The words "I love you" nearly slipped out, but she checked herself at the last minute and said, "I like you."

"I hope so," he said, looking deep into her eyes as he squeezed her fingers. "I truly hope so."

He wasn't the type of man she would discuss business with. She couldn't imagine arguing with him. What they had was uncomplicated: he made a fuss of her and she liked being with him. After Edward, she hadn't expected or looked for another man, so to find one felt like an unexpected blessing.

GOOD HOUSEKEEPING MAGAZINE ran an article about Miss Arden, along with some photographs that showed her as a much younger woman than the one Helena had seen in the Savoy. They must be decades old. It mentioned her thoroughbred horses, her health spa in Maine, and her skill at yoga. A couple of weeks later, *Cosmopolitan* ran a similar piece, showing Miss Arden in a bathing suit, looking not a day over twenty-five. Helena snorted. Anyone could pull out an old photo; readers would get a shock if they saw what she looked like now.

Helena suspected Harry had urged her to raise her profile and become a figurehead for the company, the way she was for hers.

A *Fortune* magazine article came next, and it was particularly fruitful, with a detailed breakdown of Elizabeth Arden's international operations, and lots of information that was not in the public domain. Helena learned about the holding companies and foreign subsidiaries through which they channeled profit. It listed Miss Arden's annual US turnover as four million dollars, with her Fifth Avenue salon reported to take six hundred thousand dollars on its own. This was more than Helena's made and she strongly suspected the figures had been inflated. The journalist said that it was "tops in the 'treatments' cosmetics business" and the "Tiffany of the trade." Helena was particularly infuriated that Elizabeth Arden's salon was described as "more chic" than hers.

Helena immediately called a journalist she knew at a rival business magazine and offered her own interview.

"Unlike my competitors, I have always believed in investing in my products rather than their packaging," she said when he came to the salon. "Take Elizabeth Arden's Ardena Skin Tonic, for example. The raw ingredients in an eighty-five-cent bottle cost her three cents—I know this for a fact—and the bottle itself costs one cent, the paper label less than a cent. So her profit is eighty cents per bottle—sixteen times the cost." She paused to make sure the journalist had written down every word.

"I use more expensive ingredients, ones that I know to be effective," she continued once his pencil stopped moving. "My original Crème Valaze, launched thirty years ago, uses Carpathian herbs from my native Poland. Now my new premium products are using extract of water lily." She smiled at the journalist. "It's not cheap but our tests show remarkable antiaging qualities in the sap of the water lily. So beautiful!" She kissed her fingertips and waited for him to catch up.

"My packaging costs less than Miss Arden's," she continued, "and I use my personal art collection to decorate my salons, while she spends money on fancy gilt moldings and marble floors. My products cost more to produce, but I sell them for similar prices to hers, sometimes a little less. So my profit per item is less than hers, but I believe it is a wise investment because customers come back to me time and again; they know my products work. That's the difference between us in a nutshell."

Before he left, she gave the reporter a gift set of Herbal creams for his wife. She rubbed her hands. If he printed her words as she had dictated them, the article would put a certain someone's nose out of joint!

Next, she dictated letters to the Internal Revenue Service in the US, the Inland Revenue in the UK, and to the tax authorities in each of the countries cited, pointing out the figures quoted in the *Fortune* article about Elizabeth Arden and asking them to check if full taxes had been paid on those amounts.

When she heard that workers at Miss Arden's New York factory had joined a union, she wrote anonymously to the union leader, claiming that other factory workers in the beauty industry got twenty-seven dollars a week, that the factory boss got twenty-seven thousand dollars a year, and that Miss Arden had just spent twice that amount on thoroughbred horses. Her tactic paid off when, a month later, she heard they had gone on strike.

And that was only the beginning of her revenge, she thought. Miss Arden probably didn't know the proverb "Beware of still water, a still dog, and a still enemy." But she should.

CHAPTER 37

Elizabeth

April 1937

Elizabeth spluttered with rage as she read the *Fortune* article about her company. She had let Harry talk to the journalist and he'd shared financial information that she had never wanted or expected to be made public.

"It's a financial magazine," Harry argued. "What did you think they wanted to talk about? Shades of lipstick?"

"Discussing money is vulgar," Elizabeth said. She liked to keep details of her fortune as private as possible; she squirmed to think of her clients reading the article and realizing she was richer than they were.

She was even more furious when she saw Madame Rubinstein's riposte the following week, claiming that she invested in premium ingredients rather than fancy packaging.

"Let her produce these goddamn Carpathian herbs she's always spouting on about. I simply don't believe it. Did you ever see them?" she demanded of Harry. "Does she have regular shipments from Carpathia? Does such a place even exist?"

Harry said he hadn't been involved in the production side of the business so couldn't comment.

"It's all hogwash!" Elizabeth grumbled. "Everything about her is an illusion. I don't think she has a medical degree, I don't think she uses the ingredients she says she does, and her creams can't hold a candle to ours."

Her misgivings about the *Fortune* article were compounded when she received a letter from the IRS saying they wanted to inspect her books. "I didn't believe the week could get any worse," she moaned to Laney. "Give me strength."

Three weeks later, she had a tax demand from the Brazilian revenue service and two months later her New York factory workers went on strike.

"Bounce them all!" Elizabeth demanded. "Unemployment is still sky-high. We can replace them with people who will be grateful for the work."

The factory manager argued that it took weeks to train new workers. Even Fabian Swanson, her faithful chemist, urged her to reconsider. At last a compromise was negotiated that involved increasing basic wages considerably.

Elizabeth was alarmed. Money was hemorrhaging from her bank accounts. It was as if she had opened an artery. Harry Johnson had been brought in to rescue the business but instead it seemed he was trying to bankrupt her. Could he still be working for Madame Rubinstein on the sly?

She confronted him and they had a furious argument.

"How dare you question my integrity!" he yelled. "I'm doing my best to turn sales around, but it takes time, and it's not helped when you obstruct me at every turn."

"You seem to be dragging your heels," Elizabeth accused him. "I've come across faster tortoises." Had it not been for his five-year contract, she would have bounced him on the spot. "Get on with the job, but be very sure I've got my eye on you."

Laney said she thought he was honorable—but Laney had trusted Edith so her judgment wasn't infallible. Elizabeth felt as if she were losing her mind. All she wanted to do was spend time with her horses, but how could she leave Manhattan when her company was in the hands of imbeciles, liars, and crooks?

She had to keep an eye on every last detail. No one could be trusted. No one.

WHEN ELIZABETH WAS invited to a party thrown by *Cosmopolitan* magazine, her first instinct was to worry that Madame Rubinstein might also be invited. She got Laney to check, and only sent her acceptance once she'd received firm assurances that her rival was not on the guest list.

Still, she felt nervous stepping into the ballroom at the Biltmore Hotel, with Harry on her arm. Madame Rubinstein hadn't been invited to that *Vogue* party back in 1917, but still she weaseled her way in. What would she do if they came face-to-face? Might she attack her, or scream abuse at her? Harry would have to protect her; then she'd see where his true loyalties lay.

She glanced around the room. The writers Theodore Dreiser and Upton Sinclair were chatting with each other, and she recognized some magazine illustrators, but before she could start to mingle, she was accosted by the advertising sales director, a man with whiskey breath who appeared from his waistline to have eaten too many business lunches. He began with small talk, asking after her horses, but she knew his goal was to persuade her to spend more on advertising in the magazine.

"May I cut in?" asked a tall man with broad shoulders and sleek silvery-white hair, who reminded her, incongruously, of a polar bear. He turned to Elizabeth. "I see no one has offered you a drink yet, Miss Arden. May I get you a glass of champagne? Or some other tipple?"

"Champagne would be lovely," she said. "And who exactly are you?"

"Tom White," he said, beckoning a waiter, then extending his hand to shake hers. "I'm general manager of Hearst Corporation. I was sent here tonight to rescue guests from being bored to death by our employees trying to talk business. I'm sure you get enough of this kind of pressure during working hours and prefer to let your hair down in the evenings."

"To be frank, Mr. White, I work most evenings. I expect you do too." He had good skin for a man, she noted: unlined apart from a few laughter creases at the eyes. Perhaps he was younger than the white hair indicated.

He handed her a glass of champagne from a waiter's tray and took one himself. "Shall we sit?" he asked, gesturing at some chairs set out along the side of the room. Elizabeth was glad to follow him. The hip she had broken as a teenager ached when she had to stand for long periods, and it was getting worse as the years passed.

"I've long wanted to meet you," he said, clinking his glass against hers. "I hear we are fellow horse lovers. Tell me, what drew you to the racing world?"

"I was born with a whinny in my ear," she replied. "My father had a farm just outside Toronto, and I loved helping with the horses. They were my best friends when I was young. Other girls could be treacherous, but horses were always sympathetic."

"What kind of farm?" he asked, and Elizabeth lied, telling him her father had five thousand acres, and grew wheat, corn, beets, and kale, as well as raising cows and chickens.

He whistled. "That's big," he said. "I guess you grew up around draft horses rather than thoroughbreds?"

"Yes, but thoroughbreds are my passion," she said. "They're such magnificent creatures. And once you start visiting the tracks, you get hooked on the drama. Are you a racing man, Mr. White?"

"I never have time to get to the track, but I often listen to the racing results on my radio set."

"Ah, that's not the same thing at all," Elizabeth said. "You need to hear the roar of the crowd. For me, the horses' excitement is infectious. All my babies love to race: they're straining at the bit when we lead them out."

He regarded her, with a searching expression. "Were you not worried by the reputation of some tracks? I know the industry has cleaned itself up a lot since the bad old days of race fixing, but I believe there is still horse tampering and sabotage by the kind of men you really don't want to mess with."

Elizabeth had seen some illegal tactics employed during races—barging, holding on to an opponent's saddle blanket, trying to throw a horse off its stride—and she asked if that's what he meant.

"Sure," he said, "but worse than that. I heard of a case where a sponge was inserted up the nose of a champion horse the night before a race. It wasn't detected and the horse ran, but it came in at the back of the field because the poor creature couldn't breathe properly."

Elizabeth was horrified. "I've never heard of that, but I certainly make sure security is tight at my stables. No one can wander in who isn't on my staff."

Tom sipped his drink. "The mobsters sometimes lean on jockeys and trainers, bribing or threatening them to throw a race. You need to be very careful who you hire."

"Why would jockeys agree to lose a race? Don't they care about their reputations?" Elizabeth always wanted to win, no matter what, and couldn't understand the mentality of anyone who didn't.

"I think they care more about not getting their legs broken," Tom said. "But here I am being a curmudgeon when actually I am jealous that you have the time and money to indulge in your passion. Tell me, where do you stable your horses?"

"They're currently at Belmont Park on Long Island. Why do you ask?"

He smiled at her, a warm, twinkly kind of smile. "Because I wondered if I might invite myself to see them one day. I love horses, and it would be a good excuse to spend some time with you."

Elizabeth was momentarily speechless. Was he flirting? She would be sixty the following year and felt every day of it. Could he be after her money? She supposed he must get a decent salary from William Randolph Hearst, but she undoubtedly had more. He must be married—he looked like a man who would have a wife—but perhaps he was divorced? Did she want another man in her life? She didn't trust men—or women either, come to that. All these thoughts passed through her mind in seconds.

"How about this weekend?" he asked, when she didn't reply. "I could drive us there, and bring a picnic. Would Saturday suit?"

Elizabeth was thrown by the offer and couldn't think of a reason to refuse. Did he see it as a romantic assignation? Surely not. He was a horse lover, like her. That's all.

ON THE WAY to Belmont Park, gusts of wind buffeted the car and rain obscured the view through the windshield so Tom had to slow right down or risk going off the road.

"I'm sorry," Elizabeth said. "I should have arranged better weather for our outing."

"Not at all. I came for your company and couldn't be happier," he replied.

Was he a smooth talker with all the ladies? she wondered. What did he want from her? During the drive, he asked how she had started out in the beauty business and she told him the sanitized story she always told, omitting the fights with Eleanor Adair and Mrs. Hubbard. Out of the corner of her eye, she watched his strong forearms on the steering wheel. He was a stylish dresser, even in casual clothes.

The weather had not improved by the time they reached Belmont Park. He held an umbrella to shelter her as she scurried inside the stables, then he went back to the car to fetch a wicker picnic hamper. She introduced him to the horses first: Lord Boswell, Cherry Red, Old Gold, and her first-ever baby, the gorgeous Leading Lady. . . . She had twenty-one thorough-breds now, and each was a darling.

He had brought a pocketful of sugar cubes to feed them from the palm of his hand, but she stopped him.

"Oh no," she warned. "My babies aren't allowed sugar. If you want to feed them, I'll find some carrots."

He laughed. "So your healthy ethos extends to your animals? Quite right too!"

They sat on bales of hay to eat their picnic. Tom opened the wicker basket with a flourish and she saw he had brought a jar of caviar with some tiny corn crackers, two whole poached lobsters, and a bottle of champagne, along with two crystal glasses.

"All my favorites," she exclaimed, astonished. "How on earth did you guess?"

He laughed. "I had a little help," he replied, and admitted he had telephoned Laney to ask for tips.

Elizabeth was impressed. "I like the meticulous preparation. You're a man after my own heart."

He gave her a sideways look, and she felt embarrassed. Perhaps she shouldn't have mentioned her heart.

After eating, they spent time grooming the horses, and he laughed at the way she perfumed their manes and rubbed expensive cream into their hooves. "They're almost as beautiful and fragrant as their owner," he said.

All day long, he never missed a chance to compliment her, and Elizabeth was enjoying herself but feeling puzzled at the same time. Was he like this with every woman? What did he want from her?

On the drive back, he suggested they go for dinner at a little restaurant he knew, but she hesitated. What if someone recognized her? Dining out with a man so soon after her divorce could lead to all kinds of gossip and rumors. On the other hand, she didn't feel ready for the day to end.

"Why don't you come to my apartment and I'll ask the cook

to fix us supper?" she asked, then blushed. Would he think she was inviting him to seduce her?

He kept his eyes fixed on the road ahead. "That sounds delightful," he said.

Her cook grilled steaks for them, and Elizabeth mixed two highballs, while he stood admiring the view over Central Park from her roof terrace.

She handed him his drink and they clinked glasses, then stood in silence looking out into the dusk. From the first sip, she felt giddy as a schoolgirl. What would she do if he tried to kiss her? With a start, she realized she wanted him to. She had never felt desire like this for any man: certainly not Tommy, and not even Teddy Haslam. She moved a little closer so her arm brushed his, and the sensation gave her a jolt.

Her maid interrupted them to announce supper was ready. As they ate at one end of her long dining table, he talked about his work with the Hearst Corporation, which involved a lot of travel around the country. He often flew in his employer's small planes, but hadn't gotten over his nerves about being buffeted by the wind, with thousands of feet of empty space below.

"I never look down," he said. "And I usually throw up at least once on each flight."

Elizabeth watched his face as he talked and wondered what he wanted from her. Why was he here? Could she trust him?

After dinner, they returned to the sitting room and she poured them both brandies. She had drunk more liquor in a day than she generally drank in a month, and it heightened her state of nervous excitement. Tom sat beside her on the couch and took her hand, gently, as if it were a normal, everyday thing to do. She was acutely aware of the touch of his fingers, and the bergamot scent of his hair oil, combined with a muskiness from the horses, which had impregnated his clothes.

"I could easily fall in love with you," he said, his voice barely more than a whisper.

She giggled, nervously. What was the correct response? Please do?

"There is nothing I would like more," he continued, "than to whisk you into your bedroom and make passionate love to you."

Elizabeth clasped her free hand over her mouth, feeling shy as a virgin. "Why . . ." she began.

"But I'm sure you would refuse me, and you would be quite right too. I expect you know that I have a wife, Virginia." Elizabeth scarcely dared to breathe, as she listened hard to every word. "We married very young and lead quite separate lives. Generally, we don't see each other from one week to the next." She opened her mouth to say that divorce was not the trauma she had expected it to be, when he continued: "But we are both Catholics so we will never divorce."

Her heart plummeted. Why had he spent the day with her and plied her with champagne and compliments if he wasn't free? How could it be that when she found a man she felt such an intense attraction toward, she couldn't have him? She struggled to regain her composure.

"I understand," she whispered. "But perhaps we can still be close"—she sought the right word—"friends."

He raised her hand to his lips and kissed it tenderly, making her skin tingle. "I would love that. But now I must leave before I try to do something we would both regret." He stood, leaving his untouched brandy on a side table.

Elizabeth was stunned. After he had gone, she picked up his brandy, took a gulp, then burst into tears. It was all too much. How cruel to meet someone at her stage of life, after all the years of disappointment and loneliness, and not be allowed to love them. He hadn't given her any hope of a future.

In bed she lay awake, mulling over the conversation, hugging a pillow, imagining what might have happened if she had urged him to stay. Had he wanted her to? Should she have?

Tom sent a note the following day, with two dozen fragrant

pink roses—American Beauty, her favorites. *I had a wonderful time yesterday and only hope I didn't overstep the mark. Please tell me you forgive me*, he wrote.

She telephoned him straight away. "There's nothing to forgive," she said. "Every sentiment you expressed was entirely mutual. I wondered if we might have dinner again soon?"

"Of course," he replied. "I can't wait."

She wouldn't let this man slip away, she decided. Maybe if he fell in love with her, he would overcome his religious scruples about divorce. If not, was she prepared to be his lover? *Perhaps*, she thought, with a thrill. *Perhaps I would.*

CHAPTER 38

Helena

June 1937

Helena and Archie began a transatlantic romance. He stayed with his Washington Square friends for a month at a time, then, when he sailed back to Paris, Helena visited him there, so they never spent too long apart. They had more in common than she had first realized. His knowledge of modern art proved as extensive as hers, and his tastes were similar: they both loved Picasso, Braque, and Brancusi, the new artists pushing the boundaries of form. They enjoyed fine dining, and she was glad to note that although he was a wine expert, he wasn't a big drinker. They played bridge regularly and were well matched as partners, although she was the more competitive of the two.

The building work on her Île Saint-Louis home was almost complete, and Archie helped her to choose artworks, furniture, and fittings for it. Edward had always left interior design to her, but Archie had a good eye and she liked having someone with whom to visit galleries and discuss these decisions.

He was about six inches taller when she was in heels, the perfect height for her to rest her head on his shoulder. They kissed and embraced but he didn't push for more intimate contact, and that suited her. It wasn't a wild passion, like her youthful romance with Stanislaus, or the early days with Edward; instead it felt comfortable, affectionate, and unchallenging. It calmed her to breathe in his scent, a woody, exotic one he had brought from Georgia. "Made with Georgian herbs," he teased, and she made a mental note to have it analyzed.

As the days passed, Helena had an inkling he was going to propose. On several occasions he seemed to be working up the courage to say something, then backed down. She didn't know how she felt about getting married again. Edward's betrayal had made her cynical about men.

"If you are attacked when you are walking through a park," she told Stella, "it makes you wary of walking through that park again."

"I've asked around about Archie," Stella replied, "and no one has a bad word to say about him." She said there had been one other lady he used to dine out with several years earlier, but Archie had told Helena about her, and promised it was over.

Could he be after her money? He always insisted on paying the bill in restaurants, saying it was "a gentleman's duty," even though it was obvious she was by far the wealthier of the two. She liked his male pride; he contrasted with Edward, who had never been shy about spending her money.

As she began to think seriously about marrying Archie, she decided to set her mind at rest by hiring a private detective. No one need know. She just had to be sure—or as sure as anyone could be—that he wouldn't betray her.

The detective's report made for comforting reading. It said that Archie's family's claim to the throne of Georgia was tenuous, and it was unlikely he would ever take power there even if the Soviets left. Helena wasn't bothered about that one iota. If she wanted a crown, she would buy one. It said he lived on a small stipend from a family trust and had no other source of income. He had already told her as much, and she didn't mind. Finally, and most important, it said that there was no sign of any other woman in his life, only her. That made her very happy.

When Archie plucked up the nerve to ask if she would consider marrying him, he was so tense she yearned to put him out of his misery straight away, but something held her back.

"Can we get engaged first without setting a wedding date?" she asked. "I need time to get used to the idea."

"Of course," he said, with obvious relief that he hadn't been turned down flat. "I haven't bought you a ring, as I know you have strong feelings about your jewelry, but perhaps we could choose one together?"

He couldn't have been more perfect, she thought. Letting her choose her own ring was a masterstroke. She thought of all the revenge jewels she had bought during her marriage to Edward, and vowed to get rid of them. They had negative associations and now she was ready to start afresh.

HELENA WAS QUITE content to be engaged without getting married. It meant she and Archie could spend time alone together without giving the scandalmongers any reason to gossip. They were treated as a couple and invited to dinners together, but she didn't have to share his bed. Since the hysterectomy, the thought of making love didn't appeal. She was too old for all that; her back hurt, and her digestion was cranky. Truthfully, she would rather get a decent night's sleep.

Not long after their engagement was announced, Edward wrote requesting a divorce so he could remarry. Helena asked around and found out that the girl he intended to wed was Swiss, and just twenty-two years old. That made her furious. He was sixty-eight! How dare he marry a girl who was young enough to be his granddaughter! It was sick and *wrong*. She was embarrassed for him, and embarrassed to be associated with him. Archie was younger than her but not by that much, and at least they *looked* as if their ages were similar.

"Let him have his happiness," Archie persuaded her. "And we can have ours. Who cares what the rest of the world thinks?"

He was right, of course. Helena fought off the urge to wreak one last piece of revenge on Edward by refusing him a divorce. The decree was granted in February 1938, and she made sure he didn't get a single additional cent beyond what she had already given him. In June that year, she and Archie got married, with Mala as her bridesmaid and her sons as best men, and it was truly one of the happiest days of her life.

Over two hundred American friends came to the wedding ceremony, then they held a reception in Paris for their European friends, before sailing to South America for a prolonged honeymoon. Helena was building a new salon in Rio de Janeiro and wanted to be there for the opening.

"I might have guessed you would choose our honeymoon location to tie in with your business interests," Archie teased. He didn't mind, though. He was the most easygoing, congenial man she had ever met.

She and Archie shared a bed now but, aside from a brief union on the wedding night, he did not attempt to make love to her. He massaged her back when it played up, and rubbed her feet after she'd had a long day, and there was lots of physical affection, but it seemed their libidos were compatible, like so much else.

When they discussed where they would live as a married couple, Archie said he preferred Paris to New York, but Helena felt Europe was unsafe for anyone Jewish. The antisemitic rhetoric emerging from Germany was growing ever more strident: Jews were caricatured as "vermin," as "sly and money-grabbing," and as "only out for themselves." Hitler's frequent pronouncements encouraged those who might previously have kept their anti-Jewish sentiments to themselves.

Helena was shocked when she started receiving death threats at her Berlin salon—"*We're coming for you. Watch your backs, Jewish pigs.*"—but the police took no action when she reported them. It came as no surprise when she heard her salon had been seized by the authorities. She tried to hire lawyers to take legal action against the seizure, but it was hopeless: no one would take the case.

"We will always have the Île Saint-Louis house," she told Archie, "but I think we should make our main home in New York until the Germans get rid of their terrifying madman of a leader." She decided to start looking for somewhere grander, with plenty of space where they could entertain. She didn't intend to use the title "Princess"—she was already a Queen of Beauty Science—but there was no harm in raising their living standards to suit Archie's royal status.

BACK IN NEW York, Helena invited Carmel for cocktails so they could catch up on their news. Carmel was enjoying her new role at *Harper's Bazaar*, where she had been allowed to make all the design and editorial changes she had longed to make at *Vogue*.

"I'm getting used to working with my brother," she said. "It was strange at first, because he used to boss me around when we were children. Now he holds the purse strings for the Hearst Corporation, so I need to ask his permission for any major expenditure. But he's very fair, and hasn't abused his 'elder sibling' status so far."

"He seems decent," Helena said. "But he must be tough-minded to run that vast empire."

"I heard some gossip that will interest you," Carmel said. "It seems Tom has been having clandestine dinners with Elizabeth Arden."

Helena was stunned. "But he's married!"

Carmel spread her hands in a "so what" gesture. "Tom likes women and they like him. But you'd think a woman in her position would be a little more careful. She has many clients who would take their custom elsewhere if the news leaked out."

Helena sipped her drink, mulling this over. "Do you think they are having an affair? I thought she was supposed to be a lesbian?"

Carmel laughed. "I can't vouch for Elizabeth's sexual proclivities—Tom hasn't shared that with me—but I know they are seeing each other often. Alone. At night. In her apartment."

Helena had thought she understood her rival. She had judged her to be conventional, old-fashioned, and snobbish, but this liaison showed her in an entirely new light. "Has Tom had affairs in the past?"

"Oh yes," Carmel said with certainty. "A mistress named Cissy Patterson was obsessed with him for years. She approached his wife, Virginia, and offered her a million dollars to divorce him, but Virginia refused. She loves him too, she said."

"That must have been very hurtful for Virginia." Helena's sympathies were always with the wronged wife. "Why would Tom cheat on her?"

"Virginia is beautiful and smart and kind. She's a terrific wife and mother, but my brother likes a challenge. It's all about conquest. He's broken countless women's hearts while married to Virginia, and he has a particular taste for millionairesses. It feeds his male ego." Carmel sounded almost proud of him.

"I had a lucky escape then," Helena said. "I had a feeling he was flirting with me at your party."

Carmel laughed. "I'm sure he was! I would have warned you not to get involved if I thought you were tempted. But I don't see any need to warn Miss Arden. Especially since she had no scruples about stealing your sales team."

"I have news on that front," Helena said, a grin twitching at her lips. "Harry Johnson telephoned me last week and asked if he could have his old job back. He said working with Miss Arden is insufferable. She watches him like a hawk, insisting on signing off on every tiny decision, and she loses her temper and screams if things don't go her way." The grin became wider. "I had to tell him that his former position has been filled."

"Have you found someone?" Carmel asked.

"Tell me, what did you think of Miss Arden's ex-husband Tommy Lewis?" Helena replied, cocking her head to one side.

Carmel was puzzled. "I liked him, I guess. He had good manners and could mix well in any company. Why do you ask?"

Helena was gleeful: "He is going to be my new sales director, starting next week. What do you think Miss Arden will make of that?"

Carmel snorted with laughter. "I imagine she will be foaming at the mouth. What fun! I only wish I could be in the room when she hears the news."

Helena rubbed her hands. She didn't need to be there. She could imagine.

CHAPTER 39

Elizabeth

April 1939

Tom White called Elizabeth late one afternoon to ask if she was free for dinner. "I've got something important to tell you," he said, his tone serious.

Elizabeth's heart leapt. *He's leaving Virginia*, she thought. *It has to be that.*

She had been hinting for ages that he should. They'd been meeting secretly for several months and, although he hadn't made any attempt to seduce her, romance was definitely in the air.

"I can picture you as a little girl," he'd said one evening, as they sat on the couch, faces inches apart. "I bet you worked hard at school and had big dreams that made you different from your classmates. You were always driven, weren't you? And with that came loneliness because you couldn't admit your ambition." He stroked her cheek with a finger.

She nodded, a lump in her throat. "It's as if you've known me all my life," she said.

"I wish I had," he whispered. "At least, I wish I had met you earlier . . . before . . ." His voice tailed off.

He meant before he married Virginia. If only they had met then . . . Still, she hoped she could persuade him it wasn't too late for happiness, if he could overcome his religious scruples.

She didn't miss a chance to hint at what it might be like if they were together.

"Wouldn't it be wonderful if we could spend Christmas in Maine?" she'd asked the previous December. "Just think: long snowy walks, the scent of pine trees, crackling log fires, and deep, glorious peace. Why not find a way to come with me?"

"I'm sorry," he'd replied. "It does sound idyllic, but my wife has invited our extended family to stay and I can't get out of it."

He gave her a diamond bracelet as a Christmas present, and slipped out to telephone her on Christmas Day, knowing she was spending it alone, but for Elizabeth that wasn't enough.

"How about a Caribbean vacation?" she asked in January. "A week of winter sunshine would do us both a world of good."

"It would be marvelous," he said, "but I can't possibly take the time off work. We're too busy. Maybe in a month or two."

And now he had "something important" to tell her. It had to be good news.

"Of course I'm free, dearest," she replied. "Come to my apartment at eight."

She telephoned the cook and asked her to make his favorite pot roast, and she dressed in a new pink chiffon gown, with a scooped neckline.

When Tom arrived, looking flustered, it was quarter after eight. She poured him a whiskey and soda, no ice, just the way he liked it, and they sat down to eat, since the beef was ready. Elizabeth's heart was pounding as she speculated on what he had to tell her, but she forced herself to wait.

"This is excellent," he said, licking his lips.

Elizabeth tried a tiny mouthful of beef, but nervous anticipation stole her appetite.

"I heard something today from my sister Carmel that I thought I should pass on," Tom said, taking a sip of whiskey. "Before you heard it anywhere else."

She tilted her head. "Do you mean Carmel Snow, the editor of *Harper's Bazaar*? Is she your sister?"

"I thought you knew," he said.

What could Carmel have heard, and how did it affect her? Elizabeth frowned.

"It seems Helena Rubinstein is hiring your ex-husband as her new sales manager," he continued, watching her face.

Elizabeth dropped her fork to the plate, splashing gravy on her gown. "Tommy?" She was stunned. Was he allowed to do that? She counted: yes, the five years' noncompetition clause he'd signed on their divorce was up. "Oh no!" She clasped her head in her hands in despair.

"I guessed you might be upset," Tom said gently, "but does it matter? You have Harry Johnson now, and after five years Tommy can't know any compromising information about the company."

Elizabeth felt like crying. "Is that what you came to tell me?" she asked, a catch in her voice.

"Yes, I thought I should let you know before you read it in the press." He attempted to cheer her up. "From what you've told me, it will be no time before he's bedding her beauticians."

Elizabeth pressed the heels of her hands into her temples. She couldn't decide what she was more upset about: Tommy working for Madame Rubinstein, or the fact that the "something important" Tom came to tell her was not the news she had been hoping for. She couldn't express the latter, though.

"You don't understand," she whispered. "Tommy knows *everything*: he knows how the operation runs; he knows domestic details; he knows private things about me that no one else knows." She remembered that her brother Will had told Tommy all about their poverty-stricken background; she didn't want her rival finding out about *that*. "Madame Rubinstein will use anything to her advantage. She's only doing this to get revenge because I hired her sales director."

Tom chewed another mouthful of beef. "I've met her a couple of times and found her very civilized and cultured. She
doesn't strike me as the vindictive type."

"You're wrong," Elizabeth hissed, close to tears. "She's underhanded, devious, and capable of anything. In my experience,
Jews only care about money. They don't mind who they hurt so
long as they get their own way."

Tom put his cutlery down with a clatter. "Elizabeth, sentiments like that are beneath you. Some of my closest friends are
Jewish, and I do business with many Jews, none of whom are
remotely the way you describe. I'm frankly a little shocked by
your attitude."

She shook her head, wishing she could take back the words.
"I didn't mean it, Tom. I'm upset. Just ignore me."

She found it hard to make conversation during the remainder of the meal, and didn't try to persuade Tom to stay for a
nightcap. She was cross with him. He could have no idea how
she felt about him or he wouldn't have raised her hopes tonight
by saying he was coming to tell her "something important." And
the fact that he spoke up for Madame Rubinstein was another
black mark against him. She'd thought he understood her in
a way no one else ever had, but tonight his words had been
thoughtless and hurtful.

She had been in a foul mood when she heard her rival had
married a prince. She had always considered herself the classier
of the two of them, while that woman was vulgar and common,
so it was insufferable that she could use the title "Princess."

And now she had hired Tommy. There was no question it
was revenge, designed to upset her. She couldn't bear to think
of him having cozy tête-à-têtes with that woman and telling her
all about their life together. The idea made her ill. She had to
escape New York. Perhaps she would bring forward her spring
trip to Europe. She'd go to see Gladys, then to London to visit
Teddy. That would lift her spirits; at least, it always had in the

past. And perhaps Tom would miss her so much that he'd at long last rethink his attitude to divorce.

ELIZABETH FOUND THE atmosphere in Paris charged, as if the air pressure was higher than normal. The weather was unusually warm for early spring, and Parisians were wearing summer clothing, but everyone seemed bad-tempered. She overheard arguments in the street that she couldn't make out with her poor French. Bad smells emanated from the drains, even in the smart 8th *arrondissement*. A dog snarled at her as she walked across the sidewalk to her salon, and for a moment she feared it was going to bite her.

Gladys wasn't sympathetic when she described her feelings for Tom White. "What are you thinking, Elizabeth? You mustn't encourage a married man. I'm astonished you're seeing him alone in your apartment. It's very wrong of you."

Elizabeth had been sure Gladys would understand, and was stung by the criticism. It left a bad feeling between them. "I'm lonely," she wanted to say. "I deserve happiness too." But she bit back the words. Gladys was happily married; of course she would defend the institution.

One morning Gladys mentioned that Wallis Simpson, now the Duchess of Windsor, was having a facial in a private room at the salon, and Elizabeth popped in to greet her. They hadn't seen each other since the KT hour in London a few years earlier, before the prince abdicated his throne to marry her.

"Congratulations on your marriage . . . Your Highness," she said, hesitant, unsure how Wallis expected to be addressed these days.

Wallis turned those piercing blue eyes on her. "It's been rather a furor, as you probably read in the papers. Thank goodness for the oasis of calm here in your salon." Her hair was pulled back in a turban and her skin glowed from the facial.

"Are you having any other treatments today?" Elizabeth asked. "Massage? A manicure perhaps?"

"I'd love to, but I'm meeting the duke for lunch at the Ritz, along with some German friends." She glanced at a jeweled wristwatch, then riffled in her bag and pulled out a gold lipstick tube.

Elizabeth remembered reading in the press that the Duke and Duchess of Windsor had been to Germany to meet Adolf Hitler, and asked about the trip. "What's Hitler like in the flesh?"

"The Führer is a man of great magnetism," Wallis said. "A forceful character." She shrugged. "He's certainly solving Germany's problems. My husband was very impressed with his innovative solutions to the housing shortage." She opened the lipstick and carefully painted her lips dark berry red.

Elizabeth wasn't sure what she was referring to, but she knew that many Jews had been arrested and forced to leave their homes and businesses, in a manner that sounded cruel and distressing. Surely that wasn't the solution she meant. "People seem to find him charismatic," she said.

"I wouldn't go that far." Wallis caught her eye in the mirror. "I don't think he likes women much."

"Oh really?" Elizabeth returned her gaze. "I guess no one's perfect."

Wallis peeled off the turban to reveal her dark hair scraped into a neat center parting and coiled behind each ear. "I must rush. Can't keep the Nazis waiting. Enjoy your stay in Paris."

She hurried out to a waiting car and Gladys appeared by Elizabeth's side. "She comes two or three times a week and never pays the bills. Are you sure you don't want me to send an invoice?"

Elizabeth shook her head. "No, royals don't pay. Not even royals without a throne." That train of thought reminded her of Madame Rubinstein's new husband and she scowled.

Over dinner with Gladys, Henri, and some of their friends that evening, Elizabeth repeated Wallis's views on Hitler and asked their opinion.

"The man's a genius," Henri said. "He's saving the German economy, after two decades of punitive reparations, and he's simultaneously solving the Jewish problem. I think your American friend is wrong about him not liking women. Perhaps he simply didn't like *her*."

Elizabeth glanced at the other guests, but no one demurred. "The American press seems rather alarmed at him annexing Austria and marching into Czechoslovakia. There's a lot of talk that it could lead to war," she said. "Don't you think he's gone far enough?"

"You've been listening to propaganda," another guest said. "Von Ribbentrop is a personal friend of mine and he assures me the territorial acquisitions are at an end. Hitler wants to live peaceably alongside his neighbors. War would be in no one's interests."

Elizabeth listened as one after another of the guests agreed. Hitler seemed universally popular at this table, and she didn't feel she knew enough to argue against them. A headache pressed on her temples and she excused herself early.

That night, the air pressure shifted. When she awoke in the morning and looked out her bedroom window, the sky was dark and ominous. As she watched, a streak of lightning crackled across the sky, and hailstones pelted against the glass like handfuls of grit.

The weather was foul for the remainder of her stay, and Gladys seemed distant. For once, Elizabeth wasn't sad to leave.

When she got to London, the rain was unremitting and the temperature was well below average. She bought a new mink coat from a furrier near the hotel, to keep out the chill. Teddy Haslam was wrapped in a smart camel coat, with a trilby hat.

"What do the British people think of Herr Hitler?" she asked.

"My Parisian friends seem enthusiastic, but I worry about his intentions."

"He's a bit of an oddball," Teddy told her, "but on the whole, I rather think he's good for business."

"You don't think he's planning a war? That's what the American press says."

"In the Munich Agreement, he promised not to make war on France or Britain," Teddy replied. "If he chooses to win back other territories that were once German, perhaps we should turn a blind eye."

Elizabeth wasn't sure whom to believe anymore. Everyone had different perspectives. Many of her customers in the salon seemed uneasy about the Führer. The wife of a British cabinet minister said her husband was certain there would be war before the year's end, and Elizabeth shivered.

While she was in London, advertisements appeared in all the magazines for a new product launch by Helena Rubinstein. *The world's first waterproof mascara*, they read, alongside a photograph of it being worn by swimmers performing an aquatic ballet at the New York's World Fair.

Elizabeth snorted as she showed it to Teddy. "Waterproof indeed! It's impossible. That woman will do anything for a cheap gimmick. She tells lies, lies, and more lies. Everything is appearance with no substance. I wish . . ."

She knew better than to express out loud what she wished for in that moment: she'd heard Madame Rubinstein's Berlin salon had been confiscated by the German authorities, and she wished they could find a way to close down her entire international business at the same time.

CHAPTER 40

Helena

May 1939

A few days after Tommy Lewis started working for Helena, she invited him for cocktails at her apartment. She wanted to quiz him about his ex-wife, and thought he might talk more freely in a relaxed setting.

"Elizabeth's an ogre," he told her, with a grimace. "She's a petty dictator who has grown more bad-tempered with the years. She takes every slight personally and holds grudges forever. Especially against you."

"Me? Why on earth would she hold a grudge against me?" Helena asked, all innocence. Privately, of course, she wasn't surprised.

"She's obsessed with you!" Tommy exclaimed. "She thinks you are some kind of devil incarnate." Archie handed him a whiskey and soda, and he took a quick sip.

"I don't understand." Helena pretended to be baffled. "I'm her business competitor for sure, but it's not personal." She didn't tell him about Edith spying on her; he didn't need to know that.

Tommy settled back in his chair, took a longer swig of his drink, and considered for a few moments. "I think she's scared. Elizabeth's wealth and success were hard won. She doesn't publicize it, but she grew up in extreme poverty, one of five children whose mother died when they were little. They dressed in rags, lived in a shack with no heating, and often went to bed hungry."

Helena nodded slowly. Some of the pieces clicked into place. She could see how poverty might have lit the flame of Elizabeth's ambition and made her resolve never to go hungry again. Helena's family had never been short of food. In her case, she'd been born competitive and being disowned by her father had only made her more determined to succeed. She had something to prove, to him and to herself.

"I always told her to speak out about what she had achieved coming from such a background, but she feels ashamed of it," Tommy said. "Instead, she has turned into the world's biggest snob."

Archie nodded. "In my experience, the *nouveau riche* tend to be more snobbish than those who grew up with money. I suppose it comes from insecurity that it could all be taken away from them if they don't maintain the highest standards."

"Elizabeth's brother Will told me she became a social climber as soon as she arrived in New York," Tommy said. "She reinvented her past, trying with all her might to be accepted by the Social Register crowd."

"She has been accepted by them now," Helena said. "She should be content."

"Only to an extent," Tommy said. "Her friendship with Bessie Marbury helped her get a foothold in New York society, but she doesn't have as many top connections here as she does in Paris, through her sister marrying a count, or in London through her sales director, Teddy Haslam."

"I heard that she had a lesbian affair with Bessie Marbury," Helena said. "But she was married to you at that time, so I guess it was a lie."

Tommy finished his drink before he answered. "Elizabeth is frigid. I gave up trying to have marital relations with her after months of refusals. She's a cold, unnatural woman in that way, so I would be surprised if anything happened with Bessie."

Archie took his glass and went to get him a refill from the drinks cabinet.

"Is that why you had affairs with her beauticians?" Helena challenged.

He blushed. "I don't know what you heard," he stuttered. "There were one or two girls, perhaps."

Helena smiled to reassure him. "I don't care what you did then, but you won't seduce any of mine, will you? I don't want to have to deal with tears and tantrums, never mind unwanted pregnancies."

"I wouldn't dream of it," he assured her, eyes downcast.

"I am curious why you accepted such a low figure in your divorce settlement?" Helena asked. "You could have got far more than twenty-five thousand dollars."

Tommy hesitated before answering. "Elizabeth threatened to accuse me of theft if I didn't accept. A private investigator dug up some evidence and she was going to show it to the police."

"Theft?" Helena gave him a sharp look.

"It's not what you think," he said quickly. "I'd had some company information sent to my private address for convenience and she thought I was stealing it."

"And were you?"

He hesitated. "I wouldn't call it stealing. A friend of mine was opening a new salon and I gave her advice, based on our operation. Elizabeth had fired her on a whim and I felt we owed her."

"A good lawyer would have won that case," Helena replied. She assumed he was talking about Mildred Beam; she had already heard the story of her dismissal from Edith.

He shook his head. "You don't know Elizabeth. She would never have let me win. She would have pitched her expensive legal teams against me and kept raising the stakes until I was bankrupt. I've seen her do it to others, time and again."

Helena wondered if Elizabeth would ever attempt to sue her. Let her try!

She liked Tommy, she told Archie at the end of the evening. He was affable and open. She could see that customers would like him. But he wasn't quite as smart as she had expected. She decided she would limit his areas of responsibility, without letting him feel any sense of slight.

HELENA AND ARCHIE sailed to France in the summer of 1939, to stay with friends of his on the Côte d'Azur. The news from Germany was worsening, but the sun was scorching as ever and the air was full of the scent of jasmine and lavender. These were halcyon days, when it seemed impossible to imagine a war on the horizon.

They drove to Paris after their vacation and were there on September first, when they switched on the radio to hear the long-dreaded announcement that Hitler's troops had marched into Poland.

Helena burst into tears, and Archie gripped her hand, gray-faced, listening to the words of the newsreader.

"I expected it," Helena sobbed, "but I can't bear it. What will become of my poor country?" It had so often been invaded and overrun, conquered by one power, then another, and always its inhabitants suffered. "I must cable Regina and tell her to leave as soon as possible."

Regina was the only one of her sisters remaining in Poland. Regina's three children were all employed by Helena: Mala in New York, Jacques in Toronto, and Oskar as supervisor of her Saint-Cloud factory near Paris. Regina had refused to leave before because her husband owned a company in Kraków, and she had made her life there, but surely she would change her mind now. Helena would pay for her to travel anywhere she wanted to go.

Regina cabled back, saying that she and her husband intended to stay for the time being to protect their property.

Helena replied: *I will buy you a new house, but I can't buy you a new life. Please leave. I beg you.*

Again, Regina refused, so Helena tried once more: *Hitler loathes Jews. He wants to rid Europe of them. You must get out.* There was no reply, and she hoped that meant Regina was considering it, and perhaps had left already.

She sent and received many cables that day. Ceska was in London but desperate to escape, since the British government had issued an ultimatum to Hitler saying Britain would enter the war if German troops had not left Poland within two days. Her tone was hysterical. Helena booked her a passage to New York, accompanied by Roy and Horace, who had been visiting friends in the UK.

On Sunday the third of September, the British ultimatum expired at eleven-fifteen in the morning and Prime Minister Neville Chamberlain announced on the radio, in a chilling tone, that Britain was at war with Germany. The French president, Édouard Daladier, declared war at five that afternoon. That evening Helena summoned all the family members based in Paris to her home.

"I've decided to transfer my European assets into the hands of our lawyers until the war is over," she told them. "It's just a precaution. I want the factories and salons to remain open, but you are all free to leave and I'll help you to travel wherever you want to go."

Stella said she wanted to go to Argentina, where her son was living. Three cousins expressed a desire to work at Helena's salon in Rio de Janeiro. South America seemed a safe bet, since that continent had not been drawn into the last war.

"What will you do, Oskar?" Helena asked. "Will you come to New York with us, or would you prefer South America?"

"I'm going to volunteer for the French army," he said. "If my parents won't leave Poland, I need to stay in Europe and fight to save them."

"No, you can't! I won't allow it!" Helena threw her arms around him, and burst into tears. Everything made her cry today.

Archie spoke up. "If Oskar wants to fight, he should fight. Were I a decade younger, I would join him. Hitler has to be stopped."

"He's right, Aunt Helena." Oskar gave her his handkerchief to dry her tears. "I can look after myself. You mustn't worry."

She felt a shiver of fear, like cold fingers on her spine. He was thirty-seven years old, with a first-class degree in chemistry, and he was proving an exceptional businessman, but still she thought of him as a child.

"Your mother will never forgive me if I let anything happen to you," she whispered.

"I would never forgive myself if I didn't fight," he replied, and she knew his mind was made up.

It wasn't just family members that Helena helped over the next few weeks: Edward telephoned asking if she would sponsor him and his young wife to get to the United States. She knew how much it had cost him to ask, and agreed straight away. Their sons were going to be there, after all.

"Well done," Archie said, giving her a hug. "I guess that means you're not angry with Edward anymore."

It was true. War made old enmities seem insignificant.

AS HER RELATIVES left, Helena remained in Paris, making arrangements for the business and renewing her efforts to contact Regina. Once Kraków was occupied by the Nazis, cables could no longer get through. She kept writing letters but had no idea if they were being received, as no replies came. What did that mean?

"We have to get out of Europe," Archie said. "You've done all you can."

"I want to stay in case Regina needs me," Helena said. "It will be easier to help her from this side of the Atlantic than it will from New York."

She prayed that Regina could slip across the border and catch a train to Paris—but all the countries bordering Poland to the west and south were now in German hands, while to the east lay the grim specter of Soviet Russia. Maybe she could find a boat to take her across the Baltic to neutral Sweden?

When they heard the German army had marched into Belgium, Archie said, "It's time, Helena. We need to get out fast."

They tried to buy tickets to sail to New York, but found it was no longer a simple matter. All the money in the world couldn't get them a cabin on a ship that was already full to bursting with refugees. Archie telephoned one shipping line, then another, and all the while the radio reported the German advance through Belgium, heading in the direction of Paris. Britain's expeditionary force combined with French troops seemed unable to stop them.

Helena felt constant panic, her nerves buzzing like an electric generator. She couldn't eat, couldn't sleep, couldn't think for the clamor of her worries. Oskar was out there somewhere, fighting on the front line. Any day she could get word he had been killed. And what of Regina? A Jew, in a country occupied by Nazis? What would become of her?

They finally managed to procure one-way tickets on the USS *Manhattan*, leaving on the tenth of May, 1940. Helena sobbed as she packed her belongings. Her housekeeper and caretaker, an elderly French couple, were staying to look after the Île Saint-Louis house, but who knew when she might see it again? Worst of all, she was leaving behind Regina and Oskar. She hadn't heard from either of them for months, and had no idea if they were dead or alive.

Some good friends of Archie's drove them to Cherbourg, taking a risk because German planes whined overhead like hostile birds of prey. As the ship pulled out into the choppy gray ocean, Helena stood on deck, watching the French coastline until it was indistinguishable from the cloudy horizon. She was one of the lucky ones, she knew. Millions of Jews were stuck in Europe, while she had a home to go to in America. But at that moment, she didn't feel lucky at all.

When the USS *Manhattan* arrived in New York six days later, it was like stepping into a different world. Traffic was busy, pedestrians milled on the sidewalks, shoppers stopped to gaze in store windows, and advertisements were pasted on billboards for Dorothy Gray's new lipstick and Chesterfield cigarettes: it was business as usual. The only signs of war were the news vendors' kiosks with headlines about the German advance.

Helena invited all the family members in New York for dinner at her apartment. Ceska and Manka were there, along with Mala, Roy, and Horace, and several cousins. She greeted her sons with fierce hugs, overwhelmed to see them again after almost a year apart. Roy had a degree from Oxford University, and a postgraduate business degree from Harvard, but despite his academic success he was quiet and withdrawn as ever. Horace had never completed a college degree, although Helena commented to Archie that if they introduced one on liquor, he would pass with flying colors.

Talk at the dinner table was about whether America would enter the war. Mala hoped they would, so the conflict would be over sooner and her parents could be saved. Horace argued against it, saying this was a European matter, and Roy agreed with him. Helena kept her views to herself, but privately she was disappointed in her sons. "Look at your cousin Oskar," she wanted to tell them. "He has gall."

"What news of your mother?" she asked Mala.

Tears filled Mala's eyes, and she had to compose herself before she could speak. "I just had a letter from a neighbor," she said. "It was sent six weeks ago in the hands of friends who escaped to Britain, but it only arrived yesterday. She tells me

Mama and Papa and most of the Jewish population have to wear armbands with a Star of David on them, and to report for forced labor. I would have wired you, because I know you were trying to get her out, but then I heard you were arriving in Manhattan today."

Helena felt a chill ripple through her. "Who do we know in Kraków?" she asked. "There must be someone who can smuggle them out. I will pay whatever it takes."

"I've tried everyone I can think of," Mala said. "They all say they can't risk it or they'd face arrest themselves. The friends who escaped to Britain are helping the Polish resistance. They can sometimes arrange for letters to be delivered but say it's almost impossible to get people out now."

"What to do, what to do," Helena muttered. She wondered if she might be able to track down Stanislaus, her old boyfriend. Would he help, for the sake of their long-lost summer romance? She would try anyone and everyone she could think of, and offer to make them rich beyond their wildest dreams. There had to be a way.

A military telegram arrived telling them that Oskar had been captured by German forces at Dunkirk, but had escaped shortly afterward. His commanding officer wrote that he must be on the run behind enemy lines. Helena and Mala clung to each other, too traumatized to speak. As a Jew in German-held territory, he was in great peril. She couldn't imagine Jewish prisoners of war would be treated well by that regime.

This war had always felt personal to her because Hitler was opposed to the race she had been born into, and therefore the very fact of her existence. He had sent his troops into her homeland and threatened her family, so it touched her to the very core. She felt such hatred for him that if he had been in the room and she was holding a gun, she had no doubt she would have shot him dead and hang the consequences.

CHAPTER 41

Elizabeth

June 1940

I t was a shock to read that German troops had marched into Paris and occupied the city. Hitler had invaded so many countries in quick succession, Elizabeth scarcely had time to keep track. He couldn't be allowed to get away with it, that much was clear.

Her first concern was for Gladys. Should she leave France? Henri wrote that it was perfectly safe there. The occupiers wanted businesses to run as normal and he promised to make sure her assets were protected. At his urging, she transferred the French business into Henri's name, grateful that he had high-ranking Nazi friends who would look out for them.

"Hitler is clearly a maniac," she told Tom, "but I'm sure not all Nazis are bad people. Goering and von Ribbentrop were friendly enough when I met them. I hope they will get rid of their leader as soon as possible."

"Somehow I doubt that," Tom muttered. His boss, William Randolph Hearst, had been rather keen on Hitler a few years earlier, so he was keeping a low profile and Tom was forced to deal with the press on behalf of the company.

Elizabeth was disappointed that her absence in Europe had not had the desired effect of making him miss her so much he decided to leave his wife. On the contrary, he seemed distracted and she got less attention than she had before. She guessed the international situation was making him anxious, as it was her. They were very similar types.

Her European businesses had been subsidizing the American one for some time, so it came as a shock when she realized she could no longer transfer money out of Europe—not even from Britain. She had received a tax bill in America for more than half a million dollars and had been relying on profits from the British and French businesses to pay it. The IRS was always on her back these days—ever since that stupid *Fortune* article. She hated writing huge checks to the government. It felt like pouring money down the sewer. They warned her to stop mixing her business and personal expenses but it was *her* money and she felt she should be allowed to spend it as she saw fit.

Harry Johnson had not been worth the salary she paid him, since her profits were still dropping. She was aware that he often avoided her, telling his secretary not to put her calls through and creeping out via the fire escape when she tried to confront him. She was counting the days till his five-year contract expired and she could bounce him so hard and so fast his feet wouldn't touch the ground. Just the thought of the sum she was giving him made her tetchy.

It seemed everyone was determined to thwart her these days. She was having trouble sourcing some of the raw ingredients for her products, because petrochemicals were needed for military purposes. That was baffling when America wasn't even in the war. "Solve it!" she shouted at her factory managers when they informed her of the problem. "That's what I pay you for."

Tom's visits became even less frequent through the fall, and she felt an underlying anger toward him. Why had he led her on and let her develop feelings for him if he didn't mean to marry her? She was in love for the first time in her life and she had believed he was too, even if he'd never actually said the words. He'd seemed to understand her like no one else ever had—but if that were truly the case, he would want to be by her side.

"I am a woman on my own, and I'm anxious about the war. I would have thought you would make an effort to see me more often," she berated him one night, after three glasses of champagne had loosened her tongue.

"I have a wife and family who also need me," he reminded her, his face devoid of emotion.

"How could I ever forget?" she replied, in her most cutting tone.

Not long afterward, he made his excuses and left.

Elizabeth started making late-night telephone calls to Laney again, just to hear the sound of another human voice, but she couldn't tell her about Tom. No one could know about him.

On December seventh she was at the Belmont stables, grooming the horses, when her trainer came rushing in.

"I just heard on the radio that Japanese troops are bombing Pearl Harbor," he called.

"Why would they bomb a harbor?" Elizabeth murmured, distracted.

He stared at her, as if incredulous that she didn't know. "Because most of the American navy is based there."

She clutched the mane of the horse she was grooming. "They're bombing *Americans*?" It didn't make sense. What were they playing at?

"It looks as if hundreds of planes are involved. Come and listen on the radio if you want."

She followed him to an office where three other staff members were huddled around a radio set. The words of the newscaster were chilling: "President Roosevelt has confirmed that the Japanese have attacked the American naval base at Pearl Harbor, from the air. A second air attack is being reported in Manila, capital of the Philippines. We will bring you more news as it happens." There was an interlude of music, then the same stark facts were repeated. It was clear there must be huge loss of life, but no one said as much.

Elizabeth rushed to the telephone and rang Tom's office, but his secretary told her he had gone home. To his wife. Of course he would. Elizabeth was at the bottom of his list of priorities. At a time like this, her welfare probably hadn't even crossed his mind.

THE FOLLOWING DAY, America declared war on Japan. Elizabeth decided to go to the salon, to keep herself busy. Out on the street, folk were hurrying past with a sense of urgency. When she arrived, she heard that most clients had canceled their appointments and stayed home, as if they feared that bombs would drop on Manhattan any moment. Still there was no message from Tom.

Elizabeth kept the radio set switched on as she tried to deal with correspondence, but her brain was frazzled. Some of the beauticians asked if they could go home to be with their families, since the salon was empty, and she agreed. She would have done the same if only she had a family to go home to.

When the telephone rang, she snatched it up, but it was only a Russian friend asking her for dinner the following evening. During the conversation, he didn't once mention the war. Elizabeth supposed that having survived the Russian Revolution and escaped to America, he was less shocked by atrocities than they were. She accepted the invitation, just for the company.

When Elizabeth arrived at her friend's apartment the following day, she was introduced to the other guests. One of them was a prince—Prince Michael Evlanoff—who had recently arrived in the city, having fled Paris. He was of medium height, with thinning brown hair and hazel eyes.

"Where are you a prince of?" Elizabeth asked, bluntly.

"I am descended from a long line of Tatar princes," he explained with an East European accent. "We were forced out of Russia by the Bolsheviks in 1917."

"Yes, but where exactly did your people rule?" she persisted. "I thought the Romanovs were the royal family of Russia before the Revolution."

He sniffed and she got the impression he disapproved of the Romanovs. "My kingdom is Tatarstan, in west-central Russia, and our blood goes back to Genghis Khan."

"Gracious!" Elizabeth exclaimed. "I would hardly be claiming kinship with *him*. Did your wife come to America with you?" She glanced around, but there didn't seem to be a woman accompanying him.

"I have no wife," he said. "Being in exile has made romance impossible, but now I hope to settle permanently in New York."

An idea popped into Elizabeth's head: he was a proper prince, like Madame Rubinstein's husband, and he was unmarried. He looked younger than she was, but not too much younger. Could he be worth cultivating? She contrived to sit next to him at dinner and monopolized his attention for the rest of the evening.

Before she left, he lifted her hand to his lips and kissed it. "We must meet again," he said. "Perhaps you would come to the Stork Club with me? Perhaps tomorrow evening?"

She felt a flutter in her stomach. He liked her. She gave him her address, and took a taxi home, mulling over this exciting new connection. What would Tom make of her dining with another man? Would he be jealous? That might be no bad thing.

A BOUQUET OF white camellias arrived at Elizabeth's apartment the following morning, with a card reading: *With the compliments of Prince Michael Evlanoff*. Elizabeth smiled broadly as she showed them to her maid, Molly, who was dusting the hallway.

"From a prince," she said, and gave a little twirl, feeling girlish and carefree as a debutante.

"They're beautiful," Molly exclaimed, wide-eyed, before she ran to fetch a vase.

Michael was punctual when he collected her that evening, and he took her by taxi to the Stork Club on East Fifty-Third Street. She was impressed when the doorman recognized him and said, "This way, Your Highness," before leading them to the Cub Room, an exclusive area where movie stars mingled with the wealthy and titled. Elizabeth gawped; she had never been inside before. She was sure she could see Laurence Olivier and Vivien Leigh in the corner.

The maître d' led them to a table right in the center of the room, and asked, "The usual, Your Highness?"

Michael took charge of ordering food and drinks for them both, then quizzed Elizabeth about her business. How many salons did she own worldwide? Which were her bestselling products? When would her Maine spa reopen? He had seen a brochure and was dying to visit.

After answering his questions, Elizabeth felt it was not inappropriate for her to ask about his business interests.

"I live off a trust fund set up for me in a Swiss bank," he said straight away.

"Aren't you finding it difficult to get money out of Europe right now?" she asked. "I'm told I can't transfer assets in wartime. It's so annoying."

"My fund was arranged by King Gustav of Sweden, with a special dispensation," Michael replied. "I helped Emanuel Nobel to escape from Russia, and the Swedes feel they owe me a debt of gratitude. I'm writing a book about the Nobel family."

Elizabeth was impressed: a prince and an intellectual, with his own trust fund. He was perfect in every way.

There were no awkward pauses in the conversation. Michael was relaxing company, although he wasn't Tom's intellectual equal. Elizabeth kept glancing around, hoping Tom might turn up and see her with another man. Maybe that would give him the push he needed to leave Virginia. There was no sign of him though.

For the next week, she and Michael dined out every night at the city's best restaurants. He always signed the bill, and he sent her flowers the following morning. His trust fund must be decent-size, she guessed.

Sometimes, when they arrived at a new restaurant, the maître d' took her for his wife, and referred to them as "Your Royal Highnesses." Elizabeth simply loved that. Wallis Simpson wasn't allowed to call herself HRH, despite being married to an ex-king of England, but Michael could.

Tom rang, eventually, more than a week after Pearl Harbor.

"How are you, Elizabeth?" he asked.

As if you care, she thought to herself. "I've been terribly busy," she said airily. "I have a new beau and we're dining out every night. He's a prince, in fact."

There was a pause. "I'm happy for you," Tom said. "I hope he treats you with all the respect you deserve."

That stung Elizabeth to the quick. Did he not even plan to fight for her?

"Of course he does," she insisted, her tone sharp. "He's a perfect gentleman. And, given the circumstances, I don't think it would be appropriate for me to see you anymore."

She hadn't planned to say this, and regretted the words almost as soon as they left her lips. *Argue with me!* she urged him in her head. *Win me back! It's you I love!*

Yet again there was a few moments' silence. "I understand," he said, his voice a little sad. "I hope you know you can telephone me anytime you need a friend."

Elizabeth slammed down the telephone receiver and burst into tears. She'd ruined everything and lost him forever. A moment later she realized, in truth, he had never been hers. He'd been a fantasy. She'd thought he had seen the real her, and that he had loved her for who she was, but she'd been wrong. Maybe she wasn't the kind of person to inspire love. She seemed destined to be on her own.

ELIZABETH WAS ASTONISHED when Michael proposed two weeks after they met. It was flattering, but struck her as precipitous.

"Why delay?" he said. "You are the woman I've been waiting for all my life."

He produced a ring with an enormous diamond set in platinum studded with marcasite. It was so big it was almost vulgar—but not quite, Elizabeth thought, her face flushing.

"Gracious, I don't know what to say." Her mind leapt ahead. She could post an engagement announcement in the *New York Times* society column, and Tom would hear about it. Then he'd be sorry.

"I would like us to be married before the New Year," Michael continued. "Somewhere beautiful in the countryside. Maybe your spa in Maine. What do you think?"

Elizabeth loved Maine when it was blanketed in snow. She supposed wedding guests could stay in the bedrooms, and they could celebrate the arrival of 1942 as husband and wife. But why the rush? It left her so little time to make arrangements.

Michael insisted he couldn't wait any longer to be her husband.

Her heart was still broken over Tom, but maybe this would be the cure. She would become a princess on marriage—Princess Elizabeth, like the heir to the British throne. In her fantasies, Tom arrived in Maine just in time to stop the ceremony going ahead, but she knew that was a pipe dream.

Why *not* marry Michael? He was eligible and charming.

As soon as his ring was sparkling on her fourth finger, Elizabeth telephoned Edna and asked who could produce a wedding dress for her in record time.

"Charles James is your man," Edna said, giving her his private number. "How thrilling, Elizabeth! I'm over the moon for you."

Elizabeth threw herself into a flurry of arrangements. She ordered the staff at Maine Chance to prepare the building and had food and liquor sent up in a truck, including a case of Michael's favorite vodka. She went for fittings with Charles James, who created an elegant silk-satin gown in palest shell pink, high-necked, bracelet-sleeved, and nipped at the waist, then falling in soft cascades. Michael said he would arrange a honeymoon, but she organized everything else, hiring a justice of the peace to officiate the ceremony, a florist, and lots of extra waiting staff.

They would live in Elizabeth's apartment after the honeymoon, since Michael didn't own a New York property. She gave orders that her upstairs study be converted into a bedroom fit for the prince: royals always slept in separate rooms, she had heard, and that suited her perfectly. She also asked that her best linen and towels be embroidered with the Evlanoff crest. She would commission some engraved silver on her return.

Elizabeth thrived when she was busy. Everything would go like clockwork on her wedding day because she would make sure it did. There wasn't a detail she overlooked. Guests would be whisked up to Maine on a Pullman express on December twenty-ninth, the ceremony would take place on the thirtieth, and she and Michael would slip away on the first. Edna was coming, along with a *Vogue* photographer who would capture images of the day. It would be picture-perfect.

Oh my gosh, is this really happening? she wondered. Little Florence Nightingale Graham would have been speechless if she could have looked into the future. If only those girls at school who used to talk down to her would come across the wedding pictures in *Vogue* and know she had become a real-life princess! If only Tom would see the pictures and realize what he had let slip through his fingers.

MICHAEL LOOKED DASHING in black tie. Elizabeth blinked back tears as they said their vows, promising to love and respect each other till death did them part. The war seemed so far away in this setting, with the low apricot sun glinting off crisp, icy snow leading down to the frozen lake. Sprays of white Christmas roses decorated every surface and champagne bottles stood at the ready.

What a magical life it was, she reflected, looking around the room. Maine Chance had never been so beautiful. The wedding pictures in *Vogue* would be a wonderful advertisement for her spa. She couldn't wait for Madame Rubinstein to see them and know she wasn't the only one to snare a prince.

Michael resolutely refused to give her any clue where they were going on the honeymoon until the car picked them up and drove them to an airfield. Elizabeth had been on a few airplanes before, flying to racetracks where her horses were running. Still, she felt a frisson of nerves and clung to Michael's arm as the plane soared up through the clouds. *I suppose I will be doing more flying now that I am royal*, she thought. Life was going to be very different.

Michael hadn't tried to make love to her yet. On their wedding night, he and his Russian friends had drunk gallons of vodka and danced boisterously to music played on a phonogram, as a result of which he had passed out fully clothed when he came to bed. That was a relief to Elizabeth. If he wanted to make love to her on the honeymoon, she planned to tell him quietly but firmly that she would rather not. He was seventeen years younger than she was, she had discovered: forty-six to her sixty-three. She hoped that didn't mean he had stronger sexual urges.

The sky outside was dazzling blue now, and hot white sun shone through the plane window. She began to relax. Everything was going to be fine.

The landing was a little alarming, as they bounced along the airstrip before screeching to a halt. The first thing she saw when they climbed out of the plane was palm trees against blue sky, then she noticed the sign on an airport building: Nassau. They were in the Bahamas! She whirled around and kissed Michael.

"What a wonderful surprise!" she exclaimed, genuinely pleased with his choice. The Duke and Duchess of Windsor were living in Nassau. She would send a note, letting Wallis know she was on the island. Perhaps she would suggest they meet for a cocktail.

"We're staying in the very best hotel," he said. "They've sent a limousine to meet us."

In the hotel's airy foyer, Elizabeth accepted a glass of pineapple juice from a waitress while Michael went to check in. A beautiful fuchsia-colored plant was cascading around the doorway and she stopped to examine its papery flowers. Once her juice was finished she handed back the glass and looked across. Check-in was taking a long time. Michael was in an intense conversation with a man in a suit, whom Elizabeth guessed was the hotel manager. She wandered over to join them.

"Is our room not ready?" she asked.

Michael shook his head. "It's not that. They want to be paid in advance for our stay, and won't let me wire money later, but I'm afraid I forgot to bring a checkbook."

Elizabeth gave the manager her iciest stare. "Do you know who we are? And did you realize it's our honeymoon?"

"Of course. My apologies, but it's company policy."

Elizabeth had assumed Michael would have paid in advance. It was the new husband's role, was it not? She opened her mouth to argue with the manager, then closed it again. She didn't want to spoil the holiday atmosphere. Instead she smiled sweetly.

"Why don't you give me the bill?" she asked. "I'll make sure it's paid straight away."

Michael squeezed her arm but she noticed he didn't say thank you.

CHAPTER 42

Helena

January 1942

H elena heard via Molly, the maid on her payroll at Elizabeth Arden's apartment, that her mistress had known Prince Michael for less than a month before marrying him. She raised an eyebrow, and remarked to Archie: "That woman would go to any lengths to copy me."

Word came from friends in Paris that Miss Arden's brother-in-law, Count Henri Maublanc de Boisboucher, dined out with the Nazi occupiers. Helena knew that the Duchess of Windsor had been a regular at her Paris salon, and the Windsors had shown their true colors by visiting Hitler in 1937. She had also heard a rumor from Ceska that von Ribbentrop had held Nazi meetings in Miss Arden's London salon before the war, so clearly that's where her sympathies lay. It was sickening to think that anyone could be prejudiced against her entire race, given what was happening to Jews in Europe. It was doubly unforgivable while Helena was doing her best to save her sister's life.

They heard that Regina and her husband, along with most Kraków Jews, had been forced into a ghetto in the Podgórze district of the city, and were being made to work in factories there. Helena wrote letters to everyone she could think of in Kraków, trying to get help for Regina, and sent them via the friends in Britain who were part of the Polish resistance network.

One of the letters was addressed to Stanislaus at the University Hospital, where she had heard he worked on a cardiac ward.

When his reply came, many weeks later, it was affectionate: *Dearest Helena,* he wrote, *I have very fond memories of our time together. When I read stories in the newspapers of your great success, I feel proud to have known you. It's a shame you didn't become a doctor, because I know you would have been excellent, but your talent did not go to waste. My wife uses your skin products and tells me they are the best.* . . . He went on: *I regret that personally I can do nothing for your sister. My role in this war must be to use my medical skills to treat the injured and save lives. Be assured there are those in Poland who are doing their best to help our Jewish friends. I hope and pray that you will be reunited with your sister and we will all emerge from this atrocity before much longer.*

It felt strange to see his handwriting, almost fifty years after they last met, bringing back a wave of the intense feelings she used to have for him. He would have helped her if he could; she was sure of that.

It was hard for Helena to carry on with daily life when her worries choked her. Anxiety was always there, tight as a drum beneath her rib cage, no matter what she was doing. Somehow she managed to eat, sleep, and work. Archie was a solid, calming presence she could turn to for support, but work was her real solace. As always, she kept a close eye on Elizabeth Arden's business. When her rival launched Velva Leg Film, designed to add color to bare legs when stockings were in short supply, Helena quickly followed suit with her own tinted leg cream. She even opened a Bare-Leg Bar in her Fifth Avenue salon, where women could come to have their legs colored on the spot.

When she heard from a contact in Saks that Elizabeth was launching a new perfume with the unusual name of Blue Grass, she arranged a publicity stunt for her Heaven Sent fragrance to steal media attention. Five hundred tiny samples of her perfume were attached to balloons and released from the roof of Bonwit Teller, right in the middle of the day when the street below was crowded with shoppers. The balloons drifted down, and pass-ersby scrambled to grab their free gifts. Of course, Helena had arranged for photographers to capture the scene, and it made the cover of the *New York Times* the following day—publicity money couldn't buy. Helena was especially gratified when she heard from Walter Bonwit that Elizabeth Arden had telephoned him to protest about the "cheap stunt."

She was honored when Helena Rubinstein Inc. was offered a government contract to supply camouflage and sunburn creams to the US army. President Roosevelt wrote commending her personally for her contribution to the war effort, and she would have crowed to the press about her triumph until she heard that Elizabeth Arden had also gotten an army contract and had also been commended by Roosevelt.

She didn't think that woman deserved commendation. She might be striving to appear patriotic now, but her family was pro-Nazi and Helena strongly suspected she was too.

WHEN TIME PERMITTED, Helena went searching for a new apartment. She wanted one big enough to accommodate her extended family, if necessary, somewhere to display her ever-expanding art collection, and a place where she could entertain in style. A real-estate agent showed her a three-story penthouse at 625 Park Avenue, and straight away she adored it. It was light and spacious, just two blocks from Central Park, with a vast roof terrace curving around the building. She offered the price asked for and the agent said he would confirm later that day.

When the call came, at first Helena couldn't believe her ears.

"Apologies," the agent said, "but the owner has strong feelings about Jews and refuses to let you have the lease."

"He said *what*?" Helena challenged. "In this day and age,

when Jews are persecuted across Europe? What kind of man is he?"

The agent agreed it was despicable, but insisted the owner would not be swayed.

Helena slammed down the telephone, remembering the time she was refused a Fifth Avenue salon in 1915. She would not let this happen again. She asked her lawyers to find out who owned the entire Park Avenue building, all fifteen stories of it, and how much they would accept for it. Everyone had their price. Sure, it would be expensive, but she was determined. All the loathing she felt for Adolf Hitler was channeled into loathing for this one man who would not lease his apartment to her. She was driven by rage; it was an easier emotion to handle than fear.

The negotiations took months, but Helena was steadfast. She had the money and she would not let the antisemites win. As soon as the contracts were signed and the building was hers, she served an eviction notice on the owner of the penthouse, giving him minimal time to vacate the premises. That felt good.

She hired her favorite architect, Max Wechsler, to redesign it. There would be a vast hallway with a black-and-white-tiled floor where her Elie Nadelman sculptures would be displayed on plinths; a modern living room with silk and velvet upholstery in shades of purple and magenta; a baroque dining room in white and gold, where her African art would be shown; and a card room with three murals painted by her friend, Salvador Dalí. Art by Picasso, Matisse, Braque, Chagall, Derain, Modigliani, and Miró would decorate the bedrooms and the vast top-floor ballroom. On the roof terrace, she had rows of vegetables planted to support the war effort.

When the work was finished, a *Life* reporter came to interview her, while a photographer took pictures. "Welcome to my castle in the sky," Helena greeted them, before showing them around, explaining what each room would be used for. They raved about the Dalí mural of her chained to a rock by strings of pearls, like a wealthy modern-day mermaid. They were astonished to find seven small Renoir paintings clustered above a fireplace in the sitting room.

"*The* Renoir?" the reporter asked. "The famous one?"

"Of course," she replied with a shrug.

The *Life* interview was supposed to be about the interior design of the apartment, but Helena had received ominous news earlier in the day and it preyed on her mind. It seemed a new internment camp had been built forty miles west of Kraków to house political prisoners, among them Jews, and conditions were grim. She couldn't resist mentioning it to the reporter.

"My sister Regina is the least politically motivated person you can imagine. She is not a practicing Jew—none of my family are—yet we are tarred with pervasive and completely inaccurate stereotypes." The journalist was scribbling it all down, but Helena didn't care. "And it's not just in Nazi Germany," she added. "We all know antisemitism is rife in America, although the perpetrators try to keep it veiled now that we're at war with the fascists. Henry Ford and William Randolph Hearst have often attacked Jews. So did the great aviation hero, Charles Lindbergh."

Archie was gesticulating at her behind the reporter's back, trying to make her stop, but she was too riled.

"Even in the beauty business, there are those who would have all Jews sent to internment camps if they got their way," she said.

"Helena, I think you should concentrate on talking about your art collection," Archie said, in a warning tone.

"To whom are you referring?" the reporter asked.

"It would be interesting to know where Miss Elizabeth Arden's sympathies truly lie in this war," Helena said, and Archie clapped a hand to his forehead. "Her family in Paris are Nazi-lovers, and I heard from friends in London that her salon has been used for fascist meetings. As you can imagine, this is hard for me to swallow when my sister is being held prisoner by that regime."

As the reporter scribbled it down, she knew she had crossed a line but she didn't care. In the Great War, Miss Arden had accused her of being on "the wrong side." Frankly, she couldn't see any reason to hold back now.

CHAPTER 43

Elizabeth

January 1942

On the second day of Elizabeth's Nassau honeymoon, while she lay by the pool under the shade of a beach umbrella, she was surprised to see Michael walking toward her, arm in arm with another man. She sat up and pulled a towel across her legs.

"Darling, this is my friend Burt Chose," Michael said. "Guess what? He's staying in our hotel."

Burt was deeply tanned, with movie-star looks, although he was rather short, maybe only five-four. His black hair was combed in a slightly off-center parting and he had long wolflike canine teeth.

"How do you do, Mr. Chose." She reached up and shook his hand. "It seems quite the coincidence that you happen to be staying in our honeymoon hotel."

He smiled, flashing those teeth. "I've been dying to meet you," he said. "And I couldn't make it to your wedding, so Michael offered to introduce us here. Isn't it divine?" He gestured toward the palm-tree-lined walkway that led to a white sand beach, with a glint of turquoise ocean beyond. "I love the Bahamas! I want to invite you both to a restaurant later where they specialize in seafood. You'll love it."

Michael pulled up a reclining chair so he could join them

and Burt stripped off his shirt and lay facedown on it. Elizabeth gasped at the cheek and opened her mouth to object, but Burt spoke first.

"Look! I brought some of your Ideal Suntan Oil." He held up the bottle, which was shaped like a hip flask. "Can you put some on my back, please?" he asked Michael.

Elizabeth watched, speechless, as Michael applied the oil meticulously to Burt's back, smoothing down each arm to the fingertips, not skipping an inch. He'd been much more cursory when he'd applied her lotion earlier. A hard little knot of suspicion formed inside her, but she couldn't put into words what she was thinking.

"Do we have to eat dinner with your friend?" she asked Michael once they were alone in their room. "It's not very romantic for a honeymoon couple. I'm sure he doesn't want to play gooseberry."

"We've agreed now," Michael said. "Don't worry about Burt. He can take care of himself."

All through the meal, Burt and Michael chatted about acquaintances Elizabeth had never heard of, about shows she hadn't seen, and countries she hadn't visited. She had assumed that, as a prince, Michael would be well-brought-up but his behavior was downright rude. She didn't want to argue with him in front of his friend but she was quietly fuming by the time they got back to the hotel. Michael and Burt went for a nightcap in a bar down by the beach, leaving her to make her own way to bed. This wasn't right. She wouldn't put up with it. It was disrespectful and cold.

When she awoke in the morning, Michael was sound asleep and could not be roused. He slept through her yoga routine, and didn't waken when breakfast was served on the balcony. Burt was already down by the pool when she got there, and he was never more than a few feet away for the rest of the day. He was civil to her, flashing those canines, but once or twice she saw the two men exchange glances and got the impression they were mocking her.

She lay by the pool with her eyes closed, trying to decide what to do. Michael had still not attempted to make love to her and, while that suited her, it also struck her as odd. Why had she married him so hastily? What would Bessie have said? This was exactly what she had criticized Elsie de Wolfe for.

Truth was, she hardly knew Michael. She'd assumed that his solicitous behavior before their marriage would continue: the flowers, the little romantic gestures, the generosity. Instead, he was virtually ignoring her and spending his time with Burt. What if someone saw them and it was reported in the papers that there was a third person on her honeymoon? It would look terrible. When she caught Michael alone in their room, changing for luncheon, she told him as much.

"I'm not spending the rest of my honeymoon with Burt hanging around," she said. "Please tell him to give us our privacy now."

"That would be rude," Michael replied. "He's a close friend of mine, and I won't have you making him feel unwelcome."

"May I remind you who paid for this honeymoon?" she snapped. "Although that should have been the groom's role."

Michael didn't reply. He didn't even look at her, just swept out of the room and pulled the door closed behind him. She didn't see him at luncheon, or during the rest of the afternoon. Burt was absent too. Elizabeth's suspicions grew. It couldn't be what she was thinking, could it? The idea was far too disgusting to her.

Thank goodness she hadn't sent a note to the Duchess of Windsor! What on earth would she make of this peculiar situation? Elizabeth shuddered.

With a bitter taste in her throat, she sent a cable to her housekeeper in Manhattan, telling her to stop monogramming the linen and redecorating the upstairs room; there had been a change of plan, she wrote.

ELIZABETH SPENT MOST of the remainder of her honeymoon alone. Michael walked out of their suite whenever she confronted him, and she simply didn't know what to do. She couldn't divorce him after a week of marriage. It would be reported in the press and everyone would know she'd made an idiotic mistake. Madame Rubinstein would clutch her sides laughing. Tom would think her a fool.

With any luck, Michael would behave with more decorum once they were back in New York and Burt was no longer with them. She'd just have to be patient, and avoid photographers in the meantime.

When Elizabeth got back to her Aeolian Building office and flicked through a folder of bills on her desk, she got a further shock. It seemed Michael had been running up debts in her name. He had somehow charged most of the restaurant bills during their courtship to her company, as well as all the flowers he had sent her, and the flights to the Bahamas. Even the engagement ring was on her account! How could that have happened without her permission? Laney called to make inquiries and learned that Michael had been passing himself off as her fiancé from the start.

"Michael, I thought you had a trust fund?" she asked, thrusting the folder of bills at him that evening. "How do you explain all this?"

He glanced inside and shrugged. "As you predicted, it has proved impossible to get funds out of Europe during the war. If you give me a loan, you will be fully reimbursed once I can access my money again."

Elizabeth stared at him, aghast. This was blackmail, but she had no choice if she wanted to maintain the pretense of a marriage. "I will give you an allowance," she said eventually, "but I will not have you running up debts in my name. I've never left bills unpaid. It looks bad."

Michael sulkily agreed he would live within his allowance. He was like a child, she thought. He slept in till noon, spent the afternoon wandering around the house in his robe, then went out most evenings, only returning after she was asleep.

Elizabeth couldn't bear to see a grown man wasting his life. She asked what was happening to his book about the Nobels, but he claimed he couldn't do the research without visiting Sweden, which was impossible in wartime. She asked if he wanted to start a business of his own, but he didn't seem to feel the need. Whenever the subject was raised, he simply left the room.

Helena Rubinstein seemed happy with her prince; she was often photographed around town with him and had launched a line of men's grooming products under his name. Meanwhile, Elizabeth had married a man who did nothing but squander her money, and who still spent most of his time with Burt Chose. What did they get up to? The thought made her wince. But she couldn't bear to divorce Michael and have the world find out about her foolish mistake, so the marriage limped on in name only.

WHENEVER SHE COULD tear herself away from the business, Elizabeth got her driver to take her to Belmont, where she spent time with her precious babies. Still she struggled to find trainers she saw eye to eye with. She'd lost count of the number she'd sacked because they treated her like a crazy woman and thought they could do as they wanted the minute her back was turned.

Great Union had won Elizabeth's first major race in 1939. He was a grumpy horse, given to bucking and rearing in the starting gate, but he was fiercely competitive on the field and had equaled the track speed record at Belmont. She found a jockey he took to, a scrawny Irishman, and tried him at several of the East Coast races. They came frustratingly close, often second or third, but never took the top prize again after that win in 1939. Something was missing, but she couldn't think what, and successive trainers had no suggestions.

One day, at the Saratoga racetrack, she stood watching as Great Union was led out to the paddock. She hadn't paid any attention to an old man crouching nearby, but suddenly he spoke to her.

"I wouldn't race that one today. He's got a problem with the left fetlock. Probably a tendon."

Elizabeth looked at the man, then the horse. "My trainer passed him for fit," she said.

"Put your hand on the fetlock," he said. "Betya it's hot. Needs to be rested."

Elizabeth got the jockey to hold him still while she bent to feel the fetlock, and sure enough it was hot. If he ran on that, he would damage it further.

"We need to scratch him today," she told the jockey. "Take him back to the stable." She turned to thank the old man but he had gone. "Who was I talking to just then?" she asked.

"Tom Smith," came the reply.

Tom had been the trainer of Seabiscuit, the most famous horse in America in the late 1930s. He had taken a small, skew-legged horse that no one else rated, and turned him into a legendary champion. If anyone knew what they were talking about, it was Tom Smith.

She spotted him later in the owners' enclosure and went over to chat. It was hard work, though. He wasn't a man given to small talk.

"Do you think any horse with the right breeding can be made a winner, given the right training?" she asked.

"I think any horse can be *improved* with the right training," he said carefully. His skin was grooved and gnarled like the trunk of an old oak tree.

"I've had a string of yearlings with impeccable bloodlines who never lived up to promise. Is there any advice you could give me?" she said. "Maybe there's something my trainers should be doing differently." She told him about the feed she used, her belief that their legs should be massaged before and after races, the practice runs they did, their routines.

"Every horse should be treated different," he said. "You need to penetrate the mind and heart of the animal. That's when you make a winner."

In one short conversation, Tom won her confidence so completely that she offered him a job.

He didn't accept straight away but the following week he came to her stable to inspect her thoroughbreds and watch them go through their paces.

"You don't have a great champion here," he told her afterward. "But if you've got the money, I could help you find one."

She agreed on the spot. She might be an old fool when it came to choosing husbands, but she had absolutely no doubt about the capabilities of this man. He would be the third Tom in her life, after her first husband and then Tom White. The British had a phrase "third time lucky," and she thought that in her case it was going to be Third Tom Lucky. She could feel it in her bones.

SIX MONTHS AFTER her marriage to Michael, he asked her for a hundred thousand dollars to clear his debts.

Elizabeth swallowed hard, a flutter of panic in her chest. "How on earth can you owe so much? What about your allowance?"

Michael shrugged. "These are debts from before we married. I'm being chased by the creditors right, left, and center. Some are threatening to bankrupt me, and that would be humiliating for us both, darling. You know you can afford it, so why not just pay up?" There was no apology, no hint of shame. His expression was stone-cold.

"Give me a week," she said. "I need time to think."

She went back to the private detective she had used to snoop on Tommy and asked for a full report on Prince Michael Evlanoff, no holds barred, as soon as possible.

When she read it, Elizabeth was devastated. It seemed that Michael was known in many circles as a homosexual, and that Burt had been his lover for several years. His royal title was fake—he had no claim to any throne, anywhere. What's more, he was still opening accounts in her name at stores across town: gentlemen's outfitters, clubs, even a car dealership. It was obvious she should have gotten the detective's report before agreeing to marry him, and she was furious with herself that she hadn't thought of it. She'd been swept along in the giddiness of romance, and wanting revenge on Tom. Why had no one warned her? Did she have no true friends who cared about her? She was angry with Michael, but she was angriest of all with herself.

Elizabeth was badly shaken by the news, but she threw herself into action. She called a locksmith and had the locks changed at her apartment, telling the doorman that he was not to admit Michael under any circumstance. She called her lawyer and asked him to obtain a quick divorce, citing cruel and abusive behavior. He was also to send a letter warning Michael that if he ever spoke to the press about her, she would have him and Burt arrested for sodomy. She knew people in positions of influence: Eleanor Roosevelt, for example, and FBI director J. Edgar Hoover, and she would ask for their help if need be.

Michael's perfidy hurt her, badly. He had seen her as a lonely, gullible woman he could manipulate, and she had fallen right into his trap. It made her feel as humiliated as poor Florence Nightingale Graham, the little girl with cooties in her hair. How would she explain her divorce to the world? She decided to try telling Edna first, and hear her reaction.

"He came with two suits and he left with twenty-two," she told Edna, at the end of her story. "I've been swindled, when all I wanted was to be loved."

"You poor dear," Edna said. "He's clearly a crook. Thank goodness you realized before he cleaned you out completely. I did think you were getting married too quickly, but you seemed so enchanted with him I didn't say anything. Next time I will."

"There will be no next time," Elizabeth said, and meant it. "I'm going to stick to horses; they're far easier to manage than men."

HER DIVORCE CAME through in February 1944. Michael didn't challenge it. He got a pay-off, not a huge one but decent enough, and Elizabeth imagined he would move on to some other wealthy older woman. She braced herself for mocking press coverage, but the next day some shocking news arrived from Paris that took her mind off anything to do with Michael: Gladys had been arrested and taken to a Nazi internment camp called Ravensbrück.

Elizabeth wrote to Henri in blind panic: How could this be? She had thought his Nazi connections would protect them. What was the charge against her? How could they get her out? If money would help, she would pay.

Communication was frustratingly slow. Her letters had to be sent to a friend of Henri's in Switzerland, and smuggled into France by back channels; his replies came to her by the same route. They were read by a censor's office before reaching her, and the process took several weeks each time.

I don't know the truth of it, but she is accused of helping to treat enemy airmen in the course of her volunteer work for the Red Cross. I have sent money to the commander at Ravensbrück and asked him to arrange favorable conditions for her, Henri wrote. *She will*

have enough food and decent bedding, at least, but I am trying to
get her moved to a camp that is closer to home. Fear not, Elizabeth!
Everything that can be done is being done.

How could she not be afraid when her beloved sister was in
a Nazi camp? Had she really been helping enemy airmen? Why
would she take such a risk? It didn't seem like the gentle sister
she knew. Elizabeth hadn't been following newspaper reports of
the war closely till then—she was too distracted—but now she
started to read about the Allied advance through Italy. *Hurry!*
She wanted to cry to the American troops. *Please hurry!*

One day she saw her name mentioned in a *Life* article about
supporters of fascism in the US, and she exploded with rage. She
rang the editor and screamed down the phone.

"How dare you!" she cried. "My sister is interned in a Nazi
camp. What on earth makes you think I support that hideous
regime?"

"Helena Rubinstein told us von Ribbentrop held fascist
meetings at your London salon," came the reply.

"Well, that is complete nonsense," Elizabeth said, "and I'll sue
anyone who repeats it."

"She also said your brother-in-law dines with leading Nazi
figures."

Goddamn Henri for being friends with a few Nazis. It had
seemed harmless at the time, of course. None of them had suspected it would come to this. Elizabeth ripped the cord out of
the wall and hurled the telephone across the room.

"I hate her!" she screamed, so harshly that she damaged her
throat. "I truly hate her. I wish she would just *drop down dead*!"

CHAPTER 44

Helena

June 1944

Helena was overcome when she heard on the radio on June 6 that American, Canadian, and British troops had landed on the beaches of Normandy. Her legs gave way beneath her and she slumped in an armchair. At last, they were making headway. It truly felt as if the war had reached a turning point. She wasn't aware she was crying until Archie came into the room and rushed to comfort her.

"Why are you upset?" he asked, dabbing her tears with his handkerchief. "It's wonderful news!"

Helena blew her nose, gasping to control her breathing. "I am thinking of all the people across Europe who have been living under Nazi occupation hearing this news and having hope at last. I am praying that Regina will hear it and know help is coming. She just has to hang on."

Archie perched on the arm of her chair and they listened to the radio report together. Every time the newscaster repeated, "Allied troops have landed on the beaches of Normandy," Helena got tearful again. *Please let it be in time*, she thought. *Please God*.

Not long afterward, newspapers published photographs taken by American pilots of the internment camps outside Kraków where she assumed Regina was being held. They showed long barrack-style blocks and reported they were near the village of Oświęcim, which the Nazis had renamed Auschwitz. Helena couldn't bear to imagine what it was like to be there. Reports were emerging of mass killings but she hoped they were of combatants and that women would be spared. "Hold on, Regina," she whispered into the ether. "They're coming to rescue you. I'll see you soon."

There had been no word of Oskar since the news that he was trapped behind enemy lines in France in 1940. Helena worried constantly about him and Regina; they were in her thoughts when she opened her eyes in the morning, and as she lay in bed last thing at night. In between, she worked, she finished decorating her new apartment, and she met friends, trying to keep busy. It's the way she had always survived.

WHEN HELENA READ in the press about the failure of Elizabeth Arden's marriage to her "prince," so soon after the wedding, she felt a certain schadenfreude. She had no sympathy for anyone with fascist beliefs, and certainly not that woman. When she next saw Carmel, she said as much.

"Elizabeth's started having secret dinners with my brother again," Carmel said, "so I have the inside story. She told him she'd had no idea Michael was a homosexual when she married him." Carmel gave Helena a complicit smile. "I don't know about you, but I had certainly made sure that George was attracted to me before I accepted his proposal."

Helena smiled too, thinking that Elizabeth must have been desperate for a husband to rush into matrimony with someone quite so ill qualified.

"Tom says her sister has been interned by the Nazis in France. She got back in touch with him to ask if William Randolph Hearst had any connections who could help."

Helena knew that Hearst newspapers had supported the Nazi party in the 1930s; Mr. Hearst believed they were the only government standing up to the specter of communism and that America should take a leaf out of their book. Seemingly he had met Hitler and given him advice on raising his profile in the US.

"I know Hearst campaigned for America to stay out of the war," Helena said with distaste, "but surely he can't still be in contact with German officials now?"

"I'm sure he's not," Carmel said. "I think Elizabeth is clutching at straws. Tom said she's very distressed about her sister."

Helena wondered why Elizabeth's sister had been interned when her husband was a friend to the Nazis, but couldn't find it in her heart to care. "She encouraged that regime with its vile policies," she said. "If you run with wolves, sooner or later you will get bitten."

ONE DAY THAT summer of 1944, Helena was sitting in her office above the Fifth Avenue salon when she heard a scream downstairs. She got to her feet. There was a commotion going on. Mala's voice called urgently: "Aunt Helena! Come quick!"

She rushed to the stairs and started to descend, gripping the handrail because her knees were unreliable these days. She paused halfway, looked down, and her heart almost leapt out of her chest. It was Oskar, her beloved nephew, painfully thin and with a long grizzly beard, but undeniably him. She shrieked and covered her mouth with her hand, tears welling up.

Oskar sprinted up the stairs to throw his arms around her. Mala was close behind, shrieking in a voice that was almost hysterical.

"What happened? How did you get here?" Helena asked, touching his cheekbone, his hair, his bony shoulder, to make sure she wasn't imagining it.

"Can we sit down first?" He grinned at her. "I've been traveling for the best part of a month to get here and I'm beat."

"Come—come to my office. You need food," Helena said. "What would you like? I'll send someone out to a bakery. Or we could go for lunch in a restaurant. You must eat."

"There speaks a good Jewish woman," Oskar said, taking her arm to help her back to her office. "I'd love a cup of coffee. Food later."

Helena asked her assistant to get coffee, and sat down, Oskar beside her. Mala knelt on the floor at his feet, clutched his hand, and wouldn't let go.

"I was lucky enough to get a diplomatic flight out of Lisbon yesterday," he said. "We landed this morning. It got a bit hairy in the mid-Atlantic, so I'm glad to have my feet back on terra firma."

"Lisbon! What were you doing in Lisbon?" He seemed changed, Helena thought, yet familiar too. That same grin. She remembered his long fingers and large knuckles. The bones of his skull were prominent under his skin.

"I had to escape across the Pyrenees, just after D-Day," he explained. "I'd been working for a Résistance cell that was sabotaging German troop movements: dynamiting bridges, mainly. I heard my identity had been compromised after the Allied landings and I've been on the run ever since."

"Dynamite!" Helena repeated.

"Yes, a chemistry degree turns out to have unexpected advantages," he said.

He looked exhausted and she should have let him rest, but Helena needed to hear at least the bare bones of his story. "We heard you were captured after Dunkirk, then escaped," she said. "But where have you been for the last four years?"

"I traveled around France a lot," he said, "working for one Résistance cell, then another, passing on my chemical expertise. '*Homme de dynamite*,' they called me." The coffee arrived and he inhaled the aroma with a deep sigh. "Real coffee!" He took a sip. "I can't tell you how good it is to be here."

"How is it in France?" Helena asked. "We hear stories . . ."

He shook his head. "I'll tell you later. First, I need to know: Have you heard from Mum and Dad? Did they get out of Poland?"

Helena looked at Mala, then back at him. "We think they are being held in a camp known as Auschwitz."

Oskar swore and turned his head away. He wouldn't tell her what he had heard about that place; she wasn't sure she wanted to know.

HELENA HOSTED A dinner for all the family members in the US, so they could welcome Oskar home. Jacques caught the train from Toronto, Mala and Victor were there, Manka and her family, and Roy and Horace too.

Oskar and Roy huddled in long conversation: Roy was working for the Office of Strategic Services in Washington, a bureau where they liaised with overseas agents resisting the Nazis. Helena watched them—Oskar wiry, tanned, and intense, Roy pale and podgy—and wished that at least one of her sons had signed up to fight. Horace had been declared medically unfit, due to health problems that Helena was convinced were caused by his drinking. Roy could have volunteered for the army, though, instead of seeing out the war in a desk job.

They raised their glasses that night—to the heroism of Oskar, and to his parents, whose fate was still unknown.

While she watched Oskar, Helena made a decision: she had a vacancy for a manager at the Long Island factory where Horace worked—on the days he could be bothered to show up. She would offer Oskar the job.

"Are you sure Horace won't mind me being his boss?" Oskar asked, when she told him later. "I don't want to tread on anyone's toes."

"Don't worry about Horace," she said. "He's gaga. He probably won't even notice."

Later that night, a little tipsy, she told Archie about the conversation. "Sometimes I wish Oskar, Jacques, and Mala were my children," she said. "I'm more proud of them than I am of my own sons."

"Helena!" Archie took her face in his hands and looked deep into her eyes. "Don't ever say that again. Don't think it either. Do you hear me?"

She nodded mute agreement. It was true, though.

HELENA'S ELATION AT Oskar's safe return was soon over-shadowed by horror. As the Soviet army advanced into Poland, they liberated a Nazi internment camp near Lublin, known as Majdanek, and reports about it began to appear in the American press.

"This was not a concentration camp," one journalist wrote. "It was a gigantic murder plant." In the center stood a huge stone building with a factory chimney, which appeared to have been a crematorium. There were around a thousand survivors, so thin and malnourished they couldn't walk and could barely speak. But many more were known to have been detained there. What had become of them?

Helena couldn't bear to look at photographs of emaciated survivors, or to read their accounts. She threw the paper away. Perhaps Auschwitz hadn't been so bad. Perhaps Regina had escaped and was hiding somewhere till the war's end. She tried to cling to hope as the Soviet army advanced slowly toward Kraków, taking back towns under Nazi occupation, one by one.

Auschwitz camp was liberated on January 27, 1945. Early reports said there were around seven thousand survivors, but they were barely alive. Some died after the Russian soldiers gave them food, because their digestive systems could not handle it. As she read the descriptions, Helena finally accepted in her heart that Regina was gone. She couldn't possibly have survived in that place for more than three years.

Still, she hired a private investigator in Kraków to make inquiries. It seemed some records had been found at the camp: *Sterbebücher*, or death records, they called them. The investigator discovered that Regina had died two months after her arrival there in 1942. Her husband had died six weeks later. She had been dead all that time and Helena hadn't known. She couldn't bear to think of what they might have suffered, or how they might have died. She prayed Regina hadn't been alone but had someone kind holding her hand at the end.

They mourned Regina and her husband in the traditional Jewish manner. Close family members ripped their clothes, to symbolize their loss, before they covered the mirrors and sat shiva for seven days. Oskar read the *hesped*, outlining his mother and father's wonderful qualities, and they all recited the Kaddish prayer together. Helena found some comfort in the familiar rituals. It was ironic that after so much time, the words came back to her, ageless and dignified.

CHAPTER 45

Elizabeth

July 1944

One sweltering day in Manhattan, when the temperature topped ninety degrees and there wasn't a hint of a breeze, Elizabeth received a letter from Henri, with another letter tucked inside. She scanned his first. He wrote that he had managed to get Gladys moved to an internment camp at Vittel in northeastern France, where conditions were much better than at Ravensbrück. Then he said she had written letters for both of them, and he enclosed Elizabeth's. Immediately she tore open the second envelope to find a note written in blunt pencil on a single scruffy sheet of paper.

Dearest Sister, I hope you are not worrying about me, Gladys wrote. *I am keeping myself busy and my spirits are high. We have running water, for which we are incredibly grateful, and there is sufficient food, although we joke that we will be fashionably thin, like Coco Chanel, when we emerge. Every morning I lead the other women in an exercise routine, based on the ones you do at Maine Chance, and they love it.*

Elizabeth sensed Gladys was putting on a brave face. Her sister had a cheerful disposition, and she could imagine she would cope better than most.

I've promised all the women a treatment at your salon when we get out of here, she wrote. *We fantasize about lying in a comfortable chair having a facial and a shoulder massage, then getting our nails polished. I hope it won't be much longer.*

It was wonderful to read her words, but she was still a prisoner, and Elizabeth was anxious. Might the Germans kill their captives before retreating? Or take them back to Germany as hostages? She couldn't bear to read the newspaper stories with those appalling images of the camps farther north and east where so many had been killed. It was impossible to believe that Goering and von Ribbentrop, the two Nazis she had met, could have been part of the horrendous crimes committed during this war. They must have been in the dark or they would have stopped it.

Paris was liberated by American troops on August 19, and Elizabeth prayed that Vittel's residents would soon be allowed to return home.

She had telephoned Tom White after Gladys was interned, desperate to ask if he could help in any way. They'd started dining together from time to time, but she quelled any romantic illusions and treated him as a friend. It still hurt, but she preferred being able to see him and talk to him than not.

He said he thought it could be another year before the war ended completely, because Hitler would never surrender, and the Japanese would certainly fight to the last man.

Elizabeth couldn't cope with another year of war. She yearned to see her sister. She had a physical ache in her sides just thinking about her. How much longer before they could sit side by side sipping sherry and sharing everything that had passed during the insufferable years apart?

AS ALWAYS, SPENDING time with her horses comforted her. Whenever Elizabeth visited horse auctions with Tom Smith, she was impressed by the acuteness of his insights. He could watch a horse for a mere few minutes, noting the way it moved and behaved around people, and from that brief impression he judged temperament: the ones that were shy and held back, the ones who were jumpy and spooked easily, and the ones with fire in their belly. He watched a horse walk in the paddock, observing how it balanced its weight, and the nod of its head. He could spot any tiny problems with bones and ligaments, and sensed straight away when a shoe didn't fit properly. He preferred to judge pace without the distraction of a stopwatch; he just knew which ones were fast.

Tom didn't say much, and he never smiled. Elizabeth found it hard to figure him out, but she trusted his instincts about horses right down the line.

His training methods were designed individually to suit each horse's personality. Conventional wisdom said that you couldn't change a horse's natural running style, but he managed it for several of her babies, increasing their speed dramatically. He suggested stabling the horses with compatible companions to help them relax before races. He let her use her creams and perfumes on them—"Don't do no harm," he said, gruffly—but when it came to treatments for swollen, tired legs, he used his own liniment, and Elizabeth let him.

In the first year he worked with her, Tom spent a staggering $287,000 of her money buying twenty yearlings. They had to build new stables in Kentucky and take on more staff, but Elizabeth gave him free rein, in a way she would never have allowed any manager in her beauty business. It paid off though. By the end of 1944, her horses had won prize money of almost $80,000 and she had several emerging champions.

Tom decided to enter Star Pilot into a race at Arlington Park, near Chicago. Elizabeth accompanied the team there in a Pullman express car and checked into a hotel close to the track, eager to be part of the action.

The morning of the race, Elizabeth came to the stables to see if they were ready.

"Ready as he'll ever be," Tom said, "but the jockey is being leaned on. He's been told that if he doesn't throw the race, his wife and kids will be kidnapped."

Elizabeth couldn't believe her ears. "Have you informed the police?"

"Don't work that way," Tom said. "Folks saying this have most likely got the cops in their pockets."

"Where are his wife and kids?" Elizabeth asked, thinking fast.

"They live near Belmont," Tom told her.

"Let's get them out of there," Elizabeth said. "I'll send a car and have them driven up to Maine for a vacation at my spa. Two weeks, all expenses paid. And we run the race to win."

Tom nodded, his expression inscrutable. "I'll pass that on."

"Whoever tried to put pressure on him—please tell him in future to talk to me directly." Elizabeth spoke with her steeliest tone.

Tom gazed toward the horizon. "You sure 'bout that?" he asked.

"I am," she said. There wasn't a shadow of a doubt in her mind. She had never in her entire life given in to blackmail and she didn't intend to start now.

IN MID-SEPTEMBER CAME the news Elizabeth had been waiting for: Vittel had been liberated and Gladys was back in Paris. She wrote to Elizabeth straight away.

Ravensbrück was horrendous, she said. *Least said the better. But in Vittel we were accommodated in hotels, we had cooking and exercise facilities—it was almost like being on vacation, except for the barbed wire and the guards pointing machine guns at us! The most exciting moment was when Red Cross parcels arrived. The joy of unpacking them and finding luxuries like butter and honey was without parallel.*

Elizabeth made a mental note to send a donation to the Red Cross. Perhaps she would host a fundraiser on its behalf.

Gladys's letter continued: *The atmosphere in Paris is not as celebratory as you might expect. Instead of a feeling of* fraternité, *there is a lot of accusation and counteraccusation about* collabo-rateurs *who sat down to dine with Germans, or sang for them in nightclubs, or, in some cases, had affairs with them. Kangaroo courts are meting out justice, and I have seen several poor women whose heads have been shaved, without a chance to stand up for themselves. Henri has decided to leave town for the time being, until it all dies down. He's staying at the Beau-Rivage Hotel by Lake Geneva. It's terribly distressing for him, as you can imagine.*

Elizabeth was shocked. Her brother-in-law had been friends with a few Nazis before the war, but she was sure he hadn't actively assisted them during the Occupation. Gladys had even helped enemy airmen. Elizabeth herself had dined with Goering, and conversed with von Ribbentrop, but that didn't make her a *collaborateur.* She felt incensed at the idea. Her company had supplied American troops; she had been personally commended by President Roosevelt.

Then she remembered a journalist saying that Madame Rubinstein claimed fascist meetings were held at her London salon. Why had she said that? Could there be any truth in it? She cabled Teddy Haslam.

"I let von Ribbentrop use one of our rooms," he replied. "Just a couple of times."

That's all it took in this day and age of witch hunts, Elizabeth thought. She didn't believe she had done anything wrong. She hadn't flown to Germany to meet Hitler. She hadn't given Teddy permission to host fascist meetings in her rooms. She was careful not to involve herself in the politics of other countries. Yet sometimes it was the appearance of wrongdoing that counted with the public, rather than the *actualité.* She decided she had best keep her head down for a while, stay out of the press, and focus on her beautiful horses, her babies.

CHAPTER 46

Helena

May 1945

Hitler's suicide left Helena feeling empty: she was glad he was dead, because the world was rid of a monster, but regretted there hadn't been a trial where he had to answer for his crimes before being publicly executed. She would have liked to see him grovel and beg for his life. Instead he had gotten away with murder on an unimaginable scale.

She didn't join the V-E Day celebrations in the streets of New York because she didn't feel festive: her sister was dead, and her nephews and niece were orphaned. She did her best to take a mother's place for Mala, Jacques, and Oskar, hosting family dinners every weekend, but they were somber affairs, each of them weighed down by their grief.

A week after victory in Europe was declared, Helena and Archie managed to secure places on a troop ship that was crisscrossing the Atlantic to ferry soldiers back to the US. They sailed for Cherbourg in a basic cabin, with a shared washroom—far from the luxurious first-class suite Helena would have paid for before the war. She had known worse: traveling steerage class to Australia in 1896 had been grim, and that voyage took three long months, whereas this was only five days.

They didn't know what to expect when they arrived. Helena knew her London salon had been damaged by the Blitz, but she believed Paris had been spared that fate. Most of its buildings remained intact, since the German general in charge of the city had surrendered to the Free French rather than obey Hitler's orders to destroy it.

At first glance, everything seemed normal as Helena and Archie drove along the boulevards. Café tables were set out on sidewalks, and customers were enjoying their coffees in the spring sunshine. Horse chestnut trees were resplendent with their pink-and-white flowering candles. When she looked a little closer, Helena could see that most pedestrians were stick-thin and their clothes threadbare, with few of the usual signs of Parisian flair.

She was apprehensive as they drove onto Île Saint-Louis and turned left into Quai de Béthune. Her house stood, just as it had for four centuries, surviving floods and the Revolution, but when she opened the front door a scene of wanton destruction met her eyes. The Brancusi sculpture that had hung in the entrance hallway was nowhere to be seen. The black-and-white floor tiles had been dug up, leaving craters underfoot. The oak banister had been ripped off the stairs.

Helena and Archie ascended carefully to her apartment, stepping over chunks of masonry. Her heart was beating hard, her throat dry, and the thought occurred to her that they might find a Nazi or two holed up there. She gripped Archie's arm tightly.

As she opened the door, she saw broken glass all over the floor. A huge mirror had been smashed, as had many of the windows. She stepped inside, glass crunching underfoot. Some paintings remained on the walls but they had been slashed, so the canvas flapped open. Helena clucked her tongue in despair.

"Why do that?" Archie echoed her thoughts, pointing to a Derain. "What good did it do them?"

She didn't have an answer. She could understand why someone might steal a painting but to destroy it was incomprehensible.

Most of the furniture had been ripped apart for firewood: in several places she found the charred remains of a chair arm or table leg amid a pile of ashes. Helena walked around in silence. Any one of those fires could have set the entire building alight—and its neighbors too, since houses on the island were so close-packed.

She opened the glass doors to her beloved roof terrace and shook her head in disbelief to see that before leaving, her unwanted guests had uprooted flowers and trees from their tubs, leaving soil, broken pots, and withered plants strewn across the tiles.

Helena felt violated. This was her home, and some Nazis had broken in and reduced it to rubble. It felt personal: they had almost certainly known the owner was Jewish. At least the building's structure seemed intact. She vowed she would restore it and make it even more stunning than before.

"Are you okay?" Archie asked, putting an arm around her.

"I am, but let's go," she said. She couldn't bear to stay a moment longer. They would live in a hotel until the house was habitable once more.

Next they visited the office of her French lawyers. Her three salons and her Saint-Cloud factory had been requisitioned by the Germans. They had continued to serve the few wealthy clients who could afford to look after their skin in wartime, but the profits had all gone to the occupiers. As soon as the city was liberated, her lawyers had taken charge, and they handed her the account books they had kept.

Helena examined them, and nodded approval. They'd done a good job in the circumstances, especially since it was difficult to procure the raw ingredients to make her creams and lotions.

"Business is picking up now," her lawyer told her. "Mostly from international women returning to the city, but some Parisians too."

"Did Elizabeth Arden's salon remain open?" Helena asked.

"It did. The staff kept it running, even when her sister was detained in a camp in northeastern France."

"Why was she detained?" Helena asked.

"I assume because she was a resident alien. Vittel was a camp for British, American, and Canadian citizens. She's back in Paris now, but her husband has fled to Switzerland. It seems some citizens threatened to string him up from a lamppost because of his friendship with the occupying forces."

"That doesn't surprise me," Helena said. Her face tightened with anger at the thought of him wining and dining Germans.

"Vittel also had a few hundred Jewish detainees," Archie told them, "but they were deported to Auschwitz last year."

He read the newspapers cover to cover each day and was well informed about all aspects of the war. Helena didn't read much, and was careful to avoid stories about conditions in the camps. The photographs on magazine covers made her sick and dizzy: haunted faces staring through barbed wire, and skeletal limbs that could hardly take the weight of emaciated bodies. Had Regina looked like that? Did she die of starvation? Or illness? How had Jews become so hated that other human beings were capable of doing that to them? It was clear now that what had happened in the camps was a systematic program of mass murder of millions of Jewish men, women, and children. Hitler had carried out his stated goal of trying to rid Europe of her people.

Helena stood abruptly. "Let's visit the salons now," she said, reaching for Archie's hand. If she kept moving, kept focused on work, she could stop herself from dwelling too much on the murder of her younger sister, as well as many of her friends, and virtually the entire European Jewish community.

STEPPING INSIDE THE rue du Faubourg Saint-Honoré salon was like stepping back in time. Everything seemed just as she had left it in 1940. Surfaces gleamed, mirrors sparkled, and

the air was full of the scent of her Herbal creams. There was
a murmur of gentle conversation in the background. Helena
greeted the French woman who had been running the salon for
the last five years, kissing her on both cheeks, and embracing
her. It couldn't have been easy taking orders from Nazis. She
went around the building thanking each and every member of
staff, and promising them a bonus in their pay packets to reward
them for their loyalty.

"Madame Rubinstein," said a woman with a very grand English accent, who was sitting in a massage chair.

She turned and smiled but didn't recognize the speaker.

"We haven't met," the woman continued. "Lady Diana Coo-
per, wife of the British ambassador."

Helena shook her hand, saying how do you do. Lady Diana
was a strikingly beautiful, middle-aged woman, with elfin bone
structure and finely plucked eyebrows above merry eyes.

"Have you just arrived in Paris?" Lady Diana asked. "My husband, Duff, and I came last September, hot on the tail of the
fleeing Germans. I swear your salon has been a godsend as I
strive to keep Father Time at bay." She patted the skin under her
eyes. "I'm a complete devotee of your Hormone line."

"I'm glad we could help," Helena said.

"It's so handy for me as the embassy's just down the road at
number 39. I'd be honored if you and your husband would pop
in to visit. We have open house every evening at six," Lady Diana
continued. "There's plentiful liquor, so it always attracts a lively
crowd of penniless artists and musicians." She laughed. "They'll
do anything for a free drink."

"We'll certainly try," Helena said, wondering if any of her
old Parisian friends would be there. She was dreading making telephone calls to see who had survived the war and who
hadn't.

"Oh please do! It's a shambles of a house, rather like an infe-
rior brothel in layout, but I've done my best to get it shipshape."

She lit a cigarette in a long black holder. "We only have one rule at our gatherings: no talk about the war!"

"That sounds like a good rule." Helena warmed to her.

"Would you like to go?" she asked Archie later. "Maybe for an hour on the way to dinner?"

"Why not?" he said. Whatever she wanted, he always agreed.

THE EMBASSY WAS in a large house set back from the street behind railings. The doorman checked a list and waved them inside. Lady Diana must have remembered to put their names down.

They were led into a high-ceilinged room, where a hundred or so guests were chatting in small groups. The air was thick with cigarette smoke. Archie asked a waiter what drinks he had on his tray and selected a vodka cocktail for Helena, and a whiskey for himself. She peered around the room but couldn't see their hostess.

"You are Madame Rubinstein, are you not?" a serious-looking young man asked, and when she agreed, he introduced himself: "Jean Dubuffet. My name probably won't mean anything to you. I'm an artist. I had a solo exhibition at the Galerie René Drouin last year. I'd love to show you my work sometime." He spoke in a rush, clearly nervous.

"I know your name," Helena said. "Tell me about your work."

She listened as he described his paintings, which incorporated sand, small pebbles, pieces of glass, and string into the texture of the oil paint, to create impastos. Helena asked him to note down his studio address and said she would visit sometime. She needed to replace the art that had been damaged in her home, and liked nurturing unknown artists.

Next she was accosted by a gaunt-faced man, who said he was a playwright and began to describe to her the plot of his new play. It sounded very dull and Helena's attention drifted. Maybe she shouldn't have come. It felt wrong to be at a party

so soon after hearing of Regina's death. She would find their
hostess, make her excuses, then leave.

Lady Diana was in the center of a group by the window,
wearing a slinky cerise satin dress and multiple strings of crystal beads. She was a dynamic figure, clutching a glass and her
cigarette holder in one hand and gesticulating with the other.
She caught sight of Helena and waved energetically, causing her
drink to slosh over the side of the glass. She ignored that, de-
tached herself from the group, and hurried over.

"Charmed you could make it," she said, kissing Helena and
Archie on both cheeks. "It's rather a hotchpotch of guests. I
haven't a clue who half of them are."

"You must have overflowing cellars to entertain like this every night," Helena said.

"We do!" Lady Diana agreed. "When I arrived, this house was
full to the brim of treasures left here for safekeeping by fleeing
British residents. We've been returning the valuables—paintings
and such like—but I rather felt we were entitled to keep the
booze. Quid pro quo, as they say."

"The Germans didn't requisition the house then?"

"No, they kept it safe for us—this and the Duke and Duchess
of Windsor's house are intact." She made a comic face. "Best
not to mention *them* these days."

Helena nodded sagely. Their support for Hitler before the
war, and their clumsy attempts to negotiate peace with Nazi
officials during it, had left their names tarnished.

"Oh look!" Lady Diana exclaimed. "Here's someone I expect
you'll know." She beckoned to a woman whose face Helena felt
sure she recognized.

"This is Gladys, Countess of Maublanc de Boisboucher . . ."

Helena frowned, realization dawning.

". . . probably better known as Elizabeth Arden's younger
sister," Lady Diana finished with a beaming smile. "So you two
are in the same business."

Gladys had platinum-blonde hair with a hint of gray at the roots, a square jaw, and eyes that were too close together, like Elizabeth's. Her fitted blue gown displayed a hint of cleavage and clung to the curve of her hips. She looked healthy, with flesh on her bones, nothing like the photographs from Auschwitz.

Gladys held out a tentative hand, but Helena ignored it.

"I'm amazed you would show your face here," Helena said in a low voice. "I heard your husband has fled town, and assumed you would have the good sense to do the same."

Gladys flinched. "I've done nothing wrong. Quite the opposite—I was a prisoner of the Germans."

Lady Diana had turned to talk to another guest, but she threw a worried glance in their direction, as if sensing the frosty atmosphere.

"You look rather well nourished for a concentration camp prisoner," Helena said, nodding at her figure. "It seems being married to a Nazi had its uses during the Occupation."

Gladys blanched and took a step backward, but didn't reply.

Lady Diana trilled: "Oh, we don't mention the war here. Didn't I tell you?"

Archie grasped Helena's elbow and pulled her away. She could hear her words being repeated in whispers by other guests in the vicinity.

"You shouldn't have done that," Archie said in her ear. He very rarely criticized her, but she didn't argue. He was probably right.

CHAPTER 47

Elizabeth

June 1945

Laney brought the mail while Elizabeth was in the middle of her yoga routine. She recognized Gladys's handwriting and stopped to read the letter, incensed when she reached the description of her confrontation with Madame Rubinstein at the British embassy.

"How dare she!" she cried to Laney. "If I'd been there, I swear I would have slapped her right across the face. What a bitch! After all Gladys has been through!"

Poor Gladys. She was so polite, she would never answer back when someone attacked her. Elizabeth felt protective; Gladys could easily have died in Ravensbrück because there had been a gas chamber there. She had told her she feared at first she might be executed, although her only "crime" had been supplying civilian clothes to help English pilots pass as Frenchmen while they tried to escape. She was forced to work in a textile factory at Ravensbrück and they only had one meager meal a day, of watery soup and a hunk of rough bread. She hadn't said any more, but Elizabeth could read between the lines and tell the horrors still haunted her.

She threw the letter onto a table. "What makes Madame Rubinstein think she has the moral high ground? She spent the war in New York, so she's no goddamn heroine."

"Her sister died in Auschwitz," Laney said, quietly.

"Did she?" Elizabeth hadn't known that—but still, it was no excuse for such rudeness. "Well, I don't think that gives her a monopoly on suffering. Gladys was in a camp too."

Laney cleared her throat. "They're not the same, Elizabeth," she said. "What happened to Jews in the extermination camps was a world away from what happened in prisoner-of-war camps. Hitler's goal from the start was to murder all European Jews, and he built huge incinerators to destroy the evidence. I say this as your friend of many years: don't even think of comparing Gladys's experiences to theirs."

Was Laney chastising her? Elizabeth blinked hard. Her assistant had never spoken to her with this tone. At first she couldn't decide how to respond. She knew what had happened to the Jews had been appalling; there was no question about that. Still the thought of Madame Rubinstein being rude to her sister made anger surge through her veins.

"Of *course* I didn't mean to compare them," she backtracked. "But who the hell does Madame Rubinstein think she is? She has briefed the press against me, she hired my ex-husband in a spiteful gesture, and she placed a spy at the very heart of my empire."

Laney's face was expressionless as she sat, holding her notebook and pencil, awaiting instructions.

"Everything about her is fake," Elizabeth continued. "She pretends to be a doctor, she pretends she has these miraculous nonexistent herbs, and frankly she is pretending to be civilized when under the skin she is nothing but a savage."

Laney waited, the gentle tap of her pencil against the binding of her notebook the only sound in the room.

ELIZABETH TRIED TO persuade Gladys to come to New York for a vacation in the summer of 1945, but Gladys wanted to stay in Paris, close enough to visit her husband. Elizabeth was disappointed. She didn't have time to go to Europe; she was preoccupied with launching a couture collection for American women who wanted Parisian glamour in their wardrobes once more, and she was spending any remaining time at the track.

Tom Smith had bought more new yearlings, and she loved to watch them in training. Some were quick on the uptake, while others needed dozens of repetitions before they understood what was required, but Tom was endlessly patient. He never lost his temper, working long hours with complete focus, and only selling the ones he considered beyond hope.

Two of her babies, Star Pilot and Beaugay, had a series of impressive wins, with Star Pilot becoming Colt of the Year in his age category, and Beaugay ratcheting up six wins in a row. Six! Both were stunning creatures—long-legged, with glossy coats and elegant lines.

In contrast, another of the new purchases, a big, gawky fellow called Knockdown, was the ugliest horse she had ever seen, with a cussed temper to match. He refused to let Elizabeth baby-talk and pet him, pinning his ears back and emitting a blood-curdling shriek whenever she came near.

"Why did you buy such an unattractive creature?" she demanded of Tom. "I want you to sell him at the next opportunity." She couldn't bear to have ugly staff in her salons, and she wanted all her horses to be beautiful as well as fast.

"Certainly, Miss Arden," Tom said, but next time she visited the Kentucky stables, that disagreeable horse was still there. What's more, he attempted to bite her when she approached his stall. She only just got her hand out of the way in time.

"I've entered him for the Santa Anita hundred-grander," Tom told her, "along with Star Pilot."

She frowned at that. "Make sure he knows we want Star Pilot to win," she said.

"Yes, ma'am," Tom said, without expression.

She knew he humored her. He didn't really believe in her

creams and perfumes, her hanging baskets and the music playing in the stables. He followed her orders, but carried on training the horses his own way. No matter; Elizabeth had total
faith in him. It was Knockdown's jockey she blamed when he
got in front of Star Pilot at Santa Anita and blocked him, so
that neither won.

"Get rid of that hideous horse," she told Tom again.

"Yes, Miss Arden," he replied.

"I'm just curious," she said. "Do you ever smile?"

He thought for a moment. "Not that I can recall, ma'am."

She laughed at that. With Tom at the helm, her earnings
from the track topped half a million dollars in 1945 and she was
named Owner of the Year. Tom was taciturn and gruff, but an
absolute treasure. Third Tom Lucky indeed!

ELIZABETH WAS FINALLY able to travel to Paris in the
spring of 1946. Henri was still holed up in Switzerland, where
Gladys visited him every few weeks. He hadn't been accused
of any crimes, but they felt it might take a little longer before
he could safely return. He wasn't alone. Several other Parisians
were sheltering in Switzerland, among them Coco Chanel, who
was said to have had an affair with a German officer during the
Occupation.

"But Henri did nothing wrong, did he?" Elizabeth demanded
of Gladys. "It's so unfair."

"It's appearances that count," Gladys said. "People around
here have long memories. The worst insult you can throw at
someone is *collaborateur*."

"Have you bumped into Madame Rubinstein again?" Elizabeth asked, eyes narrowed. If she came face-to-face with her, she
wouldn't hold her tongue.

"I don't think we mix in the same circles," Gladys said, turning away.

On the surface she seemed to have recovered from her wartime ordeal, but she changed the subject if Elizabeth tried to make her talk about it. They had a pleasant time together—shopping, lunching, and going to the theater—but without Henri, she seemed subdued. The shadows of the war lingered.

Next, Elizabeth traveled to London, on a whistlestop trip to catch up with Teddy Haslam. He was his old debonair self, immaculately dressed and well informed about society gossip, but she was shocked to see the devastation of the city: huge craters were all that remained of some buildings she remembered in Grosvenor Square and Berkeley Square. The John Lewis department store on Oxford Street had taken a direct hit and was covered in scaffolding, while Mount Street lay in ruins.

Teddy took her to Royal Ascot, and Elizabeth placed money on Caracalla, a good-looking bay with a white blaze and white socks, who won by two lengths.

A racing journalist sidled up to her as she counted her winnings. "Are you thinking of racing in England, Miss Arden?" he asked.

"Not at present," she said, "but I always enjoy visiting the races here."

"What differences do you notice between the American and British racing scene?"

Elizabeth spoke without thinking. "I hope it's less crooked in this country. In the States, you still come up against race-fixing, a vestige of the bad old days when mobsters controlled the tracks."

He asked for examples, and she told him about the practice of putting sponges in horses' noses to stop them breathing so well, and about the time her jockey was warned that his wife and children would be kidnapped if he didn't throw a race.

"Did he throw it?" the journalist asked.

"He didn't win," Elizabeth said, "but I believe he lost legitimately. I require integrity from all my employees."

Teddy took her arm and led her to where Her Majesty Queen

Mary and her entourage were emerging from the royal box. Elizabeth curtsied as the royal party passed, but wasn't sure if the Queen remembered her because she didn't stop to chat.

AS SOON AS she got back to Manhattan, Elizabeth rang Tom for an update. He told her he had entered three horses—Knockdown, Lord Boswell, and Perfect Bahram—in the Churchill Downs Classic in Kentucky, and the remaining twenty-eight horses had all been taken to Arlington Park, ready for the start of the Chicago racing season.

"You still haven't sold Knockdown then?" she asked.

"Not yet, ma'am."

She smiled to herself. It was clear he had no intention of selling. "I need to check on business in Manhattan, then I'll join you in Chicago," she said. "I'll be there Friday."

The first race was Saturday afternoon. She couldn't wait. Jet Pilot, one of the yearlings they'd bought the previous year, was going to race for the first time and she and Tom had high hopes for him. Beaugay was also running; he was a competitive creature who could put on a sudden burst of acceleration that took him from the back of the pack to the lead in the blink of an eye.

Elizabeth arrived in Chicago on Friday evening and took a taxi straight to the stables, impatient to see her babies. They were restless and excited, whinnying and pacing. They always picked up the atmosphere and sensed when they were about to race. She walked around with soothing words for each.

Leading Lady was there, and Elizabeth made a big fuss of her, as always; although her racing years were long past, she liked to have her around. Tom argued she should have been put out to grass, but Elizabeth maintained she had a calming influence on the younger horses.

He joined her to report on the form of the racers. They were ready, he said, and track conditions were perfect.

She traveled back to her hotel just before midnight and fell asleep quickly, exhausted from her recent travel across time zones.

When the telephone rang, wakening her, she looked at the clock: three-fifteen a.m. Was it a wrong number? She picked up, ready to snap at the caller.

"There's a fire at Arlington stables." It was Tom's voice, but he sounded strange.

"Is it serious?" she asked, trying to judge his tone.

There was a pause then a sniff. "It is," he said, and put the phone down abruptly.

Elizabeth tore off her nightgown and pulled on a woolen dress and coat, before rushing downstairs and asking the night receptionist to find her a taxi.

The stables weren't far—just five minutes away—and as soon as they reached the highway, she saw that the sky was lit up a hazy orange. She could smell smoke long before they pulled into the drive. As soon as she leapt out of the car, it filled her lungs. She coughed and choked, her eyes stinging as she tried to peer through the crowds of men rushing around.

Her stable was a mass of yellow-orange flames shooting skyward. Several men were directing fire hoses at it, but the roof had gone and the walls were caving inward. It clearly couldn't be saved. Men were yelling to be heard over the roar of the fire and the crashing noises as internal structures collapsed. It was like a vision of hell.

Where were the horses? She grabbed a stranger's arm and asked, but he shook his head. He didn't know.

She moved closer, and now the heat was scorching her face. Her babies must have been taken to neighboring stables. Suddenly she made out a dark shape on the grass, just past the barn, and rushed over, her heart thudding.

Up close she saw it was Leading Lady, lying on her side. Elizabeth crouched beside her dear head, and knew straight away she was dead. Her uppermost eye was open and staring horribly, and her teeth were bared. From her expression, she had died screaming. *Oh no, not her. Please no.* Elizabeth retched and clasped her hands over her mouth. The air was full of a sickening, almost sweet smell of scorched flesh—horse flesh. The horse's poor hind legs were charred to the bone, open wounds pink and oozing.

"I had to shoot her," a voice said, and she turned to see Tom emerging from the smoke. "I never heard an animal scream like that."

"Where was the vet?" She had to yell to be heard.

"Busy," he said.

Elizabeth leaned over, stroked her *grande dame*'s mane, and kissed her nose, below the neat bullet hole, whispering, "Sleep well, my precious baby." If she'd listened to Tom, Leading Lady would have been enjoying retirement; it was her fault she'd been there at all. Tears prickled her eyelids, but she wouldn't cry, not now. If she started crying, she would fall apart, and she still had to check on her other babies.

Her bad hip was stiff and aching. She tried to stand but couldn't manage so Tom caught her arm and pulled her up.

"Where are the rest?" she asked. Her heart was fluttering and she felt dizzy and nauseous.

"Vets are treating some down here," he said, leading her away from the barn, toward some outlying stables where the air wasn't quite so dense with smoke.

"Some." She repeated the word, scarcely daring to ask.

"Jet Pilot's fine," he said. "He was nearest the door so we got him out first. War Date and Gay Paree are okay. Blue Fantasy is injured but he will survive. Beaugay and Darcy are being treated for smoke inhalation."

She waited. Tom kept walking.

"But the rest? Where are they?" She pulled on his arm to stop him.

He turned to her, his face lit by the orange glow of the fire, and she saw that his eyes were red and so swollen they were almost closed. Was it the smoke? He tried to speak but his voice caught in his throat so he answered her question by nodding his head back toward the stable.

"*All* the rest?" She breathed hard. "Twenty-one of my horses are trapped in there?" She looked back. The barn was completely consumed by flames.

A sob burst from his throat. "I did what I could."

"I know you did. I know." The ground swayed and she clutched his arm, feeling as if she might faint.

Don't think about it now, she told herself. *There will be time for that. First, see what can be done.*

BEAUGAY WAS BUCKING and snorting in his stall, pawing the air and tossing his mane. Elizabeth approached slowly, hands outstretched, talking quietly.

"Baby boy," she said. "You're okay, Mama's here." She placed a hand on either side of his chest and pressed firmly, trying to transmit calm. "It's all over, you're safe. It's all right."

If he bucked again she risked being kicked, but she had a feeling he wouldn't. His heart was thumping hard beneath her palm and his breathing was ragged. He was petrified.

"Shhh," she whispered, stroking his nose and blowing gently in his nostrils until he stopped tossing his head and she could nuzzle him, skull to skull. His entire body was trembling, and the judders transmitted through her bones as if they were one creature and she could feel what he felt.

"Mama's going to give you a rubdown," she said, her voice shaky. "Won't that be nice?" She found a curry comb and began rubbing it in circular, rhythmic motions over his flank. Gradually she felt him go still. His eyes closed.

"Jet Pilot could use your magic touch," a vet said as he passed. "He's not hurt but he's badly spooked. Next stall down."

All night long, Elizabeth comforted her six surviving horses, going from one to the other, massaging and brushing, whispering and petting. It was all she could do. Focusing on their needs helped her to block out images of the agonizing death the others must have suffered. The expression on Leading Lady's face said it all. She knew they would have been rearing and screaming, crashing against the doors of their stalls, desperate to escape. They'd been in her care, and she had failed them.

Tom came to watch.

"How did it start?" she asked over her shoulder. "Where was the nightwatchman?"

"Gilbert Jones says he raised the alarm as soon as he spotted the flames. We all rushed to help but it was too late—the fire had taken hold. So we pulled out the ones we could reach before the roof collapsed." He was shivering, his teeth chattering, and Elizabeth realized he was in shock, just like the horses.

"Go and sleep," she told him. "I'll stay with them. You go."

He didn't argue. He'd probably seen worse sights tonight than she had. She knew he would have run back inside, time and again, until it was too late. He would have fought to the last.

She blinked away tears and focused on grooming the survivors, top to toe, soothing them till they were calm.

When dawn came, the flames had been extinguished and the barn was a smoldering black silhouette against pink-gold sky. Some police officers had arrived and one asked if she would answer a few questions.

"Of course," she said, her throat hoarse.

They walked to an office up the track and sat down. Elizabeth refused the offer of coffee because she felt nauseous and a headache had an iron grip around her skull. She looked down and realized she wasn't wearing stockings; she had forgotten to put them on when she rushed out of the hotel all those hours ago. She wrapped her coat tightly around her, although it wasn't cold in the room.

"I appreciate this is a difficult time, ma'am," one of them said.

"We've been doing some preliminary investigations and we're suspicious about the speed with which the fire took hold."

"It was a wooden structure full of straw. Barns always burn fast," she said.

He looked at his colleague. "It seems substances may have been used to accelerate the fire."

Elizabeth's brain felt cloudy. "What substances?" *What could he mean?*

"We'll establish that down the line," he said, glancing at his colleague.

"You think someone started the fire *deliberately?*" Her whole body shuddered in revulsion at the idea.

"It seems that way," he said. "We wanted to ask if you have any enemies. Anyone who might want to harm you?"

Elizabeth felt a surge of fierce anger and gritted her teeth before she replied. There was only one enemy she could think of.

"Yes," she said. "Yes, I do." And she named Helena Rubinstein.

CHAPTER 48

Helena

August 1946

Helena was in her office at the Fifth Avenue salon, checking a proof of her new Color-Spectrograph chart that helped women choose the right makeup colors to enhance their hair tones, when her secretary put her head around the door to say there were two detectives asking to speak with her. Her first thought was that Horace had gotten himself into some kind of trouble. Had he crashed another car? Gotten drunk and punched someone in a bar? Please don't let him be hurt.

"Show them in," she said, quickly covering the papers on her desk, rising to her feet and walking around to greet them.

The two men were in uniform, peaked hats in their hands, brown leather belts fastened diagonally across their chests. They towered over her as they shook hands, calling her "Mrs. Rubinstein." She didn't correct them.

"How can I help?" she asked, gesturing for them to sit, while trying to read their expressions. Was it bad news? They sat with their hats on their laps, and the younger one took out a notebook and pencil.

"Do you know Miss Elizabeth Arden, the beauty salon owner?" the older one asked.

Helena was taken aback. "We haven't been introduced," she said, and they glanced at each other. "Why do you ask?"

"There was a fire at her stables last Friday. Twenty-two of her horses died."

Helena gasped. It was horrible news, but her first reaction was relief that they didn't seem to be there about her wayward son.

"She thinks you might have been behind it," the detective continued, watching her face.

"Me!" Helena couldn't take it in. She looked from one to the other in astonishment. "But why would I do that? How?"

He cleared his throat. "I believe she thinks you might have hired someone."

She shook her head slowly. It would have been laughable if it weren't also alarming: she knew only too well that blame was often pinned on Jews for crimes they didn't commit. Discrimination against her race continued, even after the cataclysmic slaughter of the war. "What possible motive could I have?"

He glanced at his partner. "Miss Arden said you two are old enemies, and that you attacked her sister at a party in Paris. . . ."

"No!" Helena held up her hand in a "Stop!" gesture. "I exchanged a few words with her sister. I did not *attack* her. This is ridiculous. Miss Arden and I own competing businesses but there is no personal enmity—not on my side, at any rate." She kept her tone calm and logical. She didn't want this to escalate. *Stop talking, Helena,* she berated herself. *Say as little as possible.* It was a strategy that worked when cutting a business deal, but the injustice of the accusation fired her and she continued: "I have no idea where Miss Arden keeps her horses. I couldn't even begin to guess which state they might be in."

"Could you tell us where you were last Friday evening?" the detective asked.

Perhaps she should call her lawyer. Better safe than sorry. Then again, there seemed no harm in cooperating, so she consulted her desk diary and found the entry. "My husband and I dined at the Colony Club with four friends. Any of them will verify this."

He asked for the friends' names and addresses and she gave them, hesitant now. What would they think about being dragged into this nonsense?

"Did you make or receive any telephone calls while you were there?" he asked.

"Certainly not. Anyone will tell you that I seldom use telephones." She felt her face flush, and hoped they wouldn't notice. She still got flushes when she was stressed, a remnant of her menopause symptoms.

"You're sure you didn't hire someone to set the fire? Perhaps you didn't mean it to take hold like that, you just wanted to scare her?" He was testing. She got the impression he didn't believe the accusation but had to go through the motions.

She looked from one to the other, meeting their eyes directly. "Definitely not," she said. She wanted to add that she was not that kind of person, that Elizabeth Arden must be mad to think such a thing, and that she found it outrageous that they would come here and accuse her of such a heinous crime—but decided it was best to hold her tongue.

"Thank you, Mrs. Rubinstein," the older one said, standing up. "We'll be in touch if we need to talk to you again."

She asked her secretary to show them out, closed the office door, and sat down hard, clutching her head in her hands. This feud with Elizabeth had gotten entirely out of hand. *What to do, what to do.* She needed to end this. But how?

ARCHIE ADVISED HER to do nothing. "The police must realize it's an absurd accusation by a hysterical woman. I'm sure you won't hear from them again," he said.

But Helena wasn't the type to do nothing. She mulled it over for a few days, then, without telling Archie, she asked Edith to contact Molly, the maid at Elizabeth's apartment, and ask her to let them know when her mistress was next at home. A week later, a call came to say she was there.

Helena didn't want to risk being turned away by the doorman of the Fifth Avenue building. Instead, Edith asked Molly
to leave the entrance to the tradesmen's elevator open at five
in the afternoon precisely. It was accessed from the back alley,
and normally used for deliveries. Helena had the same kind of
elevator in her building.

She dressed dramatically in a red-and-gold-patterned gown
accessorized with six strings of pearls and dangling pearl earrings, and she wore large pearl and ruby rings on each hand. Red
was a statement: it said she was not to be trifled with.

When she pulled back the latticed door of the service elevator, she stepped into a large hallway decorated in French
eighteenth-century style: ornate and pretty-pretty, not her taste
at all. A man in a footman's uniform emerged through a doorway and looked startled to see her.

"I'm visiting Miss Arden," she said, with an air of authority.
"Which way do I go?"

He glanced at her regal attire and pointed to a staircase with
Art Deco–style foliage painted on the walls. The stairs curved up
to the next floor, where she could see a doorway that led into a
room with a glass wall. She hesitated outside, then stepped over
the threshold and looked around. A tiny figure wrapped in a pale
pink blanket was curled in an armchair, like a bug in a cocoon.
The figure gave a strangled scream and tried to rise, but her feet
were trapped inside the blanket.

Helena strode across till she was about ten feet away. Elizabeth shrank back into the chair, holding her arms in front of her
face as if she expected to be struck.

"I'm sorry to hear about your horses," Helena said firmly, "but
it was not me who set the fire."

"How did you get in?" Elizabeth's voice was panicked. "What
are you doing here? You're trespassing. Get out or I'll have you
thrown out!"

Helena folded her arms. "I was visited by some police officers who said you accused me of killing your horses. I will not leave until we have cleared up this matter."

Elizabeth managed to throw off the blanket, leapt to her feet, and rushed toward Helena with a roar, open hand raised as if to slap her. Helena reacted quickly, grabbing her by the wrist.

"Don't!" she warned in a low voice.

Elizabeth struggled to yank her wrist free, but Helena held on tightly, and grabbed hold of her other wrist too.

"If we fight, you know I will win." She stared hard into Elizabeth's blue eyes and detected a flicker of fear. *Good!*

Her rival's face was free of makeup, and she looked exhausted. Her complexion was good, but not as good as hers, Helena thought. There were pouches under the eyes, worry lines on the brow, open pores on the sides of her nose. The squareness of her jaw gave her a masculine look. And pink puffiness around her eyes made it a pretty sure bet she had been crying.

Elizabeth stopped struggling and Helena released her wrists, watching for signs of a renewed attack. She was taller than Elizabeth in her high heels but guessed they would be roughly the same height in stocking feet.

"I always said you were capable of anything," Elizabeth said in her peculiar upper-crust accent, taking a step backward. "Now I know it's true."

"May I remind you that you are the one who just tried to hit *me*," Helena said, still watching her warily. "But this is not the way to solve our differences. We are business rivals, that's all. Personally, I don't care a fig about you. I just want you to admit that I am not a criminal."

Elizabeth turned and walked slowly back to her chair, with a pronounced limp. She sat down carefully, as if her hips pained her. "Yet you have broken into my home," she said, "which is a criminal act."

"There was no breaking involved," Helena said. "Your staff let me in. I thought it was time we talked because you and I, we are not each other's enemies, not really." She paused, choosing her words with care. "Copying a lipstick shade or an advertisement does not lead to the murder of horses. Poaching employees is normal business practice. Tit for tat. You steal my people, I steal yours."

"It got personal when you were rude to my poor sister, who has been through hell and is still recovering from her ordeal. I thought that was beyond the pale." Elizabeth pulled the pink blanket over her bare legs.

"I apologize for that," Helena said straight away. "My husband also thought I was in the wrong. Perhaps you can understand that I am in mourning for my own sister, and the words slipped out unguarded."

Elizabeth didn't reply.

Helena realized she would get no condolences from this quarter—not that she sought them. She turned to look out through the plate-glass wall, which led to a narrow terrace and, beyond, a panoramic Central Park view. The day was muggy and overcast, with dark clouds threatening rain later.

"If I wanted to make this feud personal, I could have done so long ago," Helena said. "I learned a lot about you from Tommy, as you can imagine. . . ."

"Pah!" Elizabeth spat, dismissing this with a flick of her wrist.

"And I also know that you have secret dinners with Tom White." She watched for a reaction but Elizabeth's face was a mask. "The gossip columnists would be fascinated to hear about that, I imagine. But they won't hear it from me. It's not how I operate."

Elizabeth shrugged. "Two can play that game. I heard from Harry that your younger son is a drinker and your older one can't bear to be in the same room as you."

Helena forced a laugh. "Your information is out of date. I saw

Roy last week when I went to meet my latest grandchild—a girl they have named after me." She perched on the arm of a pink satin sofa. She wasn't sure how she felt about being a grand-mother, but the baby was very sweet. Horace had two sons, but he had divorced their mother so she hardly ever saw them. "Fam-ilies are complicated, I think we can both agree. I hear you are estranged from your brother—Will, isn't it?" She sighed deeply. "How much we know about each other! All the effort we have spent spying on each other. It's totally gaga."

She looked around the room. It was a good size, but not as big as her sitting room. The walls were painted pastel pink and hung with smoked mirrors rather than art. Plants trailed from tall pots by the window, and pink lamps stood on glass side ta-bles. *Ghastly*, she thought. *The woman has no taste at all.*

Suddenly she noticed that Elizabeth had a bell on the table beside her. She could have rung for a member of staff to throw Helena out, but had chosen not to. She clearly wanted to hear what she had to say.

"Do the police have any other suspects in their investigation into your stable fire?" she asked. "Or should I hire a lawyer to defend myself?"

Elizabeth turned to look out the window, and when she spoke, her voice was flat. "They think it was a warning shot from some Chicago gangsters who fix races. I had spoken out about it and they weren't happy."

"You did?" Helena reassessed her. She looked tiny and frail, but she was clearly a force to be reckoned with. "That was brave. I hope you will continue to speak out and won't let this fire scare you off."

"I don't scare easily," Elizabeth replied, with a sniff. "I don't imagine you do either."

It was the first compliment she had directed in Helena's direction—at least she took it as a compliment. Did it signal a softening of her attitude? "Of course not. I love a battle," Helena said. "I don't think you and I would have invented so many new products over the years if we'd hadn't been competing with each other."

"No, I suppose not." Elizabeth sounded weary. "And now there are new threats on all sides, from Charles Revson and Estée Lauder, and goodness knows who else. Every Tom, Dick, and Harry thinks he can succeed in the beauty business."

"Ah, but we came first," Helena said. "We invented an industry that didn't exist before. They should all be thanking us." She truly believed this. There had been some greasy cold creams before they came along, but she and Elizabeth had persuaded women that they had a right to be beautiful, and that beauty could be achieved by anyone with just a little effort and investment.

"Tell me," Elizabeth asked. "I've always wondered. Do you really have a medical degree?"

"Of course I do," Helena said without a moment's hesitation. She had been telling the lie for so long now that she almost believed that she had studied medicine herself, instead of Stanislaus coaching her from his textbooks.

"Yet you call yourself Madame Rubinstein rather than Doctor? I've always thought that curious." Elizabeth sounded skeptical. She tilted her head to one side, like a bird.

"It was a business decision," Helena said, standing up. She had said her piece.

"And you have never named any of those precious Carpathian herbs that give your products such *miraculous* antiaging properties. Why is that?" There was a hint of a smile playing on Elizabeth's lips.

"I protect my secrets, of course," Helena said, straight-faced. "Everything is for the business. I imagine you're the same."

Elizabeth raised herself up, chin held high, and said, "Frankly, I don't see any similarities between us."

"No?" Helena queried, curving one side of her mouth into a smile. "I think we have a lot in common. In another life—who knows? We could even have been friends."

"Isn't it pretty to think so," Elizabeth replied in her cut-crystal upper-class voice.

The delivery was flawless. Helena threw back her head and guffawed. The corners of Elizabeth's mouth twitched. She was struggling to stop herself laughing too.

Helena considered offering to shake hands but didn't want to push her luck. She was still chuckling when she got into the elevator to ride back down to the lobby—the main lobby this time—and see herself out.

Epilogue

No one was charged in connection with the fire at Elizabeth's stables, but the nightwatchman, Gilbert Jones, was fined fifty dollars for dereliction of his duty. Elizabeth continued to race, and in 1947 Jet Pilot, a survivor of the Arlington fire, won the prestigious Kentucky Derby, the country's top event. Elizabeth screamed herself hoarse as she watched the race, but the result was never in question: Jet Pilot took the lead out of the starting gate and never relinquished it, a testament to Tom Smith's exacting training.

The following morning a lavish bouquet of flowers arrived at Elizabeth's hotel suite, in her racing colors of cherry pink, white, and pale blue. Elizabeth opened the card: *Congratulations on your victory over the hoodlums*, it read. And it was signed *HR*.

Elizabeth pursed her lips. A year ago she would have sent those flowers straight back, but now? Now she appreciated the gesture.

She had rebuilt her stables, bought many more horses, and she still worked hand in hand with Tom Smith, her Third Tom Lucky, to whom she was eternally loyal. They had made it clear they would never throw races no matter what, and the threats had diminished. She hoped their stance had made a difference for other racehorse owners too.

She and Helena had not met again since the confrontation in her apartment. They were still business rivals, and they would never be friends—but perhaps they weren't enemies either. She wondered what she would do if they bumped into each other at a party, or in a restaurant. A brief nod of acknowledgment, perhaps? She didn't plan to offer a handshake, or any warmer type of greeting. Of course, it was impossible to tell what Helena would do: that woman was a law unto herself.

Eleven years later, when Elizabeth read in the newspapers that Helena's younger son, Horace, had died in a car accident, she felt genuine sadness for her. She knew Artchil had died three years prior, and Helena's loss of her son on top of her husband must have been devastating. She sent flowers and a sympathy card, which Helena acknowledged with a brief note of thanks. The exchange felt civilized: two women of a certain age who respected each other.

They remained competitive though. When Elizabeth's Eight Hour Cream was awarded a royal warrant in 1964, she whooped in triumph. This was the epitome of success for her—and the fact that Madame Rubinstein didn't have any royal warrants made it all the sweeter.

In May that year, Elizabeth read in the newspapers that Helena had stood up to three armed burglars who broke into her apartment and tied up four members of her staff. They demanded the keys to the safe where she kept her prized jewelry collection, but Madame Rubinstein refused to hand them over.

"I'm an old woman," she was reported to have said, "but I'm not scared of you. You can kill me, but I'm not going to let you rob me."

The burglars ransacked the apartment but all they got away with was a hundred dollars in cash. As soon as they left, Helena called the police, untied her staff, then got dressed and made up, ready to give a press conference about her ordeal. She looked great in the photos, Elizabeth thought. She wasn't sure she would have been as brave. True to form, Madame Rubinstein used the incident as publicity for her business. She never missed a trick.

On April second the following year, Elizabeth was still in bed when her Fifth Avenue salon manager rang to say that Helena Rubinstein had died.

"Are you sure?" Elizabeth asked.

It came as a shock; she had seemed immortal. Elizabeth rang a bell and asked her maid to bring her the *New York Times*.

The story was on the front page, under the headline "Helena Rubinstein Dies Here at 94."

"Ninety-four?" Elizabeth shrieked out loud. All that time she'd been under the impression her rival was two years younger than she was, she'd actually been six years older.

"Well, I'll be damned," she muttered to herself. "Maybe her goddamn Carpathian herbs did work after all."

AUTHOR'S NOTE

Both Elizabeth Arden and Helena Rubinstein dealt in illusion. They sold the promise of youthfulness and beauty to their customers, while both were pretending to be something they were not. Elizabeth tried to pass as upper class and to hide her impoverished upbringing; Helena pretended to have a medical degree and to have discovered herbs with antiaging properties.

They both told fibs about their age; you will find several different dates of birth quoted in biographies and newspaper archives. Wikipedia claims Helena was born on December 25, 1870, Michèle Fitoussi's biography says 1872, her 1928 *New Yorker* profile said she was forty-eight (so born in 1879), and her *New York Times* obituary in the spring of 1965 said she was ninety-four (so born in 1870). Elizabeth's date of birth is variously given as December 31, 1878 (most biographies), 1881 (Wikipedia), and 1884 (her *New York Times* obituary). Whatever their true ages, both of them looked a good decade younger, making them living advertisements for their products.

I have stuck to the facts in covering the main events of both women's stories, but I sometimes moved the timeline of events for the sake of my narrative. I dramatized scenes and invented dialogue and feelings throughout.

Lindy Woodhead reports in her book *War Paint* that the women copied each other's products and advertisements. The two adverts about success I quote are remarkably similar. I can't say for sure which came first, but I decided in this instance to make Helena the aggressor. I also don't know specifically which of each other's products they copied, but I expect they would have analyzed all the other's new releases and incorporated elements into their own. It's true that Elizabeth poached Harry Johnson and eleven members of Helena's sales team in 1937; and it's also true that Helena hired Tommy Lewis the following year, in a significant escalation of their previous rivalry. It's true that Elizabeth lost twenty-two horses in a stable fire in 1946, although there was never any suggestion that Helena might be responsible.

There is no record of the two women ever meeting, but I couldn't resist bringing them together for my novel. They had so much in common—not just their rival businesses, which they built from scratch, but their marriages too, and their sheer resilience and chutzpah (to use a wonderful Yiddish word).

For more information about the decisions I made when fictionalizing their stories, as well as a further reading list and some reading group questions, please go to my website, gillpaul.com.

ACKNOWLEDGMENTS

I was researching a "Paris between the wars" novel when I fell down a Google rabbit hole and stumbled over a PBS documentary about Elizabeth Arden and Helena Rubinstein called *The Powder & the Glory*. It wasn't available online but I was curious enough to order a copy of the DVD. While waiting for it to arrive I found footage of Patti LuPone and Christine Ebersole in the Broadway show *War Paint*, and had to order Lindy Woodhead's book of the same title, which inspired it. Two self-made businesswomen who became bitter rivals in the early twentieth century? Paris could wait.

When I did my research and began to compare Helena and Elizabeth, I realized antisemitism had to be a theme. I don't have Jewish blood (that I know of), so I asked advice from a number of people who do: Sylvia Coury, Vivi Lachs, Beeri Seema, and Marnie Riches in the UK. In the US, Jennifer North wrote a very useful sensitivity report. I wanted to make sure nothing I wrote would be offensive to Jews, and I sincerely hope that's the case.

My first readers were Karen Sullivan, Lor Bingham, Marnie Riches, Tracy Rees, Vivien Green, and my agent Gaia Banks. Huge thanks to them all for the invaluable feedback. Thanks also to my Hist Fic Zoom gang of Dinah Jefferies, Eve Chase, Heather Webb, Hazel Gaynor, Jenny Ashcroft, Liz Trenow, and Tracy Rees for the moral support and pep talks that are essential in a writer's life.

All the team at William Morrow are unbeatable: Lucia Macro, Asanté Simons, Jori Cook, and Amelia Wood are simply the best I've come across after decades in the business. A special shout-out to Kim Yeon for her stunning cover designs, Kim

Acknowledgments

Lewis for her meticulous and intuitive copy editing, Stephanie Baker for a top-notch proofread, and Lisa Flanagan for bringing my characters to life in audiobook narrations.

In the UK, the Avon team brings energy and enthusiasm to each and every book: high-fives to my editor, Molly Walker-Sharp, and to Maddie Dunne Kirby, Ella Young, and Gaby Drinkald.

Eternal gratitude to the reviewers, bloggers, YouTubers, and podcasters around the world who give up their time to spread book love. I really appreciate all your time and effort, and it's been such fun getting to know you.

Finally, huge thanks to my partner, Karel Bata, who acts as my personal photographer, filmmaker, and computer-fixer; and to my sister, Fiona Williams, for her generosity in providing me with a country retreat, complete with children and fluffy animals, when I need a break from the city.

SOURCES

Some quotations in this novel have been taken from printed sources, as follows:

Page 16: "*A Famous European House of Beauty Announces the Opening of its Doors in New York . . . the accepted advisor in beauty matters to Royalty, Aristocracy, and the Great Artistes of Europe.*" Announcement of the opening of HR salon in New York, 1915, as pictured in https://www.cosmeticsandskin.com

Page 20: "*Travelers intending to embark on an Atlantic voyage are warned that a state of war exists between Germany and Great Britain. . . . Vessels flying the flag of Great Britain or any of her allies are liable to destruction. . . . Travelers sailing in the war zone do so at their own risk.*" German government advert from the *New York Times*, Saturday May 1, 1915

Page 36: "'Have you ever noticed it is easier to persuade a pretty woman to try a skin treatment than a plain one? The plain one says, "Oh, but my nose is too big so what's the point?" or "My skin is terrible so why try?" It is our job to show them that *anyone* can be beautiful, and that not trying is pure laziness.'" Paraphrased from Helena Rubinstein, *My Life for Beauty*, 1965

Page 38: "'the most famous scientist of beauty the world has ever known. . . . In Paris, London, Sydney, and New York, her Maisons des Beauté Valaze are frequented by those who follow her instructions to the tiniest details.'" From Helena Rubinstein advertisements, as pictured in https://www.cosmeticsandskin.com

Page 70: *"There is just one right way to do a thing and you can always distinguish the Right Way by its success. Many are those who offer panaceas for all complexion defects . . . but no one has achieved a success comparable with Elizabeth Arden."* Advertisement for Elizabeth Arden beauty preparations, 1919, as pictured in https://www.cosmeticsandskin.com

Page 71: *"'Nothing succeeds like success' is an old and very true saying. Certainly nothing has ever been greeted with more success than the new and improved Valaze Beauty Preparations, the most successful and efficacious in the history of Beauty Culture."* Advertisement for Helena Rubinstein beauty preparations, 1919, as pictured in https://www.cosmeticsandskin.com

Page 187: "'spoiled, petulant schoolgirl.'" Quoted in Lindy Woodhead, *War Paint*, 2003

Page 219: *"useless people, idlers, little zeros."* Quoted in Lindy Woodhead, *War Paint*, 2003

Page 264: "'tops in the "treatments" cosmetics business' and the 'Tiffany of the trade.'" *Fortune* magazine article, October 1938

Page 325: "'He came with two suits and he left with twenty-two.'" Quoted in Lewis and Woodworth, *Miss Elizabeth Arden*, 1973

Page 367: "'Isn't it pretty to think so.'" Quoted in Lewis and Woodworth, *Miss Elizabeth Arden*, 1973